I0658410

Stolen Stars

Tim Rangnow

Published by Tim Rangnow, 2024.

Table of Contents

Prologue

Five Powers Alliance Research Facility
  Oceanica Platform 37
  512 miles off the coast of Portugal Province
"How certain are we about this data?"

"Nothing in this world is one hundred percent certain, but I'd wager my next child that what's on that report is accurate."

"The conclusions we draw are far more uncertain than the information itself. We just don't have enough data points to extrapolate from and explain what we're seeing."

The three astrophysicists stared at each other in silence for a few moments. They were part of a large group sequestered for the last week poring over every kilobyte of sensor data. That group had exhaustively explored every theory that could possibly explain what they had all seen, but none of the theories had emerged as a clear winner.

The scientist wearing a rumpled suit and a permanently worried frown rubbed a hand through his thinning hair. He felt like he'd aged a decade in the last week, and the future didn't hold much promise of letting up any time soon. "If this is what we have, then it's what I'll have to present. You might be in charge of the project before the end of my meeting, Dr. Waneeta."

A woman with gray hair tightly pulled into a severe bun and thick glasses that made her eyes seem larger than they should be shook her head and reached out to pluck a bit of lint from his lapel. "They could try, but I'd decline the honor. Only a fool would want to be in charge of this fiasco." She flashed her teeth in a quick grin.

"No arguments there," the first scientist sighed. "I guess I can't put this off any longer. They're all waiting." He fruitlessly pulled at the knot of his tie to straighten it as he shuffled out of his untidy office.

The corridors of Oceanica Platform 37 were bustling despite the late hour. The sun had set on this part of the vast Atlantic Ocean several hours ago, and normally the duty rotation would have only a skeleton crew manning each department overnight. The arrival of their visitors had stirred up the hornet's nest, however. The addition of all the aides and hangers-on wasn't helping, either.

The scientist bounced off other people hustling through the corridor. He muttered offhand apologies, but his mind was so focused on what lay ahead that he barely noticed if there was any reaction to his words. Thirty years of academic life had prepared him for stressful presentations, especially when he was trying to secure a new research grant or get one extended, but this was a situation he'd never expected to find himself in.

After too short a time, he realized that he'd arrived outside the chamber he'd been summoned to. Ten armed guards flanked the wide doors, two from each of the delegations that had arrived on the platform in the last couple of hours. The scientist picked out the pair wearing the uniform of his home country, hoping he'd get some sense of comfort from the familiar sight. He didn't.

"Are you ready for your presentation, Dr. Norman?"

The unexpected voice made him jump, and the scientist whirled to see who had snuck up behind him. It was a woman he'd spoken with many times over the last week, a senior advisor to one of the people waiting in the room. She was both shorter and more commanding in person, as if her position lent any amount of importance needed to offset her pixie features and slim build. "I- I'm as ready as I can be," he stuttered.

The woman's lips pursed as if she were holding back a smile. "You'll do fine, Dr. Norman. You were handpicked to lead three dozen of the brightest minds Earth has to offer. Just tell them what you know, outline whatever suppositions your team has come up with, and then explain what you hope to accomplish in the coming days."

With a tiny nod from the woman, two of the guards hurried to open the doors. The scientist tried to swallow the nervous lump in his throat, only to find that his mouth had gone dry. Conversely, his armpits were leaking so badly he half expected the stains to show through his jacket.

As they entered the vast chamber that had been designed for meetings more heavily attended than this one, three loud knocks echoed to announce the start of the meeting. The scientist barely noticed the archaically dressed man who held the thick staff that had generated the noise. He was shaking badly as the woman guided him forward with a hand in the small of his back.

The table he was led to held only five people, three men and two women. The power of the entire planet resided in those five leaders, however, as did the immense expectation that the scientist and the team he'd been given would solve the greatest mystery of the modern age.

"Dr. Norman will present the findings of his research team," the woman said, her voice ringing in the large chamber. Her words seemed to bounce off the rows of mostly vacant seats that rose up around them and made the scientist feel like he was on the arena floor of an old Roman colosseum.

He started when he realized that the woman had stepped back into the shadows and all eyes were now on him. "Anytime, Dr. Norman," the president of the North American Alliance said with an impatient gesture.

The pressure of standing in front of the heads of the Five Powers made his mind go blank, and the scientist's eyes darted around as if searching for any hint of reassurance. When he spotted a tray holding a glistening pitcher and several empty glasses, he almost shouted with glee. His hands were shaking so badly that more water splashed onto the tray than into the glass, but he was finally able to take a sip and soothe his dry mouth.

He set the glass down slowly, trying to force his racing brain to slow down and focus on what mattered in the present moment. Every time he tried to snatch at the words he'd practiced for the last half day, they skittered away before he could latch onto them. His mouth moved, but nothing emerged.

The lights in the room suddenly dimmed, and the scientist's head snapped up in surprise. The heads of the Five Powers were no more than dark shapes now, and that somehow made them less imposing. His racing heart was finally starting to get under control when hidden displays dropped from the ceiling and lit up to show the first frame of imagery the astrophysicists had been dissecting.

"*Intrepid*!" the scientist exclaimed, wincing at how loudly he'd barked the word. "Uh, *Intrepid* has been the focus of our orbital imaging platforms since the moment the colony ship left Earth's orbit. For four months, eleven days, nineteen hours, and twenty-seven minutes, the entire planet watched in fascination as humankind prepared to leave our solar system for the first time."

"Get on with it," a heavily accented voice snapped.

The scientist flinched, easily recognizing the voice as belonging to the general in charge of the Junta Arinallo that currently ruled South America. "Yes, uh, well..." The scientist nervously took another sip of water as he focused on the static image on the screens. "Play the video, please."

The grainy feed had been captured by two of the imaging platforms orbiting the planet. Each of the Five Powers was allowed one by the terms of the treaty that ended the Unification Wars, but the other three had been out of position at the moment of this footage.

A grainy object filled the center of the video, which was recognizable as *Intrepid* only because every person in the room had spent countless hours watching the ship's progress over the last four months. "As you can see," the scientist said, "*Intrepid* was approaching what we've long considered the outer edge of the solar system. Four months of steady acceleration had given them the speed needed to cross the light years to Proxima Centauri within the seven-year mission parameters, and everything appeared to be proceeding smoothly."

The pixelated ship on the screen suddenly flickered, as if the data stream had buffered. When the image cleared, the ship was no longer alone. A large, golden obelisk was floating in space, and it was massive when compared against *Intrepid* on the screen.

"We're still not sure what caused the flicker," the scientist said, his voice beginning to grow stronger as he fell into the comfortable flow of discussing the data. "However, we do know that *Intrepid* shed all momentum in the split second it took for the

data feed to clear up again. At the same time, this strange structure had appeared."

"Isn't that impossible?" someone asked. "Bringing such a
large ship to a complete stop in so short a time?"

The scientist forced himself not to turn and find out which
of the world leaders had spoken. "Theoretically, yes. Everything
we know about physics and the laws of motion says that such an
abrupt change in momentum should never have occurred without catastrophic damage as a result. I've tasked a small team with
finding an answer for how it might have happened, but they've
made little progress so far."

He cleared his throat and forced his mind back to the presentation he'd spent hours rehearsing. "*Intrepid* and the obelisk
remained in this position for approximately seven and a half
hours," the scientist said, raising an arm to point at the image that
appeared to be frozen on the screen. "The last messages and data
streams from the ship were received many hours later. However,
based on the communication speed between such vast distances,
we can extrapolate that our contact was cut at the very moment
the obelisk appeared."

Mutters began behind him, but the scientist ignored them.
He motioned for the video feed to be sped up, then waved a
hand when the time stamp reached a familiar point. "This portion of the feed has not been shared with anyone outside the top
echelons of the government and scientific community, of course.
The public feed was cut and scrubbed as soon as the obelisk appeared."

The scientist raised a hand to shade his eyes only a second before the screen flashed with blinding light. The men and women
at the table and scattered around the chamber uttered expres-

sions of shock and dismay, and their voices only grew louder when the light faded to reveal empty blackness on the screen.

"We've all seen this footage many times, Dr. Norman. Can you tell us what happened at that moment?" the Chairman of the Pan-Asian Coalition asked. "Where is *Intrepid*?"

The scientist ran a hand through his hair, making it stand up more wildly than it normally would. This was the question his team had been tasked with answering, and they'd spent more than a week trying to find those answers. Analysis of the stars visible on the screen verified that the imaging platforms were still focused on the same portion of space the colony ship had filled before the bright flash. They'd also gone back through decades of images captured by the space telescopes looking for any object that could have been the strange golden obelisk that appeared near *Intrepid*. The searches had come up empty, which shouldn't have been possible for a structure of that size.

His team had eventually arrived at three primary theories to explain what might have happened. One, *Intrepid* had made first contact with a strange alien craft and been destroyed. Two, a malfunction happened simultaneously on both imaging platforms focused on the colony ship, causing false images before the flash occurred at the moment the software corrected itself. The third and most contentious of the theories was that the bright flash, which had been preceded by a single image frame of a strange distortion in space around the colony ship and obelisk, was some sort of faster-than-light travel that pulled *Intrepid* away from where it had been.

The scientist turned back to the five dark shapes that were the planetary leaders. His nervousness had faded and been replaced by the confusion and worry that had run rampant in his mind over the last week. He opened his mouth to launch into the theories and explanations his team had come up with, but then he sighed deeply instead.

"Frankly, sir, we don't have any damned idea what happened." He raised both hands and shrugged. "That's why I'd like to request the use of the two unmanned research probes currently tasked with mapping Saturn's moons. It will take a few months for them to reach the position from whence *Intrepid* disappeared, but we require sensor data of the surrounding space to either verify or discard the many theories that could feasibly explain what we've just seen."

The scientist tugged on his tie again, preparing himself for angry recriminations before he was fired and his career went down in flames.

However, the chamber was silent for several long seconds. The heads of the Five Powers seemed to be communicating through mute looks, until the Prime Minister of the Western Federation spoke. "Your request is granted, Dr. Norman."

1 - Ballard

Alina Ballard sauntered through the narrow corridors of the space station, soaking in the sights and sounds of a place she never would have imagined existed half a year earlier. The air was filled with a variety of food smells, some of which repulsed her while others tempted her to draw nearer the stalls and shops they came from.

The Fleet Infantry squad she commanded trailed her, chattering between themselves about the latest training session or the delights they looked forward to experiencing during their short leave on this new space station. Alina couldn't help but chuckle at their enthusiasm to explore. It was a desire she shared, especially since this was only the third Eslop station *Intrepid* had visited. Each of the structures built and maintained by the tentacled alien species were similar in many ways, which would be expected from a species that shared a hive mind. However, there were always small differences which proved exciting to discover.

"Lieutenant, how about that one?"

Alina followed a pointing finger toward a wide doorway surrounded by flashing lights. The pictographic sign hanging to the left of the entry made it clear that alcoholic beverages were waiting inside, though few would likely be suitable for human consumption. "Really, Cantu? Nine days of hard training, and on your first leave you want to get hammered?"

The man who'd been part of her virtual combat league on *Intrepid* before they both joined the new Fleet Infantry unit nodded enthusiastically. "You know it, Lieutenant," he said through a wide grin.

She laughed and shook her head. "Just what I'd expect from a jarhead gunnery sergeant. First round is on Cantu!"

Cheers went up from the members of her squad, and she took a moment to bask in the joy those simple words evoked. Her squad. After years spent pushing paper and keeping track of inventory lists, she was finally in a role that she'd always dreamed of. *An officer in charge of grunts*, she thought fondly as she fingered the rank bars on her chest.

She followed the squad into the bar, expecting the interested stares that quickly fell on them. Her original team had been expanded to include a couple of recruits pulled from among the human colonists, and they'd also taken on some of the aliens who had been rescued from the Kr'Sal slave mines.

The pair of Panosh brothers who fought beside her in those mines had been the first to volunteer. The green-furred simian species was shorter than the average human, but their bodies carried more muscle than a gym rat could achieve without chemical help. Panosh were great at hand-to-hand combat, and she had discovered they were equally dangerous with one of the sleek rifles their race had developed during a period of inter-species war in this part of the galaxy.

The final member of her eight-person squad was perhaps the strangest. Pmnqoelashtiké, or Lash for short to save human tongues from twisting, was an insectile alien that was half Alina's height. The Tiké were a species from a distant part of the galaxy that loved to explore, and Lash was a prime example of that motivating desire. He had hopped around from planet to space station across hundreds of light years, until he had the misfortune to draw the interest of a Kr'Sal slaver. Upon being freed by the humans, he'd decided to spend time exploring this sector with them.

Alina sidled up to the bar and waved to get the attention of the Sumarong bartender. The sloth-like alien's happily dopey expression made her smile in response, as did the languid, lumbering steps it took to reach her. She motioned toward the table her squad had taken and ordered three different bottles, one type of alcohol for each of the species.

Cantu was talking when she arrived with the bottles and glasses, which wasn't a surprise. No matter how many people were added to the squad, Cantu was always the one hogging most of the conversations and filling any quiet moments with more words.

"That's what I'm talking about, Lash. Why bother with diplomacy when it's so much easier to just go in swinging and resolve everything in a much shorter time?"

The insectile alien's laughter buzzed like a wasp's wings. "Not all problems can be solved through brute force, sergeant. Look at your own history if you don't believe me. How long did your Unification Wars last? How many people died when their lives could have been spared with diplomacy?"

"Words are like pretty flowers," one of the Panosh brothers grunted.

Alina felt a faint vibration against the bone behind her ear as the translator implant worked to make the alien speech understandable. Silas had promised the feeling would fade after a few weeks, but she had to take his word for it since only those who were around aliens the most had been fitted with the implants so far. "How's that?" she asked him.

"They smell nice until you crush them in your fist," MakTur said through a grin that bared large, blocky teeth.

Lash scoffed and waved dismissively. "While I would freely admit that words have caused more fights than they've stopped, there will always be a place for diplomacy in the galaxy. Without it, this space station wouldn't exist."

"A point to the corporal," Okune said, raising his glass to Lash. "The Eslop created these little pit stops on the space lanes precisely because they offered a neutral location for various species to interact and get to know each other without having to set foot on sovereign soil. That's the first step to peaceful coexistence."

"Or a conflict that spreads across twenty-eight solar systems," Cantu said. "Don't forget that the aliens had their own all-out battle royale, just like we've had on Earth."

"Which serves as a stark reminder of why diplomacy should always be the first step, with the hope of preserving lives," Alina said, deciding it was time to turn the conversation away from such a contentious subject. "Speaking of diplomacy, which of you grunts wants to go with me to meet our contact at the WayLin Mining Consortium offices after this drink?"

Every eye at the table was suddenly drawn to other areas of the bar, and Alina smirked as they all tried so hard not to be picked. WayLin had been good for *Intrepid*, offering the human ship contracts hauling cargo for several months in the Gliese 649 system, where they'd arrived after being pulled through a wormhole. The credits they'd earned through that work had allowed them to outfit the former colony ship with much better sublight engines, increasing the speed with which they could complete the cargo runs. After nine and a half weeks of such drudge work, they'd finally accumulated the funds necessary to retro-fit the wrinkle drive from a battered old freighter they'd used to transport the freed slaves from the Kr'Sal mines.

Wrinkle drives used technology that none of the humans un-derstood to transport ships across vast distances in practically the blink of an eye. As far as Alina was able to understand when one of *Intrepid*'s engineers gushed over the drives, they func-tioned in such a way as to fold space and bring two points that could be light years apart into closer contact. She didn't really care how the wrinkle drive worked, as long as it kept making their lives easier.

"Gundar, you're up," she said, tipping her glass toward one of her newest recruits. The former colonist had joined her squad only three weeks ago, and she was still getting to know him so that she could determine how best to utilize whatever skills he might possess.

"Yes, lieutenant," Sal Gundar said through a heavy sigh. "I'm looking forward to hearing you discuss mining contracts with some mid-level paper pusher."

Alina grinned while others at the table chuckled in response. "Those mining contracts are what keep us supplied with the credits we need to buy drinks like these." She held up her glass, which contained a liquor that tasted like a mix between brandy and whiskey. It wasn't her favorite, but it was damn good.

"You know, I'm suddenly more motivated to join you," Gun-dar said.

"I thought you might be," she laughed. "One more drink and then we'll head over to the WayLin offices."

"If it's all right with you, lieutenant, I'd like to go with Mak-Tur and LoTur when they visit the local Panosh representative."

Lash's mandibles quivered in excitement at the prospect.

"That's fine, Lash. Keep these two gorillas out of trouble for me," she said with a wink at the Panosh. She'd worried they might take offense at the term, but both of them seemed to find amusement in it, instead.

"If trouble didn't want to be found, it should try harder to hide," MakTur said before flashing his teeth in a wide grin.

Cantu leaned forward to grab one of the bottles. "I'm planning to finish this, and maybe find another bar that offers a little companionship. Who's in?"

Okune rolled his eyes and released a long-suffering sigh. "I guess I have to tag along to make sure you don't end up causing an interspecies incident."

"Yeah, you totally don't want to spend a few hours with some hot alien chick hanging off your shoulder," Cantu joked, prodding his friend.

"Suarez, you're on babysitting duty with these two," Alina said, pointing to Cantu and Okune.

The woman she addressed, a botanist with an adventurous streak that made her volunteer to join the Fleet Infantry, looked at the two men with furrowed brows. "I'd rather be running herd on a flock of two-year-olds, lieutenant."

"Aw, you know you like hanging out with us, Yas," Cantu said, feigning a hurt tone. "We're fun."

"Fun is a relaxing drink and eight hours of uninterrupted sleep. Chaperoning you two around a space station is not what I'd call fun."

"Hey, I'm the responsible one," Okune protested.

"That's what makes it so much more disappointing when you follow Cantu along on what he calls an adventure," Suarez smirked.

Alina listened to the banter and let a tiny smile touch her lips. She enjoyed watching how well her cobbled-together squad got along, each of their personalities meshing with the others. When Sergeant Major Bauer had suggested accepting some of the colonists who wished to make the leap into combat roles, she'd resisted at first. Lisbet Galbraith, her counterpart and lieutenant of the other Fleet Infantry squad, had been surprisingly open to the idea, though. After all, Galbraith reasoned, they couldn't expect to face any future problems with just the six original Infantry members. The Kr'Sal would eventually come looking for trouble after their plan to enslave the humans had been disrupted, and they'd need to be ready to meet whatever force was sent after them.

She threw back the last of her drink, and then tapped Gundar's shoulder. He nodded and drained his glass before slipping out of the bar behind her.

Alina had been surprised when Captain Kerrigan tasked her with finalizing the details for a new work contract with WayLin, but he'd assured her the finer details had already been ironed out. There appeared to be some components that might require Fleet Infantry involvement, though, so he wanted her to vet that portion of the contract. Frankly, after months of training and very little real excitement, she would have been quite happy to sign on for a dangerous expedition into the unexplored regions of space.

She wiped away the smile that broke across her face at such thoughts. More than likely, the WayLin contract would involve the Infantry squads standing around on boring guard duty.

But she could dream.

2 - Wingate

Paine Wingate squeezed his eyes shut and ran his fingers over the lids, hoping to alleviate the burning sensation that had been growing in them for the last hour. There was only a little bit of work left in his day, and then he could try to find some rest.

Sleep had been elusive over the last three months, ever since his rescue from the Kr'Sal slave mines. Unless he dosed himself with heavy sedatives, which always left him feeling fuzzy and out of sorts the next day, he was lucky to get more than a couple of hours sleep in a night. Horrible nightmares would drag him into wakefulness, often with a scream of terror threatening to rip out of his throat. In those dreams, he relived the worst moments of his enslavement. He also saw the soldiers who had come to rescue their fellow humans fall time after time to reptilian brutality.

Paine took a series of deep, calming breaths before turning his attention back to the document he was perusing. It was yet another mind-numbingly boring treatise extoling the virtues of a trading partnership between Earth and one of the inhabited planets that filled this sector of the galaxy. Ever since he'd accepted the position as ambassador for humanity on Kraken station, requests such as these had taken up the majority of his time.

He leaned over and pressed one of the buttons that lined the left edge of his expansive desk. In less than a minute, the door to his office opened to admit a whipcord thin being. The Edryne, from a species whose home system was thirteen light years from Kraken, stood nearly nine feet tall, with arms and legs that seemed to have been stretched out like taffy. His grayish-blue skin was thin enough that dark veins showed through, lending a fragility to his appearance. "You summoned me, sir?"

"Yes, Bos. I was hoping you could remind me who submitted this document, which appears to be two hundred and seventy-eight pages of regurgitated enticements and promises I've already seen dozens of times before."

Bosanlek smiled as he crossed the room to bend over the desk. His mouth was very small compared to the rest of his features, so that any expression had initially sent shivers up Paine's spine. "I believe this particular entreaty for trading concessions with your world was submitted by the Dubuk."

Paine frowned, trying to remember which of the many alien races he'd come into contact with over the last half year that might be. "Remind me," he finally said through a sigh.

"I believe you likened them to the hyenas of Earth," Bos said, his hollow voice somehow forlorn despite the amusement on his face.

"Ah," Paine said, snapping his fingers as the memory sharpened. "They're the ones who build most of the starships in this sector, right? Am I correct in thinking there are a handful of shipyards around their home planet?"

"Very good, sir," Bos said with a deep nod. "Only the Acelu and Eslop persist in constructing their own vessels, but neither species has much need for ships since they so rarely travel the space lanes."

Paine tapped a finger on the datapad while he sucked on his cheeks. Finally, he flipped the device over and pushed it away. "As tempting as it would be to sign a contract to have them build ships for Earth, I don't yet know what sort of needs my people might have in the long term."

His frustration faded quickly, however. This was a subject he'd discussed many times with Captain Kerrigan since the colonists and crew aboard *Intrepid* had overwhelmingly voted to continue exploring the systems around Kraken. Both of them agreed that further exploration and contact with the alien races who populated the worlds here would greatly help to ease Earth's entry into the galaxy they had long assumed must be empty.

It was the protection of the mysterious Auricle that had kept the human solar system isolated, until they had proven capable of building starships that could traverse the distances between stars. Now that *Intrepid* had pushed beyond the strange obelisk they encountered, that protection was no longer in place. It was only a matter of time before one or more alien species discovered the location of Earth, and Paine intended to use that time wisely to make sure that humanity's best interests were served when strange visitors arrived.

"I will place this document with the others," Bos said, sliding the datapad off the desk. He stood erect, with the top of his head only a few inches from brushing the high ceiling. His face contorted briefly before he released a sound of discomfort. "I forgot to mention, sir, that a visitor has arrived and asked to see you. I was just about to inform you when you summoned me."

"A visitor?" Paine asked, his brows drawing together. In the three months he'd occupied this office, he could count the number of beings that actually dropped by on one hand. Aside from Eslop and TiTonA coming to welcome him on the first day, he'd been left entirely alone with his assistant in the suite of offices granted to them.

Bos's small mouth tightened until it had almost disappeared.

"You remember I told you F'Mosh had been recalled to the Kr'Sal home world, sir?"

"Yes, you dropped that bit of good news on me a couple of weeks ago. What does it have to do with our visitor?"

"His replacement arrived on Kraken this morning."

Paine stared at the Edryne for a few moments, and then stiffened as he realized what Bos was trying to tell him. "That lizard came here? To visit *me*?"

"X'Zak seems to be cut from a different cloth than her predecessor." Bos lifted his shoulders, a mannerism he had adopted from his human superior. "She and I spoke for several minutes before your summons, and I believe she might be sincere in her desire to apologize for the treatment you were forced to endure."

Paine clamped his jaw shut, holding back the anger that wanted to spill out in furious curses. He recognized the deep-seated fear that was driving his anger to greater heights, threatening to spiral out of control. He gripped his fingers tightly on the arms of his chair, squeezing until the pain in his fingertips chipped away at the rage within.

His first impulse was to have the Kr'Sal ejected from his offices and barred from ever returning. Every time he passed one of the rare lizards that passed through Kraken, he was forced to confront the memories and nightmares all over again. The thought of being shut up in a room with one of them was almost too much to bear.

However, he had come to trust the Edryne assigned to work with him. Bos was not only highly efficient, but a great judge of character. If he said this new Kr'Sal ambassador was different from F'Mosh, then it was his duty as the human representative to meet with her. Perhaps they could mend some of the wounds of the past, before the two races clashed again.

"Very well," he sighed after half a minute. "Show her in, but I'd like you to join us."

"Of course, sir," Bos said, stooping to pass through the doorway.

Paine used the next minute to smooth out the wrinkles in his suit and check his tie. He'd been tempted to adopt some of the flowing robes that most of the ambassadors on Kraken seemed to favor, but the suits he'd worn throughout his career had once again begun to feel like armor against the cruelties of the universe.

He was standing beside his desk when Bos reappeared, leading the Kr'Sal ambassador into his office. Paine sucked in a breath when the lizard passed through the doorway, wondering if he'd been this close to one of them since his rescue from the slave mines. It took an effort of willpower to paste a sickly smile on his face. "Hello, and welcome to Earth's embassy."

"It is a great pleasure to be granted entry," the newcomer said. Paine waited for the buzz behind his ear that indicated the implant had translated her speech, but it never came. The Kr'Sal recognized his shock and hissed in laughter. "I hope my knowledge of your tongue doesn't come as too much of a surprise. Learning your speech seemed to be the best course to smoothing the troubles between our peoples."

Paine wasn't sure how he felt about the lizard speaking English. Only one of the Kr'Sal he'd encountered had ever spoken anything but the hissing grunts of their own language, and the lizards seemed to feel that all other tongues were beneath contempt. He decided to re-evaluate this ambassador and try to judge her apart from his prior experience of her species.

For one thing, she was shorter than F'Mosh and P'Tak, the hulking overseer of the slave mines. If anything, she reminded him of the smaller lizard who had served to translate for the slaves when the overseer chose to speak to them. Her leathery hide even had the same yellowish-green color as the translator, as opposed to the darker, almost black, green of the former ambassador and slave overseer.

He waved a hand toward two chairs that flanked the one window in his suite of offices. "Would you care to sit while we talk? I'm sorry, I didn't catch your name."

"X'Zak," she said, drawing out the syllables to make them easier to understand. "I would love to sit and chat with you, Paine Wingate."

His lips twitched at the subtle jab of using his name when he'd just had to ask for hers. For a brief moment, he felt the old thrill that used to course through his veins every time he entered a delicate negotiation with the hope of winning more concessions than the other side.

"Bos, perhaps you could bring something for our guest. Do the Kr'Sal drink tea, X'Zak?"

Her head tilted as she settled into the chair. "What is tea?"

Paine chuckled and waved for Bos to gather the tea set he'd managed to borrow from one of the colonists who currently lived on Kraken. "On Earth, there are several plants which provide aromatic flavors when their leaves are steeped in hot water. That is what we call tea, and I hope you'll enjoy it." He leaned back in his chair and steepled his fingers below his chin. "While we wait, perhaps you could explain why you chose to visit me?"

"When my predecessor never would?" X'Zak asked. Her lips drew up in a smile, but he couldn't help but shudder at the memory of how threatening that expression had been in the past. "F'Mosh is what your people would call 'old school'. He and others like him refuse to accept that the practices of our past have outlived their usefulness. We Kr'Sal must evolve and change if we wish to fit in with all others who share this part of the galaxy. Wouldn't you agree?"

"Mm," Paine hummed noncommittally. He was trying his best to hide the shock of meeting a lizard who seemed willing to admit her species was not superior to all others. "There have been times during humanity's history when our ancestors were forced to confront similar issues. Some changed and prospered, while others remained stagnant and faded into obscurity."

X'Zak lifted a hand to wave toward him. "Then you understand the difficulty faced by those of us who have chosen to evolve."

Bos returned at that moment, and he bent low to place the tea set on the narrow table between the chairs. As Paine began to prepare the tea, he realized that he was actually enjoying this meeting. Perhaps he'd been wrong to judge an entire race based on the few examples he'd had the misfortune to meet.

"Tell me more about your people," he said. "I'd love to learn about the Kr'Sal from your perspective, X'Zak."

3 - Kerrigan

Captain Lyle Kerrigan leaned in, until his nose was almost pressed against the shimmering containment field. Even while not in use, the wrinkle drive was a constantly moving, humming mass of machinery. There was a strange fluidity in the way the individual parts moved. It was almost like watching a dance, with each pair moving in sync with all the others. It was hypnotic.

"You've done great work, Commander," he said when he finally stepped back. "I wasn't sure *Intrepid* would be able to handle one of these fantastic drives, but you made it work."

Commander Berger, the woman in charge of Engineering, grunted loudly. "The hardest part was keeping all these heathens from ripping that pretty little trinket apart to find out how it works," she said, waving to indicate the crew members moving around the large area set aside for *Intrepid*'s most important parts. "To be honest, I was a fair bit tempted to do the same thing."

Lyle smiled at the picture in his head. It was easy to imagine a pack of engineers rubbing their hands in gleeful expectation when they got a glimpse at the most advanced technology they'd encountered since leaving their home system. "We all appreciate your efforts in keeping the drive intact and working," he said.

"I'd appreciate knowing more about it," Berger said, her mouth pursing as she reached out to tap the containment field. Lyle had expected it to sizzle like an electronic force field, but instead he heard a faint hum when her finger touched it. "I begged for some sort of owner's manual before we left Kraken, but no one there seemed to know anything more about the wrinkle drives than we do. As long as the drives keep working, they don't seem to care what's behind their function."

"I can sympathize with that feeling," Lyle said, looking around at all the machinery and consoles that filled Engineering. He knew a small bit about most of it, but only enough to understand how to best utilize their functions in the running of his ship. If any individual piece malfunctioned, he'd have no idea how to go about repairing it.

"I tried to talk Silas into giving me something, since he was the one who helped the Kraken shipyard techs figure out how to make the drive work with *Intrepid*. The birdman went mum on me, claiming the secrets of wrinkle drive technology belong only to the species that originally built them."

Lyle's brows drew together. That was more than he'd ever heard Silas say about the drives that enabled fast travel across this sector of the galaxy. "Which species is that?"

Berger scoffed and waved her hand in frustration. "He wouldn't even tell me *that*! From the bits and pieces he did finally let go of, however, my understanding is that it's not one that lives in this sector. We'd have to explore pretty far to run across them."

"Well, that's a mystery for us to delve into at another time, I suppose." Lyle tentatively touched the containment field and was surprised by the somewhat pleasant tingle that ran through his hand and forearm. "Did Silas happen to explain why this field is necessary?"

"Eh, something about the way the wrinkle drive folds space. Without the containment field, the ship itself would be folded along with all the people in it. Pain, blood, death, yada, yada. I stopped listening once I understood it was a necessary component."

Lyle lifted an eyebrow and eyed Berger's back. He sometimes wondered if his Chief Engineer cared about anything that wasn't mechanical. "Yes, well... the wrinkle drive is performing within parameters after our first use of it?"

"As far as I can tell," Berger said, waving a datapad through the air. "The readings we're getting barely showed a blip when we activated it, though we did suffer an eight percent drain to our fuel reserves."

He winced at the steep cost of using the drive. It was one more expense he would have to factor in as *Intrepid* continued to operate under these new conditions. "We'll keep our usage of the drive to a minimum, then. Any other concerns you need to share with me while I'm down here, Commander?"

"Nothing urgent," Berger said faintly. She was scrolling on her datapad, already becoming lost in the list of tasks that she needed to check up on.

Lyle smiled fondly when the Chief Engineer drifted away, already putting him out of her mind as she approached one of her engineers and quizzed him about some maintenance work that had been requested. He cast a final look at the wrinkle drive, resisting the urge to stand and stare as the thousands of components moved through their intricate dance within the containment field.

After leaving Engineering, he enjoyed strolling through the corridors without being in a hurry to reach another section of the ship. While the bridge and cabin where he spent most of his time were in the forward section, the engines and important systems like life support and power-generating reactors were all contained in the rear section. The bow and aft sections were separated by a long, arching spine which originally held five vertical modular sections that gave the appearance of exposed ribs to an imaginative mind.

Those modular sections had housed the five hundred colonists bound to start a new life on a world around Proxima Centauri, along with the food, water, and supplies needed to sustain them through the expected seven year voyage and for the first year on their new home. After the ship was captured in the Auricle wormhole, whether intentionally or by accident, they found themselves just inside the Gliese 649 system instead. Thirty-four light years from Earth and surrounded by a variety of alien races.

Now, four of the modular sections were safely housed in cargo bays on Kraken station. A fifth had been stolen by Kr'Sal pirates, and they had no idea what had become of it once the people inside had been enslaved and dropped on a dead world that housed slave mines. It could have ended up wherever the dozen people they'd been unable to recover had been taken. *Pleasure markets*, Lyle thought sourly. Silas had feelers out in an attempt to discover a location, but so far the information they'd received had been scanty.

A trio of crew members passed by, and Lyle returned their nod of greeting. His steps slowed, and he chuckled to himself. He'd only recognized one member of the small group at first, but now he realized the other two had been recent additions.

After everyone had voted to continue exploring new worlds and space stations before returning to Earth or resuming their original mission, the colonists had faced yet another decision.

While *Intrepid* carried out cargo runs to earn the credits needed for vital upgrades and supplies, the colonists lived within the modular sections stored on Kraken station. Eslop had graciously offered to let any of the humans live and work on the space station if they chose. Many had eagerly taken the opportunity which put them in frequent contact with a variety of races, but others had expressed an interest in joining *Intrepid*'s crew and exploring the stars instead. Lyle and his XO, Commander Indira Predashi, had discussed the matter with their senior officers and finally decided to double the size of the crew.

Thinking about his XO made Lyle realize it had been a while since he'd popped into CIC. The Combat Information Center served as a secondary control center for *Intrepid*, with the officers there ready to take command in the event the main bridge was compromised. It had been placed in the aft section, buried deep within the ship's structure, where it could be well protected in the event of a ship-to-ship battle.

Lyle rapped his knuckles against the steel bulkhead before stooping to pass through the opening. CIC was buzzing, with more than a dozen officers and crew manning stations and communicating with each other or their counterparts on the bridge. The room was half the size of the spacious and comfortable bridge, but it felt like home. He smiled at memories of his time serving as XO on an Allied Fleet ship.

"Captain, what an unexpected pleasure," Predashi said, straightening up from where she'd been bent over the large table that occupied the central portion of CIC.

"Commander," he said, nodding in greeting. "I just left Engineering, so I figured I'd swing by and check in."

"How long did Commander Berger talk about her newest

toy?" Predashi asked with a cheeky grin.

He returned the smile. "I believe the good Commander recognized the vacant look in my eyes when she veered into technical details and took pity. She did mention the fuel consumption of our first use of the wrinkle drive, however."

Predashi grimaced and rubbed her neck as if trying to relieve sore muscles. "Yeah, she brought that up to me this morning. We need to find someplace to top off our deuterium tanks if we intend to use the drive more often."

"I'll bring it up the next time I talk with Silas. Maybe he can point us in the right direction." Lyle put his hands on the table and leaned forward as he lowered his voice. "That means spending some of our hard-earned credits, however, and I don't think we have much left after the purchases we've already made. The new sub-light engines were expensive, but retrofitting the wrinkle drive to work with *Intrepid*'s other systems was more so."

"Yay," Predashi said with a flat expression. "More cargo hauling jobs."

Lyle chuckled. "Perhaps not. I've been communicating with the WayLin Mining Consortium representative on this space station, and he suggested there might be an opportunity for us to transport personnel and equipment to a new asteroid deep inside this system which they've purchased the rights to mine. Lieutenant Ballard is visiting the WayLin officer while her squad is enjoying some downtime."

"You sent a Fleet Infantry grunt to talk business?" Predashi grinned and reached out to poke his shoulder. "When did you start to hate her so much?"

"More like trust her," he replied with a shrug. "Ballard has proved she has her head on straight, and I needed an opinion I could trust about the details of the job that might not occur to either of us. Such as how rambunctious a mining crew might be, and the trouble they could cause while cooped up on *Intrepid* for the two and a half weeks it would take to ferry them out to the mining facility under construction."

"We could just lock them in one of the cargo drums," Predashi said, waving her hand as if that settled the matter. "Let them cause all the mayhem they like in there. We'll just charge WayLin a cleanup and repair fee after the transport is complete."

Lyle laughed, enjoying the image while knowing it wouldn't be a feasible solution. The cargo drums had been built to replace the modular sections, designed mostly for ore crates but capable of holding almost anything. Housing living beings was not their ideal function, however.

"Speaking of downtime," Predashi said, interrupting his thoughts, "when do we start releasing crew members to enjoy the delights offered by this shiny new-to-us space station?"

"I'm planning to remain here for another couple of days," he said musingly. "My thought was two six-hour leave shifts each day, randomly assigned."

"I'd love to see what kind of bartering goes on when people want to swap their assigned leave. Some will prefer earlier in the day, but I'm sure most will want the evening leave when they can let loose and have some fun."

"Not too much fun," Lyle snorted. "It might be a good idea to group them and assign an officer to ride herd. Some Infantry escorts might not be a bad idea, as well. The last thing we need is to start something with one of the aliens that blossoms into a major incident."

"You know," Predashi said musingly, "we keep calling them

aliens. But out here, *we're* the aliens." She bent to put her elbows on the table, and their fingers brushed as if the contact was incidental.

Lyle enjoyed the softness of her skin against his and cursed the regulations for what felt like the thousandth time. He and Predashi had grown close during the voyage out from Earth, and the difficulties of their sudden arrival on the galactic scene had only strengthened that bond. "That's a valid point, commander."

Predashi smirked at him, obviously able to read his thoughts from his expression. "What do you say we adjourn to my office and hash out a leave rotation, captain?" She jerked her head to the side, indicating the closed hatch that led into her combined office and cabin just off CIC.

He glanced around, pleased to see that everyone else was focused on their own tasks and ignoring the discussion between their captain and XO. "That sounds like a good idea. We should get that completed and posted before the end of the day shift, so people can prepare for their assigned leave."

Predashi flashed him an almost predatory grin before she turned to lead him toward her office. Lyle sucked in a deep breath, and for the first time in his career he started to wonder if the regulations even mattered. After all, they were more than thirty light years from Earth and the rest of humanity. Perhaps out here, they needed new regulations.

4 - Ballard

Alina propped her boot up against the edge of the desk and pushed just hard enough to tip her chair back a few inches. With one elbow draped over the back of that chair and a bored expression on her face, she watched from the corner of her eye for the reaction of the corporate representative on the other side of the desk.

She'd been mildly surprised to be greeted by a Telbrith, a huge slug-like alien propped up on a floating platform that had an array of water misters to keep his body moist. Hearing the alien's almost guttural voice speak a greeting in English was even more shocking. It was hard to believe that when *Intrepid* first arrived at Kraken, there had been only one alien proficient with their language, and yet they now encountered more aliens speaking English every day. It had almost been a relief when he reverted to the Telbrith language, despite the vibration of the translator behind her ear with each word.

"So let me get this straight," she said, rocking the chair back and forth. "You actually *want* our Fleet Infantry squads to come down hard on your miners if they step out of line? Harder than we would for our own people?"

The Telbrith pulled a rigid pipe from his mouth, emitting a cloud of water vapor along with a booming laugh. "Very much so," he said. "Rigid discipline is a necessity in an environment such as these beings will inhabit for the length of their contracts. The slightest mistake, whether through inattention or failure to follow proper protocols, could mean the loss of many lives and many more credits."

Alina scoffed but was secretly impressed he had put lives ahead of money. "I suppose we can clamp down on them during the trip. If you're concerned about them getting out of hand, though, why not just confine them to the quarters we give them?"

"No, no," the Telbrith said. "They must have the freedom to roam the public areas and make any mistakes while they can learn from them." He puffed on the water pipe and blew out another cloud of vapor. "There is a core of experienced miners among the group, and they will need as many opportunities as possible to train the newer workers in proper behavior. In my experience, lessons learned through experience last longer than those imparted through words alone."

She raised a hand to cover the smile that spread at his words. The Telbrith reminded her of her favorite instructor back when she was going through boot camp. That grizzled old sergeant had said much the same, but with more than a few expletives sprinkled in to add some flavor. "Okay, so we let them run wild and swoop in every time someone even toes the line. Our squads can handle that, but I think you might need to add some incentives to the contract. We'll be putting in a lot of hours running herd on your workers during the trip out to the asteroid."

The WayLin representative wriggled on his sled. Alina had to avert her eyes and hold back a shudder of revulsion, reminded of earth worms that had been dug out of loamy soil when she was a child. "Would an additional five thousand credits be enough recompense for your added workload?"

She eyed him for a few seconds, wondering how far she

could push it. "Seven thousand will work better. For each squad."

The Telbrith shook as he laughed. "Done. I would have paid ten for each of your two squads, by the way."

"Funny," Alina said with a grin. "I would have accepted six." She let her chair drop and then stood to run her finger across the datapad that sat on the desk between them. Her signature was added at the bottom of the very long document in a language she could never hope to decipher, and she was glad it wasn't her responsibility to skim through all of it. Captain Kerrigan had apparently done so, or had someone do it for him before he sent her to hash out a few last details.

"It has been a pleasure haggling with you," the Telbrith said. His sled began to move around the desk, but Alina couldn't see any controls that might have been used to guide it. "Perhaps when this contract is completed, we'll have the opportunity to do it again."

"You keep paying more than you have to, and we'll keep coming back for more work," she laughed.

"I will be better prepared for you next time," the Telbrith warned, waving his long pipe in her direction. "Perhaps it will be you who has to explain an unexpected expense to her superiors then, hmm?"

"You can dream, I suppose." Alina started to reach out to slap his shoulder, but she quickly yanked her hand back. She had no idea how the Telbrith might react to contact, and she wasn't entirely sure she wanted to find out if the slug was as slimy as he looked under that coating of moisture.

Gundar rose from the chair he'd been occupying in a back corner of the room. He blinked rapidly a few times before his jaw bunched up with a constrained yawn.

Alina shot him a knowing look before waving for him to follow as she left the WayLin offices. "Did you sleep through all of it, or were you paying attention at the beginning?"

"Sorry, lieutenant," he said. The apology would have worked better without the jaw-cracking yawn that immediately followed. "I imagined a lot more excitement and fewer contract negotiations when I signed up to join Infantry."

She snorted a laugh and slapped him on the back. "We all imagined glorious battle and nonstop danger when we signed up, Gundar. They don't tell you that ninety-nine percent of the job is training and boredom until it's too late to back out."

"It's not that bad," he said with a shrug. "Spend a few weeks cooped up in tight quarters inside a modular container that's inside a cargo bay that's inside a space station. Then you'll know what boredom really is."

Alina shot him a quick glance and wondered if that had been the only reason he'd volunteered to join an Infantry squad. She knew that many of the colonists had signed on to join the expanded crew aboard *Intrepid*, while others had ventured out into Kraken and begun looking for work to occupy their time. If Gundar had merely wanted simple diversion, he could have done either of those things.

"I need to report to Captain Kerrigan, but I suppose we should go look in on Cantu and Okune first," she said.

"Sergeant Cantu can be a bit, uh, rambunctious at times, can't he?"

"That's a polite way of putting it," she said. "Cantu grew up in a large family. He was the eighth of ten or eleven kids, and always had to fight for attention. The best way he found to do that was to always be the one dominating a conversation and coming up with fun ideas."

"He's got a strange sense of what fun is," Gundar said. "He tried to talk Lieutenant Galbraith into flirting with MakTur the other day. I think she was considering doing it, too!"

Alina held her stomach as she laughed, well able to imagine the scene. Lisbet Galbraith was a woman of few words, but she was loathe to turn down any challenge. She wasn't sure who she'd feel sorry for if the woman had given in to Cantu's goading, Galbraith or MakTur.

They were passing through a crowded portion of the station, so when Alina bumped into someone she merely tossed off an apology and kept walking. She was wiping mirthful tears from her eyes when a hand latched onto her wrist. Instinct and training kicked in, and Alina spun to face the person who had grabbed her. A quick twist of her wrist broke their hold, and she flicked out her collapsible baton with her other hand.

The fight drained out of her when she was faced with wide eyes and two hands raised protectively. "Forgive me," the furred alien yipped. "I meant no harm."

Alina relaxed, but she kept the baton in her hand as she examined the person who had grabbed her. The alien was covered in thick reddish-brown fur with white streaks along the arms and up the neck. Swells at the hip and chest beneath simple clothing would indicate this was a female, while the protruding snout and sharp teeth made her think of the dogs her family had raised when she was young. There was intelligence in those blue eyes that wouldn't be found in an Earth animal, though. "Who are you?" she asked.

"My name is Tamma," the alien said in a halting voice. More words followed in what sounded like yipping barks, but Alina's implant wasn't loaded with the software needed to translate.

"She's a fox!" Gundar exclaimed, snapping his fingers as if in sudden realization. He grinned at Alina until her frown made the expression fade. "I mean that she looks like a fox, lieutenant, not that she's a foxy lady or anything. I mean... you're, uh, very attractive, ma'am. Please don't think I was saying you aren't. It's just that–"

"Gundar, shut it," she said sharply, trying hard not to roll her eyes at his sheepish expression. Then she turned back to the alien. "Why did you grab me, Tamma?"

"You are the humans, yes?" There was a hopeful expression on her foxlike face as she asked the question.

"We are," Alina said with a tight nod.

"Then you can help me," Tamma said excitedly. "Not just me, but all of my people. I am one of the Kitane. You probably haven't met any of us yet since you are so new to this part of the galaxy."

"We haven't," Alina confirmed. She looked around and noticed all the interested stares from people passing where they stood in the middle of the corridor. With a resigned sigh, she waved for the alien to follow. "Let's get out of everyone's way, and then you can tell me what you need help with. I'm not promising we can or will do anything about it, but I'll listen."

Tamma was on her heels as they moved through the crowd toward a quieter area. "You must help us," she said imploringly. "Many Kitane lives are at stake!"

Gundar shot her a confused look, and Alina motioned for him to stand on the other side of the foxlike being. "What's putting them in danger?"

Tamma's whiskers, which had been so tight against her snout

that Alina hadn't noticed them at first, twitched and stiffened. "The Golmorung," she said in a fearful whisper.

Alina waited, but no further information seemed forthcoming. "Who or what are the Golmorung?"

Tamma patted her hands against the air, looking around wildly as if afraid someone might have overheard. "Not so loud. Please! You never know where their spies might be found. I don't think I was followed to this space station, but it's impossible to say for sure."

Gundar flashed a quick grin while Alina huffed in annoyance. She supposed this proved paranoia wasn't a trait unique to humans. "I don't think we can help you with spies," she started to say, trying to find a way to extricate herself from the conversation.

"No, you don't understand." Tamma grabbed her arm with both hands while wide eyes met hers pleadingly. "They want to kill us. *All* of us. If you don't help, human, then my entire species will be wiped out!"

Alina's jaw tightened. The desire to escape faded, and she looked around for a more private location. There was a small eating establishment farther down the corridor, and she began herding the frantic Kitane in that direction. "Tell me why your people are in danger. Start from the beginning."

5 - Wingate

Insistent chimes pulled Paine up out of deep sleep, his mind responding to the sound it had been trained to listen for through years of early morning alarms. He batted his hand around until he found the tablet resting on a narrow shelf next to his bunk and shut off the noise.

Paine threw back the covers with a groan and rubbed his eyes to banish the blurriness. He swung his legs over the side of the bunk and sat there for a few moments to let his mind fully wake up. As he did so, a wide smile grew on his face. It had been months since he'd slept long enough to be woken by the alarm. It had taken a few hours to slow his racing mind and fall asleep the night before, but he'd managed nearly six uninterrupted hours of sleep without any chemical inducement. He felt fantastic!

He moved through the small suite of rooms that had been granted to him upon assuming the ambassadorship. It was while brushing his teeth that he realized he was humming. Paine froze and stared at his reflection in the mirror for a few seconds, then broke out in laughter. For the first time since he'd been dragged into the Kr'Sal mines, he was starting to feel like his old self again.

Once he was dressed and ready for the day, Paine left his quarters to begin the trip to his office. While the areas set aside for representatives of the races that passed through Kraken the most often were on the main level, living quarters were placed several levels deeper. The old Paine would have railed against what he saw as an indignity, but his new understanding of true hardship made him pause and realize that he was being treated equally with all others. He had no idea where Eslop or TiTonA might lay their head, but every other ambassador and representative he'd met had quarters not far from his own.

"Good morning," a deep voice boomed from behind.

Paine halted and turned to smile a greeting at the Telbrith representative. The sleds the race favored could move swiftly when desired, so it took only a few seconds until they were able to walk side-by-side. "Good morning, Wyeth. I haven't seen you in several cycles."

"It is a busy time for my people," the Telbrith said, waving his short arm to divert some of the mist spraying his body onto Paine. It had stunned him the first time it happened, until Bos explained that it was a great honor for one of the slug-like aliens to share their water with another being. "The Festival of Falling Skies will begin soon on my home world, and it is my duty to arrange travel and accommodations for all of our people in the surrounding systems."

"It's an important event, then?" Paine asked, making a mental note to do some research. Kraken offered many benefits, and one of them was an extensive database that detailed the customs and cultures of the various races that inhabited this sector of the galaxy. Part of his responsibilities were to fill in the information for humanity so that it would be available to the other races when requested.

"Very much so," Wyeth said. "The Festival of Falling Skies marks the occasion when our world was first visited by another race. It was twelve hundred and seventy sequences ago, but we still hold the festival every ten sequences to remember how great the change has been for our people."

Paine was growing more accustomed to using the Eslop designations for the passing of time, but he still had to do some quick math in his head. A cycle was what the Eslop called a day on the planet they originated from, which was roughly thirty-two hours on Earth. A full rotation of their primary moon was called a phase, and the time it took the Eslop world to circle their sun was called a sequence. Each sequence consisted of twenty-two phases and four hundred and eighteen cycles. That equated to roughly five hundred and sixty days on Earth, which meant it had been almost two thousand years since the Telbrith first encountered other races.

"My cousin has asked if you might like to attend," Wyeth said slowly. "He remembers you with great affection."

Paine smiled fondly. There had been one Telbrith enslaved in the mines and rescued by *Intrepid*'s Infantry squad alongside all the others. "I would love to attend and experience your festival, but I'm afraid the work here will prohibit my leaving Kraken for quite some time."

The Telbrith chuckled, his fat body writhing on the sled. "You must learn to ignore all the trade proposals being sent to you, or you'll never have a moment's peace. Within half a sequence, the newness of you humans will have worn off. Then you'll miss the days when you had so much work to keep your mind occupied."

"That day can't come soon enough," Paine laughed. "Bosanlek has been a wonderful assistant, but I'm considering bringing in a few more people to help me weed through the proposals." The idea started churning in his brain, and he wondered why he hadn't already followed through. He knew there were still some colonists living within the modular sections who hadn't found other work yet, and this might be the chance to get them out among the other races on Kraken more often. Perhaps a rotation, to expose as many of the humans as possible to those who shared this exciting place with them.

They had reached the array of platforms that were constantly moving up and down through Kraken's decks, and Wyeth guided his sled out of the main walkway. "We must part here," he said. "A transport arrived overnight, and I'm hoping I can secure berths for a handful of my people still on Kraken." The Telbrith's wide mouth turned up as he spoke the name the humans had given the space station when they arrived. There was an official Eslop name, but it was long and filled with syllables a human tongue could never hope to pronounce.

"I wish you luck and favorable transport fees," Paine said. He raised a hand in farewell before hurrying over to hop onto a platform going up.

It wasn't long before he arrived on the main level of the space station, filled with shops, offices, restaurants, and anything else the residents might want or need. Paine nodded greetings to a few of the aliens he recognized and said good mornings to a handful of humans who were hurrying toward the platforms to return to the cargo bays where their modular sections were stored.

He was still riding high from restful sleep, so he gave in to a compulsion to divert his steps and approach one of the long windows that looked out on the stars. Paine folded his arms across his chest and let his eyes roam freely, taking in bright stars, distant asteroids, and even more distant planets closer to the dim, orange sun of this system. His view was also filled with the twisting, tentacle-like arms that extended out in all directions from the flat, oblong disk of the main space station structure. Most of the protrusions served as docking points for arriving ships too large to fit in cargo bays, while some held shipyard gantries where repairs or upgrades could be carried out while the crews relaxed on the station.

Paine's thoughts turned to the people who had been lost in the short time since *Intrepid* had arrived at Kraken. He knew those deaths lay primarily on his shoulders. When the colony ship encountered a strange golden obelisk at the edge of the solar system, it had primarily been his efforts that convinced the colonists to vote to keep going. He had ignored the warnings of dangers that might await beyond the protections of the Auricle obelisks, which had kept humanity hidden from the rest of the galaxy until they were ready to leave their proverbial nest.

He spotted a cargo ship detaching from one of Kraken's arms, heading out to pick up another load of ores from one of the mining operations among the asteroids. The sight made him smile at the thought that *Intrepid* had been performing the same work for the last several months. The colony ship might have been the pinnacle of Earth's innovation, but out here it was like driving around in an outdated sedan while everyone else cruised past in the latest sports cars. Paine had been sad when Captain Kerrigan informed him they were finally beginning an exploration of the systems around Gliese 649, and he missed the company of the man he'd seen as a rival for so long. He hadn't realized how much he looked forward to their quiet evenings discussing matters on *Intrepid* and Kraken until they ended.

Shaking memories and regrets from his mind, Paine turned away from the window and resumed the walk to his office suite.

Bos would already be waiting with a list of trade proposals to peruse. He sometimes wondered if the Edryne slept at his desk, since Bos was always the first to arrive and the last to leave.

A smile touched Paine's lips as his thoughts turned to the meeting that ended the previous day. He never thought he'd enjoy spending time with a Kr'Sal, but X'Zak had proved a delightful conversationalist. They spent most of an hour talking about her home world and the history of her people, and she had left only after extracting a promise that he would visit her office soon.

Paine's smile faded, and he thought about the dozen humans who were still missing. The ones who had been destined for the pleasure markets, according to P'Tak. He was hopeful that X'Zak might be able to help him track those people down and free them, but he didn't want to broach the subject until he could be sure that she was as progressive as she seemed.

The door opened at his approach, and Paine grinned when Bosanlek rose from his desk with a greeting. One of these days he'd manage to arrive first, and he would enjoy the shocked look on his assistant's face when it happened.

"Good morning, Bos. What do you have for me today?"

6 - Kerrigan

"Are you sure we should be spending time on something trivial?"

Lyle held back a smile as he walked through the tube connecting *Intrepid* to the space station. "Weren't you the one saying we needed to learn more about the races that inhabit this part of the galaxy, Indira?"

"Sure, but that was before we had a signed contract and hard start time for the next job from WayLin."

"We don't leave the station until late tonight, and this meeting shouldn't take very long. Lieutenant Ballard feels that it's important for us to meet this Kitane and hear her story."

Predashi snorted. "If Alina Ballard said she thought it was important for you to meet in her quarters for a late-night chat, I sometimes wonder if you'd hesitate longer than a second before rushing off to do it."

Lyle smiled fondly and let his shoulder rub against hers. "There's only one cabin aboard *Intrepid* that I'd be eager to visit, and I can assure you it's not Lieutenant Ballard's." He waited for Predashi's scowl to soften before continuing. "She and Lieutenant Galbraith share command of the Fleet Infantry, so it's important that we show both our crew and their soldiers that we value their opinions. Besides, how else was I going to convince you to leave *Intrepid* and take a little R and R for yourself?"

His XO stiffened for a moment before releasing a low chuckle that sent a thrill of excitement down his spine. "Sneaky, Lyle. Very sneaky. But if I'm supposed to let go of the weight of command and relax for a few hours after this meeting, then you're going to do it with me. You need the time off more than I do."

"Fair enough," he said, trying the hide the grin that grew at the prospect of exploring the space station with the woman he was growing fonder of each day.

Their steps slowed as they left the docking tube and entered the bustling space station. This smaller outpost wasn't as busy as Kraken, but there were still more beings filling the corridors than would be found on *Intrepid*, even with the expanded crew. Lyle took a moment to get his bearings, and then motioned in the direction of Lieutenant Ballard's proposed meeting place.

"What did she tell you about this person?" Predashi asked, her natural skepticism showing through.

"Only enough to make me agree that it was important we hear the full story. The Kitane woman's name is Tamma, and she comes from a world eighteen light years from this station. Another race called the Golmorung are threatening hers in some way, but Ballard didn't share the details. She said it would be better to hear the story from Tamma."

"I don't know what we're supposed to do about any of this," Predashi grumbled. "We're not exactly the pinnacle of military technology in these parts."

"A diplomatic solution may be called for, in which case we'd be an ideal neutral arbitrator because of our newness to the sector."

They fell silent as they approached a quiet out-of-the-way eatery that catered specifically to a species which communicated through wavelengths of light. Lyle couldn't help but be impressed by the foresight of choosing this as a meeting place, since there was little chance of eavesdropping when all the other patrons didn't possess auditory organs.

He spotted Alina Ballard sharing a table with a foxlike being with a slightly smaller frame. He admired the reddish-brown fur covering the being's body which looked soft enough to make him want to pet her. Lyle wondered at the innate desire that he suspected came from thousands of years of domesticating animals into pets.

Ballard rose to greet them and make introductions. "Captain Lyle Kerrigan, this is Tamma of the Kitane."

"It's a pleasure to meet you," Lyle said, reaching out to take her hand. "This is my XO, Commander Indira Predashi. She's the second-in-command on our ship."

"Greetings," Tamma said, looking uncertainly at where he was shaking her hand. "Is this an Earth custom?"

"A very old one," Lyle told her, releasing his grip with a sheepish grin.

"So old it's outdated," Predashi said in a low voice as she poked an elbow into his ribs.

"I notice you're able to speak our language," Lyle said, hoping to smooth out his initial faux pas. "Where did you learn it?"

Tamma lifted a hand to touch the spot behind her ear where translation implants were placed. "It cost most of my peoples' credits, but I was able to purchase the Earth package at my last stop. As soon as I heard about the new race who had stood up to the Kr'Sal, I knew you were the ones who would be able to help my people."

Lyle hadn't realized the implants would allow someone to speak another language in addition to translating words spoken by others. He suspected it was much more costly than the regular software packages. "Let's all sit, and you can explain why you need our help."

Tamma looked to Ballard, as if seeking reassurance. Once the woman gave her a quick nod, the Kitane was eager to speak. "The story of my people's history would be familiar to you. We lived mostly peaceful lives for many generations, certain that we were alone among all the stars. The study of those stars was always seen as an eccentricity, and few of our people ever did more than look up and admire the beauty of them in our night sky.

"That all changed seventy sequences ago when one of our clans began to design and build ships that would allow them to sail among the stars. There was great upheaval when they succeeded, and within another ten sequences those ships were venturing farther out from our world. Soon, they encountered a strange golden object that appeared as if from nowhere."

Kerrigan traded looks with Predashi. The Kitane had been able to master space travel much quicker than humans had, but so far the woman's story sounded familiar. "Was there a warning about what would happen if your ships ventured beyond the golden object?"

Tamma lifted her hands in an uncertain gesture. "It is possible, but the space-faring clan refused to share any information of what may have transpired with those of us still bound to our planet. In any event, the ship disappeared shortly after, and we all thought it was lost to the vastness of space. The elders of the other clans said it was evidence that we Kitane should be happy with the hills and valleys of the planet we loved, and that we weren't meant to explore the stars."

"Disappeared?" Predashi asked, leaning forward with interest. "Was it sucked into a wormhole?"

Tamma raised her hands again. "We don't know what happened to that ship. It was never seen again. I wish I could say that was the end of the story, but obviously it is not, or I wouldn't be here begging for your help."

Her ears drooped and her shoulders slumped as she continued with the story. "Many sequences passed, and the folly of the lost clan was forgotten. The stars were once again a decoration in the sky to admire in quiet moments between all the things that made life enjoyable. We were content with our place once more, and the ambitions of exploration were left in the past.

"Until a strange ship appeared above our planet. Many feared that the lost clan had returned to usurp power and force us to leave our world, so that when small shuttles detached from the larger ship and landed on our planet, there was great panic. The creatures that came out of those shuttles were monstrous, like gilliwaps grown a hundred times larger than should ever have been possible."

"Gilliwaps?" Lyle asked in confusion.

"They're kind of like frogs on Earth," Ballard explained. "From the way Tamma described them to me, it's like a small garden frog with six legs and purple skin."

"Ugh," Predashi said, her mouth turned down in distaste. "That wouldn't be a pleasant thing to encounter."

"It was much more frightening when the smallest of these creatures towered over us," Tamma said, her voice high-pitched with excitement. "They introduced themselves as the Golmorung and said they had come to our planet seeking a home."

Kerrigan tried to imagine giant six-legged frogs showing up on Earth and asking if they could move in. He suspected there would be a wave of panic much like the one Tamma had described on her world, followed by the launch of nuclear weapons in an effort to end what many would see as an alien invasion. "Did they come to ask if they could live there, or to tell you they were going to do so?"

The Kitane raised her hands uncertainly again. "I have only heard of the first encounter through hearsay since it happened from my own village. Whether appeal or demand, the Golmorungs claimed they only wanted to make homes among the swamps and salt marshes that my people had little use for. The clan elders debated for many days before finally deciding to allow the small contingent of Golmorungs to leave their ship and settle on our world.

"The ship that arrived in orbit held nearly a thousand of the monstrous creatures. Some of my people protested the elders' decisions, but many of us felt there was little harm in giving up a small portion of our planet to aid these travelers from the stars. After all, it was a loss that impacted our lives very little.

"For the first few sequences, it appeared that Kitane and Golmorung would be able to co-exist in a way that profited both of us. We sold our excess crops to the Golmorungs, and in return they sold us the fish they managed to catch that had always eluded our attempts. It was a partnership that benefited both races."

Tamma's expression grew sad. "Such peace was not to last, however. Without warning, another ship arrived above our planet. This time, the Golmorungs did not ask before more of them landed to take the land they needed to make their homes along the shores of a large lake. When the clan elders protested, they were told to be glad the hills and valleys were still left to us.

"The protests that arose from this fresh invasion were more contentious than before. We are a peaceful people, and war is something that hasn't been known for many generations. Without weapons to defend ourselves or the knowledge of how to make them, there was little we could do to stop the invasion. If the Golmorungs kept sending more of their people to make homes along all of our lakes and rivers, how long would it be before they decided they also wanted the hills and valleys? The answer came much sooner than any of us could have expected."

Lyle resisted the urge to put a consoling hand on the fox woman's shoulder as tears welled up in her luminous eyes. "What happened?"

"Fire rained down from the skies," Tamma said, her voice barely louder than a whisper. "It was the middle of the night in my clan's home when the Golmorung ships began to bombard our valley. Many died before they were aware of the attack, and many more perished in the panicked flight that followed. Of the seventeen thousand who called our valley home, fewer than eight hundred survived to reach the protection of caves in the surrounding hills.

"The other clans were attacked, as well, and soon the numbers of Kitane on our world were dwindling. We had always been accustomed to looking to our elders for guidance and protection, but only a handful of them survived the night of fire. They were broken by the sudden attacks, defeated by the betrayal that had come so unexpectedly from beings we were trying to help."

Tamma's mouth tightened and her shoulders stiffened as she sat straighter. "It was then that we learned the stars were not closed off to us as we had assumed. One of the Golmorung shuttles had been abandoned after they landed on our planet, and we were able to steal it. The remaining elders were incapable of finding a solution to the Golmorung invasion, so the decision was made to seek aid from the stars which had sent such a plague down on our people.

"I was chosen to be part of that ship's crew, and we set out on our voyage to seek salvation. It took several cycles to decipher the controls of the shuttle, and several more to learn how to navigate as we sailed among the stars. The first space station we encountered was such a shock that none of my fellow crew dared leave our ship for fear that we would be attacked. I was the only one brave enough to set foot off our ship, and I moved among the strange beings there as quietly as I could while I listened and learned."

She lifted shining eyes to stare at Lyle with a hopeful expression. "That's when I heard about the new race that had come from distant stars and dared to stand up to the fearsome Kr'Sal. From all that I was able to learn, these Kr'Sal are much like the Golmorungs. They take what they want, and few are willing to stand in their way. When I heard about you humans, I knew you would be the ones to help us. You can save my people from certain extinction!"

7 - Ballard

Alina sat stiffly while she listened to Tamma's story. It was the second time she'd heard it, so she was able to keep her attention on Captain Kerrigan and Commander Predashi. Judging by their expressions, she thought there might be a chance they'd agree to the idea she'd been mulling since she first met the fox woman.

When the story came to a close, Kerrigan cast his eyes around the group. One of his fingers tapped the table while he considered everything they'd just heard. "That is quite the tale, Tamma. If you don't mind, I'd like to digest all this information and discuss it with my officers. Is there a way I could contact your ship once we've done that?"

"I already have those details, captain," Alina said, flashing a comforting smile at the Kitane shifting nervously beside her. "It will only be a few hours before you hear from me, Tamma."

"Very well," the Kitane said. Her wide eyes cast a final imploring glance at each of them, holding their gazes for a second before moving on to the next. "I will return to my ship and let the others know that I've spoken with the mighty humans. That will give them some reassurance that we might yet save our world and our people." She stood and bowed deeply before striding out of the restaurant.

"She was laying it on a bit thick at the end there," Predashi scoffed once the Kitane was gone.

"Would you do any less if you were in her position?" Kerrigan asked. There was a faraway look in his eyes, though, and Alina wondered if he was considering what might have happened on Earth if invaders had come and begun taking the land they wanted by force. It was all too easy to imagine after seeing such advanced technology in the hands of the races that inhabited this corner of the galaxy.

"We need to help them, captain," Alina said, lowering her voice as she leaned in. "I get the feeling her species is incredibly timid by nature, and they just don't have the disposition required to fight back against the Golmorungs."

"How are we supposed to do that?" Predashi asked. "Setting aside the fact that *Intrepid* is contracted to start a new job for WayLin tonight, our ship has no weaponry. If we rushed into a system to face off against armed alien ships, we'd be blown to bits before we got close to the planet."

"Nor do we have a large force of Fleet Infantry with which to fight off these invaders," Kerrigan added. "There are only sixteen trained soldiers on *Intrepid*, lieutenant, as you well know."

"And some of us are needed to complete the terms of the WayLin contract," Alina said, waving a hand dismissively. "I'm the one who hammered out those details, captain, so I'm well aware of them. As much as I'd love nothing more than to race to Tamma's home system and push those frogs off her planet by force, I agree that we're not equipped to do that."

"Then what other option is there?" Kerrigan asked. The corners of his lips twitched, and she hoped that was a good sign that he was willing to listen to her proposal.

"I spent a couple of hours with Tamma yesterday," she said. "She told me the same story you just heard, but then I spent half an hour questioning her to learn more about her world and these invaders. From everything Tamma has seen and heard from others, it doesn't appear the Golmorungs who live on the planet are any better equipped than the Kitanes. They might have some handheld weaponry that was out of sight every time a Kitane was around, but I expect their primary means of attack are the ships themselves."

"Which we can't do anything about," Predashi reminded her firmly. "Unless you're proposing leading your squad on some sort of forlorn hope attack to board and disable them."

Alina grunted and shook her head. "I won't deny the thought is very appealing, but there are far too many unknowns about those ships to even consider a boarding action. Until we know more about them, at least. That's why I'm proposing something a little different."

"Go ahead, lieutenant," Kerrigan said when she paused for several seconds. "We'll hear you out."

"Tamma's ship is small, captain, akin to the original space shuttles that were sent up from Earth at the end of the Twentieth Century. There are nine Kitane crew members, and the quarters are too tight to fit anyone else in." She licked her lips, hoping the officers didn't react badly to this next part. "What I propose we do is swap out eight of those crew with my squad. The Kitane shuttle is small enough to pass undetected by the Golmorung ships in orbit around her world, so we have a very good chance at getting past them to the surface."

"And then what?" Predashi asked sternly. "Do you think you can lead your squad on some glorious crusade to push the invaders from their world?"

Alina chuckled but shook her head. "No, ma'am. I'm not foolhardy enough to think we're that good. What we *can* do, though, is teach the Kitane how to fight back. Maybe pass out a few weapons at the same time and train Tamma's people in how to use them, giving the Kitane the self-sufficiency to protect themselves in future."

Predashi snorted contemptuously, but Kerrigan placed a restraining hand on her arm. "We have no idea how many Golmorungs are on the planet, lieutenant. Nor do we know how many warriors might be stationed on the orbiting ships, ready to land and crush anyone who dares to fight back?"

"Why bombard the planet from orbit if they have warriors?" Alina asked. "You've served on Allied Fleet warships, sir. What kind of energy or ammunition drain is required to fire on a planet and cause the sort of damage Tamma described?"

"A great deal," Kerrigan said, dipping his chin approvingly at her logic.

"More than any sane leader would waste if the same results could be attained by a landing of armed troops," Alina said. "I'm not saying those ships are defenseless, but they must not have enough trained warriors to risk sending them down to the planet. Which is saying a lot from what we know of the Kitane from Tamma. They seem like the sort to roll over and show their belly at the slightest show of force."

"She does have a point," Predashi conceded with a shrug. "We don't even have half an Infantry platoon, but if we had to attack a planet populated only by people like Tamma, I'd favor sending down the soldiers we do have rather than wasting reactor fuel on an orbital bombardment."

"That's all well and good," Kerrigan said, "but how long have the Golmorungs on the planet been able to entrench themselves? Several sequences at least, based on what Tamma told us.

Those first arrivals must have known the locals would eventually fight back no matter how tentative the Kitanes might be. They'll be prepared for any aggressive action against them."

Alina held up a finger. "One, they might expect the Kitane to eventually fight back, but they'll also probably think the bombardment cowed any elements urging such action." She lifted another finger. "Two, my squad and I can teach strategies the Golmorungs would never expect to face from what they know of the foxes. That will give us a leg up on overcoming their defenses and hopefully lead to fewer casualties in the process."

"Three," Predashi said, "you're going to need someone along on this fool's mission who knows ships. Because you'll need them to tell you if it's possible to either incapacitate both of the orbiting vessels or take one and use it as leverage to prevent the other from bombarding your position from orbit once you show yourselves."

Alina bit her lip and nodded agreement as she eyed the XO. She'd expected Predashi to be the biggest obstacle against convincing Captain Kerrigan to go along with her plan, but it seemed she'd swayed the woman to her side. "That's true, commander. Those orbiting ships are going to be the largest threat we face on the ground from everything Tamma says. They could also be the key to forcing the Golmorungs to capitulate without too much of a fight."

Predashi huffed out a deep breath. "Before we explore this idea further, is it something we really want to do? If we help the Kitanes, then how many other planets are going to come running to us begging for aid?"

"Who else do they have to appeal to?" Kerrigan asked. "As far as I can tell, there's no form of law enforcement out here. The

Eslop might qualify, but they don't seem to care much about anything beyond their space stations." He chuckled and ran a hand through his hair. "Hell, I don't know if there are any laws out here to be enforced. As Tamma said, we didn't get a lot of support when the Kr'Sal abducted our people and forced them into slavery. If we tell the Kitanes that we can't help, aren't we just saying that we only care about ourselves?"

"Silas helped," Alina said. "The Panosh and Sumarongs did as well."

"Yeah, two cases of guns and a couple of warriors." Predashi scoffed and waved her hand dismissively. "Fat lot of good either of those would have done if the Kr'Sal had been prepared for someone to actually go in and attack one of their slave mines. We merely took advantage of their complacency."

"But that also gave us a reputation for being willing to fight back," Alina pressed, leaning in to lend force to her words. "Aiding the Kitanes might reinforce that reputation and make the Kr'Sal or anyone else think twice before targeting humans again."

Kerrigan slapped a hand on the table and stood up. "Very well, let's get back to *Intrepid*. I want to call the senior officers together and discuss this matter with them. Lieutenant Ballard, I'd like you and Lieutenant Galbraith to attend, as well. Before I agree to this mission you're proposing, I want to make sure we're seeing all the angles. Agreed?"

"Yes, sir," Alina said, holding back a grin as she stood and tossed him a salute. Relief flooded her body as they began the walk back to *Intrepid*'s docking tube. She didn't have the green light yet, but she seemed to have convinced Predashi, and the captain was willing to listen further.

She thought about the long weeks of training. The months of getting to know her new recruits and slotting them into the squad in a way that would benefit everyone. A little action would help to cement those skills and advance them further than any amount of training could.

Alina chuckled softly. The biggest fight would be the one between her and Galbraith to decide which squad would go with Tamma and which would be left to babysit miners on *Intrepid*.

8 - Wingate

Paine drummed his fingers on the arm of his chair. "I understand your desire to help, captain. These Kitane people sound like they've found themselves in a terrible situation. Does *Intrepid* really have the resources to offer much in the way of aid, though?"

"That is what our senior officers spent two hours discussing before we made the decision to help as much as we can. We're only sending a single squad," Kerrigan said, his voice coming through the video connection as clearly as if he were in the room. "Eight soldiers, which is more than we had available for the slave mine rescue."

Paine winced at the reminder of the predicament he'd been in not so long ago. He'd spent many restless nights wondering what might have happened if he hadn't been on the modular section that was stolen by the Kr'Sal, along with nearly two hundred others. Would he have fought Kerrigan's attempts to mount a rescue? He liked to think he wouldn't, but he also wasn't blind to how stubborn and conceited he had been before the ordeal.

He turned away from the display showing Captain Kerrigan to type out a search string on a tablet. "I'm not finding anything about either the Kitane or the Golmorung in Kraken's database. I'm still getting used to the strange logic behind the arrangement of all their information, though, so that doesn't mean there's nothing here to be found."

"You doubt Tamma's story?"

"Not entirely," Paine said. He rubbed a hand over his face,

fighting a desire to be back on *Intrepid*. He was incredibly grateful for the near instantaneous communication available between the Eslop space stations, but it wasn't the same as being in the thick of decisions like this one. "What I find hard to accept is that a woman from such a backward culture would just happen to come across someone from *Intrepid* while she's looking for help. That's a big coincidence."

Kerrigan shrugged. "Coincidences do happen, Paine. Not all of them require conspiracy theories and shadowy motives to explain them."

He chuckled and tossed the tablet back onto his desk. "You're probably right. I'd still like to schedule an appointment with TiTonA to see if she might know anything about either of those races. I'd try to get in to see Eslop, but I haven't even seen the squid around Kraken in the last couple of days so he must be busy with some other project."

"That's an excellent idea. Silas speaks highly of the Panosh, so TiTonA should be able to provide us any information they have to help out. You'll have to route your message through this space station, however, and it might take some time for me to send a reply. *Intrepid* is departing in two hours to begin ferrying the WayLin miners out to their new operation."

"That reminds me," Paine said. He dug around in a stack of tablets pushed off to one side of his desk until he found the one he wanted. "The local representative for the WayLin Mining Consortium visited this morning. She mentioned how pleased the company has been with *Intrepid*'s ability to exceed contractual terms. They'd like to discuss bringing us into the fold in a more permanent capacity."

Kerrigan frowned through the screen. "We're only working

for them to earn the credits we need to upgrade the ship. I don't think any of us are interested in becoming cargo haulers full-time."

"You might change your mind once you look over the terms they're offering." Paine waved the tablet in the air. "Ownership stake, Lyle. A very tiny one, but we're talking about establishing long-term cash flow simply by delaying further exploration of the surrounding solar systems for another sequence or two."

"An ownership stake in a mining company doesn't sound that appealing to me," Kerrigan said through a smile. "I'll bring it up at the next senior officers' meeting, however, and see how everyone else feels about it."

"Do that. I've already forwarded the details to Yumi, so she can go over them at length for you once she's had time to digest everything." Yumi Nakutora had been his assistant during the trip out from Earth, and she'd taken on his role as political consultant aboard *Intrepid* after he took on the ambassadorship.

"I'll invite Ms. Nakutora to the meeting," Kerrigan promised. "Don't get your heart set on the idea, though. The crew is used to following orders and staying on mission, not setting up business interests thirty light years from home."

"What is the mission?" Paine asked, almost laughing at the expression on the captain's face. "There are more than six years left before we were supposed to arrive at Proxima Centauri on our original course, Lyle. That's a journey we could make in less than a day now that you've procured a wrinkle drive, though I'm still waiting to find out what political repercussions there might be from settling in a currently unclaimed system. What harm could there be in establishing roots here in the meantime and helping to advance humanity's cause before Earth finds out just how much larger the galaxy has become?"

Kerrigan held up his hands in surrender. "I'm not the one you have to convince, Paine. I'm just pointing out that not everyone is quite so excited at the prospect of our new circumstances."

The sound of chimes came through the connection, and Kerrigan glanced away from the screen. "That's station docking control. I need to take this, so send me any information you manage to find about the Kitanes or the Golmorungs."

"Will do," Paine said just before the connection was terminated and his screen went black. He sat back in his chair and took a moment to marvel at the fact that he'd just had a real-time conversation with a man several light years distant. He'd tried to get Bos to explain how the communication system worked between the Eslop space stations, but the only details his assistant knew was that it used technology akin to the wrinkle drives that allowed ships to traverse great distances in very short amounts of time.

The door to his office slid open with an almost inaudible hiss at that moment, and the willowy Edryne entered carrying a tray. "You worked through lunch again, sir," Bosanlek said solemnly as he set the tray on Paine's desk. "I had Manuel run out to pick up that soup you enjoyed last week."

Paine smiled as he bent forward to breathe in the aroma from the steaming bowl of pho. Finding a restaurant on Kraken that served a dish similar to what he'd always enjoyed on Earth had been a pleasant discovery. "How is Manuel working out?"

"Quite well, sir," Bos said. "He is reading over proposals for trade delegations this afternoon, to see if any of them merit your attention."

He picked up a shovel-like spoon and scooped up some noodles and broth. "I'm sure he's regretting volunteering to come work for us," he laughed as he slurped the pho. When he'd raised the idea of bringing in a few of the colonists to assist with his work, the response had been surprisingly enthusiastic. Manuel Ortega was the first of twenty-three people who had signed on for the rotation.

Paine closed his eyes and savored the salty broth before swallowing. "Bos, have you ever heard of a race called the Kitane? Or the Golmorung?"

The Edryne hummed in thought for a second, then shook his head. "Neither are familiar offhand, sir. Would you like me to search through the Eslop database for any information on them?"

"I had no luck there but see if you can find something I didn't. Also, can you get me an appointment to meet with TiTonA at the earliest available slot? She might be able to shed some light on either or both races."

"I wouldn't hold your breath," Bos said, his small mouth turning up in amusement at the human phrase he enjoyed being able to use. "With Eslop in seclusion for the bi-sequence hive mind communion, she has a lot on her plate."

"Is that why I haven't seen Eslop around lately?" Paine asked. He found the concept of a species with a hive mind fascinating. If the squid-like race had been filled with the slightest amount of territorial ambitions, their ability to share thoughts would have given them a large advantage over all others.

"There are three days remaining, and then Eslop will leave seclusion and return to his duty running the station." Bos moved around the office, tidying up while Paine focused on finishing the pho. "The communion allows all the members of the Eslop race to catch up on what is happening throughout the portion of the galaxy they have built space stations in. It's a fascinating time, and one all of us eagerly await to hear news from."

"How far have they spread?"

"None of us knows for sure, but it was the Eslop who first encountered the race that builds the wrinkle drives. Considering that no other known race has yet encountered them, it must be a considerable distance."

Paine slurped up the last noodles, lost in thought about how much he still didn't know about the alien races who shared Kraken with him. This sector of the galaxy comprised what he would have thought impassable distances only a year ago, but it was only sixty or seventy light years from one side to the other. Beyond those nebulous borders, there were other alien races that had yet to be encountered by all but the most well-traveled. When seen in that light, it was hardly surprising that *Intrepid* had encountered yet another race they hadn't known existed.

"Now that you've taken in sustenance, a representative of the Monolith Transport Collective has requested a meeting. You have half an hour open this afternoon, so should I let them know you'll meet with them?"

He set the empty bowl on the tray and tried to hold back a groan of dissatisfaction. As much as he'd talked up the prospect of establishing a corporate presence in the space around Kraken, he didn't look forward to the meetings with company representatives. All too often, they were trying to sell him on some idea that would use human labor to enrich themselves. That's when they weren't trying to wriggle any tidbits about Earth from him, as a means of discovering where his home system might be located. There would come a time when their home world would have to be alerted to the wonders that awaited them beyond their borders, but Paine wanted to make sure everything was set up for success before that moment came.

"Very well, let them know I'll see them this afternoon. They probably want to offer their services at an inflated price for any of our people who wish to travel beyond Kraken."

Bos retrieved the tray and swept out of the room, leaving Paine alone to begin slogging through yet another trade proposal that had made it past Manuel's gatekeeping. He kept hoping he'd come across one that offered intriguing prospects for the colonists languishing in Kraken's cargo bays. Placing them in positions that suited their skills and benefited all of them as a whole would help to improve Earth's chances of success once they learned that aliens were real.

Paine chuckled at the thought of the disappointment so many people on Earth would feel when they learned there were no little gray men waiting out here. Then he paused and wondered if such a race might exist just beyond the borders of this sector, lurking and waiting to be encountered.

He shook off such fantastic thoughts, returning to the work ahead of him.

9 - Kerrigan

Lyle smoothly stepped aside, clearing the corridor for a pair of crew members out for a jog while not on duty. They raised their hands in greeting as they passed, barely breathing any harder than they would have at rest.

"Young pups have too much damned energy," Predashi growled beside him.

"We were the same twenty years ago," he said with a fond smile. "Back before the strains of command sapped away our free time and the energy required to spend quiet hours in vigorous exercise."

"I can think of another kind of workout that's just as effective and far more fun." She arched a brow and shot him a smirk.

Lyle cleared his throat and patted the rank bars on his chest. His XO always knew exactly what to say to leave him disconcerted and speechless. They continued on their path, and he tucked his hands behind his back to keep them from nervously toying with his uniform. "I'm still not entirely happy about this situation, by the way," he finally said after a minute of silence.

"Yeah, well I wasn't happy about letting you charge in with the grunts to rescue our people from the Kr'Sal slavers. There's not a chance in hell I'm going to let you do that again."

"That doesn't mean you had to volunteer so quickly to go along with Lieutenant Ballard's squad."

Predashi snorted contemptuously and bumped her shoulder against his. "It's not like I'm going to be toting around guns and rushing toward danger. My role in this little mission is simple. Observe the Golmorung ships, look for any weaknesses we could exploit, and then aid a boarding attempt if we decide such is warranted."

"It all sounds so easy," Lyle chuckled. "Until you're in the thick of it and having to find a quick solution for a problem you never could have anticipated."

He slowed as they neared the airlock, and Lyle steered his XO toward a small alcove between two bulkheads. "Indira, I still think we should accept Commander Berger's offer to send one of her engineers. They'll have more experience with digging into mechanical systems and be better suited for deciphering any equipment on the Golmorung ships we have no experience with."

"They'll be shit for tactical thinking, though." Predashi put a hand on his shoulder as she leaned in. "Having me go along on Ballard's little crusade to help the Kitane is the right decision, and you know it. I'd gladly take along an engineer if we had the space, but it's going to be crowded already."

Lyle frowned but couldn't deny her words. There were a thousand scenarios where the knowledge and experience of his XO could prove crucial to the success of the mission. Unfortunately, there were also a thousand scenarios fraught with danger and an elevated risk that she might not come back at all.

Predashi's smirking expression softened, and her hand slid across the back of his neck. Before he realized what was happening, she pulled him in and their lips met in a brief kiss. "Stop worrying about me, Lyle. I'm a big girl and I can take care of myself."

"I know you can," he said in a near whisper, "but that won't stop me from worrying until you come back through that airlock safe and sound."

She ran a hand down his chest before stepping back. "I'm more worried about you," she laughed. "*Intrepid* is already full of roughneck miners, and now you'll have a pack of Kitanes roaming around with gaping expressions at every new thing they see. You're in for a fun time while I'm away."

Lyle chuckled, glancing over just as a pair of Kitanes were escorted onto the ship by one of his junior offices. The foxlike beings were wide-eyed as they looked around the corridor, and they spoke rapidly to each other in the high-pitched yipping bark that was their language. "I've already received complaints that a few of them wandered into Engineering and started to poke around our reactors. I don't think it will be long before I'm eagerly awaiting your return so they can be herded back onto Tamma's ship. They might be harder to keep corralled than those miners."

"It'll be good practice for Lieutenant Galbraith," Predashi said through a grin. "She'll be babysitting a lot of new recruits in the future if we keep expanding the Fleet Infantry unit."

"Which will be a necessity if we continue to find ourselves in situations like this one." Lyle let out a deep breath as they resumed a slow walk toward the airlock. "I guess I didn't expect the galaxy to be a peaceful place, but I certainly didn't think we'd be the ones trying to maintain order."

"Lead by example, that's what my father always told me. If we keep showing these aliens how it's supposed to be done, maybe they'll fall into line and start helping out more."

Lyle grunted but wasn't sure if he shared her optimism. He'd read up on the devastating war that had raged between almost a dozen different races for more than forty sequences. The peace that had been brokered by the Eslop continued to hold, but it seemed to be propped up on shaky foundations. One slightly aggressive move by any of them could cause the entire house of cards to tumble down.

He stopped just outside the airlock chamber. "Last chance to change your mind. If anyone should be risking their neck on this mission, it's me."

"I should stay here to play nanny for a bunch of miners and foxes while you're out having all the fun? Not a chance." Predashi laughed and slapped his arm playfully. She stepped over the raised lip of the doorway, then glanced over her shoulder. "Oh, and Lyle? We're picking up where that kiss left off when I get back. Count on it."

Commander Indira Predashi was wearing a wide grin as she ducked down and shuffled through the constricting tube that connected *Intrepid* to the Kitane ship. Kerrigan's cheeks had been flaming after her parting words, and she hoped he would spend a lot of time thinking about them until she returned. A few more incentives like that, and maybe he'd finally forget the regulations and give in to the feelings they both knew were growing between them.

She grunted when she finally left the tube and was able to stand upright, then yelped in pain when the top of her head collided with something hard. "Careful, commander," Lieutenant Ballard called out. "There's not a lot of headroom in this tin can."

Predashi grumbled and rubbed her scalp as she looked

around. Comfort had clearly been the last thing on the minds of the ship's designers. The low ceilings were compounded by bare metallic surfaces and red-tinted lighting that was already giving her a headache. "Ten people are supposed to fit in this thing?"

"The rear compartment is slightly larger," Ballard said, poking her head out from where she was going over the crates of gear her squad had already carried onto the ship. "Honestly, though, I don't think these shuttles were intended for long trips. The Golmorungs probably only used them to ferry people to and from their larger ships."

"I guess we're lucky it even has a wrinkle drive." Predashi walked forward, careful to keep her head bowed as she watched for anything else that might present an obstacle. "Has Tamma explained why the Golmorungs abandoned it?"

Ballard reached out an arm to tap against a darker spot on the wall. "Hull breach, which must have happened while the shuttle was transporting the frogs down to the planet. It wasn't too large, so Tamma's people were able to repair it before they left to seek help."

Predashi ran her hands over the darker metal, surprised at how smooth the welds were. She hadn't gotten the impression the Kitane were metalworkers from Tamma's story, but this patch job showed an expertise that would only come from years of experience. "I guess it'll hold for the trip back to her world. What's it called, by the way?"

"Tamma's home world? She called it Waldruun at one point."

Predashi grimaced at the name, but she suspected it came from Kitane legends just as many of the planet names in their home solar system had. Those would sound just as strange to many of the races out here, she suspected.

While Ballard continued double checking equipment and verifying that her squad had everything they might need, Predashi wandered over to a pair of consoles filled with buttons and switches. Both were at waist height, with narrow rectangular bench seats placed in front of them. She tried to imagine a six-limbed Golmorung using these consoles, which made her shudder in revulsion. Frogs had always been one of her childhood terrors, and she still had nightmares of the time one of her older sisters had left a particularly warty amphibian under her sheets just before bedtime. Her screams when the toad had bumped her leg under the covers had woken the entire household.

"These systems look almost primitive," she said, waving a hand toward the buttons and switches. "It's hard to believe a race capable of traveling between solar systems built all this."

"That lack of highly advanced technology is the only reason Tamma and her people were able to figure out how to fly this rust bucket," Ballard said. "I was struck by the same thing, though. The shuttles in *Intrepid*'s docking bays look almost magical compared to this."

Predashi thought of the quote from a famous historical author, a man whose books she'd devoured in her teenage years. "If this is the best the Golmorungs have to offer on their ships, then this mission of yours might be easier than I feared."

"Don't jinx it," Ballard snapped. Predashi started to laugh, but then she noted the seriousness of the other woman's expression. "Superstitions exist for a reason," Ballard told her. "The biggest one is that you *never* say a task is going to be easy. That's just asking for trouble!"

"I meant it's going to be Herculean and nearly impossible,"

Predashi said, raising her hands in surrender.

"Better." Ballard relaxed enough to give her a tight smile. "Sorry for biting your head off, commander. I guess I'm more tightly wound about this than I thought I was."

"It's understandable. I'm not even going to be fighting those frogs, but I'm a little tense, too."

"Well, at least we have enough gear for almost any situation. We broke out the heavier armor for this mission, just in case the frogs have better weaponry than we're expecting. There's enough ammo to hold off an entire battalion of hardened troops, too." She sighed longingly. "I wish the Panosh hadn't demanded we return their rifles. Those were incredibly effective against the Kr'Sal and should work just as well against these Golmorung."

"From the quagmire that is the intertwining peace treaties that stopped the massive war out here, I'm guessing the Panosh didn't want those weapons used at the wrong time. Or against the wrong people. I can't blame them for not being entirely trusting of us just yet."

"I suppose so." Ballard dropped the lid of the crate and flipped the latches shut. Her fingers moved surely as they locked and secured the crate, so that only she or another member of her squad could open it again. "We'll make do with what we have and hope it's enough."

Tamma appeared only a few moments later, and she was able to move swiftly through the ship. Predashi noted sourly that the fox was short enough that she didn't have to be afraid of bumping her head on any of the protrusions. "We are ready?" the Kitane asked eagerly.

"Everyone's onboard and the gear is checked," Ballard confirmed. "There are fold-down seats in the rear compartment, commander. We should head back there and strap in."

"Yes, go do that." Tamma waved them away as she began working with one of the control panels. The engines cycled up with an almost deafening hum mere seconds after the airlock closed with a loud bang.

Predashi frowned as she followed Ballard into an even more cramped space. With herself and the Infantry squad, there was barely enough room left to breathe. She foresaw much bumping of elbows and knees in her near future, along with a longing for the open spaces on *Intrepid*. She took one of the two open seats, and her expression soured further when she realized how narrow it was. These seats had clearly not been designed with human bodies in mind, and this journey was going to be incredibly uncomfortable.

"No good deed goes unpunished," she grumbled, another saying her father had been fond of trotting out when she was a child.

10 - Ballard

Alina's hands tightened on her thighs when the ship lurched suddenly, not for the first time. The sound of the engines had grown even louder when Tamma poured power into them, and she was starting to regret not packing better ear protection. The waxy earplugs every member of her squad had inserted into their canals did little to lessen the overwhelming din.

She flinched back when there was a loud bang that seemed to come from the bulkhead at her back. The one with nothing but the vacuum of space on the other side of it. Her eyes squeezed shut and she tried to stop the images that flooded her mind of the ship falling apart piece by piece until they were left floating in the black emptiness between the stars.

Her eyes met Predashi's, and Alina returned the woman's sickly smile. Seeing *Intrepid*'s XO just as disconcerted by the strange noises as she was made Alina think about her squad. They all had to be feeling nervous and jumpy in that moment. "This ship survived a journey to another space station before this one," she shouted to be heard over the engine noise. "It'll make it back to Tamma's world."

"We'll be deaf and senseless from all the noise by the time we arrive," MakTur yelled in reply. Both of the Panosh looked miserably uncomfortable, shoved into narrow seats that were an even tighter fit for them than the humans.

Lash was the only one who looked remotely unfazed by the continuing hums and bangs. The Tiké almost lounged in the seat that was slightly too large for his small body, and he stared around with a captivated expression. His mandibles were held open in what Alina had come to recognize as a smile. "I've traveled on many ships in my lifetime, but this might be the most dangerous one to attempt space travel in."

"Why are you so happy about that?" Cantu asked with a stupefied expression.

"New experiences should always be greeted with joy at the thrill of discovery. This is exactly why I decided to stay among you humans, because you keep putting yourself in situations most rational races would happily avoid."

Alina rolled her eyes, and then chuckled when she heard a loud snort of amusement from Predashi. Lash had said something similar to her when he'd applied to join an Infantry squad, but she'd thought he was joking at the time. Now, in this precarious situation, she wasn't so sure.

The flight finally smoothed out after another ten or fifteen minutes, and the loud bangs became infrequent surprises. The deafening hum of the engine that was making Alina's molars ache lessened to a dull roar, and she began to entertain hopes of surviving the trip to see a new world.

When the wrinkle drive engaged, everyone in the room shivered in reaction. There was a stinging sensation that began in the fingers and toes before racing through the rest of the body, and Alina hated the feel of it. Thankfully, the sensation lasted no more than a handful of seconds, and then faded instantly once the drive shut down.

"Is it just me," Predashi asked, "or was that worse than when *Intrepid* used the wrinkle drive?"

"Much worse," Okune said, shaking his hands out to relieve

them of the remembered sensations. "That felt like being stung by a thousand wasps at the same time."

"Yeah, the last time we did that it felt more like my body had fallen asleep." Predashi flexed her fingers, staring at them as if searching for reassurance that the stinging sensation hadn't left behind any visible marks.

Alina unbuckled the strap that crossed her chest and stood up. "Everyone hold here for now. I'm going to go check in with Tamma and see if I can get a look at the Golmorung ships."

"I'm coming with you," Predashi said. "This might be our best chance to observe those ships without them noticing our presence."

"Why can't we get up and stretch our legs?" Cantu whined. "I'm sure MakTur and LoTur would love to have some space to move around."

"Not yet," Alina said sternly, giving her most calcitrant soldier a glare. "I'll let you know after I've had a chance to assess our current situation."

Without waiting for another word, and knowing Cantu couldn't stand to keep his mouth shut for long, Alina quickly left the compartment. It took only a dozen steps to reach the front of the shuttle, where Tamma was hunched over a console and flicking switches at apparently random moments. "We're in your home system?" she asked.

Tamma looked up with a sharp yelp, and her wide eyes took in the two women for several seconds before the stiffness in her body began to relax. "Yes, we are approaching Waldruun now. My calculations were a little off, but it will only take half a cycle to reach the planet."

"Fifteen or sixteen hours?" Predashi asked under her breath.

"That's more than just a little off." She brushed past Alina to approach the unused control console, seemingly looking for something that might equate to the systems on *Intrepid*.

"It is only a small delay," Tamma said defensively.

"It's fine," Alina reassured her, placing a hand on the Kitane's shoulder. The bones beneath her clothing and fur felt thin and fragile, and they gave yet another reminder that this woman was far from human. "Do you have some sort of viewscreen? So that we can see the planet and the Golmorung ships in orbit?"

Tamma's eyes ran over both consoles. "Yes, it's here somewhere." She reached across to the other console to press a couple of buttons and flip a switch. Nothing seemed to happen, and Alina was about to assure her they'd make do without the screen. Then a steady whirring noise came from below and a thick display rose up from behind the second console.

Alina dropped onto the narrow bench to get closer to the tiny screen. It couldn't have been more than ten inches diagonally, barely larger than the tablets she'd carried around while working in the Quartermaster department on *Intrepid*. The screen flared to life with a faint popping sound and fuzzy static that slowly resolved into an image of a distant planet.

"Can we get a better view?" Predashi asked, leaning over her shoulder. "Maybe zoom in?"

Alina shrugged as she looked at the buttons and switches in front of her, none of which appeared to be labeled in any way. "I'm afraid to touch anything, commander. For all I know any one of these things could pop open the airlock door and suck us out into the black."

Predashi laughed and patted her shoulder. "I think any race foolish enough not to clearly label that particular button or switch wouldn't have survived long enough to cross the stars."

The XO's assurance didn't make Alina feel any more comfortable with the idea of pressing buttons or flipping switches without knowing what they might do. She reached out and touched the tiny display, hoping she could zoom in by spreading her forefinger and thumb the way she would on a tablet. Nothing happened when she tried it, and pinching her fingers together didn't do anything, either.

"This ship could have come out of late Twentieth Century Earth," Predashi said, her voice pitched low enough for only Alina's ears. "How did those frogs ever manage to leave their solar system, much less travel to another?"

"They have wrinkle drives," Alina said. "Stolen or purchased, they must have run across some other race willing to part with them."

"Lieutenant Syun would have a field day digging into their history to figure it out," Predashi said.

Alina chuckled in agreement. Everyone on *Intrepid* had run across the distracted science officer at one time or another since the ship had first arrived at Kraken, often when he bumped into them while investigating some fascinating discovery. He'd also sent long questionnaires to anyone who set foot on the Eslop space station, with hundreds of questions about how the air felt in their lungs and what any food they'd sampled had tasted like. "He's going to hate that he missed this opportunity to explore the issue firsthand."

"I'm sure he'll be after me to answer tons of questions when we're back on the ship," Predashi scoffed. "Maybe the Kitane will let him interrogate them before they leave."

"He's probably chasing the ones we left on *Intrepid* right

now, hoping to find out every little detail about their planet." Alina grinned at the image of the overly enthusiastic officer cornering one of the foxes and peppering them with questions about how their air smells or their soil tastes.

"That's one more reason I'm glad I came along on your little crusade, Ballard. I don't have to deal with all the complaints that will flood in from his interactions with the miners and the Kitane."

Tamma glanced over at them, clearly eavesdropping now that their voices had been raised to normal levels. She looked away when Alina shot her a wink and began to mumble to herself while she focused on the control board in front of her.

"Those smudges," Predashi said, extending a finger to point them out on the small display. "Do you think those look like ships in orbit?"

Alina turned her attention back to the screen, leaning forward and squinting as she studied the objects. "Maybe? Hey, Tamma, is there any way we can focus the image on the Golmorung ships?"

The Kitane sighed loudly as if they were interrupting important work. She leaned over to flip switches and press buttons, and within half a minute the image on the screen had shifted and zoomed in on the smudges Predashi pointed out. The picture of the ships was fuzzy at the edges, but sharp enough to make out most of the details.

The XO whistled as they studied the ships. "Not what I was expecting."

"Definitely not what I imagined," Alina murmured. The ships on the screen looked tiny against the backdrop of the planet, but what really stood out was the multi-colored skin of their hulls. It was as though the vessels had been cobbled together using whatever materials were available and been repaired in a similar fashion over the course of decades. "I don't know how those things haven't already fallen out of the sky, commander."

"Don't judge a book by its cover," Predashi said.

"I suppose, but I can't imagine anyone going to that much effort to make their ships look like near derelicts if the interiors are in better condition."

"We'll have to wait until we're closer to the planet, but I'm interested to see if we can pick out the weapons they used to bombard the planet." Predashi leaned closer to the screen, almost hanging on Alina's shoulder. "It might be feasible to board one of them, after all."

"What?" Tamma asked sharply, looking up from her console. "No! You must help my people on the planet, not worry about these ships and whether you can take them for yourselves."

"That's not what we're planning," Alina said, trying to soothe the Kitane. "If we can board those ships and stop them from being able to bombard the planet again, that would go a long way to saving more of your people."

Tamma's eyes narrowed and her lips pulled up in a near snarl. "Foolish," she said. "You will wait and meet the elders. We will all decide the best way to fight the Golmorungs."

Predashi's mouth tightened into a disapproving frown. "You came to us for help, remember? Are you going to let us do that, or tie our hands out of the gate?"

"Why would I tie your hands?" Tamma asked in confusion. "You can't fight if I do that. No, you will wait and speak with the elders. We will all decide on the best way to push the Golmorungs off our world. Once they are on those ships, they can fly away to some other world for all I care."

Alina shared a look with her XO. She was confused by Tamma's sudden change in behavior when they'd discussed boarding one of the ships, but she supposed it could be understandable in some small way. The Kitane woman could be worried that her squad would be bogged down in a fight aboard one of the Golmorung ships, and then they'd be unable to help the people on the planet. Or it could be as simple as a desire to let the frogs leave once they realized the Kitanes had found others to help push the invaders off their world.

She tucked those thoughts into a corner of her mind for now, to be pulled out later when she had more information about the situation they were facing. "I'm going to let the squad know it's safe to move around for a while. If that's okay with you, Tamma?"

"Yes, yes," she said, waving a hand dismissively. "Just keep them away from me so I can focus on the task at hand."

Alina stared at her, wondering what had happened to the timid and submissive woman she'd met on the space station. Then her frown relaxed as she looked at the display. They were getting closer to the Kitane's home world, and Tamma must be feeling the pressure of the expectations her people would have. Freedom could be just around the corner, but there was a lot of planning and fighting to do before they got there.

She glanced again at the hodge-podge Golmorung ships. It was stupefying that any race had traversed space in those junkers, and she wasn't exactly fond of the idea of forcing anyone into them to brave the void between solar systems once again. But she would always fight against anyone who tried to take what didn't belong to them.

These bullies were about to learn they weren't the biggest kid around.

11 - Wingate

Kraken was a busy space station, with bustling corridors and busy shops at all hours. Paine thought it was much like his brief visits to the Oceanica Platforms in both the Atlantic and Pacific back on Earth. Those facilities were shared by all of the Five Powers, with different groups accustomed to different time zones so that there was never a lull while everyone slept. That constant hum of activity had been somehow soothing to him, and he'd often strolled through hallways while his mind wandered over whatever was troubling him when he couldn't sleep.

His mind was already lost in a multitude of thoughts while he wandered along Kraken's promenade, which circled the main deck and was lined with shops, restaurants, bars, and anything else visitors to the station might desire. The hum of voices, all speaking languages he couldn't understand without the aid of his translation implant, washed over him like a soothing blanket. A faint smile touched the corners of his mouth unconsciously.

The meeting with the representative from Monolith Transport Collective had been more interesting than he'd expected. The formally dull Sumarong had droned on for half an hour, reciting an obviously well-rehearsed corporate pitch. Paine had been on the verge of conveniently remembering another meeting he needed to attend when the sleepy expression on the Sumarong's face deepened with a wide, dopey grin. That's when the sales pitch shifted into high gear.

"I can see that our many advantages leave you unenthused,"

the Sumarong said in a slow voice. "Perhaps you'll feel differently if your people can experience our services firsthand? I've been authorized to offer you twenty free tickets, good for passage to any port we visit within wrinkle drive range of this space station."

Those words had blown away the boredom and made Paine perk up instantly. It had taken all of his willpower not to grin like a simpleton at the offer, while he instead pretended to mull it over for half a minute before accepting. The culmination of one of his goals was within reach now. Once he selected the colonists who would have the best skills to explore and evaluate the destinations on offer, humans would be able to experience more of what this sector of the galaxy could provide. They would be one step closer to smoothing the entry of Earth onto the galactic stage.

Paine finally rose up out of those thoughts only to realize he was on the far side of Kraken from his embassy offices. He slowed to a stop and took the opportunity to examine the many entertainments on offer. Food and drink were the big draws, of course, but there were also a few gambling establishments that catered to races with more than two hands or primary appendages. A now familiar strobe of purple light, barely visible to eyes not able to view to the infrared spectrum, told him there were delights of a carnal nature being offered behind another storefront. Farther along was a tech emporium, offering wonders such as translation implants and individual software packages to add new languages to devices already in use. Paine touched his pocket and the credit chip stowed there, momentarily tempted to see if the shop offered anything for the languages of the two races *Intrepid* had encountered, before remembering he was running low on credits. The embassy wouldn't receive a new infusion until after *Intrepid* completed their current job.

The smell of fried food with a hint of sweet flavoring drew him across to a small eatery set between a packed-to-the-brim bar and a raucous dance club. Paine smiled when he caught a glimpse of the crowd through the smoky windows of the club, still amused that dancing was just as popular out here as it was on Earth. His jaw dropped when he saw an Acelu performing a series of moves that were reminiscent of late Twentieth Century breakdancing. The avian's colorful feathers were highlighted by a spotlight, and other beings stood around watching with wonder as the dance continued.

Paine shook his head and chuckled at the display he'd just witnessed. He made a mental note to ask Silas if all his people were so enthusiastic the next time he passed through Kraken. The avian had been the first alien *Intrepid* encountered, and he'd proven to be a great friend to all of them.

"Mr. Wingate!" a voice called out when he entered the tiny restaurant.

"Over here," a woman said, waving her hand to get his attention. "Come join us."

Paine noticed that all of the half dozen tables shoved into the cramped space were full, so he gladly accepted the offer to join a trio of colonists in a back corner. He pulled back an empty chair and greeted them all with a smile. "Enjoying a night out before heading back to your quarters?"

"This is breakfast before work for me," the woman laughed.

"Some of us get to sleep while others work late into the night," the man to his left said playfully.

"And some of us are night owls who are perfectly happy with the late shift," the woman on his right responded.

"Better you than me," the other man sitting across from him added. "It took months for me to get used to the schedule on *Intrepid*, and I don't plan to suffer more exhaustion while training my body to a new schedule."

"Kraken is more fun at night," the woman insisted. She turned to Paine and placed a hand on his arm. "I was able to get work at one of the gambling dens, and you wouldn't believe the sorts of people who come through there while everyone is sleeping back in the cargo bay. I don't know if I'll ever get used to how many different types of aliens there are."

"She carries drinks to the tables, so the gamblers don't have to stop spending credits," one of the men confided. "Before you start to think they put her in a skimpy outfit or something, it's apparently interesting enough that she's human."

"We're new and different," the woman said. "All the races that pass through the station love to talk and ask me what my people are like. They leave me big tips just for the pleasure of a minute's conversation. You fellas should have listened when I told you to apply there, but now they're not hiring any more of us."

Paine was fascinated by how happy and vibrant each of them was. There was an excitement that had been missing during the long voyage out from Earth, when everyone had faced years of travel to reach a world that was only projected to have a seventy-nine percent chance to sustain them and provide a new home. "Where are you two working?" he asked the men.

"I'm working in a place like this for now," the man across from him said, waving a hand to indicate the restaurant. "There was some food humans could safely eat when we arrived on Kraken, but with so many of us living and working here now, there's a demand for better options. I spent my college years wait-ing tables, and I picked up a few things from the chefs I worked with. Enough to let me teach the local cooks how to prepare a few dishes, like spaghetti or lasagna."

"Just don't ask him where the meat comes from," the woman said in a loud whisper.

"It tastes just like beef," the man protested before turning his attention back to Paine. "A few worlds around here raise a variety of animals. I've seen pictures of them, but I don't think I'd ever want to visit those farms in person. They look nightmarish, but a few of them taste quite good. You'd never know the meat didn't come from a cow."

The man sitting to Paine's left shuddered theatrically. "I'll stick to plant-based foods, thank you very much. There's a place on the other side of the station serving kebabs that are to die for. I'd swear it was peppers, zucchini, and tomato picked from my grandparents' garden."

Paine laughed along with the others, surprised at how much of the stress had bled from his body in such a short time. He re-solved to get out and socialize more. "Have any of you tried the soup restaurant near the embassy?"

"That place is great!" the woman enthused. "The broth is kind of salty, and the noodles are just like my grandma used to make. All it's missing are carrots and little chunks of chicken."

They spent some time discussing the various dishes they'd sampled around the station, laughing at the stories of friends try-ing to eat food that wasn't compatible with human palates. Paine shared a story of the one time he'd stopped at a Dubuk restaurant to try something that looked like fried bread filled with meat and cheese. His mouth had been flooded with a vomitous flavor that was worse than any sickness he'd ever suffered, and it had taken every shred of willpower to keep from spitting the food out and offending the cook who was watching him eat.

"What about you?" he asked the man to his left once the laughter died down. "What sort of work did you find on Kraken?"

"Right now, I'm working at an electronics shop down the way, but I'm hoping to get a position with the station's technology division. I signed on as a tech specialist for the *Intrepid* mission, so I want to find something that would suit my skillset."

"Hey!" the woman protested. "I would have been happy to find a job in my field, but Kraken isn't exactly a geologist's playground."

"Not much work for entomologists, either," the other man said laughingly. "I haven't seen any insects on Kraken at all, unless you count the ones being served in some of the restaurants."

"Better a job that doesn't use our skills than nothing at all," the woman said with a shrug. "It's that or being bored and wandering the modular sections all day because we don't have credits to spend."

Paine chewed on the inside of his cheek and examined his companions. Perhaps he'd been guided to this restaurant by fate. "How would you all like to put your skills to use?" he asked.

They all looked at him with interested expressions, and over a meal that he barely tasted he began to explain about the opportunity to travel to new worlds on a Monolith transport. The prospect of not only getting off the station for a while but also being able to employ their hard-earned skills invigorated his companions, and several hours passed as they discussed the opportunities presented by what Paine was offering.

Before he left to stumble back to his quarters deep in Kraken, Paine had secured their agreement to use some of the free tickets he'd been provided. They were also going to talk to other colonists they knew, with the goal of assembling two expedition teams with a variety of expertise that would allow them to fully explore and learn about the worlds they visited.

When his head finally hit the pillow in his bunk, he drifted off to sleep with a sense of satisfied accomplishment. He was one step closer to improving the future for the entire human race.

12 - Kerrigan

Lyle settled into the command chair that was in the center of *Intrepid*'s spacious bridge. After more than half a year in charge of the ship, it almost felt as though the padding had molded to his shape. He ran his hands along the wide arms, which contained a variety of displays allowing him to monitor the ship's systems without having to wander around to the various consoles.

The first thing he checked were the specialty cargo modules that had been constructed specifically to fit *Intrepid*'s frame. Three of the five had been detached and hauled to another part of the space station over the last couple of days, where a variety of heavy mining equipment and prefabricated shelter sections were loaded. A fourth had been repurposed to house the miners they were transporting out to an asteroid deep within this solar system. All of the modules were showing a good connection, and the ship's Quartermaster department had gone over the contents thoroughly to ensure nothing would shift unexpectedly during the trip.

He also pulled up the crew manifest, just to doublecheck that everyone was on board and accounted for. It was a cursory inspection, but one he'd never failed to perform after leaving a pair of crew members behind during his third voyage as captain. The hapless pair had visited kiosks on the Mars Research Facility to communicate with family back on Earth, and they'd lost track of time. He had then lost several hours turning back to retrieve them once someone realized the crew complement was two short, and the earful he'd received from several superiors had ensured he never again forgot to check before departure.

The task was doubly important considering the present circumstances. They were more than two hours late and already behind schedule for the WayLin transport job. *Intrepid* had been clearing for departure earlier when Lieutenant Galbraith informed him a handful of the miners had slipped past her squad and disappeared. It took most of an hour to track them down to a bar in the space station, where they'd gone to slam down drinks celebrating a departure that hadn't happened yet.

"Status report," he said, once his own checks were complete.

"Engineering is green and ready for departure," Lieutenant de Windt said. "The reactors are warmed up and the engine is purring, according to Commander Berger."

"Course is set and plotted in the navigational charts," Ensign Poehl said.

"The station dockmaster has cleared a flight path for us," Lieutenant Stebbins said. "Again."

Lyle grunted a response, but there wasn't much amusement in the noise.

"CIC is showing green across the board," Ensign Larkin reported from the Comms station.

Lyle's mood lightened for a moment, until he remembered that Commander Predashi wasn't holding court in CIC for this trip. He hoped that it hadn't been a mistake to allow her to go along on Lieutenant Ballard's mission to help the Kitane. "Very well. Take us out, Helm."

"Aye, captain." Lieutenant Stebbins' hands moved across his console with the surety of years of experience. *Intrepid* barely shuddered as the ship detached from the space station, and the deck plates began a subtle vibration as the engines powered up. Within a few minutes, there was enough separation from the docking arm to increase the power to the engines.

Lyle couldn't hold back a grin as *Intrepid* jumped forward. The new sub-light engines WayLin had helped them procure were a vast improvement over what they'd had before. It would take two and a half weeks to reach the asteroid the equipment and miners were destined for, but that journey would have been at least three times as long before the upgrade.

He'd asked about using the wrinkle drive to vastly cut down on the amount of time the job would take, but Commander Berger had launched into a lecture filled with technical jargon that nearly put him to sleep. The gist of it was that using a wrinkle drive for travel within a solar system was not only a massive fuel drain, but there were increased risks and dangers involved with folding such a small amount of space that only the most desperate or idiotic would attempt it. Minimum range for the drives was universally agreed to be a light sequence, which equated to a bit less than two human light years. Inconvenient if your journey only required a single light year, since you'd have to make one long jump and then a smaller second jump to backtrack to the desired destination.

"We have cleared the space station's area of influence," Lieutenant Stebbins finally announced. "Permission to increase power to the engines, captain?"

"Granted. Let's go to eighty percent."

"Aye aye."

The vibration of the deck plating increased, and Lyle wriggled his toes in his boots. Most people who served on starships lost awareness of that vibration a few weeks into their first trip, but he'd always enjoyed the feeling. It told him he was on the move once again, venturing out to places no other human had ever explored.

An hour passed quickly as he watched over his bridge officers. They'd been serving together long enough to mesh and complement each other perfectly. Lyle had no doubt that these men and women could keep *Intrepid* running without him, and that any one of them could step into a leadership role at the drop of a hat. Not for the first time, he wished he was in communication with the Admiralty on Earth to request promotions for those who had been in their current ranks for the required amount of time.

His left armrest vibrated a moment before he heard a soft chime. Lyle wasn't surprised to find a message from Lieutenant Galbraith, asking to meet with him. He cast a final glance around the bridge, letting his eyes linger on the viewscreen and the strange stars that filled it, before standing and tugging his tunic to smooth out any wrinkles. "I'll be in my quarters if I'm needed. You have the bridge, Lieutenant Stebbins."

It was a short walk to reach his cabin, placed so that the captain could respond to the bridge for emergencies with minimal delay. Entering the quarters, he stepped into a room set up as an office space to carry out his duties while not on the bridge. His private area was accessed via a door at the rear of the room.

Galbraith arrived five minutes later, and she rapped her knuckles against the open steel door. "Reporting as ordered, captain."

"Come in, lieutenant." Lyle finished off a few lines of the report he was working on, which would eventually be forwarded to his superiors whenever they reestablished communication with Earth. "You asked to see me?"

"Yes, sir." Galbraith took one of the chairs across his desk while maintaining a stiff posture. The look on her face warned him she was about to say something he wouldn't like. "Captain, I have to apologize for the lapse that allowed those shit-brained miners to get past my soldiers. If you've lost confidence in me and wish to demote me, I won't fight it."

Lyle stared at her for several moments before responding. "Lieutenant, you did absolutely nothing wrong. You have eight soldiers, including yourself, to watch over more than fifty rambunctious miners. The fact that we've only had the one incident so far speaks highly of your skills."

Galbraith's mouth turned down in a frown, but the stiffness in her shoulders lessened a fraction. "If we just had the miners to worry about, captain, my squad could handle it fine."

"The Kitanes," he said, nodding agreement. "Have they been causing you problems?"

"Not just me," she said. "The foxes seem to have a highly developed sense of curiosity, and they love to poke their snouts into anything and everything. The fact that none of them speak or understand our language isn't helping, either, since they don't seem to grasp that some areas of *Intrepid* are off limits to them. I've had complaints from half a dozen departments since they came aboard."

Lyle waved toward the display he'd been working at when she entered. "I've seen them. From everything Tamma told us, the Kitanes are a relatively primitive race by the standards of this part of the galaxy. Their technology seems to be about half a century behind our own, which means they're probably feeling overwhelmed by all the fantastically advanced systems on this ship. I suppose we can't blame them for wanting to know more."

"That doesn't mean we can let them roam freely, sir. It also doesn't help that I'm having to assign one of my people to follow the foxes around when they leave their assigned quarters, which they always do in pairs. That means half my squad has to be dedicated just to watching over them, which leaves me very short-handed for dealing with the WayLin mining personnel."

"No," Lyle agreed, "we certainly can't allow any of our visitors to freely roam the ship. I hadn't realized you were stretched so thin, Lieutenant."

Galbraith snorted in disgust. "Frankly, sir, this is partly my own fault. Alina wanted to expand our Fleet Infantry unit months ago to include a third squad, but I didn't see the point while we were still training our current recruits. If I'd listened to her, we'd have more hands to help out with the work."

"Lieutenant Ballard mentioned something similar to me a few months back," he admitted. "I didn't see the need for it at the time, either. So, our current predicament isn't all on you."

She shrugged and blew out a deep breath. "It's a problem I'll remedy in the future, but we need some sort of solution to help out *now*, captain."

Lyle hummed in thought for a moment. "How about this, lieutenant? I'll approve the formation of a provisional security team, to last until Lieutenant Ballard and her squad return from their mission. You can recruit some of our crew to help out, and they should be able to at least ride herd on the Kitanes and free up your people to watch over the miners. Would five be enough?"

"Ten would be better," Galbraith said, arching an eyebrow.

He fought back a smile at her steady expression. "Let's settle on eight, lieutenant. I'll send out a ship-wide message shortly, and have any volunteers contact you for temporary reassignment with the approval of their senior officers."

"Thank you, captain. It won't take all the weight off my shoulders, but after a day or two of training they'll certainly help to lessen the workload for my squad."

"It's for the good of the ship, lieutenant. If you need any further support, or if you encounter any issues that require the attention of a senior officer, my door is always open to you."

Galbraith stood and snapped off a sharp salute. "I won't fail you again, captain. These two and a half weeks will go smoothly, even if it means my people are only getting a few hours of sleep every night."

"Let's hope it doesn't require that much effort," he laughed. "I think the miners will test your limits in the early days before settling down to whatever they consider a normal level of rowdiness. The Kitanes will likely grow bored with their exploration inside of a week, as well."

"That would be wonderful, but I'm not holding my breath."

Lyle escorted the Infantry officer out of his cabin, and then glanced along the corridor that led directly from the elevator to the bridge. A handful of doors opened off the corridor on either side, leading into the cabins of his senior bridge officers. He breathed a sigh of relief at the knowledge that he wouldn't have to deal with any roughneck miners or inquisitive Kitanes intruding here.

He returned to his desk to begin composing a concise message to call for volunteers to join the temporary security team. As he did so, he thought about Lieutenant Ballard and the mission that had taken her away from *Intrepid*. He hoped the issues she and Predashi were dealing with were just as minor as the ones that faced him.

13 - Predashi

Indira perched on the narrow bench seat, with her chin propped on her palm as she leaned on the console. Her eyes ached from studying the images on the tiny screen in front of her, but she refused to give up. During the long approach to Waldruun, the view of the Golmorung ships had sharpened in incremental stages, until she could now pick out details that had been hidden behind fuzzy pixels before.

If anything, her assessment of the ships had solidified as the clarity of the image improved. It was plain that these ships were on their last legs, and that all the patchwork repairs had been done either with haste or an uncaring attitude for cosmetic appeal. There was none of the precision or loving care that would be given by dedicated shipyard crews.

She had also noticed within the last hour that the profile of each of the ships was subtly different. While the nearest one had a rounded bow with spiky protrusions at the rear that looked to be engine nacelles, the ship still mostly hiding behind it had a boxy bow and blunt edges. Her first thought had been that the ships were constructed by two different races, but the differences could have been explained away by a variety of other reasons.

What was worrying her most, however, was her inability to pick out any weaponry so far. It was conceivable that whatever guns had been used to bombard the planet were tucked away when not in use, but any armed ship would practically bristle with weapons. The appearance of strength was often the best defense, but these ships instead looked like ripe targets for anyone with a mind to take them.

Indira groaned and rubbed her eyes, deciding it was time to take a short break from her unceasing observations. She stood and arched her back, trying to relieve sore muscles. A quick glance reassured her that Tamma was still deeply involved with her tasks piloting the shuttle. Not wanting to disturb the Kitane, she decided to check in on the Infantry grunts.

She followed the sound of Ballard's voice toward the rear compartment, where the lieutenant was running her squad through a variety of exercises. "I have to keep them loose in case we hit trouble on landing," she'd explained not long ago.

Indira leaned against the doorway with her arms crossed over her chest and watched the soldiers perform deep knee bends followed by twisting at the waist. There was something amusing about the contrast between the diminutive Tiké in the middle of the group and the hulking Panosh near the back. The humans mixed among them laughed and joked with the aliens, and a casual observer never would have known they had all met only a few short months ago. She never would have anticipated that such a mishmash of races could join together and work as a cohesive unit.

"Down on the ground!" Ballard barked at her squad. "I want fifty pushups from each of you." There was a round of protesting groans, but none of the soldiers wasted much time dropping to the ground. While they grunted through the exercises, the lieutenant stepped closer. "How's it looking, commander?"

"I'd guess we're about half an hour out from hitting atmosphere. So far, those Golmorung ships don't seem to even know we're here."

"I'm not shocked by that," Ballard scoffed. "I'm not an engineer, but it's plain to anyone with eyes that those two ships have seen a lot of hard use and haven't been cared for as well as they should."

"That's putting it mildly," Indira said with a quick smile.

Ballard leaned in and lowered her voice. "We could have Tamma divert our course, ma'am. Having seen those rust buckets, I'm confident we could board and take one without much resistance."

"It's a tempting thought," she admitted. "But there are still too many unknowns, lieutenant. For one thing, we don't even know what these Golmorungs look like. I'm sure we all have a similar image in our head after Tamma's description, but for all we know they could be like that assistant of Wingate's back on Kraken."

Ballard grinned at the image. Everyone who had met the tall and extremely fragile-looking Edryne working at the embassy had felt the urge to treat him with kid gloves. Bosanlek had proven their concerns unfounded by engaging in a wrestling match during a training session, easily tossing one of the Panosh off his back and reversing a chokehold until the simian tapped out. "Point taken, commander. I'm still highly tempted to give it a shot. If we managed to take both of those ships, this whole thing could be over with a few well-placed shots."

Indira frowned at the thought of bombarding the Golmorungs from orbit with their own ships. She had no doubt the frogs would capitulate quickly if it happened, but she wasn't sure she entirely liked the idea when they had yet to even meet one of them. There could be a multitude of good reasons behind their actions on Waldruun, as heinous as they seemed from her current perspective. Still, it was an idea that had to be considered. "Show me how you'd do it," she said.

The lieutenant looked back to make sure her squad was completing their assigned exercise. Lash was already standing up, and his mandibles writhed in mirthful amusement as he watched the others strain through the last of their pushups. "It's time for a rest period," Ballard told them. "Hydrate and catch your breath for a few minutes, then start checking your gear."

They wandered back toward the control consoles, which was a short journey. Indira couldn't get over how small the shuttle's interior was and how many of them were packed into it. It looked twice as large from outside, but she suspected much of the walled-off space held the wrinkle drive and engine components.

Ballard dropped onto the bench with a quick hello for Tamma. The Kitane didn't acknowledge it, too wrapped up in her own work. Indira had no idea what that might be, but it seemed to involve a lot of flipping of switches and pressing of buttons at seemingly random moments. The information on the small screens that were spread across the control console was gibberish to her eyes, though.

"See this area, commander?" Ballard asked, pulling her attention back to the display showing the patchy ships.

"All I see is a darker shade of metallic gray," Indira said wryly.

"Right now, it's in shadow," Ballard said with a nod. "A few hours ago, though, the light from the sun was hitting the ship just right to highlight a small depression in this spot. I'm ninety-eight percent certain that's an airlock."

Indira leaned in and squinted at the image. "I'll take your word for it, lieutenant. How does that help us?"

"The location of the airlock is the important thing. It's way back near the rear of the ship, which means it has to be close to their Engineering compartment. Even if we faced stiff resistance, my squad could penetrate that far before anyone on the bridge was alerted to our boarding and had time to do more than start locking down essential systems." Ballard swiveled on the stool to look up at her. "Five minutes, commander. Ten at the outside. That's how long I estimate it would take for us to have control of the engine room, which gives us control of the ship."

"You can't control any weapons from the engine room," Indira pointed out.

"No, ma'am, we couldn't. We could make sure those frogs weren't able to use them either, though." Ballard gave her a predatory grin. "I'd leave half my squad in control of Engineering and lead the rest forward through the ship until we reached the bridge. Depending on the number of frogs we'd have to wade through and how prepared they are to fight off a boarding party, that could turn out to be the trickiest part of the operation."

Indira chewed on her lower lip for a moment. "*Intrepid* has five-inch steel bulkheads surrounding the bridge, with carbon fiber laced throughout to slow any efforts to cut a way in. There are weapon lockers beneath forward and rear consoles, each holding half a dozen stun guns. Anyone trying to breach our bridge would face a long, hard fight."

"Yes, ma'am, they would. But do you think the crew of these ships would be as organized and prepared?" Ballard asked, tapping a finger against the patchwork ship on the display.

Indira had to admit the lieutenant's confidence was beginning to sway her. The fact that the sensors on the Golmorung ships hadn't even detected their shuttle as they approached the planet made it all but certain they could get close without being seen. The question was how close, because latching onto the hull and getting through the airlock would be a tense and dangerous time if the frogs were waiting for them to come through the door.

"No!" Tamma growled. She reached across to slap her hand against the console the women were huddled over. "Always the ships! Why do you focus so much on something that doesn't matter? I brought you here to help my people on the planet! Fight the Golmorungs, push them off our world, and that's all that matters."

Ballard jerked back at the venom in the Kitane's voice. "We *are* helping your people, Tamma. Trust me, boarding one of those ships could be the fastest way to end this situation with minimal bloodshed."

"No!" Tamma stood up and thrust her snout forward, showing sharp teeth in a snarl. "The ships don't matter, only the planet. You will help us on the planet!"

"We're going to do everything in our power to help your people," Ballard assured her in a soothing voice. "You have my word, Tamma. Okay?"

The Kitane glared at her for several seconds before finally relaxing and taking a few steps back. "I'm sorry for my reaction, but you have to understand how much pressure I'm under to save my people."

"We get it," Indira said, reaching out to squeeze her shoulder. "Lieutenant Ballard's squad will lend their expertise to that cause. If we discuss options like boarding those ships, it's only because we're trying to find the fastest solution to your problem."

Tamma's eyes flashed at mention of the ships, but she shook

off whatever words she'd been about to say. Instead, she waved them away and returned to her console. "I'll be landing shortly. It may take some time to get through the valleys to reach the caves where my people are hiding, and you should be strapped into your seats in case the trip is rough. Within the hour, you'll be able to meet with the elders who survived the bombardment. You can discuss options to push the Golmorungs off our world with them."

Indira followed Ballard back to the rear compartment, but she paused in the doorway. "Boarding one of those ships is a good option," she insisted. "Why is Tamma so adamant we not even consider it?"

"Her people have been through a lot, commander. They opened their home to refugees from another world, and then got stabbed in the back when those newcomers decided they wanted everything. That kind of shock and stress can leave emotional scars that might not make sense to anyone else."

"Maybe," Indira said. She had a feeling there was something else about those ships that made the Kitane woman so resistant to any discussion about them. She'd have plenty of free time on the planet while the Infantry grunts scouted the planet and trained the Kitane to fight, and she intended to use that time to dig into the issue.

"Gear up!" Ballard barked, making Indira jump at the sudden shout. "We're strapping in for landing, and I want each of you ready to fight in case that door opens on a horde of frogs pointing rifles."

"Yes, lieutenant!" seven voices replied instantly.

Indira snorted as she watched the men, women, and aliens hustle to strap on armor plating and check over their short but deadly NK70 rifles. She'd watched the Infantry squads drill on *Intrepid*, but it was still impressive to see them in action. Within the space of two minutes, all of them were armored, armed, and strapped into their seats.

"I wouldn't want to be one of the Golmorungs," she chuckled to herself as she fell into her own seat.

14 - Ballard

Alina clenched her jaw as the shuttle banked through yet another hard turn. If not for the straps, every member of her squad would have been tossed around the compartment like ragdolls. When Tamma had said she needed to fly through valleys to reach the hiding place of those who survived the orbital bombardment, she hadn't thought it would involve such aerial acrobatics.

Cantu whooped with joy as the ship suddenly swung into an abrupt turn in the opposite direction of the last one. Alina winced when one of their gear crates slid across the deck and slammed into a bulkhead. She cursed herself for not thinking to strap those down, as well. If Lieutenant Moore was around, he'd never let her forget the lapse. Only three months in Infantry, and she was already forgetting the hard-earned lessons from her many years in the Fleet Quartermaster corps.

"I think I'm going to be sick," Okune said raggedly. His dark skin had paled considerably, and there was a greenish tint around his cheeks that didn't look promising.

Suarez tried to edge away from him. "If you barf on me, I'm going to return the favor. I won't be able to help it."

"If you two start, we're all going to be joining in," Cantu laughed. "It's human nature."

"But not Tiké nature," Lash told them matter-of-factly.

Okune swallowed hard, until he was able to speak again. "What? Your race doesn't vomit?"

"There is no need," Lash said. "Our stomachs are highly efficient and able to process any food intake without difficulties."

"We don't vomit much, either," LoTur said, grinning widely enough to bare his teeth. "Looks like it's just you humans who have that weakness."

"Great, we'll add that to the visitor brochures," Alina laughed. "Hang tight, Okune. We have to be close to our destination by now."

As if her words had been a prophecy, the shuttle pulled out of yet another turn. Moments later, the loud noise of the engines began to wind down, and a minute after that they were all jostled when the ship touched down for a rough landing.

"Thank every god in the universe," Okune moaned in relief. "Another minute of that, and I really wouldn't have been able to hold back."

"That's okay, buddy," Cantu said, reaching over to pat his friend's knee. "You made it, and now you get to look forward to the flight out when it's time to leave." Okune paled at the idea and gulped loudly.

"That flight will be much smoother if we do our job," Alina told them. She released her straps and then motioned for everyone else to do the same. "Now, let's get out there and meet the people we came all this way to help."

Commander Predashi led the way into the front portion of the shuttle, where Tamma was already standing beside the hatch. The Kitane pulled a lever as soon as she saw them, and the seal popped with an audible hiss. She grabbed another lever set into the hatch door and yanked up on that one. The door slowly began to crank open, and the interior of the shuttle was flooded with dry, dusty air.

Cantu coughed as he covered his mouth and nose. "That's

rank, lieutenant."

Alina hissed him into silence, grateful that he'd pitched his voice low enough that it hadn't carried to Tamma. The scent that met her nostrils really was foul, however. It smelled like unwashed bodies clustered together in a tight space, which she guessed was exactly what caused it.

Tamma had returned to her timid nature, and the worry in her eyes was evident to all of them. "I will go first, to let my people know that I've brought mighty warriors to assist us in our darkest hour. Please don't come out until I give the signal."

"What signal?" Predashi asked.

The Kitane was already stepping through the hatch, though. They could hear a smattering of voices, which doubled and then tripled in volume at the sight of the shuttle's first occupant. Alina heard Tamma begin speaking in her language, and she tapped the implant behind her ear unconsciously. Being unable to find the software to interpret Kitane speech was going to slow their efforts to train the foxes to fight back against the invaders.

Loud cheers suddenly broke out, echoing throughout the tight confines of the cavern the ship had landed in. "I guess that's the signal," Alina said. "Keep a tight formation and try to look formidable. First impressions go a long way toward setting the tone, and we need these people to trust that we can do what we've promised."

"I don't know about the rest of you," Cantu said haughtily, "but I always look formidable and impressive."

"Formidably stupid and impressively foolhardy," Okune muttered.

Alina let a smile touch her lips, but she smoothed it away when she stepped forward. She had to duck slightly to get through the opening, and then she paused when she found herself at the top of a short set of stairs. She looked out over the cavern, but it was so dimly lit that she could only make out shadowed figures for the most part. Only the first few rows of the crowd were visible, copper-furred faces watching her expectantly. She led her squad out of the shuttle and down the stairs, and they fanned out to either side. Commander Predashi stepped forward to fill the final spot to Alina's right.

Tamma walked over and grabbed Alina's hand. She threw it high into the air, and the crowd watching them released another cheer as the Kitane launched into a speech in her yipping language. Alina tried to keep a fierce but not overly angry expression on her face, all the while wishing she had some idea of what Tamma might be saying.

When Tamma released her hand, Alina let it drop to rest comfortably on the weapon slung across her chest. She was hoping the pomp and ceremony was almost over, but then Tamma bowed her head and took several quick steps back. At the same moment, a trio of Kitane stepped out of the crowd and approached the Infantry squad.

These were clearly the surviving elders, she thought. Their fur was a dull brown color, almost sandy instead of copper, with larger streaks of white shooting off from the narrow lines that ran up their outer arms and necks. One had a notched ear, evidence of a wound taken in the distant past. Alina suspected it was a battle wound of some sort since there were also a few crisscrossing scars on his face where fur no longer grew.

The elders stopped a few paces in front of Alina, where they gave her and the squad a thorough examination with their eyes. The crowd of Kitane had fallen into an anticipatory hush, so that the cave was deathly silent for long seconds. Alina fought the desire to shuffle her feet under the weight of that silence and the gazes of the elders.

The scarred elder finally raised his snout and spoke a single word. Whatever he'd said caused the rest of the crowd to howl in response, making Alina stiffen up. Her finger slid over the trigger guard and onto the trigger itself, ready in case they needed to defend themselves.

She jumped when two hands clamped down on her shoulders. "Your offer to help us has been accepted," Tamma breathed into her ear. "The elders will want to meet with you later tonight, but first there will be a celebration to welcome mighty warriors into our fold."

Alina was astonished by the idea of a party at such a late hour. Her body was still on *Intrepid*'s clock, and it was telling her that it was only a few hours short of the beginning of day shift. The very idea made her fight back a yawn. "Can we meet with the elders first? I'd like to get my people situated so they can grab some sleep before we set up a program to train whoever wants to fight back against the Golmorungs."

"The elders will let me know when they're ready," Tamma said, stepping out from behind her. "A space is being prepared for you, but for now you must celebrate with us. Come. Come!"

Alina glanced over at Predashi, only to find the commander being urged forward by a pair of Kitane that looked smaller and younger than Tamma. Their eyes were bright with eagerness, which also showed through the wide grins on their snouts. Predashi didn't seem to be fighting them, so Alina decided they could give in and enjoy the celebration for a short time. A quick nod over her shoulder was enough to let her squad know they could relax.

"Party time!" Cantu trumpeted. "Whoop whoop!"

"I'll stick close to him, lieutenant," Okune said before racing to keep up with his friend.

"And I'll stick close to both of them," Suarez groaned. She scowled as she delved into the crowd of Kitanes, but Alina hadn't missed the glint of joy in her eyes at the same time.

"We'll stay with the ship, lieutenant."

She looked down into Lash's face. His insectile features made it almost impossible to read emotion, but she thought his voice was more earnest than usual. "It's their ship, Lash. No need to stand guard."

"But our stuff is on it," MakTur said. He and his brother were flanking the Tiké, and neither looked enthused at the crowd of Kitane filling the cavern. "Besides, partying isn't something we Panosh particularly enjoy."

Alina gave them a quick nod, respecting the dedication to duty that each of them was showing. The fact that their human squad mates had already delved into the celebration made it even more impressive. "Fine, but you three get extra bunk time once we have a place to bed down."

Tamma's tugging on her arm had grown more insistent, and she could no longer ignore it. "Come," the Kitane urged her through a wide grin. "My people want to meet the mighty human warriors who have come to save us."

She clenched her hands on the rifle as she was led into the crowd of foxes, but she was soon relaxing and letting the weapon hang at her side. Clumps of Kitanes were gyrating wildly in what she thought must be some form of dancing, while others banged on makeshift drums or played wooden instruments that looked like forked flutes. Her eyes had adapted to the dim lighting in the cave, so that she was able to make out more of the features on the people around her. Every face was suffused with joy and fresh hope, and Alina couldn't help but be swept up in their celebration.

It felt like hours had passed when Tamma reappeared at her side. Alina was holding a small cup of some drink that smelled like lemons but tasted sweet like strawberries. It was delicious and she was on her fourth helping. "The elders are ready to speak with you," Tamma said, leaning in to shout the words over the noise of the party.

Alina threw back the last of her drink and looked around for Predashi. The commander would want to be included in this meeting, but she couldn't find her amidst the Kitanes. Cantu was leading his squad mates in a dance not far away, all of them easily visible over the heads of the shorter Kitanes, but Predashi must have been sitting somewhere to be so well hidden.

"The elders wait for us," Tamma insisted, jerking on her arm. "They will be angry if you delay."

Alina continued to search the crowd as Tamma led her toward a far corner opposite where the shuttle was parked. Predashi's dark hair would fade into the dimness of the cavern, but her uniform would stand out against the leathery clothing worn by the Kitane. She still hadn't spotted the commander by the time Tamma ducked through the opening of a large tent, however.

She turned in a circle, doing a final scan of the crowd, then followed Tamma into the brightly lit tent. Alina had to blink against the bright light emanating from globes set into each corner. Once her vision adjusted, she scoffed at the sight of Predashi already sitting across from the three elders. "Commander, I was looking for you."

"You found me," Predashi said, shooting her a quick grin.

"Please, human, sit with us," the scarred elder said, motioning to cushions beside the commander.

Alina pushed her rifle so that it hung at her back, then crouched down and tried to get comfortable. Sitting while wearing body armor wasn't exactly easy, and it wasn't one of the things they practiced in training. "Thank you for seeing us," she said. *Finally*, she thought.

"We wanted to observe you humans before we spoke," the elder explained. "Seeing how you interacted with our younglings told us much about you, and it has verified much of what Tamma claims."

"They are mighty warriors," Tamma said, her voice small but insistent. "They will help us."

Another of the elders snapped at her in their language, making Tamma drop her gaze and shrink in on herself. The scarred elder placed a hand on the other's arm, stopping the harsh words. "Forgive me, but I failed to introduce myself. I am Elder Hamman. To my left is Elder Torrel, and on my right is Elder Bitnat. I am the only one able to speak your words."

"We apologize for not being able to speak your language," Predashi said. "We tried to find a Kitane software module for our translation implants, but there wasn't one available on the space station where we met Tamma."

Elder Hamman barked a laugh filled with bitterness. "I doubt many have heard of our people beyond this world, so what you say doesn't surprise me." He picked up a cup that sat on the table that separated them, eying them over the rim as he sipped whatever was inside. "Now, humans, tell me why you wish to help our people."

"We believe in freedom for all races, and we would never hesitate to fight to ensure that freedom," Predashi said.

"After Tamma told us what had happened here," Alina added, "we couldn't have done anything else."

Elder Bitnat began to speak, quieting only when Elder Hamman patted the air. "What payment are you expecting for the aid you offer?"

"Payment?" Alina asked, her brows drawing in. "We're not asking for payment. We just want to help your people fight against the invaders to your world."

Elder Hamman eyed them as he drank from his cup again. "You will leave our world once the Golmorungs have been destroyed? Without demanding something in return for your efforts to save our people?"

Predashi shook her head. "First of all, we're not here to just wipe out the Golmorungs. I'd like to scout their nearest settlement first, then try to approach and open a dialogue with them. The goal is to make them leave your planet, hopefully with as little bloodshed as possible. Diplomacy is our first step, with force only to be used if that fails. Once the invaders have departed, our people will return to the space station where Tamma found us, and you won't have to worry about being indebted to us or expecting a bill for our services."

"Diplomacy?" Elder Hamman asked, his face flickering with disgust. "You would try to speak to those monsters who have killed so many of our people? That will do nothing but get you killed, as well. The Golmorungs are a vicious and savage race, and only extreme violence will stop them from spreading like the plague they are."

Alina frowned at the rage in his voice. She shot a glance at Tamma, but she still had her eyes downcast. "We'll fight them if we have to, but you must understand that we're not here to help you commit genocide. The goal is to remove them from your planet, and if diplomacy can make that happen, then that's the method we'll use."

The elders on either side of him began to speak loudly in their yipping language, but Hamman's eyes met hers and never wavered. The crosstalk continued for more than a minute, until Elder Hamman slapped a hand on the table. The tent fell silent, and he finally ripped his gaze away from hers. "It is late. Perhaps after you've rested and had a chance to see what it is we are truly facing, then you will not be so quick to dismiss what I am saying. Tamma, show the humans to the area that has been prepared for them."

"Yes, elder," she said, rising quickly and motioning for Alina and Predashi to follow her from the tent. They walked in silence for several moments, and when she spoke it was almost too quiet to hear. "You should not speak in such a way to the elders."

"Yeah? Well, then your elders shouldn't be such bloodthirsty morons," Alina said.

Tamma's spine stiffened, but she said nothing more as she led them through the cavern. The celebration was dying down, and there were only a handful of small groups remaining in the large open area.

Alina raised her hand to cover a yawn, and she was grateful when Tamma finally ushered them into a smaller cave opening off the main cavern. The Kitane woman walked away as soon as Predashi entered the cave, and Alina frowned at her back for a few seconds before following the commander.

The squad was already there, with sleeping bags rolled out around the crates that had been stacked in the middle of the room. She snorted when she heard Cantu's snores. "I guess everyone is already settled in."

"Suarez and I drew first watch," Okune said, appearing from the shadows beside the entry. "I made sure Cantu is on the last watch, lieutenant."

"Good work," she said. "I guess bedrolls will have to do for tonight, but let's hope we can make better arrangements tomorrow."

"It seems we have a lot to look forward to tomorrow," Predashi said wryly. "If those elders don't loosen up, I don't think we'll be on this world for much longer."

"They will," Alina assured her. "They've been under a lot of strain, not the least of which was sitting here for countless weeks waiting for Tamma to return and hoping it was with good news. Give them the night to realize our methods can work, and they'll stop being so angry."

"Maybe," Predashi said. She was already wriggling into one of the sleeping bags, shifting around to find a comfortable position. "If not, we've wasted a lot of time and effort for nothing."

15 - Wingate

"We have not heard of these Kitanes you speak of," Eslop told Paine, the alien's voice a high-pitched squeak that seemed odd coming from a large body covered in tentacles. "That is not surprising if they have only recently emerged from Auricle protection, however."

"Wouldn't that ship have been transported here, just as we were?" Paine asked.

Eslop's central body shook with laughter. "The Auricle seem to have no real reason for why or where they transport those who first leave their protections. We believe the purpose is to ease their entry into a galaxy filled with many other races, but it's not always done in the most expedient manner."

Paine was glad *Intrepid* had been brought to this space station. He tried to imagine what might have happened if the Auricle obelisk had sent them to the Kr'Sal home world instead, and shuddered at the disaster that would have befallen. "What about the Golmorungs who have begun to invade their world? Do you know anything of them?"

"Unfortunately, they are also unknown to us. It is likely they have come from a great distance. While we have explored farther than most and built our space stations outside of what's locally considered to be 'known space', there are many races and people we have yet to meet."

That was a gentle reminder that the galaxy was a vast place, Paine assumed. While this sector of it felt like a massive territory ripe for exploration, it was only a tiny part of the whole. Even with wrinkle drive technology, it would take entire lifetimes to explore all the wonders the galaxy had to offer.

"You say the Kitane woman your people encountered left that space station a few days ago?"

"She did," Paine agreed. "Only a few hours before *Intrepid* departed to carry out their latest contract with the WayLin Mining Consortium. Thank you for recommending us to them, by the way."

"It was the least we could do to smooth your entry into the galaxy," Eslop said, waving several tentacles in dismissive gestures. Paine thought that's what he was doing, anyway, since many of the tentacles were always in motion. "We will commune with the hive mind this evening to see if there is knowledge of the Kitanes elsewhere."

"Thank you. My assistant and I have been searching Kraken's database, but we've found nothing so far. I appreciate your efforts to delve deeper."

Eslop released a deep, watery chuckle that was incongruous with his speaking voice. "You are satisfied with Bosanlek?"

"Very much so! Bos has been a wonderful assistant. I sometimes think he knows what I need before I do."

"The Edryne are talented administrators, and we make use of their services in many capacities. They are rumored to have some level of empathic abilities, but such has never been tested nor proven."

Paine began to laugh off Eslop's words, but then he saw that the alien's expression hadn't changed. He didn't think it was meant to be a joke, but rather a serious comment. "Well, whatever the case, Bos has saved me many hours of work with his efficiency. I, uh... I don't suppose I'll be able to afford to keep him once your generosity comes to an end."

Eslop's tentacles writhed more than usual for a moment, but then the squid-like alien turned aside. "We explained your situation to Bosanlek when he expressed a desire to work in your embassy, and he agreed to defer all payment for a period of one sequence. At that time, the total amount of his salary will become due. We discussed this with Captain Kerrigan."

Paine sat with his mouth open for several seconds. All this time he'd thought Eslop had been paying for Bos's service, and it turned out the humans would foot the bill. Why hadn't Kerrigan discussed this with him? It was a decision they both should have been part of.

"Captain Kerrigan has already forwarded a considerable number of credits to us, which are being held in a secure account until Bosanlek's payment is due. Kraken, as you call our home, is considered the safest place within a handful of your light years. More than half a dozen banks have chapters here, and I chose the most reputable to safeguard your assets."

The mention of the name the humans had given to the space station upon first arriving made Paine flush with embarrassment. He had been the one to first speak the name, because the many tentacular protrusions from the central disk made him think of the giant sea creature out of myth and legend. He was relieved that Eslop didn't seem offended by it. "Thank you, again. You have been very kind to us since we arrived in this part of the galaxy."

"Peace, harmony, and cooperation are all that we wish for the races who share the galaxy with us. Sometimes, maintaining those things requires a bit of hot-headed forcefulness. Which is something you humans are very good at."

Paine thought he detected a hint of amusement in Eslop's voice. "Yes, well, we do have our moments, I suppose."

"You will have many more, we think." Eslop's tentacles twisted and several of them began activating screens set up all around the alien. "We must return to our work, but we will inform you once we've communed with the hive mind and learned anything there is to be learned about the Kitanes or the Golmorungs."

"Of course," Paine said, scrambling to stand up and give the station owner a short bow. "I'll wait to hear from you."

As he left Eslop's office, which was situated just beside one occupied by TiTonA, Paine cursed his awkwardness at the end of the short meeting. After all of his years assisting politicians and handling negotiations with power players, he still felt awed by the tentacled alien who operated Kraken. There was something strangely intimidating about dealing with a hive mind, when each member of the race would share thoughts and memories with every other.

They, he reminded himself forcefully. Several times during the meeting, he'd referred to Eslop with singular pronouns. The fact that the alien was one part of a vast entity meant he should have referred to them as he would a group rather than an individual. He resolved not to make that mistake again, for fear of insulting their host.

Paine shook off the aftereffects of the meeting and made his way to the nearest platform, which he rode down to the main deck. It still alarmed him that there were no railings or walls around the floating platforms, but Bos assured him they were entirely safe. The air cushion that pushed the platforms higher or allowed them to descend would keep anyone from falling off between decks. Paine was always careful to stand as close to the middle of the platform as he could, however.

He had only taken a few steps off the platform when he saw a large group of humans approaching in the distance. Paine's lips pulled up in a joyful grin, and he raised a hand in greeting. "I almost missed you," he called out.

The trio he'd met in the restaurant a few evenings ago were at the head of the small group, and they returned his greetings. Introductions were made, but Paine let the names flow over him. He'd met far too many people throughout his career, and names had become slippery unless he encountered individuals often. This group was about to leave Kraken for at least a week, so he'd have forgotten their names by the time they returned even if he did try to remember them.

"Are you looking forward to your trip?" he asked.

"Absolutely," the woman from the restaurant said. "The casino manager wasn't very happy when I told him I needed a few weeks off, but he gave in when I said I'd find a new job after I got back if he didn't like it."

"She also talked him into paying a 'retention bonus,'" one of the men snorted. "You should have gone into sales, Sue, because there's no way haggling skills like that come in useful for a geologist."

"You'd be surprised," she smirked. "I spent a couple of years working as a surveyor for a mining company back on Earth, and it's amazing how many landowners I had to sweet talk to gain access to their property. Almost all of them wanted cash up front, but I was only given a tiny budget to cover that plus the equipment I needed to hunt for whatever mineral the company wanted to mine out of the ground."

"You should have mentioned you have experience with mining," Paine said. "I could have spoken with the WayLin representative here on Kraken about getting you out to one of their asteroid operations. There are likely many jobs you'd be qualified for there."

"No thank you," she said, raising a hand to fend him off. "I only worked that job for the paycheck. My real love is volcanic rock formations, and getting a research grant to spend a year or two studying them was impossible without decades of accreditation or friends in the right place. I had neither, so I had to fund my own research."

"And then you signed up for *Intrepid* instead?"

She laughed and shook her head. "That was a drunken dare with some old classmates. We all signed up for the colony expedition, and two of us actually got selected. I almost turned it down, but the idea of being one of the first people to study rock formations on a new planet was impossible to resist."

"The ten thousand bucks upfront was hard to say no to, also," someone added, setting off a round of chuckles.

Paine frowned, wondering if all the colonists had been paid a bonus. His own incentives had been different, the promise of political power and influence over shaping a new colonial administration. He still had those dreams, but his priorities had shifted so that they were less about himself and more about serving all of humanity's interests.

"We should get moving," Sue said. "Our transport is scheduled to leave in less than an hour, and I want to get good seats."

"Enjoy the trip," Paine told them as they began moving past him. He noted that all of them were carrying backpacks stuffed full of clothing and whatever equipment their various specialties might require. "I'm looking forward to hearing all about your experiences when you return."

He stood in the middle of the walkway, watching the group until they disappeared through a wide set of doors past the platforms. A pair of Dubuks flanked those doors, checking each person to verify they had tickets for the transport. The uniforms they wore had the Monolith logo plastered over their stomachs, a large, black obelisk that made him think of the Auricle structure which had greeted *Intrepid* on the edges of their solar system.

Paine apologized when someone bumped his shoulder, and he moved across the corridor to stand in front of an oblong window. He tucked his hands against the small of his back as he studied the stars and picked out the dark shapes of asteroids close enough to be seen from Kraken.

His mind drifted for a while, until he saw the transport come into view as it departed from the space station. The ship was half as long as *Intrepid*, with a fat, low slung belly that was filled with passenger compartments. The Monolith representative had told him each compartment would hold up to twenty passengers, and the company tried to keep the groupings as varied as possible. That ensured mingling between the various races that used their services, and provided an experience which could help entice customers back in the future.

He envied the men and women who had boarded that ship. They were bound for a planet seventeen light years distant, on the very edges of known space. That planet was on the far side of Kraken from Earth, which would give the group the distinction of exploring farther than any other human up until this point. They'd have a hell of a story to share with the people back home.

"A penny for your thoughts."

Paine startled at the voice behind him, and he whirled to find a Kr'Sal hovering nearby. "I'm sorry?"

"Isn't that the human expression?"

He stared for a few moments, until his mind made the connections. "X'Zak. I apologize, but I didn't recognize you at first." He laughed nervously and darted his eyes around. The Kr'Sal ambassador was alone, which helped to quell his sudden nervousness at being so near one of the lizards again. "Yes, you have the expression correct. I'm afraid my thoughts wouldn't even be worth a penny, though."

"Perhaps," she said, stepping forward to stand beside him at the window. "One day, you'll have explain what a penny is and why someone would trade it for another's thoughts. It mystifies me."

Paine laughed quietly. "It's a very, very old saying among our people. It's from a time when a penny was worth far more than it is these days.

"As for what I was thinking," he sighed, switching his gaze back to the transport that was growing smaller as the engines flared to push it away from Kraken. "I suppose I was just feeling a little melancholy about being stuck here on Kraken while other humans are out experiencing what this part of the galaxy as to offer."

X'Zak hummed acknowledgement. "I often feel the same, Mr. Wingate. The demands of my position tie me to whatever planet or space station I'm assigned to, leaving me with little time to enjoy other pleasures."

"Call me Paine, please."

"Paine," she said slowly, as if tasting the word.

"And you have to understand that Kraken is the only place

I've seen since leaving Earth. Unless you count the slave mines run by your people, of course," he added bitterly.

"The slave mines my people *used* to run," she said, lifting a finger to emphasize the point.

Paine narrowed his eyes as he turned to her. "What happened?"

"The faction I'm part of managed to gain enough sway in our government to force the slave mines to shut down. There was only one left, really, after you humans ravaged our operations at the other." A small smile touched her lips. "To be honest, it was your actions more than anything my faction did that convinced our government to shut down the slave mine in our home system."

"You freed the slaves?"

X'Zak flinched back. "Unfortunately, no. They were sent to the slave markets on Tn'Gun, where they will be sold to work elsewhere."

"Then you didn't really accomplish much, did you?" he asked spitefully. Paine clenched his jaw, grinding his teeth together. There had been a brief spark of hope that they'd finally be able to recover the dozen humans who had been taken to the so-called pleasure markets, but he should have known better. Nothing ever changed that much without years of hard work. "I'm sorry," he said through a deep sigh. "I know it's not your fault."

Her hand lightly touched his arm. "No, it's I who am sorry, Paine. I know you still suffer from your time in our slave mines. I wish there was something I could do to erase the dreadful memories you must have."

He was tempted to tell her that helping him find the remaining enslaved humans would help, but Paine wasn't sure how much he could trust her. She was still a Kr'Sal, after all. A member of the race that saw slaves as an acceptable part of the labor force, and further embraced the degradation of the slaves they saw as sexually desirable. It would take more than a few kind words to change his mind and open up to her.

"Please, I feel like I've soured your day," X'Zak said kindly. "Why don't you come back to my offices, and I'll return the favor you so graciously provided when I visited you. My people don't have anything similar to your tea, but we do have a drink that I believe you'll find delightful. It's made from the secretions of insects on my world, similar to the bees that you said produced the honey we added to our tea."

Paine pursed his lips for a moment, then nodded. "I'd enjoy that, X'Zak. I have a meeting in an hour, but I'd be glad to spend time with you until then."

"Excellent," she said, wrapping an arm around his. X'Zak began to lead him away from the window. "I spoke of my people and my world last time, so it's your turn now. Tell me more about humans. What is the world you come from like?"

"It's beautiful," he said, smiling fondly at his memories of seeing Earth from orbit when *Intrepid* began their voyage. He began to describe that view and the way it had made him feel, and she listened attentively.

16 - Kerrigan

Bzzz bzzz bzzz!

The insistent vibrations pulled Lyle out of the light doze he'd fallen into while perusing reports at his desk. He rubbed his eyes and blinked to try and relieve the gumminess behind the lids.

Bzzz bzzz bzzz!

The trio of vibrations made him groan as he reached for a tablet resting on his desk. It was an alert tone, and the three quick vibrations told him it was coming from Fleet Infantry. That could mean only one thing.

"We're not getting paid enough for this," Lyle muttered to himself as he rose from his chair. A quick glance at the time on his tablet told him it was much later than he'd expected. His nap had lasted for several hours, and it was nearing the end of *Intrepid*'s day.

He pressed a button below the alert on his screen, and within seconds Lieutenant Galbraith was staring back at him. "Captain, I'm sorry to disturb you, but there's a bit of a kerfuffle over here in cargo drum four."

"Kerfuffle?" he asked with a tight smile. "Is that what we're calling it now when the miners get rambunctious?"

"I've decided to institute a five-tiered scale of rowdiness," she said. "Kerfuffle is the second rung on that ladder."

He chuckled as he passed through the doors of his quarters. "I'm on my way, lieutenant. Keep a lid on things until I arrive."

"We'll do our best," Galbraith said, just before she cut the connection.

Lyle tugged on the hem of his tunic, knowing the gesture was futile. Falling asleep at his desk would leave the uniform hopelessly wrinkled until it could go through a sanitation cycle. He probably should have taken half a minute to change, but if the lieutenant felt the need to reach out for his assistance, then the issue almost certainly required his attention as soon as possible.

Intrepid's corridors were almost empty at that late hour. The evening shift was winding down, and the first of two night watches would soon begin. A skeleton crew would be manning each department, ready to call in the day shift in the event of an unlikely emergency.

Lyle enjoyed the peacefulness of the quiet that fell during the late night and early morning hours. Too many captains failed to even think about the crew members on those shifts unless something went wrong, but he always worked at least one shift each month on the bridge during the overnight hours. It allowed him to get to know the officers and crew who kept *Intrepid* running smoothly while his senior officers slept, instead of only being familiar with the normal day shift.

He stepped into the elevator, which was inappropriately named since it was also capable of traveling horizontally along *Intrepid's* spine. The transition from normal up and down movement came with a short jolt, but he was already holding one of the bars placed around the car for such moments. Lyle still marveled at the system that had been designed to connect both halves of *Intrepid's* primary hull while also allowing smooth movement between the decks of the bow and aft sections. The early designs for the ship had called for normal elevators, with a procession of moving walkways along the spine since it had been assumed that only the members of the Quartermaster department would need access to the modular storage compartments. When the decision was made to house the colonists in those sections, as well, there was a sudden budget infusion that covered the cost of the streamlined elevator he was now riding inside.

The elevator slowed to a smooth stop near the top of the arching spine, and he stepped off to find Lieutenant Galbraith waiting for him. "It's that bad?" he asked, eyeing the ripped seam of one uniform sleeve.

Her icy blue eyes blazed with suppressed rage. "One of those bastards snuck a few bottles of hooch onto the ship, sir. He decided to share it with half a dozen of his friends this evening, and several other miners didn't like being excluded from the festivities."

Lyle winced. He'd seen enough brawls in bars involving off-duty crew members to guess what had happened next. "Any injuries?"

"At least four of the miners are down, but we haven't been able to get close enough to see how badly they might be injured. Those still on their feet are looking worse by the minute, but they're so pumped up on alcohol and whatever else was in those bottles that they don't seem to be feeling it."

"Lead the way," he said with a heavy sigh. Lyle had been impressed when Lieutenant Ballard managed to secure bonus payments for each member of the Infantry squad. It was only the second day of the trip, however, and those payments looked to be smaller than the effort required to earn them.

Galbraith led him into the cargo drum and through a maze of corridors. These walls were designed to be easily pulled down and reassembled, so that the drum could be reconfigured for whatever purposes might be required. Right now, this drum was arranged to house the mining crew and store all the personal gear they wanted to have for the length of their contracts with WayLin.

He could hear the fight long before they reached the common area that had been set up for recreational purposes. When they passed through the door, Lyle came to a sudden halt. More than two dozen miners were involved in the brawl, with half a dozen races represented.

There seemed to be three different factions involved in the scuffle, but he couldn't pick out any rhyme or reason for the groupings. The full Infantry squad remaining on *Intrepid* was lined up between the fight and the doorway, with eight crew members wearing the red tunics of the provisional security team interspersed between them.

"I thought you were going to run the volunteers through some training before throwing them into action?" he asked, having to raise his voice to be heard over the noise of the fight.

"We were in the middle of some drills when I got the call," Galbraith explained. "They wanted to come see the kind of issues we have to deal with, and I didn't expect it to grow into... this." She waved her hands toward the riotous miners. "I think this has moved up a few rungs on the ladder into brouhaha territory, sir."

"Duck!" someone yelled, only a moment before a chair flew through the air in Lyle's direction. He barely managed to jump out of the way before it crashed into the wall just behind where he'd been standing. There was enough force in the throw that the plastic snapped in several places, and he didn't like to think what it might have done to him if he hadn't moved in time.

"Simmons!" Galbraith yelled.

A man wearing sergeant's stripes on his Infantry uniform hustled over. "They're not listening to reason, lieutenant. Even after someone knocked out that big Sumarong who started everything, they just seem to want to fight."

"They've been cooped up for less than two days," Galbraith said through gritted teeth. "What the hell is it going to be like after a week?"

"They'll calm down," Lyle said, hoping he sounded more confident in that statement than he really was. "I'm sure this is just them working excess energy out of their system before they reach the asteroid and have to buckle down and start working."

A trio of fighters broke off from the main group, with two Panosh pummeling a Dubuk that was giving just as hard as he was receiving. They veered into the Infantry line, however, some-how wrapping up one of the provisional security team members into the fight. The man yelped with surprise at the first blow, and then was forced to fend off flying fists and glancing blows.

"That does it," Galbraith snapped. "Simmons, deploy the ba-tons."

"Are you sure, lieutenant?"

"Do it, sergeant," Lyle said. The soldier nodded and hurried over to pass the order, and he stepped closer to the lieutenant. "Sorry to butt in, but this is already getting out of hand."

"That's what I wanted you here for, sir. My people are going to have to bash some heads, and you'll need to soothe some bat-tered egos when it's all over."

"Do what you have to, but try to keep the injuries to a mini-mum," he said, wincing when two of the Infantry soldiers flicked out their collapsible batons and went after the trio of fighters. Well-placed blows made the pair of Panosh back away from the

Dubuk, which also gave the security crewman a chance to break free.

"I put in a call for a medical team right after I called you, sir." Galbraith smirked at him for a second before flicking her wrist to extend her own baton. "Now, I'm going to go join the fun before it's over."

Lyle grunted in amusement as she hurried over to join a pair of red-shirted crew members who were trying to separate a Telbrith and a Sumarong. Both of the aliens were larger than the humans trying to restore order, and he was impressed that the disadvantage didn't slow the response of men and women who likely hadn't expected this level of violence when they volunteered to join the security team.

The flash of colorful feathers made him turn to watch as an Acelu who had joined *Intrepid's* Infantry unit fought alongside one of the human sergeants. The cooperation between his people and the alien races they had only met several months prior was a gratifying sight. It reinforced his hope that Earth could join the galactic community once they found out humans weren't alone.

He was forced to step in when he saw a Dubuk stoop down to pick up shards from a broken bottle. The miner was obviously beyond inebriated, swaying and lurching with each step, but that wouldn't stop him from using those shards as potentially deadly weapons. With the Infantry squad and provisional security team already engaged, he was the only one who could stop it from happening.

Lyle raced forward and chopped his hand down against the Dubuk's forearm, hoping to make the miner drop the shards. The hyena-like alien only squeezed the glass tighter and bared his teeth in a low growl. He moved faster than Lyle had expected from his inebriated state, slamming a fist forward.

The blow to his stomach made him cough explosively and bend over in reaction. He saw a flash of movement in the corner of his eye just before the Dubuk slammed a fist down on his back.

Lyle dropped to the ground, taking some of the power out of the blow as he moved with the punch. He quickly rolled onto his feet, coming up beside the Dubuk. The drunken miner blinked in response to his opponent appearing in an unexpected location, and Lyle took advantage of the slow reaction.

He kicked out, slamming the heel of his boot into the back of the Dubuk's knee. The miner's leg buckled under the kick, and he dropped into a kneeling position.

That gave Lyle the leverage he needed to grab the arm holding the remains of a broken bottle. He smashed that arm down against his raised knee several times, until the Dubuk's fist finally opened and dropped the sharp glass.

The miner yowled in protest, swinging an arm through the air and catching Lyle just under his chin. The blow was more surprising than painful, but it gave the Dubuk time to jump back to his feet and barrel forward to wrap him up in a bear hug.

Up close, the smell of rancid meat and strong alcohol on the Dubuk's breath was almost overpowering. Lyle tried to hold his breath as he struggled to break free, but the Dubuk miner was too strong. He grunted as the arms around his chest began to squeeze.

Lyle jerked his head forward, hoping to slam his forehead against a nose or something delicate, but he hit the top of the Dubuk's head instead. The miner's skull was hard enough that Lyle's ears were ringing after the collision, and he had to blink stars from his eyes.

He tried to suck in a breath, but his chest was so constricted now that his lungs couldn't hold enough air to stop the burning need that was growing by the second. Lyle threw his head forward again, jerking his arms at the same moment in the vain hope the Dubuk might relax his hold.

Suddenly, the squeezing grasp was relaxed, and Lyle was able to stumble back a few steps. He took deep breaths as he raised his fists for whatever the Dubuk might try next.

"It's okay, captain," Lieutenant Galbraith said. She was standing over the apparently unconscious Dubuk, her baton poised in case he rose unexpectedly. "Sorry it took so long to come help out, but these miners are tough."

"That they are," he said in a croaking voice. His head was ringing, and now he felt a trickle of blood sliding down his forehead. A glance around the common area showed that the Infantry squad and security crew were getting the fight under control, however, so he allowed himself to slump back against a nearby wall.

"Are you okay, sir?" Galbraith asked, lifting his chin and looking into his eyes.

"I'll be fine," Lyle said. He had noticed two medical crews arriving to take care of any injuries, but he didn't want them to waste time with him when others had likely fared worse. "Get back in there and reign those miners in. I want them confined to quarters for the next forty-eight hours. We'll decide what to do after you and I are able to talk with their leaders about this mess."

"Aye aye, captain." Galbraith tossed him a quick salute before turning to hurry back into the fray. The fighting was dying down quickly now, and the miners still on their feet seemed to be going through the motions rather than genuinely hoping to exchange blows.

Lyle started to walk over to check in with the doctor leading the medical crews, but he stopped after a few steps when his head began to spin. Deciding discretion was the better part of valor, he slumped into a nearby chair instead. Galbraith was getting everything under control, and she seemed to be enjoying herself in the process.

"Not getting paid enough at all," he muttered, not protesting this time when one of the medical team rushed over to check his injuries.

17 - Predashi

Indira watched the Infantry grunts roll up sleeping bags and stow them in one of the crates they'd brought along from *Intrepid*. She tried to surreptitiously rub her sore back while they worked, and she scowled at their laughter and morning cheerfulness.

"Here you go, commander."

She turned to find Ballard holding out a small metal cup, which was filled with steaming liquid. "Is that coffee?"

"The nectar of the gods," Ballard said through a smile. "I made sure we packed a small container of instant packets, because the caffeine withdrawal headaches are a bitch."

"That they are," Indira agreed. She blew on the cup before taking a sip, and then closed her eyes in bliss as the bitter taste washed through her mouth.

"You know, that's the first time I've had to sleep rough since a camping trip to Yosemite." Ballard paused to take a drink, then snorted at the memory. "It was five years ago, and the last time I was able to spend time with some friends I met in Basic Training. They loved camping, but I can't say I much enjoyed tossing and turning all night while trying to find a position that was comfortable."

"Those bedrolls aren't so bad," Indira conceded, nodding toward the gear being stowed away. "Almost as much padding in those as in our bunks."

Ballard laughed. "And here I thought you senior officers

lived in luxury with feather beds and all that."

Indira rolled her eyes, but she couldn't restrain a snort of amusement. "The only luxuries we get to enjoy are the stress and worry about every decision we make affecting the entire crew."

"You know, I would have laughed at that statement a few months ago. I've had a small taste of command, though, and now I understand better what you mean. Any decision I make could lead to one of my squad being hurt or even killed. That's a lot of weight to carry."

"I wish I could say it gets easier, lieutenant, but it never does."

They were silent as they both sipped their coffee. Indira tried to hide a grin when Cantu snuck up behind MakTur and threw a blanket over his head. The Panosh roared with mock rage as he chased the laughing man around the room, sending everyone else into paroxysms of laughter.

A figure appeared in the small opening that led into the main cavern, and Ballard's face instantly sobered. "I guess that's our cue," Indira said, guessing what the Kitane had come to tell them.

Tamma spotted them and hurried over, giving the laughing squad a wide berth as she eyed them nervously. "The elders have asked to meet with you again," she said once she reached them.

"Lead the way," Indira said.

The main cavern was as quiet as a tomb when they left the small cave that had been set aside for the squad from *Intrepid*. She saw small groups of slumbering foxes, intertwined with each other in such a way that it was impossible to tell how many were in each pile. The idea of being wrapped around others while trying to sleep wasn't appealing to her, but she supposed it was what they'd grown up with.

"Did they say anything about our meeting last night?" Ballard asked, pulling Indira's attention back to her companions.

"The elders do not share their thoughts with me," Tamma said, sounding horrified by the notion.

"Okay, but did they seem open to listening to our ideas for how to handle the Golmorungs?" Ballard persisted.

"I would never presume to speak for the elders," Tamma said in a small voice. Her steps quickened, as if she were trying to get far enough ahead that any attempts at conversation would stop.

Indira pursed her lips as she eyed the Kitane, unsure of how to feel about these elders. When she first met Tama on the space station, she'd been under the impression that the elders had been the ones to send the shuttle out to seek aid against the invaders from beyond the stars. After meeting them, however, the elders seemed to want to dictate strategy and be in control of every step in the process. Her impression was that they would have been happier with mercenaries willing to follow any orders in return for payment.

Tamma led them to the large tent again, but this time they were met by a pair of Kitanes standing guard at the flap. The guards wore the same leather clothing as all the other Kitanes, but they carried primitive spears as tall as they were. Leather slings hung from their belts, beside a pouch that seemed to be filled with ammunition of some sort. Tamma spoke a few words in their yipping language, and the guards stepped aside to let them pass. Ballard eyed each of them critically, as if assessing their skills.

"A pleasant beginning of the day to you," Elder Hamman said once they were in the tent. He was alone at the table, holding a bowl filled with what appeared to be green and pinkish-white vegetables. "You may leave us," he said, waving Tamma away as if she were a pest.

Indira frowned at the obsequious manner Tama adopted as she skittered out of the tent. She didn't like the casual disregard being shown to the woman who had bravely led a crew off world for the first time in search of help. Tamma should have been hailed as a hero, not treated like a servant.

"Have you eaten?" Elder Hamman asked around a bite. "These vegetables are plain but filling. Sadly, it is the best we can offer in present circumstances."

"Thank you for the offer, but we have our own supplies," Ballard said. "We didn't want to be a burden on your resources."

Nutrient bars, Indira thought sourly. That's what she had to look forward to for breakfast, lunch, and dinner for however long they remained on this planet. Each of the densely compressed meal bars was formulated to provide necessary calories and vitamins, but the artificial flavors left much to be desired. Those without any flavor at all were often the most desired because they lacked the horrid aftertaste.

Elder Hamman eyed them over his bowl as he finished off the chunks inside. Once he'd eaten the last of it, he set the bowl aside and rubbed a sleeve across his snout. "I wished to speak with you again in the light of day, to see if you have considered my words and changed your minds."

"Shouldn't the other elders be here?" Indira asked, eying the empty spaces where they'd sat the evening before. "If we're going to talk about what our people can do for yours?"

"Elders Torrel and Bitnut have agreed to let me handle negotiations, since I have more experience in matters such as these. It was for that reason that I was given the implant which allows me to speak and understand your strange language."

"Negotiations?" Indira narrowed her eyes as she met his gaze. "I thought we were here to help you reclaim your planet."

Elder Hamman's lips pulled up in a smug-looking smile. "My people are facing the threat of extinction. We have been lied to, we have been attacked, and we have been forced to turn our backs on generations of peaceful existence to face the reality of becoming the aggressors. While we do seek aid in destroying the Golmorungs, it must be done the right way."

"You sent Tamma to find someone who could help your people," Ballard said, leaning forward and softening her voice. "We're here to do that, but you must at least listen to our recommendations for how to proceed. Trust me, we'll resolve this situation in the best way possible for everyone involved."

"The death of every last Golmorung is the best way possible," Elder Hamman said sharply.

Indira grunted and shook her head. "I understand the anger you have toward them for the way they've treated your people, but do you really want to carry the weight of a decision like that? Wiping out an entire species is heinous on so many levels, and once your anger is gone you'll be left with only guilt and regret."

"You would have us *talk* to them instead?" Elder Hamman asked, sneering at the word.

"Possibly," Indira told him. "The first thing we need to do is send out some of our people to scout the Golmorung position and observe them. That will give us some idea of whether they might be open to initiating a dialogue." How they were supposed to overcome the language barrier was a larger issue, but one she could broach when it became necessary.

Elder Hamman snarled and tossed his head in disgust. "Tamma told us you were mighty warriors, and yet all you want to do is *watch* and *talk*. Is this how you reacted when your own people were attacked? I was under the impression that you fought back and took your vengeance."

"Sure, we fought," Ballard said, her mouth tightening at the memories. "But only because we were forced to do so. The Kr'Sal who took our people refused any attempts at diplomacy, leaving us with no other option than to free our people by force."

"We'll do the same here, but only if it becomes necessary," Indira said. "Violence is not and will never be the first option. You have to let us handle this situation in our own way. If that's not acceptable to you, then our trip here was wasted and we would ask that Tamma return us to the space station where she found us."

The elder leaned back and eyed them in silence, his face shifting through a variety of emotions as he considered their words. "What would you do if I agreed to these terms? What would be your first steps?"

Ballard nodded as if relieved that he appeared to be open to listening. "The first thing we need to do is send some of my people out to scout around, preferably with a Kitane or two who could guide them to the nearest Golmorung encampment. I want to know where they can be found, how many we can expect to encounter in each location, and what sort of weaponry might be available to them. My people would also be looking for weak points in their defenses, in case this does turn into a fight.

"While they're gone, the other half of my squad will begin training some of the Kitanes in case the need to fight arises. We'll run them through basic combat techniques and strategies, and also assess the weapons available to you. We brought along some extra rifles, also, which we can train them to use in the event they're needed."

"While Lieutenant Ballard is doing that," Indira said, "I need access to the shuttle that brought us here. Tamma told us you managed to steal it from the Golmorungs, so the technology on that ship could tell us a lot about them. That knowledge will go a long way in helping us beat them, whether through diplomacy or battle."

Elder Hamman grunted in response. "There is no need to send your people to see the Golmorungs. Many of the Kitanes have been in their presence, and they can tell you anything you need to know. I also can't risk your people leading the Golmorungs back to these caves, where we have found some measure of safety."

Ballard was already shaking her head before he finished. "Anything your people can tell us will be invaluable, but you don't possess the experience and mindset that my squad has. What we see when observing the Golmorung encampments will be vastly different from what any of the Kitanes might have picked up on."

The elder's lips pulled back in a snarl again, but he quickly calmed himself. "I will have to discuss the issue with the other elders since the safety of all our people is at stake. It may take a few days for us to come to a decision, but in that time you can begin training our people in how to fight. Agreed?"

Ballard met Indira's eyes. Neither of them was enthused by the idea of hoping the Kitane elders would reach the right decision, but they both recognized there would be no further negotiation on the point at the present moment. "Very well," Ballard said finally. "I want that decision by the end of tomorrow, though."

"I'll do my best," Elder Hamman said noncommittally. He turned his attention to Indira. "As to your request to examine the ship we procured from the enemy, I'm afraid that won't be possible."

Her lips tightened, pressing down into a thin line. "You don't understand what sort of knowledge that ship might have for us. Not just the technology onboard, but also the database that must be buried in the computer. If I can figure out how to access that, we could tap into information that could open up diplomatic avenues or give us the schematics for the ships in orbit in the event diplomacy fails."

Elder Hamman held up a hand to stop her. "Tamma told me that you humans were obsessed with this idea of getting your hands on those ships. Remove such ideas from your head now, because I will not entertain them. Your task is to remove the Golmorungs from this world, and that is the extent of it.

"Regardless, the shuttle is unavailable to you because it is no longer here. It has been dispatched to procure needed supplies for those of us forced to live in these caves."

Indira sat back in stunned amazement. She thought back to their trip through the cavern, and realized she hadn't even picked up on the absence of the shuttle. "But... Tamma said she and her crew only figured out how to use the ship after days of trial and error. I know she's still here since she brought us to see you, and the rest of the crew is back on *Intrepid*, so how is someone else flying the ship?"

"Tamma spent the night teaching them what they needed to know," Elder Hamman said dismissively. "Now the shuttle is out of sight and should be put out of your mind. Focus on training my people to fight, and especially how to use the weapons you brought for us. That will suffice while I confer with the other elders."

His hand motioned to someone behind them, and Indira turned to find that the two guards were standing inside the flap. She hadn't heard them enter the tent, though her mind had been focused on the conversation.

Elder Hamman spoke sharply. "I have other matters to attend to this morning. I'll speak with my fellow elders when I can, and let you know what we decide about your request to send a scouting mission. Some volunteers have already been selected for training, and I'll have them sent over to you within the hour."

Ballard opened her mouth to protest the sudden dismissal, but Indira put a hand on her arm. She stood without a word, turning her back on the elder as she followed the guards from the tent. The meeting had given her a lot to think about, and she wanted to process it someplace quiet and out of the way.

She had a feeling there was more going on than they'd been led to believe. Ballard's crusade was looking like it might turn out to be a lot messier than they'd expected.

18 - Ballard

Tamma was waiting not far away, wringing her hands as the humans exited the tent. Without a word, she turned and began leading them back to the cave where they'd slept.

Alina glanced at the commander's stormy expression and decided not to try discussing what had just happened. She knew Predashi had to be just as fed up with this situation as she was by now. When she'd promised to come help the Kitanes against the Golmorung invaders, she hadn't expected her every move to be subject to discussion by committee. She was starting to regret not letting Galbraith's squad take the assignment. Instead, her fellow lieutenant was probably enjoying a leisurely cruise out to the asteroid mining complex with only the minor annoyance of standing watch while the miners enjoyed some leisurely downtime.

Cantu was waiting outside their cave with Lash, MakTur, and Suarez. Each squad member had a small pack at their feet, and they were laughing as they shared stories. They spotted Alina approaching, and Cantu straightened up. "We're ready to head out, lieutenant. I packed two days' rations for each of us, and we have portable water filtration bottles so that we can refill from streams or lakes."

"The scouting mission is on hold," Alina said. "Only for a day or two, but the elders want to discuss it before giving us the green light to explore beyond this cavern."

"But we're wasting time just sitting around here," Cantu

protested. "We should be out there, lieutenant, getting the lay of the land and mapping out where the Golmorungs are located."

"Especially since there was no view of the planet provided during our landing," Lash added. "We have no idea of the environment we may be forced to fight in without a scouting mission. There could be forests covering the land for miles around, or snow-capped peaks with barren scrubland that will give us no place to hide if forced into retreat."

Alina held up a hand to stop their protests. "I don't like it any better than you do, but you have to look at the situation from their point of view. Can you imagine being woken in the middle of the night to an orbital bombardment, hearing the screams of the wounded as you're forced to run away and hide in caves with the few other survivors of your people? It must have been terrifying, and I'm sure the Kitanes are all frightened that it could happen again if the Golmorungs figure out where they're hiding."

Cantu's shoulders slumped and the fire in his eyes dimmed. "You have a point, lieutenant. At the same time, they can't hide here forever. How can we help them if they don't let us out to gather information about the enemy?"

"I'm sure they'll come around," Alina said. "I'll have an answer by end of day tomorrow."

"They'll agree to the scouting mission," Commander Predashi said firmly. "Because if they don't, then we're packing up and heading back to *Intrepid*. There's no point in staying here if they're going to fight us at every step."

Alina glanced over at Tamma, who was standing meekly off to the side and listening to every word. The Kitane woman startled when she noticed Alina was watching her, and she stirred into motion. "I will leave you to enjoy your morning meal," she said. "Once I've gathered the volunteers, I'll return with them to begin training."

Predashi muttered a few words as the Kitane hurried away. "I'm not hungry, so I'm going to take a look around. Elder Hamman may not let us scout the surrounding countryside, but he can't stop us from exploring this cavern." She wandered off in the opposite direction from Tamma.

Alina jerked her head in the commander's direction. "Go with her, Cantu. The XO's not in a great mood right now, so I don't want her wandering around alone. You, too, Lash. You have experience communicating with races whose language you don't know. The commander might need that skill."

Cantu dropped his pack with a groan, but he knew better than to argue about his orders. He and Lash hurried to catch up with Predashi, while Alina turned to MakTur and Suarez. "You two are going to hang around here with me. This training session is going to be our first real chance to observe the Kitanes in action. That will give us some idea of what they're capable of, which will aid your scouting mission once the elders approve it."

They nodded wordlessly, then followed her into the smaller cave. Okune greeted her and tossed a meal bar, which Alina snatched out the air. She peeled back the wrapper and took a quick sniff. "Blueberry?" she guessed.

Okune laughed and shrugged his shoulders. "That's what the wrapper says, but it tastes more like what you'd get if someone described the taste of blueberries to someone else who had never even heard of them. And then that person described the taste they imagined to someone else. Keep that chain going for fifteen to twenty people, and you might get the flavor in these bars."

"At least we have plenty of water to wash the taste out of our mouths," Gundar said, holding up a flask. "A Kitane brought a couple of jugs over while you and the commander were off visiting with the important people."

"Only one person this time," Alina said. She bent to examine the large metal containers that had been delivered. Each appeared large enough to hold ten gallons of water, and an experimental heft told her they were nearly full. "No idea where they filled the jugs?" she asked.

"Nope," Okune said, shaking his head. "I sure haven't seen any faucets or streams around here, but it's not like we saw much of our temporary home last night."

LoTur snorted loudly. "You saw nothing but what Cantu called 'stone cold literal foxes' last night."

Alina fought back a grin when Okune tried to look offended. "Stone cold foxes? Really?"

"There's something attractive about the Kitanes," Gundar said. "I don't know why, but I get what Cantu was talking about."

"Let's try not to let our libidos start a diplomatic incident, guys," Alina said, rubbing her forehead to hide her amused expression. "We have no idea what sort of importance their culture might give to something as simple as a longing glance or a kiss. The last thing I need is to suddenly be facing a horde of angry Kitanes because one of you couldn't keep it in your pants."

"My pants are firmly closed," Okune protested. "You, uh, might want to talk to Cantu, though. He was laying down the pickup lines pretty hard last night, and it's probably a good thing none of the people here can understand our language."

Alina sighed and made a mental note to tell the sergeant to tone down his attitude. She didn't think Cantu would really try to have sex with an alien species, but she certainly didn't need a

Captain Kirk situation on top of everything else she was dealing with.

Tamma poked her head into the cave, and Alina nodded to let the Kitane know that she'd been seen. She finished off the last bite of her meal bar and tossed the wrapper into the trash pouch inside the open crate. "Okune, Gundar, and LoTur. With me."

The three squad members finished off their own meals quickly and were on her heels when she left the cave. More than twenty foxes were milling around not far away, and Tamma motioned toward them. "These are the first group the elders wish you to train."

"First group?" Okune asked. "How many have volunteered to fight?"

"We will all learn," Tamma said. "The elders have commanded it."

Alina pressed her lips together in disapproval. She didn't like the idea of people being told they had to fight. It would make some of them resentful, which would close their minds to any lessons her people might have to impart. Others might be too afraid of the danger involved in a fight to put their heart into training. She had to accept that this was the way it worked here, though.

"Are these the only weapons your people normally use?" she asked, motioning to the spear and sling carried by several of the Kitanes.

"We were peaceful," Tamma said with a shrug. "The spear and sling are useful for hunting, though, and many are proficient in their use." She barked out a string of words, and one of the Kitanes stepped away from the group.

The man raised his spear so that it was horizontal at shoulder height. He held that pose for a few seconds, then snapped his arm forward in a blurring motion. The spear sliced through the air until it hit a boulder. Chips of stone flew up at the impact before the spear dropped to the ground with a clatter.

Without pausing, the man pulled the sling from his belt. He reached into the pouch that hung beside it, pulling out a rounded metal sphere as large as a ripe grape. Once the ball was inside the sling's pouch, the Kitane began to whirl the sling through the air until it was whistling. When he released the ball, it flew unerringly at the same boulder the spear had. The impact was in almost the same spot, and it dug out another chunk from the stone.

"It's like the Middle Ages or something," Gundar grumbled. "How are they supposed to fight off invaders with advanced weaponry?"

"We don't know what weapons the Golmorungs have," Alina reminded him. She didn't say what they were all thinking, though. Any race capable of space travel, even on ships that looked like they belonged in a junkyard, would also have weaponry vastly superior to slings and spears.

"He was damned good with those prehistoric weapons, though," Okune said. "That kind of aim is hard to teach, and the power behind those attacks was impressive. Both of their weapons are ranged, as well, which gives them a better chance against an enemy."

"There's not a spear or sling in existence that can attack from as far away as our guns," Gundar said. "If they came at us with that nonsense, we'd pick them all off before they could get close enough to use them."

"That's why we brought extra guns," Alina said. She'd had to work hard to convince Sergeant Major Bauer to release the older model rifles from *Intrepid*'s armory, but now she was glad she'd put in the effort. The semi-automatic rifles were a good half century out of date, but they'd be a vast improvement over slings and spears.

Alina eyed the twenty Kitanes arrayed in front of her. Each of them wore simple leather tunics and trousers, which seemed to be the entirety of the Kitane wardrobe. "Do your people have any sort of armor?" she asked Tamma.

"There has never been a need," she replied with a shake of her head. "Our clothing protects us from the elements while allowing free movement and comfort."

"I was afraid you were going to say that," Alina muttered under her breath. Sending the Kitanes into battle without any protection would be almost as bad as doing so with primitive weapons if their opponents were better equipped.

"This is why we need to scout the Golmorungs," she said in a voice pitched low enough for only Tamma to hear. "I need to know what we're up against so I can devise the best strategy with which to face them using what we have out our disposal."

Tamma's eyes dropped to the ground as she seemed to curl in on herself. "The elders will make the decision. I have no say."

Alina's jaw clenched, but she forced herself back into calmness. "Okune!"

"Yes, lieutenant," he asked, jerking into a stiff posture.

"Let's run these people through a basic calisthenics workout and see what we have to work with."

Alina stood with her arms crossed while Okune and Gundar moved among the Kitanes. With Tamma's help, they were able to communicate what they wanted, but it took far longer than it should have before the foxes began to act as requested. They seemed to question every order and wanted to discuss every command until it had been beaten to death with words.

There was a lot of work ahead of them, especially if diplomatic attempts failed and they were forced to fight the Golmorungs. Alina squeezed her eyes shut against the headache beginning to pound in her temples.

19 - Wingate

Paine stepped into the crowded restaurant and went up on his toes to try and see over the heads of those standing in front of him. It didn't take long to spot the person he'd come to see, so he began making his way through the mass of diners waiting for a table.

"Excuse me," he said, narrowly avoiding stepping on a Telbrith's thick tail. "Pardon me."

He was out of breath by the time he'd navigated the crowd and reached the table he was aiming for. There was one empty chair across from the lone diner, and Paine reached it just before a Dubuk was able to snag it for another table. "Silas, thanks for making time to see me."

"This one is always happy to see his human friends," the Acelu said, honking laughter as he stood and patted Paine's back in an approximation of a hug. "It was lucky this one's ship was passing near Kraken when your message came through."

"I appreciate your willingness to make a side trip to stop here so we could talk. I suppose it could have been handled over the comm system since you were within range, but..."

"But you humans are still new and interesting enough that everyone is trying to find out what you are doing or saying," Silas said, his beak dropping open in a grin.

"Exactly." Paine slumped in relief that the Acelu was understanding of his need for discretion. "Although, I feel like I've asked these questions of so many people that what I'm searching for is probably common knowledge by now, or soon will be. I had hoped to find some answers quickly, but the information I'm searching for is proving elusive."

They were interrupted when a server arrived at the table, carrying a bowl of what looked like leafy greens with stubby, wriggling worms sprinkled on top. "Would you like to order, sir?"

Paine eyed Silas's meal and shook his head. "No, thank you." The server gave him a pinched look before leaving, obviously disappointed at a seat being taken up by a non-paying customer.

"Tell this one what you are trying to discover," Silas said before scooping up a bite of his food.

Paine went through the story of Lieutenant Ballard's encounter with a Kitane on the space station, and the appeal that had been put forward for *Intrepid's* help against invaders. "Have you heard about either of these races before?"

Silas chewed silently for a minute, then shook his head. "Neither is familiar, but this one has been plying the trade lanes far from that space station for many phases. This one's people may have some information in our databases, but it will take some time for a request to be forwarded and a response to arrive."

"How long?" Paine asked impatiently. He winced at the seeming harshness of his question. "Not that I'm trying to rush you, but it's been almost eight cycles since one of our Infantry squads left for the Kitane home world. I'm starting to feel like I'll never find answers to who any of these people are."

The avian reached across to pat his arm with a feathered hand. "This one understands the haste you must be feeling, Mr. Wingate. With luck, it should only take a cycle or two for my people to respond with any information we have. I can forward it to you here on Kraken as soon as I have it."

That would likely add half a cycle since the ship Silas was serving on was headed off toward a distant planet. That would make for a long wait, but one that Paine could handle. This was likely his last avenue to find out anything about the Kitanes or the Golmorungs. "Thank you, Silas. You've been a great friend to us since we arrived here, and I don't know what would have happened to *Intrepid* if you hadn't been around."

"This one has only done what anyone would have, to welcome a new race to the galaxy."

"Maybe," Paine said. Privately, he wasn't so sure everyone would have acted as altruistically as the Acelu had, but he knew his opinion was skewed by the harsh treatment he'd suffered under the Kr'Sal. "Have you enjoyed working on a proper ship again?" When *Intrepid* first arrived in the Gliese 649 system, the Acelu had been piloting one of the small tugs that helped guide the large ships that regularly passed through Kraken. After assisting the operation to free the slaves from a Kr'Sal mine, he'd been offered several different assignments on larger vessels.

"It has been an adjustment," Silas said, his feathers ruffling with amusement. "This one has had to learn to follow orders again, but that is no hardship. The captain and crew are good and honorable people, and it is a great privilege to work with them."

"What's the name of the ship again?" Paine asked, trying to dredge it up from memory.

Silas honked a laugh, loud enough that several heads turned in their direction. "It would be meaningless in your tongue. The closest translation might be *Bulwark*."

"That's an interesting name for a ship. Is there a meaning behind it?"

"Isn't there always a meaning behind the names given to

ships?" Silas asked cryptically. His beak dipped open in a brief grin before he scooped up more leafy greens and wriggling worms.

Paine looked away so that he didn't have to watch the Acelu slurp the writhing worms into his beak. It took an effort of will to suppress the shudder that wanted to run down his body at the idea of eating live food. "Do you ever miss Kraken?" he asked, trying to cover his repulsion.

"Often," Silas said. "This one spent many phases on this station and made many friends during that time. Do you ever miss *Intrepid*, Mr. Wingate?"

"All the time," Paine admitted. He flashed a smile as he realized how deeply his longing for the ship he'd once loathed truly was. "My position here as ambassador for the human race is important, though. Far more important than remaining where I was comfortable and complacent."

"Just so," Silas said, poking his fork-like utensil in Paine's direction. "This one felt the same when the offer came to serve on *Bulwark*. Sometimes, the greater good must come before personal preference."

"On that we agree." Paine's curiosity about the mission the Acelu's ship served was growing with the conversation, but he knew well enough that any questions would be deftly avoided. Captain Kerrigan had tried to probe Silas about why he'd chosen that ship above others that had wanted to employ him, but the answers had been vague and unhelpful.

Silas shoveled the last bite of his meal into his beak, then pushed the bowl away. "This one's ship is waiting impatiently."

"Of course," Paine said, scraping his chair back to follow Silas from the restaurant. "It was good seeing you again. I'll look forward to hearing from you in several cycles. Good luck on your journey."

"Luck will be greatly needed if we are to succeed," Silas said before snapping his beak shut suddenly. "Events are moving at a faster pace than this one had expected, but all hope is not yet lost."

Paine eyed the Acelu as they entered the wide corridor outside the restaurant. He noticed that the Acelu's vivid blue feathers were pressed tight against his skin, which was the opposite of how they fluffed out when he was laughing or happy. He opened his mouth to ask what might be worrying Silas so deeply, but then caught himself before he could speak. His weren't the only secrets that needed to be closely guarded.

Silas raised a hand in farewell before striding toward the docking port where his ship was parked. Paine watched him leave, feeling a twinge of disappointment that one of the few people he considered a friend was leaving so soon.

Shaking off unhappy thoughts, he turned away and began walking toward his embassy offices. Bos had been perusing a stack of documents when he left for the short meeting, and Paine had no doubt his afternoon would be stuffed full of work. The flood of trade proposals was beginning to subside, but now he was having to deal with various companies and individuals who wanted to establish resorts and other recreational establishments on Earth or in orbit around it. They were promising mountains of credits, more than enough to enrich the newest planet to enter the galactic scene.

Paine sighed deep in his chest. It would still be many months before he would be ready to entertain the idea of breaking the news to the people back home that they weren't alone in the galaxy. Perhaps years, if he wanted to have a solid foundation ready for humanity to build upon in the future. Releasing the location of Earth now would just open the floodgates for exploitation by those with little thought of anything but filling their own pockets.

He glanced through one of the oblong windows in the outer wall as he passed, wondering how the exploration was going for the small group that had taken a Monolith transport to a new world. They were investigating the planet and any resources found there, but they would also gather important intel about the races they encountered along the way. That was the sort of information he required to better judge when it might be time to move to a new stage of the program. He was able to interact with hundreds of people on Kraken, but the spacers and merchants who passed through the station had different goals than the everyday civilians on the many inhabited planets spread across this sector.

A flash of yellowish green in the distance jerked Paine out of his thoughts, and he began to raise a hand to call out a greeting. The throng parted just enough for him to see that what had drawn his attention was merely a form-fitting outfit, and not the scaly hide he had first thought it to be. He scoffed at the eagerness he'd felt when he thought it had been X'Zak. His few meetings with the new Kr'Sal ambassador had been pleasant, and it was almost disturbing how much he looked forward to the next.

When he passed through the doors of his embassy suite, all thoughts of pleasant visits were banished by the sight of his Edryne assistant carrying a stack of datapads. Paine tugged to loosen his tie and passed by to enter his office. There was work to be done, and he had to focus on it if he hoped to get back to his quarters before the end of the cycle. "What's next on the agenda, Bos?"

20 - Kerrigan

Lyle ducked as he passed through the narrow hatch and entered the restrictive confines of CIC. There was something comforting about the dim lighting and tight spaces in the room that served as *Intrepid*'s heart, ready to take over and keep the body alive if the brain of the bridge was compromised in any way.

The man leaning casually against the central plotting table stiffened when he spotted the new arrival. "Captain Kerrigan. What can we do for you, sir?"

He waved the man back to his relaxed posture. "I was just feeling restless and decided to take a tour of the ship, Lieutenant Commander. While I was in the aft section, I thought it would be a good time to check in with CIC. Everything going well?"

Lieutenant Commander Cottlen, Predashi's second and the temporary XO until she returned, eyed his captain warily. "Every department is running smoothly, captain, with no problems reported over the last twelve hours. Was there any specific concern I might be able to address for you, sir?"

Lyle held in a weary sigh, wondering how long it would take the man to warm up to his new role. "There are no concerns, commander. If you don't mind, I'll just observe for a few minutes."

"Of course, captain." Cottlen straightened up and moved away from the central table, until he was bent over one of the consoles clustered around the edges of the room. It was clear the officer felt uncomfortable about standing around while the captain was present.

Lyle ran his hands over the smooth edges of the table, which housed holographic emitters. In the event of an emergency, or if the ship was placed under a battle alert, this table would display a three-dimensional map of *Intrepid*. The XO could easily pinpoint problem sections and dispatch emergency crews while the captain and primary bridge crew were handling other tasks.

He smiled fondly as he reminisced about his time spent serving as Executive Officer on other Allied Fleet ships. The first vessel in which he'd assumed the XO role had been a tiny workboat, tasked with ferrying personnel and supplies between various Fleet outposts on Earth and the surrounding moons and planets. He'd been a young buck back then, full of piss and vinegar and sure that he was being slighted with such an obscure posting when his talents were better suited on larger battleships. Little did he know that his career would lead him to becoming captain of the most important ship in several decades.

His memories began to shift to other times he'd visited this same room. Commander Predashi had been an unknown factor when she was first selected to serve beneath him. Each of them came up through different Fleet arms of the Five Powers that held sway on Earth; Lyle had served under the flag of the North American Alliance while Predashi came up through the Western Federation. The Unification Wars which had ravaged the planet for decades and ended only shortly before his service began had left many scars and ill feelings between the various navies of the Powers, despite the alliance that bound them all together in one service in the name of peace.

The *Intrepid* project had been complicated by the politics that bound the Five Powers together in one common goal.

While each government contributed to the building of the ship and provided an equal portion of the crew, there had been political wars fought behind the scenes to decide who would lead the expedition. Lyle was chosen from a pool of seventeen captains, primarily because he had no real ties to any significant player in the political scene. That fact, which many had seen as his biggest weakness, was what led the heads of the Five Powers to feel comfortable with appointing him captain. Indira Predashi was chosen as XO to appease the Western Federation, the last holdout to a unanimous selection of the ship's captain.

In the beginning, he'd been uncertain about how far he could trust his XO. Both of them were all too aware of the eyes on their every move, especially while *Intrepid* was still undergoing the final stages of construction and provisioning in Earth orbit. Launching the ship for the expected seven-year voyage to reach a new home around a distant star had allowed them to finally start getting a feel for each other as people instead of just representatives of their respective Power.

They had grown to respect and trust each other during the four months the ship accelerated away from Earth. Those feelings had only deepened after the encounter with the Auricle obelisk and the wormhole that had sucked them across thirty light years to a distant star.

Perhaps those feelings had deepened too much, Lyle thought now. There was an ache in his heart whenever he realized it wouldn't be Predashi's voice in his ear when he reported to the bridge and inserted the earpiece that maintained a constant connection with CIC. He missed seeing her face at senior officer meetings, and he also missed the private moments they'd been able to steal with increasing frequency over the last few months.

His eyes strayed to the door that led into her office, located just off CIC for convenience and a quick response when needed. Unlike his office, hers wasn't attached to her quarters, but it was still a personal space where she and her captain could retire to discuss serious matters in privacy.

Matters such as the kiss she had given him before boarding the shuttle for the Kitane world. That had been the first moment that he'd become aware that his growing feelings for her might be returned, and it had been impossible to get the feel of her lips against his out of his thoughts. He was eager for her return to *Intrepid*, to find out what she'd meant by her last words.

Lyle realized there was a goofy smile plastered on his face, and he quickly forced his features into a sober expression. "Carry on, commander," he said before ducking to exit CIC.

He almost jumped in startlement when he was greeted by Lieutenant Galbraith just outside. She was leaning on a bulkhead with her arms crossed, staring at the doorway. "Lieutenant," he said with a nod. "More problems with the miners?"

"Not this time," she scoffed. "They've been quiet since the last drunken brawl we had to break up." The heavy bags under her eyes told him just how little sleep she was getting while dealing with the ongoing antics of the WayLin personnel, so it was a relief that she hadn't come to drag him off to yet another negotiation to soothe frayed nerves.

"The Kitanes?" he asked.

"The foxes have also been quiet today, thankfully. After we found a pair of them poking around the computer core yesterday, I told my squad to sit on them extra heavy for a few days. They won't slip past us so easily again."

Lyle wished he had her confidence, but the Kitanes left behind on *Intrepid* had proven to be as slippery as the Earth animals they resembled. "They didn't cause any damage before your people found them, I hope?"

"Not that we could see, but the techs are going over everything today to make sure." Galbraith shook her head and pushed off the bulkhead to walk beside him. "Sergeant Simmons found them staring in fascination at one of the server nodes. He said they appeared to be mesmerized by all the blinking lights."

He chuckled along with her at the image. "I didn't expect them to be so inquisitive when I agreed to house them on *Intrepid* until our people returned."

Galbraith waved a hand dismissively. "Either of us would be just as eager to get a look at advanced technology in their position. Ballard told me their world sounded like it might be behind Earth's technology level at the time of our first moon missions. Maybe far behind that, which is incredible when you consider they were able to launch a spaceship that made it far enough to encounter their own Auricle obelisk."

"If you haven't tracked me down to deal with either the miners or the Kitanes, to what do I owe the pleasure of your company?"

The Infantry officer smirked at him for a moment before coughing to cover her impertinence. "Well, sir, I was wondering if I might be able to convince you to let me bring the provisional security team into the Fleet Infantry full-time."

Lyle's eyebrows climbed his forehead, but he had to admit he wasn't entirely surprised by the request. In the week since they'd been formed, the security team had proven to be an effective addition to the Infantry squad charged with keeping the WayLin miners and Kitane guests under supervision. "What if those men and women would prefer to return to their current departments after the temporary assignment is over?"

"Nah, that's not a problem. I talked it over with them last night. I took the liberty of approaching their commanding officers, as well, and they all indicated they would agree if you chose to make their posting permanent. *Intrepid* has more crew members than she really needs, and I have a feeling no one was volunteered for the security team if they filled a critical role, so we won't be leaving any holes in the departments the security team members came from."

He mulled over her request as they strolled through the corridors, until they reached the elevator that would take him back to the forward section and the bridge. They paused there, and he gave her a quick nod. "Request approved, lieutenant. Talk to Sergeant Major Bauer and see if the Armory has enough gear to outfit the members of your third squad."

"That brings me to the second reason for tracking you down, sir." Galbraith's lips pressed together for a moment before she plowed forward. "The Armory lockers are beginning to look pretty barren. The need for a security team once we reached our expected home at Proxima Centauri was anticipated, but no one back on Earth could have expected that we'd ever need to build a Fleet Infantry unit from scratch. We're lightly armed as it is, and trying to outfit another eight members is too much of a stretch for the supplies *Intrepid* possesses."

"I wondered when we might encounter that issue," Lyle said. "How would you begin to address it, lieutenant?"

"Well, sir, Lieutenant Ballard and I spent some time knocking around shops on Kraken the last time we passed through, and I think we could pick up a lot of what we need there. For one thing, I know a place that can provide us with something akin to power armor suits. Those would give us a lot more protection than the armor plating we're currently issued." She rapped her knuckles against the solid breastplate she was wearing. The lightweight armor was designed to protect the wearer in close combat situations, mainly against blunt weapons or knives. It offered minimal protection against firearms and had proven to be woefully ineffective against the alien weaponry they'd encountered so far.

Lyle allowed a tight smile to touch his lips. "How much would these power armor suits cost us, lieutenant?"

"Um... ten thousand, sir."

"Oh, that's not as bad as I–"

"...per person," she finished, meeting his eyes with a pained expression.

Lyle frowned and shook his head instantly. "There's no way we could afford that, lieutenant. Our profits from this current job are already ninety percent allocated toward *Intrepid*'s needs, and that doesn't leave us much for other purposes. I might be able to stretch the budget to purchase two of those suits, possibly three."

"Three would be great, captain," Galbraith said, brightening instantly. "That would allow each squad leader to be outfitted in better gear and let us learn what it can do before we purchase suits for the rest of the squad members. I knew you'd be able to help, sir. Thank you so much."

She was already walking away as she spoke, and she raised her voice to drown out his own attempts to speak until she disappeared around a corner. Lyle could only chuckle, impressed at her ability to snatch a victory by whatever means necessary.

He reached out to press the call button for the elevator while he began moving numbers around in his head to make the purchase of powered armor work. If he could talk Commander Berger into lowering the number of spare parts she wanted to keep on hand, that might free up enough credits to swing the Infantry upgrades once they received payment for this contract.

His mind was still working over the issue by the time he entered the bridge, and he had been seated in his command chair for several minutes before he realized that Lieutenant Galbraith's request had promptly ended his gloomy descent into bittersweet memories. For that alone, he thought she deserved to get what she'd been asking for.

It didn't hurt that the constant threats which seemed to be popping up for his people to handle didn't seem to be lessening. Even something as seemingly trivial as watching over the WayLin miners would be made easier with more advanced armor to outfit his soldiers. The frequent brawls and arguments would then end swiftly and with fewer injuries.

Lyle grinned at the idea of what Indira Predashi would have to say to the proposal. She'd be the first to point out that the galaxy was a dangerous place, and that humanity needed to show they were prepared to defend themselves. She'd say that if spending credits could do that more effectively, then find the credits to spend.

21 - Predashi

Indira sat perched atop one of the boulders that butted against the wall of the large cavern. She wondered how many of them the Kitanes had had to roll out of the way after they'd been forced into hiding. The majority of the cavern floor was now smooth and free of all but the largest and most immovable boulders for the most part. It baffled her that all the makeshift shelters hugged the walls or extended out into branching caves like the one shared by the people from *Intrepid*.

"Pivot! Strike!"

The group of prospective Kitane warriors were slow to react to the orders barked by one of Ballard's sergeants, which led to the inevitable collision when one of the trainees bumped into another and kicked off a chain of failure. Indira snorted with amusement when the foxes began arguing with each other, in what she assumed was an attempt to assign blame to anyone else.

The sergeant in charge of today's training plowed into the group, pushing and shoving the trainees back into position. Okune. He was more serious and focused than the other sergeant, Cantu. That man seemed like the sort who wanted to turn everything into a joke, regardless of how anyone else might be feeling.

She scowled darkly and slid off the boulder. Her own disgust with the situation had been growing by the hour. When she'd volunteered to come along on the mission with Lieutenant Ballard's Infantry squad, she'd done so with the idea that her expertise would be required to observe and plan a boarding action for the orbiting ships. Instead, the Kitanes seemed set on ignoring the vessels that had brought invaders to their world, and Tamma still refused to even discuss the possibility that taking one of those ships could end everything much quicker and cleaner than this cycle of training and scouting.

Indira growled deep in her chest as she paced around the boulder, spitefully kicking any small stone within reach. The real problem was that she was bored. She had taken a brief course on ground-based assault tactics in Officer Training School, but it had only covered the bare essentials. There had been little interest in learning more, and now she was stuck watching someone else train an alien race in the techniques she never bothered to study.

Her eyes touched on the dented and battered shuttle that rested just inside the cavern's wide mouth. The ship had returned while they slept, but her one attempt at getting close enough to examine it had been thwarted by Tamma's insistence that she remain near the small cave set aside for use by the people from *Intrepid*. Her hands itched to touch the controls inside the shuttle, to pick apart the purpose behind each switch, button, and dial she'd seen during their trip to this world.

"They're back!"

The shout followed a flash of bright light as the mesh of vines and leaves covering the cavern mouth pulled aside for a minute and then dropped back into place. Ballard's head popped out of their cave, and Indira quickened her pace to catch up to the lieutenant when she started to jog toward the wide opening.

They passed within a few yards of the shuttle, and Indira eyed it intently until she almost tripped on an errant stone and face planted in front of everyone. She forced her attention to the ground in front of her but couldn't hold back a tiny smile of victory. The shuttle's hatch was open. Only a few inches, but it meant that she could sneak into the ship if she could only get close enough without one of the Kitanes spotting her. Her boredom would be quickly banished if she had a new ship and new technology to study, regardless of how outdated and inferior it appeared.

"Cantu," Ballard called out, waving her hand to get the attention of her sergeant. He stood with the half of the Infantry squad that had left several days earlier on a scouting mission, and they were all surrounded by a growing number of Kitanes. "How did it go?"

The man grinned at his lieutenant before shifting the expression to Indira. "You wouldn't believe how beautiful this world is, lieutenant. With so many hills, there are vistas that will take your breath away. Just when you think you've found the best vantage point from which to see it all, you walk a little further and... boom! An even better one."

"Give us the travel guide version later," Indira said. "Did you put eyes on the Golmorungs?"

Cantu glanced at Ballard for a quick nod before responding. "We did, commander. The nearest encampment is about eight miles away by my reckoning. It could be as far as ten, though, since we were taking a very circuitous route both ways to maintain our stealth approach."

Ballard glanced around, then motioned for Cantu and Indira to follow her to a quieter area. It took some pushing and shoving to get through the ring of curious onlookers, all of whom seemed to be pressing for details from the Kitanes who had helped guide the scouting expedition.

"Okay, give us the rundown," Ballard said finally, dropping her voice so they wouldn't be overheard.

He started off talking about the rolling hills and towering trees that surrounded the area around the cavern, but Ballard motioned for him to skip it. "It was around noon on the second day when we finally got a glimpse of the marshland." Cantu paused and gazed off into the distance. "I say noon, but it's hard to tell where the sun is a lot of the time because of the trees. You wouldn't believe how dark it can be inside the forest during the brightest part of the day. It doesn't help that the planetary rotation here seems to be a few hours shorter than back on Earth."

"The Golmorungs," Indira growled impatiently. "What did you see?"

Cantu blushed and ducked his head. "Sorry, commander. Well, first of all, the marshlands spread out for miles. I couldn't see an end to them from where we set up. It's clear that the land there is pretty useless for hunters like the Kitane, unless they devoted years of effort to building dikes or whatever. I understand now why they were willing to part with it when the Golmorungs first arrived.

"Anyway," he said quickly, noting the rising anger in her eyes, "it didn't take long to pick out the huts the Golmorungs built for themselves. They're wooden structures atop poles to raise them above the murky water, and I have to admit I felt a little bad for anyone forced to live in them. Not one of those houses looked like it would stand up to a gentle breeze, but I guess they're stronger than they look since they've been standing for at least a year.

"We had eyes on the village for about twenty minutes before

I saw the first frog." Cantu shuddered at the memory. "Tamma described them well, but it still didn't prepare me for the sight of them. The Golmorungs could easily tower over any of us if they stood upright, but they move in a sloping crouch. Their legs are massive, bent at the knee just like an Earth frog, and it wouldn't surprise me if they could leap twenty feet in the air. Both sets of arms are pretty small by comparison. The middle pair, which would be about stomach level for us, are smaller than the upper pair. The fingers on them seem to be longer and more delicate, as well."

"How many did you see?" Ballard asked.

"During the four and a half hours we watched them, I counted at least a hundred. I think. All of the frogs look alike, right down to the same purple color, so it's impossible to know if I was counting the same ones over and over again."

"What's the most you saw at a single time?" Indira asked.

"Right before our Kitane guides forced us to pull back, I saw around forty Golmorungs at one time. They seemed to be gathering in a clearing between their raised huts, where this big stone looks like it's growing out of the water. When I wanted to stay and watch what they were doing, one of our guides almost bit my head off.

"I've gotta be honest, lieutenant." Cantu lifted his shoulders in a shrug. "They seemed like peaceful folk to me, but we didn't get to hang around long enough to really make a judgement on what the Golmorungs might be like. Our Kitane guides set up our observational post about three quarters of a mile out from the village, and they argued every time I tried to suggest we move closer. I assume they argued, anyway, since I still have no idea what any of their language might mean."

"Did you see any weapons?" Ballard asked. "Or any hint of communication with the ships in orbit?"

Cantu shook his head. "No to both. The closest thing I saw to a weapon was a two-pronged wooden spear that a couple of the frogs were using to fish around the edges of their settlement. The things they pulled out of the water looked like thick lobsters." He held up his hands, shoulder length apart. "Definitely crustaceans, and they definitely looked like they would be delicious."

Indira's mouth flooded with saliva at the thought of dining on lobster. A week of eating nutrient-rich but flavor-deficient meal bars was causing a cascade of cravings for all the food she normally enjoyed in the officer's mess on *Intrepid*.

"I was hoping you'd come back with more information that we could use in our planning," Ballard said after mulling over what they'd heard.

"Sorry, lieutenant. I would have preferred to stay out for another couple of days and set up observational posts in multiple locations, but the Kitanes seemed very nervous about being so close to the Golmorung encampment. They couldn't drag us back here fast enough."

They were interrupted by a knot of Kitanes wandering in their direction. Indira was surprised to see Elder Hamman at the center, the first time she'd seen him outside the tents set aside for use by the elders since the night of their arrival.

"You are satisfied?" he asked. "Now that you've seen our enemy, you will know how to fight them?"

"Not quite," Ballard scoffed. "I'll lead the next scouting mission myself, and I want you to inform the Kitanes who guide us that we'll be staying out for longer."

Elder Hamman frowned, his eyes narrowing in response to her request. "Why do you need to see the enemy again? Did your man here not do as you ordered him?" he asked, giving Cantu a withering stare.

"My sergeant performed admirably, but his mission was rushed by the insistence of your people that they return far too quickly. We've made a start, but there's much more to see before I can decide on the best course for getting the Golmorungs to leave your world."

Indira watched a variety of emotions flash across the elder's face, and she noted a snarl that rippled across his snout before it was smoothed away. "Very well. If you humans must see more, then I will authorize another scouting expedition. But only one! When you return, we fight."

"Or we talk with them," Indira said. "Speaking of which, if I can get into that shuttle, there may be a way to open communications with the ships in orbit. We may not understand their words, but I know some of your people can communicate with the Golmorungs since you were able to speak with them when they first arrived."

"No," Elder Hamman said, knifing a hand through the air decisively. "I can't risk that any communication with those ships will allow the Golmorungs to pinpoint our location. However..." His words trailed off as he looked toward the shuttle. "The ship was damaged during the trip to gather supplies. The pilot suffered harsh turbulence that seems to have scrambled some of the systems. Perhaps you could work with Tamma to see what repairs can be accomplished. We require the use of that shuttle if we're not to starve."

Indira suppressed the joy that leapt up inside of her. "I'd be glad to lend a hand. I have some experience with the systems on our own ship, so I should be able to help locate the problem areas and fix them." *And if I do a little poking around at the same time, no one will know,* she thought.

"I will have someone retrieve you tomorrow morning, then."

"Why not start now?" Indira asked, eager to get inside the ship.

He turned away before she could push the issue further, calling over his shoulder. "Tonight is for restful sleep. The next scouting expedition will leave at sunrise."

Ballard turned away as soon as the elder disappeared into the crowd surrounding the Kitanes who had been part of the scouting mission. "Cantu, I want a full report from each of you tonight," the lieutenant said. "Tell me everything, from the shape of leaves on the trees to the smell of the water in the marsh. I'm leading the next scouting mission, and I won't let the Kitanes dictate where I go or when I go there."

Indira nodded her approval at the fire in the other woman's voice. She shifted her gaze to the shuttle and began working out ways to probe the systems while repairing it with Tamma. If she could keep the woman distracted, then perhaps she'd find a way to access whatever databanks were aboard and learn more about the Golmorungs in a few minutes than any scouting expedition could hope to gain in a week.

22 - Ballard

Alina squinted against the harsh orange light of the setting sun, which was reflected hundreds of times across the patchy surface of the marsh not far away. She dropped her binoculars and then crawled backwards until she was below the rise of the small hill.

"I counted seventy-three," she said softly.

"Seventy-six," Okune's voice said through her earpiece. He and LoTur were set up half a mile south of the Golmorung village, while she and Gundar had posted up to the north. "There was a trio of them watching from the windows of a hut, but they were outside your line of sight."

Alina grunted in response. Seventy-six was a large number, but not as many as she'd been expecting. "What do you think they were gathering for?" she asked.

"It kind of looks like some sort of sun worship, doesn't it, lieutenant? The way the Golmorungs are clustered in total silence while the sun sets, it's almost like they're praying or something. That huge stone monolith they circled could be some form of altar, I suppose."

She'd had similar thoughts, but it seemed so incongruous to what she'd been expecting to find based on everything Tamma and Elder Hamman had told them about the invaders taking over their planet. This was almost the opposite of the armed encampment she'd been expecting, bristling with weapons and a sturdy wall constructed as defense against attacks.

Alina ran the tip of her tongue across her lips. Nothing about this world matched her expectations. From the moment they'd set out at dawn the day before, there had been a series of discoveries forcing her to shift her view of the situation.

The first had been the stunning vistas, which had taken her breath away as soon as her small scouting party stepped foot outside the cavern. From their position, they'd been able to see for at least a mile, and the land around them was filled with tall trees marching up and down hills that seemed to spread out like ripples on a pond. Those trees made her ache for home, with their orange and yellow leaves that vividly reminded her of fall. The blueish color of their trunks had been slightly unsettling, though.

"I don't see any scorched areas," Okune had remarked in a whisper only she could hear. The six Kitanes tasked with guiding them and ensuring they didn't stumble across the Golmorungs wouldn't have understood their words, but she felt the same desire to keep their comments under wraps.

"Perhaps the bombardment occurred on the other side of the mountain?" she'd asked, glancing over her shoulder at the gentle peak rising above them.

"Why would they travel that far to find a safe place to hide?" Okune responded. "We should be able to see at least some sign of the orbital bombardment from here."

That concern had been swiftly banished by the steady concentration she had to give to the ground in front of her feet when they began trudging through the forest. When Cantu had told her it took a day and a half to reach the edge of the marshes, she'd been confused at such a slow rate of travel. Breaking through waist-high undergrowth and dodging bramble patches had helped explain it.

The forest had provided other surprises, in the form of animals that could be heard and occasionally seen in the distance. Flashes of brown and white fur had left them guessing at the shape of the animals that passed too quickly to be deciphered. LoTur had ventured the names of several found on the Panosh home world, while Gundar and Okune had guessed the creatures might resemble the deer or rabbits of Earth.

What had been missing was the birdsong that Alina would have expected. She didn't realize it was missing until they'd stopped for a break after several hours of exhausting travel. The air was filled with the buzzing of insects, but no matter how hard she strained her ears, there were no bird chirps or calls.

The first night was spent in a hollow between two sloping hills. The Kitanes watched warily as Gundar and Okune began to gather fallen wood, and started to protest when Alina produced a small butane torch with which to start the fire. She only waved them to silence, however, and the barks and yips of the Kitane language trailed off after a few minutes.

Okune had tried to initiate a form of communication with a few of the Kitanes, using his hands to gesture and make shapes while he asked which direction their homes were in. If the Kitanes understood any of it, they chose not to respond with anything more than guarded looks. The foxes had bedded down in a pile on the far side of the fire from Alina and her people.

The second day's walk was just as tiring, and when the trees and undergrowth began to thin out, Alina was grateful for the reprieve. The sun had been hanging high in the sky when they broke free of the forest, and she estimated it had taken another hour to reach the first vantage point that allowed them to see the marshland spread out ahead. Another couple of hours had been wasted while she convinced the Kitanes that splitting the group was a good idea, a process hampered by their inability to understand each other's language. She had wanted Okune and LoTur to head north, but their Kitane guides swooped in to prevent any move in that direction. They'd finally agreed to letting them go south, but that only left her with more questions than answers.

"Keep watching and let me know if you see anything that might be important," Alina told Okune over the radio. They were using a tight-beam communication system, which would be next to impossible to detect if the Golmorungs were scanning for any electronic communications.

"Will do, lieutenant. I'll have LoTur relieve me in an hour."

Alina motioned to Gundar, who was waiting for her in the small camp they'd fashioned at the base of the hill. There would be no fire tonight, but the air was warm enough that it wasn't needed. The humidity was powerful enough that she was already sweating just from the short climb down the hill, so the added heat from a fire would have been unwelcome for all of them.

"Take over," she said, passing the binoculars.

Gundar crawled up the hill, dropping to his belly and slithering the last few feet to stay hidden in case any of the Golmorungs happened to be looking in their direction.

The three Kitanes who had stayed with them were eying Alina as she dropped down to sit on her bedroll. She wished she knew even a few words of their language, so that she could communicate in some way. With Tamma engaged in repairs on the shuttle, there had been no option of dragging her along to facilitate communication.

She sighed with resigned disgust as she tore open a meal bar and took a bite. This one had a hint of tartness that was probably supposed to be lemon flavor, but it left a foul taste in her mouth long after she swallowed. Alina was tempted to put the bar back in her pack, but her stomach was grumbling and growling after the exertion of the long march through the forests.

While she ate, she considered everything she'd seen during the short hours since they'd set up their observation post. The Golmorungs appeared to spend most of their time in leisurely activities, such as fishing and using their dexterous middle appendages to weave stringy marsh grass into ropes and baskets. They worked alone for the most part, and the largest grouping she'd seen until the sunset ritual was a trio of frogs that had been plying their pronged spears to catch crustaceans.

One thing that had drawn her attention was when a Golmorung exited a wooden hut, stood on the rickety balcony, and craned their head up to the sky. It had happened several times during the short period when she'd been watching, and each Golmorung had come out of a different hut. Short of the frogs possessing long-range telepathic communication with the ships in orbit, she couldn't decide why they would be so interested in scanning the skies.

As she chewed the last bite of her meal bar, grateful to be done with the necessary task, Alina shifted her focus to the night ahead. Instead of cooling down with sunset, the air was growing more sweltering by the minute. She was going to sweat buckets, and she imagined LoTur and the Kitanes would be suffering under fur which had to add to their misery. She pulled her water bottle out of her pack and shook it. Still almost full, thanks to stopping at a stream just outside the forest earlier that day, but she expected it would be empty by dawn.

"Gundar," she called out softly.

"Yes, lieutenant?"

"Do you see any water sources from up there? Besides the marsh, I mean."

There was silence for a few minutes, and she glanced up to see the man scanning around the terrain with the binoculars. "Nothing but that stream we used a couple of miles back."

Alina threw her head back in frustration. That left them with two options; hiking back to the stream and wasting hours to re-fill their water bottles, or sneaking closer to the marsh to see if their filtration units could handle the task of turning the murky water pure. She ran the pros and cons of each option while she drank deeply from her bottle.

She had traded off with Gundar to take over the scouting for the second time since nightfall before she came to a final de-cision. Waldruun's two moons had appeared over the horizon, both half the size of Earth's moon, providing just enough illumi-nation for her to pick out vague details in the landscape. There hadn't been a hint of movement in the Golmorung village since the sunset gathering had dispersed. To top it all off, the air was heavier and more humid than it had been when they approached the marsh. Alina sucked down the last of her water, and she'd heard the pathetic swish of mere dregs in Gundar's bottle before he crawled down the hill to grab a nap.

With her mind made up, the wait for her shift to end was in-terminable. Alina was twitching with impatience when she heard the scuff of Gundar crawling up the crown of the hill before he came to a rest beside her. "Your turn to grab some sleep, lieu-tenant."

"Not this time," she said as she passed over the binoculars. Alina snatched his water bottle at the same time and waved it in the air. "We're going through this stuff faster than expected, so we need a refill."

"You're not going to hike all the way back to the forest in the dark, are you?" Gundar asked in astonishment.

"That's too long of a trip," she said through a tight smile. "Especially when there's water much closer."

Gundar's eyes grew wide as he followed her pointing finger toward the marshy waters only a few hundred yards away. He glanced over his shoulder at the Kitane guides, who were huddled together in a sleeping ball. "They'd go ballistic if they knew you were even thinking of doing that."

"That's a damned good reason to do it now, while they're asleep. Better to ask forgiveness than permission, right?" She chuckled as she shoved Gundar's bottle through a belt loop beside her own. "Besides, the Golmorungs all seem to be sleeping, as well. There hasn't been a stir of movement in hours. I can make it down to the water and back in no time."

"I should go with you, lieutenant, just in case there's trouble."

Alina scoffed and rolled her eyes. "If there's trouble, Gundar, I'll be relying on you to spot it from up here and give me a warning before I'm in danger."

"Oh," he said, slapping his forehead. "I should have thought of that, I guess."

"You're technically still a trainee, so consider that a teaching moment." Alina chuckled as she rose up on her fingers and toes. "Here goes nothing."

With a lunge, she rolled over the gentle hilltop and several feet down the other side. Once she was sure her profile wouldn't be visible to anyone who happened to glance in that direction, Alina began slithering down the hill. While they hadn't had to worry too much about noise on the other side of the hill, any sound she made here was likely to echo out across the marsh. The need for greater stealth kept her movement slow and deliberate.

After at least ten minutes, she'd finally reached relatively flat ground. Alina crouched there for a moment, letting her eyes take in as much of the landscape as she could in the low light. Tufts of marsh grass poked up here and there, and she knew any one of them could be hiding a hole just waiting to snap her ankle if she stepped into it wrong.

Alina moved forward in a crouched jog, leaping over gravel and rocks whenever she encountered them and using the grass to muffle her footsteps. Sweat was beginning to pour down her face from the exertion, and several of her armor plates were rubbing her skin raw where sweat-soaked clothing was providing little protection against the harder surfaces.

She was breathing hard by the time her foot squelched on the beginnings of the marshy surface. Gravel and dirt had given way to brackish puddles, and a little farther on those puddles grew into small pools. Alina leaped from one grassy island to another, navigating her way deeper into the marsh until she reached a point where the water was deep enough that it was affected by gentle currents.

Her lips puffed out to release deep breaths as silently as possible when Alina knelt down. The smell coming off the marsh was enough to make her nose twitch, but she knew it was only the scent of decaying vegetation. The water itself wouldn't be pleasant to drink in its current state, but it shouldn't be life-threatening. Once it ran through their filtering units, it should be potable enough to keep them hydrated for another day. Then they could refill at the stream on the hike back to the Kitane cavern.

Alina quickly spun the lid off Gundar's bottle and dipped it into the water. She watched as the liquid began to seep through the filter and estimated it should only take a few minutes for each bottle. Five minutes, and she'd be on the way back to the safety of their hidden observation post.

"Still clear?" she asked, barely breathing the words.

"No movement from the village, lieutenant," Gundar said immediately, his voice hushed in her ear.

Her eyes slowly rose to scan the Golmorung village. She was halfway between it and the hill where Gundar was watching over her, close enough that she could pick out the huts in the wan moonlight. There was no light coming through the cracks of the wooden walls, and so far there had been no evidence that the frogs possessed any sort of electrical capabilities. Alina was baffled that they wouldn't have brought generators or a solar array down from their ships.

She pulled Gundar's bottle out of the water once it was nearly full and slid it back through a belt loop. Her own bottle came free easily, and she began to twist the cap off.

The only warning was a soft splash off to her left. Alina had barely started to twist in that direction before there was a wet splat to her right. When she changed direction and whirled, she was met by a horrifying sight. The Golmorung staring directly into her eyes was a hulking brute, with warty purple skin that gleamed under the silvery moonlight.

"Lieutenant!" Gundar yelped a warning through her earpiece. *Too little too late*, she thought wryly. The Golmorung must have glided through the water to reach her, hidden from sight of her squad mate.

Alina dropped her hand to the stun gun strapped to her

thigh, cursing herself for leaving her NK70 behind despite the noise it might have made on her stealthy trip. She snapped open the strap that secured the gun, but before she could wrap her fingers around the grip, something sharp jabbed into her back.

She froze into unnatural stillness. The two points digging into the clothing between cracks in her armor plating weren't breaking skin, but she knew it wouldn't take much more force to do so. The Golmorung in front of her opened his mouth and released a croaking string of words.

Alina was stunned when the implant behind her ear began to vibrate. Seconds passed by, and she didn't dare to breath as the device continued to churn over a language it shouldn't have been able to interpret. Such a thing had never happened around the Kitanes when they were speaking their language.

When the buzzing vibration stopped, she assumed the implant had failed to interpret the Golmorung's words. She was opening her mouth to warn Gundar that she was being taken prisoner when the tinny voice of translated speech rang in her head. There were only a few understandable words broken by incomprehensible static, but it was enough to leave her gaping in surprise.

"Who.... you?"

23 - Wingate

Paine gazed through the window, barely noticing the ships that were approaching or departing the tentacled arms of the space station. The ship he was waiting for wasn't scheduled to arrive for a few more hours, but he'd been so restless with anticipation that he'd given up on work when he noticed he was reading a document for the fourth time without taking in any of the meaning.

It had been ten cycles since the small group of explorers departed on a Monolith Transport Collective ship, and they were finally on the way back to Kraken to report on their discoveries. It had been a relatively short trip, but Paine hoped it was merely the first of many that the former colonists would be taking in the future. Rather than languishing in Kraken's storage bays, they could be out exploring the planets and moons that were open to them through a contract with Monolith to provide transportation. Not only would it keep restless people occupied, but it would also expand their knowledge of this part of the galaxy much faster than *Intrepid*'s explorations alone.

He jerked his gaze toward an approaching ship with a familiar design, but it took only a cursory examination to confirm it wasn't the transport he was waiting on. Paine's palms were itching with anticipation, and he snickered at his own impatience. He wondered if his overwhelming desire to greet the group on their return was driven by his fervent wish that he could have joined them.

"Stargazing again, I see."

Paine smiled at the voice and glanced at the reflection of the person who appeared beside him. "More like ship gazing."

X'Zak pulled her lips up in a grin that would have looked like a snarl if he hadn't come to know her so well. "Ah, the group of explorers you told me about returns today?"

"In another hour or so," Paine nodded. "I know it's pointless to stand here and wait to catch a glimpse of their ship when Kraken's systems could easily alert me to their approach, but..."

"But you found yourself unable to focus on anything else." The Kr'Sal ambassador shrugged her shoulders, making her flowing robes shimmer in the light. "I feel much the same when one of my clutch mates comes to visit wherever I'm posted."

Paine raised an eyebrow as he glanced at her reflection. "Clutch mates?"

She hissed laughter. "Yes, it's exactly what you're thinking. Unlike you humans, we Kr'Sal don't confine ourselves to having only one partner. I have seven mates, and together we form a familial clutch. There are nineteen children in our clutch now, or were when I left for this posting. It could be twenty by now."

Paine was fascinated by this glimpse into Kr'Sal culture, more so because it diverted his attention and made the wait more bearable. "Not all humans restrict themselves to only one partner," he said with a grin. "There are cultures on Earth that believe in sharing their mates with others in a variety of circumstances. Some are patriarchal, with husbands having multiple wives. Others are more equal, with both partners keeping lovers on the side."

"Indeed?" X'Zak tilted her head as she absorbed the information. "You humans continue to be so confusing. How has your planet survived for so long with such a fractious populace?"

"We all wonder the same thing sometimes," Paine laughed. "The world seemed a lot larger before we developed space travel, and much more so when travel was confined to our own feet or the distance a horse could carry us. That made it much easier for a patchwork of cultures and societies to spring up around the globe."

"One of your cultures didn't dominate all others and absorb them into the clearly superior society?"

"Such a thing has happened here and there," Paine admitted. "The conquered almost always maintained a core of independent spirit, however, and often rebelled against their oppressors. Often, those conquered cultures broke free and restored their own way of life after some time."

"So very confusing and unproductive," X'Zak said. "And yet it is equally fascinating at the same time. I value these meetings and the many interesting things I learn about your people."

"I've come to look forward to them, as well," Paine admitted softly. "You're not the only one who enjoys learning about the other's culture, X'Zak. Every time I pick up some new information about your people, it helps to dispel the enmity that threatened to develop between us after our first encounters."

The Kr'Sal ambassador dipped her head in agreement, and silence fell as they enjoyed a moment of contemplation. They gazed out at the stars, lost to their own thoughts.

"I have something that I must admit, Paine."

"Oh?"

"I didn't happen upon you by accident just now. I've been walking the promenade for an hour, hoping I would encounter you."

Paine's eyebrows rose in amazement. "I'm not sure if I should be flattered or frightened," he said through a shaky laugh.

X'Zak placed her hand lightly on his forearm. "Flattered, I hope. I know that we've known each other for only a short time, but I feel a closeness with you that I've never felt for someone of another race. Please tell me you understand what I mean."

He gulped, unsure of how he should feel. Paine had dreaded every meeting with another Kr'Sal after his time in their slave mines, but now he had come to consider their new ambassador a friend. Could she really be hinting that she wanted their relationship to become more than that?

"You don't have to say anything right now," she hissed in a voice barely above a whisper. "I know I have no right to burden you with my feelings, especially after the cruelty you've suffered at the hands of my people. Whatever your thoughts, whether or not you would be open to exploring this connection between us, I hope above all that we can remain friends.

"You are a kind man," she continued, her hand clutching his arm tightly as she leaned closer. "But still so strong and forceful. It is a rare combination among Kr'Sal, and I find it intoxicating. I've seen the way you humans interact with other races here on Kraken, so I feel you won't react to my confession with disgust. Perhaps I'm wrong, but I hope that I'm not."

Paine opened his mouth, but words refused to come out. His palms were sweating, and he hadn't felt this discombobulated since he'd been confronted by a woman in his college days. She'd poured out her feelings just as X'Zak was, and he'd been so frozen by disbelief that she'd taken his silence for disgust at her confession.

"This is much to think about, I know," X'Zak said, her breath warm on his cheek as she leaned in even closer. "If you say that we can only be friends, then I will be elated to have that much of a relationship with you. If you choose to become closer, know that I will feel joy unlike any I've experienced before. I will wait to hear your decision."

With startling suddenness, her rough lips pressed against his cheek. She nuzzled against him for a heartbeat, and then she was gone. Paine was slightly saddened by the loss of her warmth against his side, but the overwhelming feeling racing through his body was confusion. This was the last thing he could have ever expected to happen, and yet there was a small part of him that was exultant at the prospect.

The possibilities flooded him with a conflicting array of emotions. When Paine snapped out of the torrent of thoughts racing through his head, he realized nearly an hour had passed. He could feel the phantom presence of X'Zak by his side, and his nose twitched as he inhaled the slightly peppery scent that seemed to follow her around.

A sudden loud chime startled him, and Paine hastily pulled his tablet from a pocket. The message that had come through was marked urgent. Bos wanted him back at the embassy immediately. Paine wondered what could have gone so horribly wrong in his short absence. After a last glance through the window, he strode the short distance to his offices.

The moment the door opened, he knew the urgency of the message had been understated, if anything. Bos's expression was more somber and serious than ever, and something in his eyes spoke of suppressed rage. "You received a message, Mr. Wingate. It was routed through a handful of ships in order to reach Kraken and originated from a vessel named *Bulwark*."

Silas's ship! The Acelu's people must have discovered some-

thing in the search of their database. He doubted that yet another lack of success would merit such a critical step as sending a
message leapfrogging through ships to reach Kraken.

Bos held out a tablet, one of the embassy devices secured by
top level encryption. The short message was already open on the
screen, and Paine read it quickly. He sucked in a breath as he
read through it more slowly a second time, and then the blood
drained from his face when he looked up to meet Bos's eyes.

"We have to warn them," he said in a strangled voice.

24 - Kerrigan

Lyle breezed onto the bridge shortly after the beginning of the day shift and settled into his wide command chair. He studied the reports that had been generated by the evening and overnight shifts, then moved on to the current status of *Intrepid*'s various departments.

"Give me a course update, Nav. Am I reading these coordinates correctly?"

"Aye, captain." Ensign Poehl swiveled to face him. "The map of the system we were provided was slightly outdated. Once our sensor scans were uploaded and used to correct those charts, I was able to calculate a better course to take advantage of the current positioning of planets and asteroids."

Lyle hummed appreciatively. "Then we really are ahead of our projected schedule?"

"By seven hours and forty-one minutes at the current moment," Poehl said proudly. "We should arrive at our destination more than eleven hours ahead of initial projections."

"Excellent work, ensign. That goes for you, too, Ensign Nuñes. Collaboration like that is what *Intrepid* needs if we're going to continue to succeed out here."

"Thank you, captain," the woman at the Sensors station said.

"Now, if you can shave just as much time off our return trip, I might even consider granting each of you an extra couple of R&R hours as a token of my appreciation."

Poehl's eyes gleamed with eagerness as he matched gazes

with his counterpart at Sensors. Within seconds, they had their heads together as they began poring over the star charts and plotting out their return to the space station.

Lyle watched his officers with a fond smile, pleased with how well each of them was able to work together. He'd served on ships where cliques and factions had formed in the crew, creating schisms that made effective cooperation nearly impossible. *Intrepid*'s crew had avoided such things, perhaps because of the unique challenges they'd faced from the very beginning of the voyage.

"Comms, how long until we're within communication range with the WayLin outpost?"

"We should be within effective range in thirty-four hours, captain," Ensign Larkin reported. "The signal will be rather spotty for the first few hours, though, since we'll be at maximum range of the comms gear."

"Noted. Thank you, ensign." Lyle made a mental note to compile the various reports of incidents involving the miners they were transporting out to the asteroid. Once it was all collected and collated, he would be able to forward the report to the local facility administrator. WayLin had been very specific that the clauses and restrictions in the contracts they negotiated with the miners didn't begin until they set foot on WayLin property, but their behavior on the trip out would provide some warning of what the miners were capable of.

Lyle would be glad to have those men and women off *Intrepid*. They were being paid well to ferry personnel and equipment out from the space station, but the miners themselves had proven to be a much larger headache than anticipated. Drunken fights were becoming less common as the smuggled alcohol was quickly depleted, but that didn't stop temperamental flare-ups when conflicting personalities rubbed up against each other.

On a positive note, the time shaved off the trip by the efficiency of his Navigation department would mean they burned through less fuel and supplies. It wouldn't be a huge savings, but it would help in his goal to scrape together the necessary credits for the power armor suits Lieutenant Galbraith was slavering for. She and the Fleet Infantry squads had more than earned such a reward for their efforts.

He was in the process of putting together his report for WayLin Mining Consortium when the screen set into the arm of his chair flashed with an incoming alert. Lyle put down his tablet to focus on the words which scrolled across the screen, and his lips tightened with frustration.

"Lieutenant Stebbins, you have the bridge."

"Aye, captain."

Lyle tugged on the hem of his tunic as he marched off the bridge. There was more than a little annoyance in the gesture, and he worked to calm himself as he stepped onto the elevator. By the time he'd reached the midpoint of *Intrepid*'s arching spine, he was the cool and collected captain everyone expected to encounter.

One of the Infantry soldiers was waiting when he stepped off the elevator. "Captain, the lieutenant asked me to meet you."

"Lead the way, sergeant," he said, motioning for the man to get moving. "Sergeant Cho, correct?"

"Yes, sir," the soldier said, his shoulders stiffening with pride that the captain had remembered his name.

"What's the situation? The lieutenant's message requesting my presence was scant on the details."

"It's the miners, captain," the sergeant said.

"Isn't it always?" Lyle asked under his breath.

"Apparently a pair of the Dubuks are mated, which their race considers a sacred lifetime commitment. Well, during the morning meal, an Engineering crew member started up a conversation with the miners sitting near her table. Everything seemed to be congenial and friendly, but something she said set off an argument. The Dubuk female is adamant that her mate was being propositioned, and she's demanding that the crew member be punished."

"What exactly could have been said to elicit such a strong reaction?"

Cho shot him an amused glance. "Apparently, sir, the crewwoman asked if the mated pair had any children."

"That's all? They took offense at something that simple?"

The sergeant gave a confused shrug. "The Dubuk female seems to have interpreted it as a slight on her ability to produce offspring for her mate, captain. She insists the crewwoman was openly hinting that she would be able to provide as many children as might be desired. Lieutenant Galbraith has tried to explain how that likely wouldn't even be possible given the biological differences, but the Dubuk woman's not exactly open to being reasonable at the moment."

Lyle pinched the bridge of his nose, wondering if the miners would ever stop finding new ways to disturb the equanimity of his ship. "We have witnesses to the conversation?"

"We do," Cho nodded. "Unfortunately, so does the Dubuk."

"Let me guess, some of the other miners agree with her interpretation of the conversation, while our crew view it in a different light?"

"Exactly, captain. We've got a Sumarong and two other Dubuk miners who claim our crewwoman was overstepping the bounds of decency. Their words, sir, not mine."

"Fantastic." Lyle rubbed his temples as they reached one of the rooms inside the cargo drum. After two days of only minor disturbances, he had begun to hope the rest of the trip out to the asteroid might pass smoothly. He should have known better.

Lieutenant Galbraith was standing in the middle of the room, which was devoid of furniture aside from a table and two chairs. A Dubuk was seated in one chair, while a young crewwoman wearing an Engineering uniform was in the other. They were glaring at each other across the table, and the crewwoman had her arms crossed over her chest.

"Captain, thank you for coming." Galbraith waved her sergeant out of the room and waited for the door to hiss shut before she continued. "I was finally able to convince both parties to accept mediation, but it damn near became a brawl."

"This——is trying to steal the affections of my mate," the Dubuk woman shouted. Lyle flinched at the word his implant was unable to translate, certain it would have been quite strongly vulgar.

"All I did was ask if you two had kids," the crewwoman insisted, throwing up her hands. "I even offered to show you a photo of my son."

"Ah," Lyle said, beginning to understand how the situation had spiraled.

"Yeah," Galbraith sighed. "I've tried to explain that showing off photos of our kids is a human custom, but that's not flying."

"You were trying to demonstrate your fecundity as a way to make my mate more interested in you," the Dubuk raged, slamming her fist on the table. "I demand this... female be punished."

"No one is getting punished," Lyle said, stepping forward to lean against the table. "This is simply a misunderstanding of each other's cultural norms. I guarantee that no one was trying to steal your mate."

"As if I'd want that hairy oaf anywhere near my bed," the crewwoman snorted.

Lyle held back a groan as the Dubuk's eyes flashed with rage. Any chance of damping the emotions in the room fled with that comment.

The Dubuk female jumped to her feet, and likely would have tried to leap over the table if the lights hadn't suddenly shut off. When they snapped back on half a second later, they were strobing yellow.

Galbraith had her hand to her ear, and her expression grew grim at whatever she was hearing. "Emergency situation in Engineering, captain. We need to respond immediately."

"Return to your quarters," he snapped at the feuding women. "Remain there until I have the opportunity to speak with you again."

The Dubuk protested and the crewwoman tried to insist that she would be needed at her station, but he was already out the door and jogging down the corridor after Lieutenant Galbraith. "What's happening?"

"Commander Berger hit the alert, captain. Someone has locked down access to the reactor room, and they're tampering with our systems from inside."

Lyle pressed his own earpiece to initiate a connection with the ship's comms. "Bridge, lock down all computer access inside the reactor room."

"We're trying to do that now, captain," Lieutenant Stebbins reported. "Lieutenant de Windt is facing some difficulty, however. Whoever is in there seems to be very proficient with our systems, and they're thwarting her attempts to block access."

"Shut down computer access to the entire aft section if you have to," he barked.

"That can't be done easily or quickly, captain. Commander Berger has been working on isolating Engineering from all other ship's systems, but she said it could take as long as twenty minutes to deactivate all the redundancies and safeguards in place to prevent such a thing happening accidentally."

He bit off a curse, skidding to a halt as he and Galbraith reached the elevator. The door opened almost instantly, and seconds later they were zipping along *Intrepid*'s spine toward the aft section of the ship.

Half a minute later, Lyle and Galbraith were thrown forward when the elevator came to an abrupt halt. He heard a sharp snap, followed by a cry of pain. His forehead throbbed from where he'd collided with something sharp, and he could feel blood beginning to seep down his face.

The flashing yellow lighting shut off, encasing them in darkness.

Lyle was feeling around for the earpiece that had popped out during the collision when the lights snapped back on.

They were flashing with a dangerous red glow that instantly sent his heart sinking down into his stomach.

25 - Predashi

Indira ran her hands over the scorched surface of the shuttle's hull. Tamma had told them the initial damage occurred during landing to disgorge more Golmorungs intent on taking over this world, but she thought it looked and felt more like the result of an incendiary strike. Carbon scoring left the dull steel almost black where it had rippled and bubbled under extreme heat.

"I believe I've found the problem," Lash said, pulling her attention back to the work at hand. The Tiké had happily volunteered to help with repairing the shuttle, and his tiny stick-like arms and hands were proving to be quite an asset.

"Faulty wiring?" Indira asked, bending to look into the cavity exposed behind a removed hull plate. It was only waist high for her but perfectly placed for the insectile Tiké who was half her height.

"These leads appear to have been corroded," Lash said, pointing to a handful of connections that were ringed with what looked to be rust. "This much corrosion could only result from many phases of neglect, however."

Indira reached in to pull one of the disconnected leads out of the narrow opening. It tugged to a stop after only a few inches, but that gave her enough space to get a good look at it. The thick bundle of wiring inside the mesh sheath twisted into the metallic ring that served to connect two lengths of cable together. That ring was spotted with rust and other residue that she was reluctant to touch. "That's definitely going to cause some systems to misfire."

"More than that," Lash said in a disapproving tone. "The corrosion is bad enough that these connections could fail mid-flight, killing all aboard in a crash. This level of neglect should be criminal."

"It certainly wouldn't pass even a cursory inspection at a shipyard," Indira said. She reached for an oil-stained rag that had been in the small toolbox they found inside the shuttle. No mechanic in the universe seemed to be able to resist leaving scraps of cloth like that laying around, and this one came in useful as she used it to scrub around the metal ring. Small flakes of orange rust came off, as did some foul greenish gunk that made her nose wrinkle in disgust. "At least the metal hasn't been compromised too badly underneath the corrosion."

"Yes," Lash scoffed. "We can repair these leads and restore functionality to the affected systems, but I'd still be leery of traveling far in this shuttle until all the wiring has been fully inspected."

"This rust bucket is our ride home," she laughed. "Or did you forget?"

"Unfortunately, I did not," the Tiké said in a somber tone. He poked his tiny head back into the opening, prevented from going farther by the carapace that flared up around his neck like a cobra's hood. "I believe I can repair these leads and connector rings, if you'd like to check the results of the diagnostic we started earlier."

"Give a shout if you need another hand," Indira said as she stood up and brushed off the knees of her uniform pants. She entered the shuttle through the open hatch and winced when she forgot to duck. Her head bumped against a low-hanging junction box, and she spat out a string of curses as she rubbed thankfully unbroken skin.

Tamma looked up from where she was hunched over the control console. She quickly flipped a few switches, turned a knob, and then pressed three buttons in a rapid sequence. Whatever she'd been working on disappeared from the tiny displays set into the console by the time Indira could look over her shoulder. "Have you fixed the thrust modules?" the Kitane asked.

"Lash is putting the final touches on them now," Indira said, peering suspiciously at the blank displays. "You should consider yourself lucky the Golmorungs are such poor mechanics. Judging from the state of this shuttle, I'd bet those orbiting ships are hanging together by a hope and a prayer."

"Perhaps they didn't have the opportunity to maintain their equipment as well as they'd like," Tamma said defensively. She seemed shocked by her own outburst, but she covered any embarrassment by waving toward the second console and addressing a question Indira had asked almost an hour earlier. "I've told you many times that the communication array was damaged beyond repair. The diagnostics you wanted to run have been completed, however, since you are so untrusting of my opinion."

"You also told us your people were peaceful hunters and gatherers with no experience in space travel before the Golmorungs arrived, so I think I might have a better idea of what can be repaired on this *space* ship and what can't." She emphasized the word out of irritation, but immediately felt petty for doing so. Indira knew that a large part of her prickliness came from worry about Lieutenant Ballard and the other three members of her squad. The scouting expedition had been gone for the greater part of three days, and she was itching to find out what they might have discovered.

"I'm sorry," she sighed. "I didn't mean to snap at you, Tamma."

The Kitane glared at her for a moment, but then her expression softened. "It is forgiven. If you can find any solution my people might have missed, we will of course be grateful to you."

Indira felt a little better with the air cleared, and she shifted her focus to the various switches, dials, and buttons in front of her. Even after three days of Tamma trying to explain the basics of the shuttle's operation, she still understood little of what purpose most of them served. It was amazing that a crew of Kitanes had been able to board the shuttle and decipher the controls well enough to not only get it off the ground but also fly it out to a distant space station in search of aid.

Two switches flicked in different directions powered up the three palm-sized displays in front of her. Indira studied each of them in turn, trying once again to decipher the writing that filled the screens. The script was sharp and scratchy, almost like lines slashed in anger to form a pattern.

When she twisted a knob beside one of the displays, the data shifted into a graph with peaks and valleys. The line was still moving, jumping and dropping at apparently random moments, and it told her the power output from the shuttle's reactor was still not meeting all the demands placed on it by the ship's systems. She wondered if that might be one of the causes for the cascade of failures that lit up the screens any time she tried to activate the communications array.

"I need to get into the maintenance area to take a look at the reactor," she told Tamma.

The Kitane blew out a long breath. "I already explained that we have no way to access that area," she said, waving dismissively at the bulkhead at the rear of the two compartments. "Whatever tools are required to open it were not in the ship when we took it."

"We may have to cut through the bolts then," Indira said. She motioned to the display with the jittery line flicking up and down. "If I can't get a look at the reactor, then we won't be able to repair the power management systems."

"Do it here," Tamma said, slapping her hand against the console. "You see the system, so fix it."

"That's not how it works," she said, fighting the urge to throw up her hands in frustration. "I can't even read the words on this screen, much less figure out how to manipulate the computer system to know if any changes are possible from this console. If I can get my hands on the reactor, though, I might be able to-"

"We've never needed to get into that compartment before," Tamma said firmly. "You'll figure it out from here."

Indira pressed her lips together, wondering why everything with the Kitane had to be a constant battle. Whether it was here in the shuttle with Tamma or in the elders' tent with Elder Hamman, every suggestion and request was met with instant obstacles.

She spent half an hour trying her best, but with such a basic understanding of the controls there was little she could do to adjust the power management system. By the time Lash had completed his cleaning and repair of the wiring, she was ready to just chuck the whole project and let the Kitanes figure out how to fix the ship on their own.

The Tiké took her seat with an air of patience that Indira knew she could never match, even on her best day. His small hands moved across the controls with a surety that came from many decades of exploration and travel throughout this corner of the galaxy. Indira often wondered how old Lash might be and how far his travels had taken him, but any attempts to broach the subject were met with deft maneuvering to shift the conversation onto other topics.

"Well?" she asked after a handful of minutes. "Any luck?"

Lash's mandibles shivered with amusement. "I've only begun, Commander Predashi. It may take hours to decipher these systems, or it could take weeks."

"We don't have weeks," she said flatly.

"Then let us both hope it's not as complicated as it first appears." He bent over the displays with an air of intense concentration.

Indira decided that the best thing she could do was leave him to the work. She drifted away and ducked to exit the shuttle. Finally able to stand up straight again, she stretched her back and rolled her head on her shoulders.

A wave of Kitanes moving quickly for the wide mouth of the cavern caught her attention, and she twisted to look in that direction. The view was obscured by the shuttle's bulk, so she had to pick her way through the scattered tools and parts that had been spread out during their labors over the last several days.

Cantu appeared out of the crowd and arrowed toward her. "What's the fuss about, commander?"

"I'm trying to find that out, myself," she said, going up on her toes to see over the heads of the foxes.

"Could the lieutenant be back already? I wasn't expecting her until tomorrow afternoon at the earliest."

"I don't know, Cantu. How about we go over there and find out?"

He jumped up to try and see over the heads of the Kitane in front of them. "That's a good idea, commander. Follow me."

Indira almost lost him the moment he plunged into the crowd, but he was tall enough that she was able to follow his head over those of the Kitanes clustering around them. Before long, she had to push and shove to get through knots of people. She muttered apologies even though she knew they wouldn't be understood.

Finally, they reached an area that was empty, a cleared space around Elder Hamman and two sweaty, exhausted Kitanes. Their fur was matted and filthy, with leaves and twigs caught in the snarls as if they'd been forced to sprint through the densest parts of the forest. One of them was speaking in high-pitched yelps and growling barks, while the other nodded their head now and then to accompany whatever was being said.

"Those two were with the lieutenant," Cantu said in a low voice. He went up on his toes and craned his neck to look past them. "I don't see anyone else who left on the scouting mission."

Elder Hamman turned to look at them, and at first Indira thought the sergeant's eager searching had drawn his attention. His lips were pulled back in rage, however, and she could feel the force of his anger even before he pointed to them and motioned others to bring them forward.

Indira's arms were roughly grabbed, and Cantu protested loudly when he was treated in the same fashion. Without a word, they were shoved forward until they were no more than a few paces from the elder.

"Did you know anything about this treachery?" he asked. "Think carefully before you respond."

"What are you talking about?" Cantu asked.

"What treachery?" Indira asked at the same moment.

"Your Lieutenant Ballard disobeyed the strictures of her mission," Elder Hamman spat at them. "She left her guards behind."

"Guards?" Indira asked, narrowing her eyes at what he'd said. "Don't you mean her guides?"

"Your choice of words doesn't matter here!" Elder Hamman swept a hand through the air. "I was very clear that none of you humans were to leave sight of my people, and yet you've done just that."

"If the lieutenant slipped your leash, then she had a good reason," Cantu insisted. "What does it matter, as long as she gets the intel we need to know how to fight the Golmorungs?"

"It matters," Elder Hamman said through clenched teeth, "because Lieutenant Ballard has been captured by the Golmorungs."

Indira sucked in a breath. "You're certain of that?"

The elder motioned to the two exhausted guides. "They've seen it with their own eyes."

"We need to mount a rescue," Cantu said urgently. "I'll gather the rest of the squad, commander, and we can double time it to the observation post. Once we meet up with Okune and the others, we'll have a plan in place to break her free within an hour."

"You're staying here," Elder Hamman scoffed. "You humans have done enough damage, and now it falls to me to mitigate this situation before disaster falls on the heads of my people."

Indira had been watching the Kitane elder's face while Cantu spoke, and she didn't like what she'd seen there. He was angry, but something told her it wasn't for the reason he claimed. "What are you going to do?"

"What you should have been doing this entire time," Elder

Hamman said. His shoulders stiffened until he was glaring down his long snout at her. "We're going to wipe out that Golmorung village before they can gain any information from their captive to lead them to this cavern. I'll lead the attack myself."

"That's not necessary," Cantu said, his eyebrows drawing in with confusion. "Not to mention it'll be very chaotic. How are going to keep from injuring Lieutenant Ballard during that kind of a battle?"

"She got herself into this predicament," Elder Hamman said, looking completely unconcerned with her fate. "Now she'll have to face the consequences."

26 - Ballard

Alina was careful to keep her hands at shoulder height while the two Golmorungs who had snuck up on her guided her toward their village. She glanced once toward the hill where Gundar was watching through his binoculars, but then kept her eyes away from that direction so she didn't give away where she'd come from.

The frogs spoke to each other in croaking voices, and her translation implant continued to buzz as it worked at turning their speech into English. She had purchased a software package for herself and the Infantry squads that had included eight of the most common languages in this part of the galaxy. One of those languages must be close enough to that of the Golmorungs to allow a few words to come through.

They seemed to be less concerned about her sudden appearance in the marsh than in her lack of fur. "No hair.... hands.... face," were the words that came through her implant. One of the Golmorungs reached out to poke the back of her hands with a warty finger, almost causing Alina to jerk her arms away.

"I'm not one of the Kitanes," she said.

The reaction to her words was instant. The frog holding a fishing spear raised it while he searched wildly for an enemy, and the other rose up on his powerful legs. He threw back his head, sucked in enough air that his cheeks bulged, and then released a booming call that reverberated across the marsh.

Alina ducked her head in reaction, wanting to protect her

ears but not wanting to move in any way these Golmorungs might read as hostile. "*Not* Kitane," she said loudly. "I'm human. From Earth."

She had no idea if any of her words were making sense, but the frogs clearly recognized the name of the race they had come to steal this planet from. Alina clenched her jaw as she reminded herself that any state of war between the two races had been initiated by these fearsome frogs.

The still, predawn air was broken by an array of calls, seemingly in response to that of her captor. The Golmorung dropped down into the crouch that appeared to be a comfortable posture for them, and then waved all four of his hands in the direction of the wooden huts.

"You want me to go with you?" she asked. Alina snorted at her own idiocy. "Of course they want you to go with them, Alina. Did you think they'd just release you so everyone could go on their merry way?"

The pronged spear poked into her back, prodding her to start moving. Alina tried to pick the best path to stay out of the brackish water, but the Golmorungs didn't seem concerned about whether she got wet. When she tried to turn left to leap to another grassy island, the spear poked into her side until she resumed her straight-ahead course.

By the time they'd reached the first wooden hut, which rose out of the marsh on stilts taller than Alina, water had seeped inside her boots. Every step was met with a squish, and her heels were rubbing against the wet material uncomfortably. "I'm gonna have blisters," she muttered darkly.

Alina remained observant enough to take in the barnacles clinging to the lower foot or so of the wooden supports when she passed by. The wood had a greenish-red moss growing in patches, as well. Both were signs that these huts had been in place for far longer than a year. Perhaps longer than five or even ten years. How was that possible when Tamma said the first invaders arrived much later than that?

The first hints of orange light were touching the hills at her back when Alina reached the central clearing in the middle of the village. Her captors croaked out greetings to other frogs waiting there, as well as to some who appeared through doorways in the huts. Those openings were covered with woven curtains of marsh grass, which she thought was poor protection against the insects buzzing around her head in annoying clouds.

The spear poked into her back when her steps faltered at the sight of the largest frog yet. The Golmorung standing at the center of the clearing had to be at least seven feet tall. If he stood erect, she wouldn't have been surprised if the top of his head was as high as the stone monolith in the center of the cleared area.

Alina squinted at the plinth as she approached it. The light was still too dim to make out much detail, but it appeared as if the surface of the stone had been carved. Some of the marks appeared fresh, with white stone standing out starkly against the darker, aged surface.

"Stop," the massive Golmorung rumbled, holding out one of his upper arms. His hand was splayed wide, with the fingertips rounded like spoons.

"I'm not here to hurt you," she said, speaking slowly and feeling stupid for doing so. "Let's talk about what your people would need in return for leaving this place peacefully."

Half a minute passed, and she felt certain none of the Golmorungs had understood any of what she'd said. But then the large one, who must have been a chief of some sort based on the looks every other frog cast in his direction, shook his head. He patted his chest and then pointed at the ground. "Home."

Alina was starting to be less surprised every time her implant successfully translated a word, but that one left her stunned. "This can't be your home," she said, enunciating every word. "It already belongs to someone else."

The chief shook his head more violently. He patted his chest with all four hands this time, then threw them out to encompass the land all around. "Home," he said. "Golmorung home."

"This planet belongs to the Kitanes," she said, wondering if there was any way to reason with him using the few words they could each understand. "My people can help to find you another one, though. Some place suitable for your race that isn't already inhabited."

The chief stared at her, and Alina thought she saw frustration in those eyes. He spoke again, but this time his croaking speech was meant for all the Golmorungs gathered around them. Alina glanced around and sucked in a breath when she saw that every person in the village must have gathered to watch this moment. She spotted a handful of smaller frogs, which she suspected were Golmorung children.

Dark mutters passed among them, which then rose into angry exclamations. Some pointed in her direction while others pointed up to the sky, and Alina tried her best to follow along. The implant was having a hard time with so many voices, and even the occasional translation had ceased as it was overwhelmed by the cacophony.

"Home." That was the one word she clearly heard repeated from many mouths.

The chief waved his people into silence, then pointed to Alina and motioned for her to step forward. She did so hesitantly, uncertain of how he might react when they felt so strongly about not leaving the world they'd come to take as their own.

The sun was peeking out above the hills behind her, and she had to squint against the reflections sparkling across the marshy water. Her eyes were so dazzled that she hadn't realized the chief moved until she felt heavy hands drop onto her shoulders. She stiffened in response, but he merely guided her closer to the monolith.

The Golmorung leader tapped his chest with a splayed finger and then pointed to the ground. "Home."

"Yeah, yeah. You're not going to give up easily. I get it."

Then he surprised her by tapping the towering stone. "Home," he said again.

Alina stared at him in confusion, her eyebrows drawing in as she tried to make sense of this last assertion. Was he trying to say the monolith was their home? She bent forward to get a better look at it. She studied the faint lines of very old carvings for several seconds, and then gasped.

The carvings were crude, but it was clear that the image she was looking at was a Golmorung. The representation of water was at his feet, and a crude hut stood at his back.

The chief then pointed to the carving on the left, motioning for Alina to view them in that order. This one showed a pair of Golmorungs. One was spearing fish and crustaceans while the other hovered over a pile of what looked to be small circles. "Eggs?" she asked herself. It seemed to make some sense.

The carvings continued, looping around the monolith and showing everyday scenes of a peaceful life. She was beginning on the second ring, above the first, when those slice of life scenes shifted to something that looked like a meeting between tribes. Two large Golmorungs faced each other, while a dozen or so smaller figures stood at their backs.

Alina reached out to touch the next carving, which appeared to be a crude map. Inverted V's denoted mountains, while wavy lines indicated the marshlands she stood in. There were circles on the other side of the mountains filled with wavy lines, as well. Lakes, she suspected. Small huts clustered along the shores of those lakes in villages that were larger than this one. Lines curved between the inverted V's to connect the widespread villages. Either roads or trade routes, Alina suspected.

The images continued, with the third and fourth rings depicting larger and larger settlements and maps that showed much more land than the previous ones. The last map appeared to show half of a continent, with only small shapes to show where Golmorung villages might be located in marshes, near rivers, and along the shores of lakes which seemed to dot this planet.

When Alina reached the beginning of the fifth ring of carvings, she had to crane her neck to look up at them. These were some of the freshest carvings, with exposed stone that looked almost starkly white against the age-darkened exterior of the monolith.

The first of the images showed a cluster of Golmorungs looking up into the sky. Faint lines seemed to depict something falling down towards them.

She ran her fingers along to the next, which showed a pair of boxy ships in the middle of Golmorung figures. Those shapes were very similar to that of the shuttle in which she'd flown to this world.

Alina froze when she saw the next carving. Figures were stepping out of those boxy ships. They were tall and thin, with pointed snouts and triangular ears that poked up out of short lines denoting fur.

The Golmorungs were showing their new arrivals a forested scene in the next carving. She could almost imagine the large frog at the head of the pack pointing to a Kitane and saying, "Home."

Next was a scene that she'd heard about, but the roles had been reversed. There were more small, boxy ships disgorging more figures with canine faces. The Golmorungs watching them didn't look as happy or as welcoming this time.

The last that she could touch showed a single boxy shuttle coming down from the sky. This one was met by Golmorungs waving weapons, however. Those weapons were long tubes with a scoop at the end, which made her think of an obscure sport back on Earth. It was hard to be sure, but it appeared as though the Golmorungs were using the scoops to fling balls of fire at the shuttles in an attempt to prevent more interlopers from arriving on their world. A crude but effective attack based on what she'd seen.

The final carving, so high that she couldn't even reach it, showed a dozen Golmorung figures fleeing in terror as fire rained down from the sky. Wavy vertical lines now rose up out of the horizontal ones. *Steam rising as the water was cooked off*, she thought.

Alina stared at that last carving, then slowly turned to face the Golmorung chief. She knew now what he'd been trying to tell her without having the words to say it. They'd been lured to this planet with a story that was mostly true, but the heroes and villains had swapped places.

"Golmorung home," she said, pointing to the several of the Golmorung and then down at the ground. She was going to make sure it stayed that way.

"Okune," she said as she pressed a finger against her ear. "I want you to listen very carefully." As she began to speak, a plan for what needed to happen next started to come together in her head. Alina was pissed off, and that was bad news for the Kitanes.

27 - Wingate

Paine paced his office, his hands clenching and unclenching at his side with each step. Several hours had passed since he'd received the distressing message from Silas, and the inability to act on that information was killing him. Despite all the near-magical technology they'd found out here, there were still limitations that reared up at the worst moments.

He whirled when the door of his office opened. "Any luck?"

Bos shook his head gravely. "*Intrepid* is too far from all known communication nodes. Our contact with WayLin Mining Consortium tells me their new mining facility is in possession of an array capable of communicating with all others inside a three light sequence radius, but they have yet to make contact with *Intrepid*."

"No contact at all?" Paine asked, fearing the worst.

"Which is not unexpected," Bos cautioned him. "Based on my calculations, it will be another cycle or two before *Intrepid* is close enough to initiate short-range communications."

"There has to be some way to warn them sooner than that," he said in a strangled voice. "They need to know the Kitanes are dangerous."

The message from Silas had been short, but to the point. The gist of it was that the Acelu intelligence apparatus had received reports from beyond known space of an aggressive species that had tried and failed to take a planet from a race that had only recently ventured beyond the protection of the Auricle. They were repulsed with help from a nearby system, during which the invaders' fleet had taken large amounts of damage. One of their three ships had been obliterated, while the other two had barely managed to engage their wrinkle drives and escape. The descriptions of that species matched Captain Kerrigan's description of the Kitanes.

"I have little personal experience with Captain Kerrigan or his crew, sir, but from the way you've spoken about them, I have no doubt they will be able to handle an unexpected development such as this."

"Not if they don't see it coming until it's too late," Paine moaned. He dropped into one of the chairs meant for visitors and put his face in his hands. "Those fox bastards came to us with a sob story about their world being stolen, and we bought it hook, line, and sinker. All the while, they're the ones doing the stealing. And now they've convinced us to help them do it."

"No one would possibly blame you humans for what has transpired," Bos said.

"Maybe not, but they'd sure think we were saps and suckers for falling for it. If the people we sent out to that planet succeed in pushing the Golmorungs off their own world, Bos, who would ever trust us again? We'd be seen as the fools who helped thieves and murderers, if not as thieves and murderers ourselves."

They were on the precipice of a diplomatic disaster, and he didn't know if there would be any hope of salvaging relations with the other races in the event the worst were to happen. Many would likely view them as cold, heartless mercenaries. Other reactions would be much more severe and have dire consequences for the prospect of humanity being able to expand beyond their home world to join those who shared this part of the galaxy.

Paine was especially worried about the crew of *Intrepid*, the friends who were now in danger because of their desire to help. His thoughts turned to Yumi Nakamura, the young woman who had served as his assistant during the trip from Earth. She had taken over his role as political consultant on *Intrepid*, charged with ensuring that the needs of the colonists were being met as the ship took on jobs to earn the credits required to facilitate the survival of every human out here in this vast galactic sector they had been thrust into.

He groaned deep in his throat. "If I ever get my hands on Lieutenant Ballard, I'm going to throttle her for convincing Captain Kerrigan to go along with that foolhardy idea to play white knight."

"You supported it yourself at the time." There was a tinge of amusement in Bos's voice, mixed with reproach.

"I know, but that doesn't help me feel better about the possibility that none of those brave soldiers may ever come back because of it."

"You need something to take your mind off these concerns," Bos said, reverting to his Edryne efficiency. "Zenobia has found some promising proposals for a trade and recreational mission to Earth. Let me grab those tablets, and we can peruse the details to see if you agree with her assessment."

Paine looked up in confusion, and it took several seconds for him to remember that Zenobia was the colonist selected to help out in his office that week. "I really don't feel up to reading through flowery language and circular reasoning, Bos. I know you're just trying to help, but I'd rather worry than deal with another long-winded proposal."

The Edryne chuckled hollowly. "Fair enough, Mr. Wingate.

In that case, perhaps you'd like to meet with the exploration team who recently returned to Kraken?"

He perked up at the suggestion. With the fear and worry brought on by Silas's message, he'd completely forgotten about the Monolith transport that had been so close to arriving when he was called back to his office. "They're already on the station?"

Bos dipped his head in a nod. "I believe they are celebrating their return in the restaurant that serves the soup you enjoy."

"Really?" Paine was on his feet before he realized he was going to stand up, and he almost laughed at his own eagerness. "I suppose I should show my face and congratulate them on a successful trip."

"I'm sure they would appreciate it, sir." Bos gave him a serene smile, his small mouth barely moving as the corners of his lips pulled up. "I'll know where to find you in the event of another emergency."

"Keep trying to get me an appointment with Eslop," Paine said, standing in front of the mirror to verify that his tie was straight and his hair wasn't too mussed. Primping and preening so that he always presented the best image was second nature after so many years in politics. "If anyone could possibly have a way to contact *Intrepid* as soon as possible, it will be them."

"I will, sir," Bos assured him.

"I won't be gone long, but you know where to find me if I'm needed."

"I do, sir."

"Go ahead and reach out to Monolith Transport Collective, too, just to verify there's nothing they could do to facilitate faster communication with our people. I'm aware it might mean rerouting a ship through several wrinkle drive jumps to reach

Intrepid's current projected position, but if they want to secure transport rights with Earth badly enough, they might go for that."

"I will, sir."

Paine paused in the doorway of his office. He patted his pockets as if searching for something, but he knew the only thing he needed was the small tablet in his breast pocket. That was his lifeline to Bos and any hope of being able to stop a catastrophe before it could happen.

"Please eat something while you're out, sir," Bos said, giving him a gentle verbal push. "You've had nothing since breakfast."

He wanted to insist that he was too worried to be hungry, but his stomach chose that moment to rumble loudly and betray him. "I might do that."

The vision of a steaming bowl of pho made his mouth water as he left the embassy. Paine could already taste the salty broth, slippery noodles, and chunks of what he preferred to think of as chicken. He was grateful to the returned explorers for choosing that restaurant as the place to gather.

Paine shivered as he passed through a draft of cold air. As he quickened his steps to escape it, his thoughts turned to the warmth that had remained after X'Zak left him. That brought her words cascading back into sharp focus, after they'd been pushed to the back of his mind by the message from Silas.

He knew that there would be several sleepless nights in his near future. One thing he was sure of, though, was that the proposal she'd left him with would not be the cause of them. The danger and threat his friends were now facing sharpened his focus and made him realize how short and precious life could be. Why not take any opportunity for a little joy along the way?

Paine decided that he would have Bos reach out to the Kr'Sal embassy after he returned. It was time to meet with X'Zak again, to see if that spark of feeling between them could possibly grow into a burning flame.

28 - Kerrigan

Engineering was in a state of pandemonium when Lyle limped in. One of his ankles had been sprained when the elevator slammed to a sudden and highly unexpected stop. It would have to wait until after he resolved the current emergency, though. *It only hurts when I put weight on it*, he told himself with a silent chuckle as he hobbled toward a group of engineers.

Lieutenant Galbraith kept pace with him, one of her arms tucked tightly against her chest to protect a wrist that had likely been broken. "It's not my shooting hand," she had told him tersely when he suggested she should report to the aft medical bay to have it treated.

The trip through *Intrepid*'s corridors had been surreal. The red flashing lights had given everything an eerie cast, especially against the dim illumination of only the emergency lights. They had passed nearly a dozen people during the trip from the elevator, all of them practically sprinting to reach their destinations. Lyle had wanted to stop someone and ask for an update, but he also didn't want to keep them from a task that might be vital to *Intrepid*'s security.

"Commander Berger," he shouted upon spotting her bird's nest of graying hair across the room. "What's the status of the reactor room?"

The chief engineer continued talking to the knot of people around her for a minute, passing out orders with a gruffness that was heightened by the emergency. When the last of her engineers was on the move, she finally turned to greet him. "Captain, the shit has well and truly hit the fan."

Galbraith snorted beside him as she stepped to the side to allow a pair of crew members to pass. "Do we know who's holding the reactor room hostage, chief?"

Berger shook her head. "Whoever is in there is smart. They shut down the interior feeds before they started locking down the systems, which is what triggered an alert. We have no way to get eyes on them."

"Any luck regaining control of the reactor?" Lyle asked. He feared he already knew the answer based on the hive of activity around them.

"The opposite," Commander Berger admitted. Her mouth twisted as if she'd tasted something vile. "The reactors have begun to spin down, sir."

"They're shutting down?" he asked. The blood drained from his face. Without the power from the reactor banks, it wouldn't take more than half an hour for all the energy reserves to be depleted. Life support would be the last system to shut down, but they would be facing certain death if they couldn't get into the reactor room within a few hours to spin them back up.

"Have you tried breaching the room?" Galbraith asked.

"Lieutenant Saunders attempted to get in via the emergency access panel," Berger said with a nod. The panel opened onto a narrow crawl space barely large enough for an adult to shimmy through. There was a winding complex of them throughout *Intrepid*, designed to allow access to any area in the event of a hull breach or other emergency. "We lost contact with him just after he popped open the panel inside the reactor room. That was six minutes ago, and his comm line still isn't broadcasting."

Lyle pressed his lips together in frustration. He had to hope that whoever was in that room hadn't harmed the lieutenant. "There's been no contact with the hostiles?" he started to ask. His earpiece buzzed in his hand, and he realized with a start that he'd been clutching it since retrieving it in the elevator. He popped it back into his ear and was immediately assaulted by a cacophony of voices.

"All engines are powering down," Lieutenant de Windt said, her voice tight with stress.

"Confirmed," Lieutenant Stebbins said sharply. "Helm is non-responsive, and we are adrift."

"This is a bad time, sir," Ensign Poehl said breathlessly from the Nav station. "We were in the final stages of calculating a course correction to avoid an asteroid drifting into our path."

"How long until we reach it?" Stebbins asked.

"At our current speed, I estimate we have forty-nine minutes. The navigational plotting puts a ninety-three percent certainty on collision with the asteroid if we can't alter our course before then."

Commander Cottlen burst in from CIC. "Helm, do we have any maneuverability at all?"

"Only the docking thrusters are still responsive, XO."

"Work with Navigation to determine the best way to use those thrusters to alter our course. You have forty-eight minutes, and I only want good news."

The comm link fell silent for the space of several heartbeats. Lyle realized he was holding his breath when Lieutenant Stebbins finally spoke. "Aye, commander."

His temporary XO began calling for status reports from other departments, but Lyle tuned them out and returned his focus to Commander Berger. "I'm sorry, chief. I didn't catch what you said."

"Whoever is in there isn't talking to us, captain. They killed the comms in the reactor room right after the camera feeds, and we've had no response to our attempts to get even a text response back from them."

"Time is not on our side, commander." Lyle winced as he inadvertently put weight on his injured ankle. "With the reactor shutting down, our engines don't have the power to keep burning. *Intrepid* is adrift."

Berger grimaced as she nodded. "Aye, captain, I was about to get to that part. I was forced to order the engines shut down to prevent them from being damaged while trying to operate without enough power."

"We need to slice that door open, sir," Galbraith said. "And we need to start now. It will take at least half an hour for a plasma cutter to create an opening large enough for an assault."

Commander Berger was already shaking her head. "That won't work, I'm afraid. The reactor room was one of the spaces on *Intrepid* that were recognized as possible targets in the event of a hostile boarding. The walls and door are extra thick and shielded with titanium alloys and carbon-fiber mesh. You might be able to cut through in an hour, but it would likely take much longer."

"We don't have that kind of time," Lyle said. He was picturing the asteroid in their path, just waiting to take them out. Even if it was small and a collision only opened a hull breach, that would be disastrous in their current situation. The systems designed to seal off breached sections to protect the rest of the ship would likely be shut down by that time. "I need a solution here, and I need it within the next thirty minutes."

"I'll do my best, captain." Commander Berger didn't wait around for more discussion. She quickly moved to a nearby console and began coordinating the information coming in from her people.

Lyle turned to Galbraith, but she had also moved aside. He could hear her talking over the comms in a low voice. From the words he could pick up, she was ordering a head count on the miners. He nodded approvingly and wished he'd thought to have that done sooner.

"Commander Cottlen," he said, breaking into the flow of communications on the bridge and in CIC. "I want an immediate check of all *Intrepid* personnel. Location and status."

"Aye, captain, it's already underway." Cottlen's voice was calm, not betraying any surprise or irritation at his captain's reappearance after an unexpected absence. "At present, there are only seven people we've been unable to account for."

"Dispatch as many crew members as necessary to find them. Were any of them last reported to be near Engineering?"

"Only three of them last pinged in the aft section."

"They're the priority, then. I want an update within the next three minutes. Lieutenant Galbraith's Infantry squads are currently in the process of doing a headcount on the miners. Let's allocate a few off-duty personnel to do the same for our Kitane guests."

"Aye aye, captain."

Lyle's hands clenched tightly as he listened to the constant flow of information between his bridge and CIC officers. He itched to be on the bridge, but with the elevators out of commission it would take far too long to reach it. Especially on a bum ankle that was beginning to throb even when he didn't put weight on it.

"Miners are all present and accounted for," Galbraith reported five minutes later. "Sergeant Simmons is assigning third squad to keep them locked down in the cargo drum. Second squad is on the way to Engineering."

"We might need them," Lyle said. "Commander Cottlen just reported that he's tracked down all but one of our crew members now. Crewwoman Janisson isn't responding to her comms, and she was last seen in the mess after her shift ended three hours ago. Her post and cabin are both in the forward section, though, so I don't see her being involved in this."

As if his words had triggered it, the ship-wide comm system emitted a loud screech. Everyone around them reacted in the same way, by instinctively ducking their heads and clapping hands over ears. The screech tailed off after a few seconds and was replaced by heavy breathing.

When the first words spoken were in high-pitched barks, Lyle clamped down on his tongue to keep from spitting out a string of curses. The same recognition flared in Lieutenant Galbraith's eyes, and her lips pulled up in a snarl. "The Kitanes," he said, wondering how such a seemingly primitive race could have taken over *Intrepid*'s reactor room.

The yips and barks finally ended, and then he was treated to an even bigger surprise. "Humans, we have taken control of your ship's power systems. There is nothing you can do to stop us. This ship now belongs to the Kitanes."

"Since when do those bastards speak our language?" Galbraith snarled.

He waved her into silence as the halting speech continued.

"All humans will leave the forward and aft sections, to gather in the empty cargo drum. We will leave you here but will tell others how to find you. You have thirty minutes to comply."

"Yeah, I totally believe their promises," Galbraith snorted.

Commander Berger stormed over, her face clouded with overpowering rage. "I told those damn dogs over and over to stay out of Engineering. I should have known they were up to something when they kept coming back to snoop around."

"Foxes," Lyle said distractedly. He was still trying to grasp how the Kitanes could possess the technical skills to decipher their systems, much less take control of them. The only way it made sense...

"Tamma told us everything backward," Galbraith growled. "It wasn't her people being invaded. They're the invaders."

"That's the only way this would make sense," Lyle agreed. "Lieutenant, I want the rest of those foxes detained and under guard. Enlist some of the WayLin miners to assist, if needed. Their lives are just as much as stake as ours right now."

"Will do, sir."

"Lieutenant? I want them alive. We might need them if we can't breach the reactor room in the next," he lifted his tablet to check the time, "twenty-three minutes."

Galbraith's face writhed with disappointment, but she gave him a terse nod. "Permission to requisition explosive charges from the Armory?"

"Granted."

"Hey, now!" Commander Berger protested. "You can't go blowing up Engineering, captain. These systems are incredibly delicate and vital."

"Not Engineering," he said, "just one small section of it." Lyle didn't want to have to damage his own ship, but it was a decision he would easily make if it came down to it. Hundreds of lives were at stake.

"Give me time to come up with a better solution," Berger said. She patted the air and whirled to hurry back to her console before he could respond.

Lyle watched her spool out commands to underlings, inwardly crossing his fingers in the hope that she'd find a better method of entry into the reactor room. The fact that the Kitanes likely had a hostage hadn't escaped him, and the man's lifespan would almost certainly be measured in seconds if they had to breach with explosives or other brute-force methods.

As he waited for Lieutenant Galbraith's squad to arrive with their equipment, he asked himself if he'd been stupid to fall for the story Tamma had told them. Had it been too good? Too sympathetic? He wondered if he would have been able to see through her tale if he'd had more time to consider it.

Now Lieutenant Ballard and her squad were stranded in the heart of the enemy's territory. He hoped the woman whose skills he had come to trust would be able to ferret out the truth quicker than he had. Soon enough to keep the Kitanes from turning on her.

At least she had Commander Predashi at her side. Indira's common sense and ability to view situations from every angle would keep them ahead of the treacherous foxes.

He hoped.

29 - Predashi

Indira paced restlessly, something she'd been doing for the last hour. Ever since Elder Hamman had ordered that everyone from *Intrepid* be confined to their small cave, before he set out with half the Kitanes on their mission to destroy the Golmorung village.

"We should be out there doing something," Suarez said discontentedly.

"They won't let us," Cantu said angrily, jerking his chin toward the opening that led into the main cavern. Six Kitanes were standing guard over them, and to make things worse they had been among the first groups who had received training from the Infantry squad.

"I don't understand why they won't let us help," LoTur said, not looking up from the rifle he was stripping and cleaning for the third time. "We have the skills and training necessary for a successful rescue operation."

"God only knows what those frogs are doing to the lieutenant," Suarez said through gritted teeth. She was occupied with cleaning some of the armor plating at Cantu's direction, but that chore was so routine that it did little to keep her mind off current concerns. "They could be torturing her right now to find out where the Kitanes are hiding out."

"Don't jump to conclusions," Indira told them. She had her hands clasped tightly together in a futile attempt to project calm toward the four squad members who were worrying about the fate of their leader. "Lieutenant Ballard has proven to be as capable as any soldier I've encountered. No doubt she's already planning an escape from the Golmorungs."

"Whatever they do to her, we're going to do right back twice over," Suarez seethed.

"Damn straight," LoTur said, reaching out to bump fists with her.

"Stow that nonsense right now!" Cantu said suddenly. The sergeant stood from where he'd been poring over the contents of their small weapons container. "It's bad enough the damned foxes are hell bent on wiping out the frogs. Lieutenant Ballard would never allow us to even contemplate something so heinous, and I won't let you even joke about it right now. Are we clear?"

"Yes, sergeant!" three voices said simultaneously.

Indira gave the man a quick nod of approval. He was showing why Ballard had been confident enough in his abilities to promote him to sergeant. For a long time, she'd thought it had only happened because he'd been one of the original six members of the makeshift squad formed to rescue the slaves in the Kr'Sal mining complex.

"Now, the first thing we need to do is get out of these caves," he said next, surprising everyone.

"Sarge?" LoTur asked, his eyes wide.

"I have no doubt the lieutenant can take care of herself, but would she ever sit back and allow someone else to mount a rescue if the roles were reversed?"

"No, sergeant!"

"You've all seen what the foxes are capable of over the last couple of weeks. They're good with those spears and slings, but those are the only weapons I've seen since we landed on this planet. Do any of you really want to leave her rescue in their hands?"

"No, sergeant!"

He glanced in her direction, and Indira studied the sergeant for a few moments. It was madness to even consider going against Elder Hamman. Not only were they supposed to be working with the Kitanes, but they were also vastly outnumbered even though several dozen of the foxes were on the way to the Golmorung village. She held her breath for a few heartbeats, then gave him another quick nod.

Cantu's lips quirked in a quick smile to acknowledge her approval of his actions. "LoTur, you and I are going to gear up. I don't like leaving anything behind unless we have to, so we're going with full packs. Understood?"

"Yes, sergeant," the Panosh soldier replied, quickly reassembling his rifle.

"Lash –"

"I need him with me," Indira said, stepping forward.

Cantu looked at her in confusion. "Sorry, commander?"

She pointed in the direction of the old shuttle she and Lash had spent the last several days repairing and studying. "Elder Hamman's group has a head start of several hours. We need to reach that village before they do if we hope to stop their genocidal inclinations. Unless you somehow figured out a shortcut through the forest in your one scouting trip, that shuttle is our best hope."

Cantu's lips pulled up in a wide grin as he considered the idea. "You think you can fly it, commander?"

"Lash?" she asked, turning to the Tiké.

He was still for a moment before his mandibles chittered in

excitement. "Well enough to reach the lieutenant, yes."

"Good enough for me," Indira said. "We'll need a distraction so that Lash and I can get into the shuttle without being seen. Do you think you can manage that, sergeant?"

Cantu eyed his soldiers for a few moments, then a mischievous grin flashed across his face. "Suarez, see what you can do to draw off a couple of those guards."

"I feel the need to visit the little girls' room," she said, brushing off her knees as she stood up. She bent over the open crate for a moment, then walked over to the cave mouth and spoke in a very loud voice while making gregarious motions to let their guards know what she needed.

Indira almost laughed out loud when the woman motioned to her midsection and then blew a raspberry. Anyone on Earth would have been able to guess at the distress she was feeling, and the Kitanes caught on almost as quickly. Several of the guards traded looks, and it was clear that they were trying to pass the issue off to someone else.

"C'mon, man, this is urgent," Suarez complained, holding her hands against her stomach as she bounced from foot to foot.

One of the Kitanes finally barked something and pointed to two others. He then pointed to Suarez and made a sweeping motion with his hand.

"Thank you," she said with an overly dramatic sigh of relief as she followed the pair of Kitanes away from the cave.

"Two down, four left," Indira said under her breath. She began to wrack her brain for an idea to draw their attention before Suarez returned.

Cantu took matters into his own hands. With no more than a quick gesture, the three members of the Infantry squad raced forward. The Kitane guards were watching their compatriots lead Suarez across the cavern, so they didn't see the sneak attack coming.

LoTur swiftly swung his arms through the air, smashing two heads against each other with a hollow thump. The two Kitanes slumped down almost immediately, making the others turn to look at them in confusion. Cantu and Lash had looped around to the opposite side, and they leapt forward to jab stun guns into the backs of their remaining guards.

With all four Kitanes incapacitated, Indira jumped forward to help drag them into the cave. "You could have warned me you were going to do that," she hissed.

"And ruin the surprise?" Cantu laughed. "I didn't really think it would work, commander. Better you looked innocent if it hadn't."

"It did, though," Lash said matter-of-factly. "These four will be unconscious for only a short time. We should be ready."

Indira looked between the three of them. "Ready for what?"

"No spoilers," Cantu said, shooting her a wink before he and LoTur returned to the task of loading all their gear into four backpacks.

She huffed out in disgust but began to help out. She insisted on carrying Suarez's pack until the woman was back with them. It was an offer she regretted almost immediately. LoTur held the bag while she slid her arms through the loops, and when he let go the weight almost brought her to her knees. Indira groaned under the strain, but she managed to stay upright while the others loaded up.

Cantu moved to the cave opening and leaned out to sweep the area. "The path to the shuttle is mostly clear."

"We'll be seen as soon as we start running in that direction," Indira said.

"Not when they're too busy looking over there," Cantu said, pointing off to his left without taking his eyes off the shuttle.

Her brows furrowed with confusion. The direction he was pointing was the same direction Suarez had been led by two of the Kitane guards. What sort of diversion could she possibly cause to draw the attention of all the other Kitanes in the cavern?

The answer came less than a minute later when there was a loud explosion followed by bright, flashing light. Indira jumped in shock, but the others only chuckled with amusement.

"Flash bang," Cantu said.

Indira remembered when Suarez had bent over the crate. The woman must have grabbed one of the grenades and hid it beneath her clothing.

"Let's move." Cantu waved for them to follow, then began jogging toward the shuttle.

Indira followed the Infantry soldiers, sweeping her eyes around for any sign that a Kitane might have noticed them. There were only a few of the foxes visible, though, and they were all looking in the direction of the explosion. The distraction had worked.

When they reached the shuttle, Cantu and LoTur took up positions beside the hatch. Lash poked his head through the opening, then disappeared into the ship. There was a yelp of surprise, followed by the sound of something heavy hitting the ground.

"Clear," the Tiké called out. Indira hurried through the hatch and paused when she saw a Kitane slumped near the control consoles. Tamma. "It appears she was running diagnostics," Lash told her. "The shuttle's engines are already warmed up and ready for use."

"I guess the repairs worked," Cantu said happily as he pulled the hatch door shut behind him.

Indira was about to ask about Suarez when she noticed the woman was already in the shuttle. She was breathing hard and her face was shiny with perspiration, but she looked exultant. "I'll take that from you, commander," she said, pointing to the pack.

"Everyone should hold on to something," Lash said. He was bent over the console, and his hands moved surely across the buttons and switches. "This might be a little bumpy."

"As long as it's fast," Cantu said, reaching out to grab onto a conduit snaking along a bulkhead.

"You're sure you know what you're doing?" Indira asked the Tiké as she bent close to him. "Tamma was very tight-lipped about too many of the systems on this shuttle."

"I could have flown this ship from the first moment I stepped foot on it," Lash told her solemnly. "I've spent many days wondering why it seemed so familiar, and the answer finally came to me while we were confined in our cave."

He looked up at her seriously, and Indira was surprised to see a spark of anger in his beady, black eyes. "I've encountered a ship with controls like this before, but it was tens of sequences ago."

"You've met the Golmorungs before?" she asked, wondering how he could have neglected to tell them something so important.

The small alien shook his head. "This technology is not native to this part of the galaxy. The race that flew ships like this were wiped out shortly before my wanderings brought me to this sector."

Lash glanced at the unconscious Kitane at his feet. "Now, I believe I know who was responsible for that act."

30 - Ballard

"You need to come up here, lieutenant."

Alina lifted her head at the voice in her ear. "What is it, Gundar?"

"There's movement in the trees. I think we're about to have company."

She muttered under her breath while she finished with the task she'd been working on the last several minutes. Her knife was beginning to dull, but it had lasted long enough to complete another sharpened spike. A glance at the pile at her feet made her cramping hands hurt even worse. There had to be at least a dozen two-foot-long spikes there, and those were only the ones that hadn't already been buried in the expected path of the attack.

Not far away was their one Kitane prisoner, securely tied with vine ropes provided by the Golmorungs. Her first orders had been to capture their so-called guides, but the foxes had proven slippery. MakTur caught this one while the others melted away into the early morning mist that rose up around the marshland. She'd been tempted to question the prisoner, but it had been clear the Kitane had no understanding of her words.

Alina slid the knife back into its sheath before pumping her legs to move quickly up the low hill. She barely noticed the sound of the two Golmorungs who had taken to following her everywhere.

Gundar held out the binoculars once she crawled to the top

of the hill, and then he pointed off to the right. "Over there," he said softly, as if afraid his voice might carry.

The trees jumped into vivid crispness the moment she put the binoculars to her eyes. Alina scanned the area, but the only movement she saw was tree branches swaying with the wind. She swept the area a second time and was about to rib Gundar for being jumpy when she spotted a flash of coppery color between two bluish tree trunks.

Alina held her breath as she focused on that area. She dialed back the magnification on the binoculars so that she could observe a larger area, and then growled deep in her throat when she saw the first group of Kitanes march out of the forest.

"They're not even trying to hide," Okune said in her ear. He was placed on a hill several hundred yards closer to the forest, which gave him a better view of the approaching forces.

"They have to know the cat's out of the bag by now," she replied. "Elder Hamman would have guessed that once I was captured I'd either find a way to communicate with the locals or see something that made me doubt the story Tamma told us."

"Or both," Gundar said at her side.

"Or both," she agreed, thinking of the barnacles and mold growing on the huts. "Okune, how many do you count?"

"Uh, fifteen," he said uncertainly. "No! There's another group coming out of the forest farther south."

Alina swept her binoculars to the left until she found them. She chewed on her lip as she waited until she was certain all of the Kitanes had emerged from between the trees. "Elder Hamman is among them, so that must be the main group. Forty-three in total?"

"I get the same number," Okune said, while Gundar grunted

agreement at her side.

"It could be worse," she said, twisting to stare in the direction of the village. The Kitanes outnumbered the Golmorung warriors, but she hadn't seen anything to make her think either side had a technological advantage over the other.

"Lieutenant," Okune said sharply. "Am I seeing what I think I'm seeing?"

"Where?" she asked, pulling the binoculars up to her eyes again. She scanned the small group, which was closer to them than the main force. Everything looked just as it had the last time she'd seen them.

"The other group," Gundar said softly, tapping her shoulder.

Alina shifted the direction she was scanning, and then froze when she spotted what Okune had seen. Half of the Kitanes surrounding Elder Hamman were carrying bulky weapons. They were at least three feet in length, with large rectangular barrels that had wires running along them. "Where the hell did those come from?" she asked under her breath.

"I think those foxes were holding out on us," Okune said. "I guess it shouldn't be such a surprise, since they were lying to us from the start."

She passed the binoculars back to Gundar as she tried to incorporate this new wrinkle into her planning. Alina had expected the Kitanes to come at them with spears and slings, weapons that would require them to climb the hills near the marsh to attack effectively. The wooden spikes they'd spent the last couple of hours sharpening and hiding under a thin layer of dirt would have thinned out their ranks as they trudged up the far side of those hills.

Now the Kitanes were carrying more advanced weaponry.

Worse, she had no idea what those guns were capable of. Based off only the look of them, she expected some sort of electrical attack similar to the Panosh rifles they'd been loaned during the slave mines rescue operation. Those guns had been fairly short-range, but they'd also been fighting in tight quarters without the need to test their full capabilities. It was possible those Kitane weapons would enable them to attack from two or three hills farther back from the village.

"It's too late to change the plan now," she said after half a minute. "Those Kitanes are moving at a fairly slow pace, so we have twenty minutes until they reach our position. Okune and Suarez, pull back to the hill just north of ours. Everyone check your rifles, because I think we're going to need them soon."

There was a chorus of voices from her three soldiers. She knew they'd already cleaned and checked their rifles during the morning, possibly several times, but the familiar process would help to soothe any fears and get them into a proper mindset ahead of battle.

Alina slid down the hill until she could jump to her feet and jog to flat ground. Word of the approaching Kitanes must have already reached the village, because she could see the large chieftain quickly moving her way. His powerful hind legs pushed him forward with explosive leaps that chewed up the ground, so that it was only half a minute before he reached her.

"They're here," she told him, wishing she knew just how much he understood of what she said. "If your people have any weapons beside those fishing spears, now is the time to pull them out." Alina lifted her rifle and shook it to indicate what she was talking about.

The chief looked up to the top of the hill for a moment,

then turned and spoke in rumbling croaks to the pair of Golmorungs who had been keeping close to Alina. She felt the vibrations of his words in her chest at the same time that the implant pulsed behind her ear. A few words were translated, but they were meaningless without the context of everything that couldn't be deciphered.

She watched as the two Golmorungs hurried back toward the village, but the chief soon motioned for her to follow him in another direction. It didn't take long until they were wading through the brackish water of the marsh. Alina leaped from grassy hump to grassy hump, trying to keep out her boots dry. She'd spent nearly an hour barefoot after her pre-dawn march through the marsh to the village, while her boots and socks were hung next to a small fire in order to dry them out.

When the chief stopped moving, she looked at him in confusion. They were standing in a part of the marsh that contained no more than a foot of water, and she could see no reason for him to have taken her there. The Golmorung's amphibian face was an emotionless mask to her eyes, and it was impossible to get a read on his thoughts.

Alina watched as the chief dipped his head down into the water. It was submerged to the point that his eyes were just below the water level, and he remained motionless there for several seconds. When his lower set of arms darted forward, she jumped back in surprise.

The chieftain reared up to his full height, towering over her as he stared down with a wide smile. One of his small lower hands extended out, opening to show her a small pearl-like object resting in a small puddle of water on his palm. "Glormp," he said proudly.

Alina stared at the object and lifted an eyebrow. "What exactly is glormp supposed to be?" she asked.

The chief's smile slowly faded as he looked at her, at the object, and back to her again. He finally released a deep sigh and motioned for her to step back. When she'd done so, he dropped the small pearlescent object and retreated hastily.

Alina opened her mouth to ask what they were doing, but then just gaped as the substance the chief had pulled out of the marsh ignited. The flames that flared up were almost blinding in intensity, and she could feel the heat even twenty feet away. She raised a hand to protect her eyes, but the fizzing flames began to die out within a few seconds.

"Glormp!" the Golmorung chief said triumphantly, waving all four hands toward the blackened patch of grass.

"Okay, that was impressive," she admitted. Vague memories of her high school chemistry classes bubbled up, and she wondered if this glormp was similar to phosphorus on Earth. That substance would ignite on contact with oxygen, but the results were far less spectacular. "You have more glormp?" she asked, turning her focus to the chief.

His only answer was to leap away in the direction of the village. Alina was tempted to follow and see what he was doing, but Okune's voice drew her back to the imminent threat. "They sent out scouts, lieutenant. I've got two Kitanes on the summit of the hill next to ours."

"On my way," she said, shoving her rifle around so it bounced against her back while she quickly jogged to the observation post.

Gundar had his rifle sighted on the hilltop a few hundred yards away. His finger was resting against the guard around the trigger, but it was twitching with eagerness. "Two o'clock," he whispered.

Alina focused her gaze in that direction. She had to stare at the hilltop for several seconds before she was able to pick out the tufts of fur that were nearly hidden among the weeds. "Only two scouts?"

"So far," he said.

"Permission to engage?" Okune asked over the comms.

"Denied. We wait until they get closer. I don't want to warn Elder Hamman that we're prepared for them until it's too late for him to slither out of our trap."

"I don't think retreat is an option," MakTur said. "Look to your eleven o'clock, lieutenant."

Alina moved her eyes without turning her head, not wanting to make any errant movements which might give away their position. Her lips pressed together when she saw what the Panosh had picked up on. Flashes of coppery fur passed between hills as a group moved to circle around the observation posts.

"There are more coming around us from the north," Okune whispered into the comms.

"They're trying to flank us," MakTur said.

"No." Alina visualized the area around them, and she followed the likely directions of the Kitane movements. "Not us, but the Golmorungs. They must suspect the frogs would be expecting an attack from the same direction I had come from when they captured me, so they're trying to get around the village without being seen."

Okune grunted in her ear. "That's not good, lieutenant. If they keep moving around our flank, they're going to spot us while also avoiding those spikes we placed."

"I know," she said through clenched teeth. The Kitanes were displaying a tactical awareness that shouldn't have been possible from what her squad had seen while trying to train them. It was a brutal reminder that the foxes were proving to be skilled liars, and it made her wonder what other surprises might be in store. "Change of plans," she said, pulling her rifle around and getting into a comfortable position from which to fire. "Prepare to engage the enemy on my mark. We can't let them reach the Golmorung village."

Alina barely heard the confirmation from each of her soldiers. Her mind was already churning through the possible routes Elder Hamman might use to send his Kitanes to attack the village. After what she'd learned, she knew this wouldn't be an attempt to rescue her. The approach the Kitanes were taking only confirmed that they had no intention of rendezvousing with her troops to come up with a plan to get her out of Golmorung captivity. If the frogs had proven hostile, she would have merely been one of many casualties when the Kitanes unleashed their bloodthirsty desire to wipe out the native inhabitants of this world.

It wasn't the first time that morning that she wondered what Tamma had really hoped to accomplish by bringing them to Waldruun with her sob story of an invading race. Had the Kitane woman truly expected the humans would go along with a plan to exterminate the Golmorungs without question?

The first of the Kitanes emerged from behind the hills south of her position. At first there were only two, but the bulk of the pack wasn't far behind them. She waited until she had counted at least a dozen. "Warning shots," she said, slipping her finger onto the trigger as she tracked her chosen target through the small scope. "Now."

Four rifles barked almost simultaneously, firing off short three-round bursts. Puffs of dirt flew up only a few feet ahead of the leading Kitanes, making them jump back and scan around to see where the attack had come from. Alina watched them, refusing to even blink despite the burning sensation in her eyes.

Elder Hamman suddenly appeared from behind the hill. He strode forward to look down at the divots left by her shots, then glared in her direction. He began speaking, exhorting those around him to move forward. Alina had hoped the warning shots might make the foxes hesitate, but she was disappointed to realize that they had no intention of being diverted from whatever they planned.

Alina chewed on her lip, wondering how far she was prepared to take this. She was tempted to fire more warning shots but didn't expect any different result. It was time to either put down the hammer or back off and leave the Kitanes free to prove their intentions.

Her dilemma was solved when Elder Hamman waved toward the hills where they'd set up observational posts. The Kitanes around him raised their strange looking rifles, aimed them in her general direction, and then began to fire. Instead of arcs of electricity, though, globs of super-heated plasma shot out of the barrels.

"We're taking fire," Okune reported through her earpiece.

She snorted in disgust, but there was a smidgen of relief as the decision was taken out of her hands. "Return fire," she said. "Focus on the shooters first."

Gundar had clearly been anticipating the order, and he pulled the trigger almost immediately. Alina saw puffs of dirt as his shots tracked toward the Kitanes who continued to send bursts of plasma in their direction. So far, the closest had landed more than twenty feet to her left.

One of the Kitane shooters went down as she joined in, but their shots were giving away their position. The plasma bursts began to land closer and closer, until a lucky shot hit the ground only a few inches from Alina's cheek. She flinched back as sizzling droplets burned into her skin, and she dreaded finding out what might happen if one of those plasma globs hit her full-on.

There was a pained roar in her ear only a few moments later. "MakTur's hit," Okune shouted.

"How bad?" she asked, keeping her focus on the Kitane in her sights. She pulled the trigger to send another burst of bullets, and she felt gratified when the Kitane flew backward with a spray of blood.

"Most of it was stopped by his armor, but the rest burned through his fur and skin. These things make a nasty wound, lieutenant."

"I'll be fine," MakTur insisted in a pained voice. "Pain sharpens the mind."

Alina wasn't so sure that was true, but they didn't have the option of pulling back to treat his wounds. There were nearly a dozen Kitanes shooting at both their hills, pinning them down while the rest of their forces continued toward the Golmorung village. She risked a quick glance in that direction and hoped the chief was preparing to face them.

A glob of plasma landed on her shoulder plate at that moment. Alina's cheek and neck were splashed by tiny droplets again, but the light armor plating was holding up against the burning plasma so far.

She redoubled her efforts to take down the Kitane shooters. Every time they killed or incapacitated one of them, another of the foxes would quickly jump in to pick up the fallen weapon and continue pinning them down. Alina noticed that Elder Hamman had disappeared at some point during the last several minutes, using the distraction to slip away.

There was a grunt beside her, followed by a pained groan. Alina glanced over to see Gundar laying on his back. He had one hand pressed against the side of his face, and she saw blood streaming out between his fingers. "I'm okay, lieutenant," he said through teeth that were clamped tightly shut.

"Where are you hit?" she asked. Alina fired off a few random bursts before she dropped her rifle and slithered over.

Gundar lifted his hand reluctantly, and she tried to hold back any expression that might give away how bad the wound looked. A glob of plasma had hit near his temple, and at least some of it had gotten into his eye. Alina knew that he was likely to lose it if they didn't get medical aid quickly. Unfortunately, medical bays and doctors were in short supply out here.

She was pulling open a first aid kit when the plasma began to rain down around them, forcing Alina to throw herself on top of Gundar in an attempt to protect him from further harm. "I'll take care of it," he said tightly. "Shoot those bastards for me, ma'am."

Alina lifted her head just long enough to see several Kitanes racing toward their position. She must have given away their location when she moved to check Gundar's wound, if they hadn't already placed where the shots were coming from. It wouldn't take more than a minute for the Kitanes to swarm up the hill, and she suspected that taking prisoners wasn't on the agenda.

"Okune, pull back."

"What?! We're not leaving you, lieutenant."

"You have to," she said sharply. "Get back to the cavern and let the commander know what we've learned. She needs to know the Kitanes are the bad guys here."

"If they haven't already turned on her," Gundar said quietly.

"I'll send MakTur," Okune said. "I'm heading your way to help push back the Kitanes advancing on your position."

"Pull back!" she told him firmly. "That's an order, sergeant."

There was silence for a moment, and she thought she could hear the crunch of boots on gravel as the foxes climbed the hill to reach them. It wouldn't be much longer before they came over the top, and she scrambled to pick up her rifle. She was determined to take a few of them down before they had a chance to kill her.

"Yes, lieutenant," Okune finally said, his voice somber with the weight of what he knew would happen. "I'll bring Cantu and the others back as soon as I can."

"Too late," Gundar said, his voice little more than a croak.

Alina glanced at him and thought he must be delirious with the pain. He was lying on his back, with one finger pointing up at the sky. She craned her head back, and then felt as if she'd been crushed. "They brought reinforcements," she said dully as the shuttle dropped down out of the sky.

31 - Kerrigan

"What about using gas?" Sergeant Cho asked. "We could pump some kind of sedative into the reactor room and put the foxes to sleep."

"They'd feel the effects before they were incapacitated," Sergeant Simmons replied. "Which means they could kill Lieutenant Saunders before they went to sleep."

"If he's still alive," Cho said. "They could have killed him the moment he popped out of that emergency access hatch."

"And give up the leverage having a hostage would provide?" Simmons scoffed loudly.

Lyle had been trying to tune out the two Infantry sergeants while they tossed possible solutions to the current crisis back and forth, but it proved hard to do. Especially since his mind was only partly occupied by studying readouts at one of the Engineering consoles.

"It's about damned time," he heard Lieutenant Galbraith shout. "Get over there and start cutting."

He raised his head to see two of her soldiers carting a heavy plasma cutter assembly toward the reactor room door. Another had arrived ten minutes earlier and was already in use. Galbraith had sent for the second cutter in hopes of slicing an opening through the door in half the time.

It wouldn't be enough, Lyle thought. "Progress report, Lieutenant Stebbins."

"Captain, the maneuvering thrusters are allowing us to divert our drifting course as we'd hoped."

"But?" Lyle asked, expecting a qualifier from the tone of his Helm officer's voice.

"But it won't be enough," Stebbins said through a deep sigh. "The current Nav projections show that the asteroid will still collide with *Intrepid* as we pass. The damage won't be catastrophic and could be repaired in normal circumstances."

"These are far from normal circumstances," Commander Cottlen chimed in from CIC. "I've put the Emergency Response teams on alert, and I'll dispatch them to the expected impact locations well in advance, but without power our options are severely limited."

"I'm aware of that," Lyle said, trying not to let his frustration come through in his voice. "Commander Berger's people are working on options now, as is Lieutenant Galbraith's Infantry squad."

"They need to find a solution within the next... seventeen minutes," Cottlen said. "Any longer than that, and we won't have time to spin up the reactors and engines to hopefully avert the collision."

Lyle clenched his jaw, understanding his XO's urgency. Hundreds of lives were at stake. "Any luck finding the rest of the Kitanes?" he asked, changing the subject.

Commander Cottlen grunted in disgust. "None, captain. Those foxes are slippery and very good at hiding. Every member of the crew not currently on duty is sweeping *Intrepid* from bow to stern. It's slow going, though, especially with our elevators shut down."

"The cameras didn't catch their movements?"

"Their friends in the reactor room took care of that," Cottlen said. "I'd love to know who taught these Kitanes how to use our systems, because they managed to shut down nearly a third of our internal feeds just before they set off the alert conditions."

Lyle glanced up at the soft lighting overhead. The strobing red lights had finally been shut down, leaving them with only the low-power emergency lights. "Yellow alert started half an hour ago, correct?"

"Thirty-eight minutes," Lieutenant Stebbins reported.

"Which means the Kitane have had plenty of time to hide somewhere we may never find them," Cottlen added. "They had almost twenty uninterrupted minutes before we realized they were the source of the danger. Until you dispatched an Infantry squad to lock them down, they had nearly free range of the ship while everyone else was responding to the alerts."

"Continue searching," Lyle said. "Let's break out the emergency oxygen tanks, as well, commander, in the event we can't avert the collision and a hull rupture sucks out the oxygen from part of the ship. I want every member of the crew carrying a canister within ten minutes."

"Aye, sir. What about the WayLin personnel?"

Lyle considered their passengers for a moment. *Intrepid*'s designers had included enough emergency supplies to last through several hours of extreme disaster events. They hadn't counted on his doubling the size of the crew and bringing in passengers, however. There had been emergency supplies for the colonists, but all of that was still in the modular sections that had been left behind on Kraken. "Make sure they get canisters. They may have to share, but we should have enough to give every person on board at least an hour's worth of oxygen."

"Aye, captain."

"I've got it!" Commander Berger suddenly yelled from the other side of Engineering.

"It looks like we might have something," Lyle said hopefully. "Carry out those instructions, commander, and I'll update you as soon as I know for sure."

Lyle muted his comms as he hurried over to where his chief engineer was surrounded by a dozen other people. They were discussing something with voices full of excitement, and his spirits rose as he began to push through them. "What is it, commander?"

Berger gave him a radiant smile. "I know how to smoke out those Kitanes, sir. We should have control of the reactor room within ten minutes."

"That's great news," he said, matching her smile. "What's the plan?"

"Coolant leak," Commander Berger said, jerking her chin down in a triumphant nod as if that explained everything. The excited chatter from the engineers around him meant that it apparently did to them.

"A coolant leak would be a bad thing, wouldn't it?" Lyle asked.

"In normal circumstances it would, sir. It's the solution to our current problem, though." Berger glanced up at him and finally realized he was lost. "There are three different coolants used by *Intrepid*'s reactors, captain. One is simple water, which can be circulated through narrow tubes in order to negate some of the heat generated when the reactors are in normal operation. The second is molten salt, but we only use that in extreme circumstances if the reactors are being pushed too hard for too long."

"And the third?"

Commander Berger shot him a mischievous grin. "The third coolant is gas-based. Highly effective, gets better results than simple water cooling, but the canisters required to hold the gas are very large and bulky. *Intrepid* had the space for them, however, and it's a good thing for us that she did."

"This helps us how?" Lyle asked. He held up a hand when she started to speak. "Keep it simple, commander. I don't need technical specs or detailed schematics of how the coolants work with our reactors."

She twisted her mouth for a moment as if disappointed that she couldn't use this opportunity to delve into the intricacies of *Intrepid*'s reactors. "The short and sweet of it, captain, is that a failsafe system was necessary. The gas is an effective coolant but becomes dangerous if it mixes with oxygen. The resulting concoction is a mild paralytic, and an extremely fast-acting one. If we can fill the reactor room with that, then the Kitanes will be neutralized within seconds, before they have a chance to recognize what's happening and do anything to Lieutenant Saunders."

Lyle stared at his chief engineer and experienced a momentary desire to have never learned that information. He was well aware that there were thousands of dangers on a starship, but this was a new one. "I don't see how that helps up when we're still locked out of the reactor room, commander."

"I do," Lieutenant Galbraith said at his shoulder. "Can one of your people point us to the best target?"

"I can," one of the engineers around them said, raising his hand.

"You're with me," Galbraith told him, waving for him to follow as she headed toward the soldiers trying to slice open the door with plasma cutters.

"Give us five minutes, captain," Berger said. "The Kitanes in there will be neutralized, and we'll be able to regain control of the reactors very quickly without their interference."

Lyle felt like throwing up his hands in frustration, but he knew it was imperative that he keep his cool. The captain didn't always have to understand every stage of an operation, but he had to make it seem like he did. "Excellent work, commander. If this succeeds, I'll be putting you in for a commendation."

He left the gaggle of engineers to their very excited and very detailed discussion of the plan. As he settled on the chair at the console he'd taken over, he wondered if this was the way the Kitanes normally operated. Did they bounce around from planet to planet, station to station, manufacturing a reason for people to take them in so they could steal ships? If so, why were they also trying to invade a planet and kill the inhabitants? Perhaps they were tired of a restless existence and hoped to settle down for a while.

His thoughts shifted to the other Kitanes on board his ship. They still didn't know how many were hidden somewhere in *Intrepid* and wouldn't until they could get into the reactor room to find out how many were involved here. Commander Berger had assured him the space was too small for all seven, and she suspected at least half of them were elsewhere.

Lyle had put up a timer on one screen, counting down to their collision with the asteroid that had wandered into their path. Time was not on their side. It would take at least ten minutes to cycle the reactors up again to the point where the main engines could be reignited. Maneuvering around the asteroid would take another couple of minutes, which further reduced their margins. If Commander Berger's plan didn't work, they might be out of options to save the ship.

"We're ready, captain."

He looked up to find Lieutenant Galbraith hovering at his side. "Don't wait for me, lieutenant. Get us into that room."

She smiled wickedly as she snapped off a quick salute. His eyes followed her progress as she hurried over to where her squad was huddled around a section of the bulkhead surrounding the reactors. Both plasma cutters were ignited and used to slice open a ragged hole.

Lyle rose to his feet when one of the soldiers yelped in surprise, wondering if they'd just failed in their task. Galbraith's sergeants moved forward quickly, though, slapping a roughly cut metal plate over the hole. The edges were quickly sealed to the bulkhead with quick-drying adhesive, and then the Infantry squad stepped back.

An expectant silence fell in Engineering, until Lyle felt he almost shouldn't breathe and disturb it. The wait was interminable, and every second that passed seemed like it was an hour. He walked forward on silent steps until he was standing beside Galbraith. Her face was shining with expectation, and he noticed for the first time that she was carrying one of the snubnosed NK70 rifles. He wondered when she'd sent one of her soldiers to fetch weaponry.

The emergency lights flickered for a moment. Lyle would have expected gasps of dismay at the failing power, but instead there were scattered cheers and laughs.

"The failsafe has engaged!" Commander Berger called out.

"Those bastards deserve worse than they're getting," Galbraith said under her breath. Lyle knew he was the only person close enough to hear it, but he frowned at her bloodthirsty words.

"The systems are reporting an airtight seal," Commander Berger shouted. "Gas levels are at fifty-nine percent and dropping fast."

"How do we get in there once the Kitanes are dealt with?" Lyle asked, leaning over so Galbraith could hear him over the cheers around them.

"Commander Berger said that once the Kitanes are no longer countering her attempts to retake control of the reactor systems, she should be able to open the door from out here."

"I hope she can do it fast," he said, glancing at the countdown on his console.

"Three minutes," Galbraith said, sounding confident of the commander's abilities. "It'll take that long for the gas leak to be contained and fully cleared from the room, anyway."

Lyle's hands clenched at his side. They would be cutting it very close, but if the timeline was correct then they'd have a few minutes to spare. The asteroid could be avoided, which would allow everyone to focus on finding the other Kitanes before they could cause more damage to *Intrepid*.

His earpiece began to vibrate urgently with an emergency communication, reminding him that he'd muted it earlier. Lyle tapped it to unmute, and his knees almost buckled in shock.

"Repeat, the bridge is under attack by Kitane hostiles," Lieutenant Stebbins yelled frantically. His voice was high-pitched with fear and alarm, and there were loud bangs in the background as if someone were forcing their way through the doors that led into the bridge. "Again, the bridge is under–"

The comm feed shut off suddenly, leaving only deafening silence.

32 - Predashi

The shuttle dropped for half a second before leveling out again. Indira's hand gripped the console so tightly that her knuckles were starkly white from the strain. "I thought you said you could fly this thing!"

"I am flying it," Lash said calmly, not losing focus on the controls in front of him.

"You sure about that, bro?" Cantu called out just as the shuttle jerked to the side, throwing everyone against a bulkhead. "Because I've been in crashes more controlled than this."

Lash ignored the ribbing that continued to be thrown in his direction as the shuttle shook and dipped for another minute. Finally, the flight smoothed out to the point where minor turbulence was an uncommon occurrence.

Indira was finally able to release her breath and unclench all the muscles that had been straining to keep her upright against the jerky movements. "Figured it out?"

"It was not a simple matter," Lash said, lifting his shoulders in an apologetic shrug. "The race that built these ships had three primary appendages, and therefore they designed their control systems for use by three hands."

"Tamma didn't seem to have any problems with it," Cantu muttered behind them.

"The Kitane also had much more experience with these systems," Lash replied, his calm equanimity never breaking. "*Much* more experience, if what I suspect is true."

Indira followed the direction of his gaze to the crumpled mass of the unconscious woman. "You said something earlier about the race who built these ships being wiped out. It was a genocide?"

"One that was perpetrated by an unknown aggressor," Lash confirmed. "There were only rumors left by the disappearance of a young race and most of their ships."

"Most of, but not all?"

"The Qualtide race was fairly primitive among those of us who have left the safety of our home systems, more so than even you humans. They had only been exploring their sector for a handful of Eslop sequences before they encountered whatever race attacked them. When the remnants of the battle were discovered by a trading vessel, only two derelict ships were found. One was of unknown origin and severely damaged to the point that it had been abandoned, while the other was the shattered remnants of a Qualtide ship. Two others known to be in their small fleet could not be found, and it was assumed at first that the Qualtides had fled the field of battle."

"Sounds like a good assumption to me," Cantu piped up. "If they lost a third of their ships to the attack, I would have fled for safety, as well."

"Many would do so," Lash nodded. "That assumption lasted less than a phase, however. When salvage ships arrived, they discovered bodies floating amidst the wreckage. Many bodies."

"Qualtide bodies?" Indira asked quietly.

"All of them, yes. So many bodies that the only conclusion which made sense was that the entirety of all three ships' crews were accounted for. Their attackers must have gathered their own dead before fleeing in the ships they stole."

Indira frowned as she glanced back at Tamma. "You think it was the Kitanes, because this shuttle is of Qualtide make?"

"Yes."

"Couldn't it have been the Golmorungs who were responsible? Tamma's story of their arrival here on Waldruun would make it a feasible explanation."

Lash's mandibles chittered in dismissal as he waved his small hands over the switches and buttons. "You've seen how difficult it was for me to master these controls, Commander Predashi. I'm not bragging when I tell you that I have flown many hundreds of ships in my lifetime, and that there isn't a being within a dozen light sequences who could match my skill. How, then, could a primitive race of hunters and gatherers have deciphered these systems in such a short time as Tamma would have us believe?"

"He's got a point there," Cantu said.

"He does," Indira conceded. Her thoughts had been running along similar lines, but she'd hoped she might be wrong. "That would mean we've been backing the wrong side in this fight."

"It explains why the Kitanes were so clingy during the scouting trip," Cantu said. "They didn't want us going off on our own and stumbling across any clues which might make us question who this world really belongs to."

"That must be why they reacted so harshly to the lieutenant being captured," LoTur added. "Elder Hamman wouldn't want to risk her escaping and bringing back information from their village."

"We need to get there before the Kitanes do," Indira said. "Can you push this thing harder, Lash?"

The Tiké shook his head regretfully. "The repairs we made

are allowing flight, but the power management issues you pinpointed are still a problem. If I try to push the engine any harder than I already am, the risk of catastrophic failure rises exponentially."

"Uh, catastrophic like falling out of the sky?" Cantu asked.

"If we are lucky. Much worse if we are not."

Cantu's eyes grew wide as he looked around at his squad mates. "I vote we don't push the engine."

Indira snorted a laugh, but she couldn't hide her frustration. They were already hours behind Elder Hamman's warband, and she'd been counting on the shuttle to help them reach the Golmorung village well ahead of the Kitanes. At their current speed, however, she wasn't sure how much of that lead they might be able to erase.

She settled on the awkward stool that was attached to the deck in front of the console, while the Infantry soldiers performed yet another weapons check. Cantu and LoTur helped Suarez strap on her armor, as well, which helped to lighten the load in their backpacks.

"We've got three extra rifles, commander," Cantu said after a while, interrupting her dire thoughts. "If you'd like to use one of them, ma'am?"

"I wish we had three extra soldiers to carry them." Indira swiveled on the stool and held out a hand. "I guess I'll have to do as a replacement in the present moment."

"I'll take all the support we can get," Cantu told her, his expression sober and serious for one of the rare times since this mission had begun. He passed over an NK70, along with several spare clips of ammunition.

"We're approaching the edge of the forest," Lash said.

"Finally." Indira turned back to the small displays on her console. "Can we get any view of what's outside the shuttle?"

Lash was silent for a few moments as he searched the switches and dials. Indira seethed at the delay, simultaneously wishing she could dredge up a clear memory of how Tamma had activated the screen when they approached Waldruun.

She tensed in anticipation when the Tiké finally found the right combination to activate the screen. It rose up from behind her console, lighting up after a few seconds to show a view from the nose of the shuttle.

"They're under attack," Cantu said, pointing at the figures moving on the screen.

Indira batted away the hand that was obscuring her view. She was relieved by what she saw. "Lieutenant Ballard is on that southern hill. She must have already escaped from the Golmorungs."

"I think that's Gundar with her," Cantu said as he bent to get a closer look at the small screen. "Look! Okune and MakTur are on the hill just north of them. They seem to have figured out what was really going on faster than we did, because it looks like they were dug in and prepared for an attack."

"I don't think they expected these numbers, though," Suarez added. She put a finger against the screen where a handful of Kitanes were sprinting toward Ballard's hill. Others to the north were just beginning an approach on Okune's location. "Are they carrying guns?"

"It damn sure looks that way," Cantu said gruffly. "Drop us down on those foxes, Lash. Let's show them what happens when they try to stab the Fleet Infantry in the back."

The soldiers moved toward the hatch in the side of the shuttle, each of them grabbing onto something to steady themselves as the shuttle swooped in and began to descend. Indira watched the images sharpen on the screen as they got closer. Ballard rolled onto her back to look up at them, and it seemed as though her face clouded with hopelessness at sight of the shuttle. Indira realized the lieutenant would be expecting the worst; Kitane reinforcements arriving to crush any hope of preserving the Golmorung village.

She growled deep in her chest as she grabbed her rifle and hurried over to join the others. "What's the plan, Cantu? Fire from the ship?"

"We're going to drop, commander," he said calmly, as if jumping out of a hovering ship into the midst of the enemy weren't incredibly dangerous. "If you could cover us from up here, that would be great."

"I won't claim to be a marksman, but I've spent enough time on ranges to hit my target more often than not."

"Just keep shooting," LoTur said. "That's enough to keep them from focusing solely on us, since they'll have to keep an eye in two different directions."

"This is as low as I can get without damaging our own people," Lash called out. "Go quickly."

Cantu didn't hesitate to spin the wheel that retracted the locks on the hatch door. Within seconds, it was swinging inward. He tapped his fingers against his brow in a quick salute, shot Indira a wink, and then jumped out.

She quickly moved into the opening after LoTur and Suarez followed their sergeant. Indira was relieved to find that they had all landed on or near the crown of the hill. LoTur was right beside Ballard, shooting down at the Kitanes who had been close to overrunning the position.

Several of the Kitanes holding weapons shifted their aim up at the shuttle. Indira had to duck back quickly when a glob of some burning substance hit the hull near the opening. She blew out a breath before leaning out again and firing back, not bothering to aim as she sent three-round bursts toward the Kitane shooters.

The shuttle wasn't a stable platform from which to fire, and it continually dipped, rose, and shook as Lash struggled to control it. Indira kept up a steady rate of fire as the Kitanes began to pull back down the hill. She wasn't sure how many times she hit her targets, but she saw at least four of the foxes go down under the heavy fire from herself and the Infantry squad.

"They're secure. Take us down," she called to Lash. "Closer to the edge of the marsh."

He complied immediately, and she almost fell out of the opening when the shuttle banked unexpectedly before it continued dropping to touch the ground with a jarring shake. Indira was out of the door a second later, racing toward the hill in a crouching run.

Cantu met her near the bottom. "Stay low, commander! We've got several Kitanes pinned down on the far side, but they could break in this direction at any moment."

She dropped to one knee beside him. Indira's heart was racing from the action she'd just faced, but she felt more alive than she had in weeks. "How's Lieutenant Ballard?"

"The lieutenant is fine," he said, his mouth tight with emotion. "Gundar took a hit to the face, though. Whatever those guns shoot, it burns like lava."

She winced at the image that flashed in her head. "Will he

survive?"

"He will, but his eye might not."

A shower of stones and gravel rolled down the hill toward them at that moment, and Indira swung her rifle to point up at what she thought might be an attack. She smiled when she saw Ballard sliding toward them, but then sobered when she saw Gundar right behind her. Half of the man's face was covered with bandages, which were already turning red as blood continued to seep through.

"We're clear," Ballard said sharply. "The Kitanes ran for cover behind another hill, but they'll head for the village next. We need to get there before they do."

"Screw that," Cantu protested. "Gundar and MakTur are hurt, lieutenant. We were lied to, and those Kitane bastards would have happily killed you to keep their secret safe. I say we all load up in this shuttle and get out while the getting's good. We can bring *Intrepid* back to finish this off with greater force."

"We're not leaving the Golmorungs to fight alone," Ballard said, stabbing a finger into his chest. "I don't care if I get killed doing it, at least I'll die knowing it was for the right reason."

Cantu held up a hand helplessly. "Okay, you win. I just didn't want to rush in without taking a moment to consider our options."

Ballard glared at him for a second. "There. I considered. We're going into that village to protect the frogs."

The full Infantry squad assembled around her, and Ballard pointed out the best path through the boggy marsh. Then she turned to Indira. "Thanks for bringing the cavalry, commander. I think it's best if you stay with the shuttle. It's going to get hot and hectic very soon."

She gave the lieutenant a flat stare. "Lash, can you lock down the shuttle to keep our prisoner contained and the other Kitanes out?"

"I can, commander," the Tiké said as he appeared through the hatch.

"Do it." Indira ordered before she turned back to the lieutenant. "I'm coming with you."

Ballard flashed her a quick grin. "I won't turn down an extra gun. Just stay on my six so I can cover you."

Indira gave her a curt nod, and then took up position in what felt was the center of the squad. She didn't like the idea of being coddled, but she also knew her lack of experience in ground combat could be their biggest liability.

"Move out!" Ballard barked. She set off at a light jog, leading them along a path through the marsh which would keep them mostly dry.

Indira could see coppery Kitane fur around the village ahead of them, and there were flashes as their bulky rifles shot out burning gobs of plasma. She only hoped the Golmorungs would be able to huddle somewhere safe until they could arrive to push back the attack.

33 - Ballard

Alina popped out the expended cartridge from her NK70 and smoothly slid one of her spares into the slot. Her breath was loud in her ears as she leaped and ran through the grassy islands dotting the marsh. The sound of eight pairs of boots following buoyed her spirits as they raced toward a fight that she expected would be harder than the one she'd survived on the hill.

She'd been certain that death had found her when the shuttle appeared. Seeing Cantu jump out of it like a braindead adrenaline junkie had made her laugh with palpable relief. With the help of her squad, the Kitanes had been turned back only feet from the top of the hill. The tide had turned, their attackers fled, and the first victory of the day had been secured.

She just had to hope it wouldn't be the last. After what she'd seen in the Golmorung village, the guilt of what she'd almost helped accomplish drove her to rectify the situation. Whatever it took, she planned to keep the Golmorungs safe and eject the Kitanes from a world they never should have set foot on.

There was a yelp right behind her, and Alina dropped into a crouch as she scanned the area for any sign of an attack. Seeing nothing, she twisted around to find out what had happened. While she'd half expected to find that Commander Predashi had stepped into a depression and twisted her ankle, it was instead MakTur who had made the pained sound.

"I'm fine," he grumbled as his brother ripped off his chest plate to expose the wound beneath it. "A little bit of the plasma seeped under, but it's just a small burn."

"Small burn?" Cantu asked. He pointed to the large welt running across the Panosh's chest, where his green fur had been singed and burned away. The exposed skin was red and inflamed, with blisters already forming around a deep gouge where the plasma had eaten through skin and into muscle. "That's gotta hurt."

"Pain—"

"...sharpens the mind," Alina said, finishing the mantra for him. She looked over her shoulder at the village, which was only another hundred yards away. "It can sharpen your mind right here, MakTur. Gundar, you're staying with him. Any Kitanes who flee should come this direction to reach the safety of the forest, so you can pick them off and keep them from returning to the cavern to gather reinforcements."

"I can fight with you, lieutenant," MakTur said through clenched teeth. The pain on his face was apparent to everyone as LoTur rubbed an ointment across the burns to minimize any infection.

"You'll cover the rear as the lieutenant ordered," Okune said sharply. "Is that clear, corporal?"

MakTur's eyes widened in a flash of rage, but he slowly nodded. "Yes, sergeant."

Okune gave him a wan smile and patted his shoulder. "Good man. Gundar, I'm holding you responsible for keeping this big ape from trying to follow us."

"Count on me, sarge," Gundar replied. He was resting on a lump of dry grass, and his pale face made it clear the pain from his wound was worse than he would ever let on. "Just promise you'll call us off the bench if you run into any trouble."

"Absolutely," Alina told him. She waited restlessly while Lo-Tur finished treating his brother's burns, then got back to her feet. "Standard formation but stay low and keep your eyes on a swivel."

There were nods of acceptance, and then she set off at a quick pace again. The short rest had let them all catch their breath, so she didn't have to worry about them being exhausted when they reached the village and encountered hostiles.

Alina sniffed in disgust. It was hard to think of the Kitanes as the enemy after several weeks spent living among them as friends. Harder still to realize she'd been so easily fooled when she first met Tamma. Without her urging, Captain Kerrigan might never have authorized this mission to support what would have been a genocide in the making if she hadn't tried to save time by filling their water bottles in the marsh.

She was more than ready to take revenge for the lies and deception. Elder Hamman was the main focus of her anger, because she knew his was the mind behind it all. His scars showed that he had been in battle before, likely against some other race practically helpless to resist the Kitanes. If she could take him out of the fight, it might make the others retreat in confusion.

They reached the first hut within minutes, and Alina held up a hand to bring the squad to a halt. There was a dark shadow between the stilts, which resolved into one of the Golmorungs when they got closer.

The frog croaked a few words at them, and her implant vibrated as it churned through the translation. The only word that came out was "Protect."

"Fascinating," Lash said excitedly. "This language is quite similar to an old dialect of Telbrith. That would suggest that there might be–"

"We can ponder the possibilities later," Alina cut him off. "Preferably after the battle."

"Of course, lieutenant."

Cantu rubbed the spot behind his ear where the translation implant had been placed. "What does he mean by 'protect', lieutenant?"

She shrugged as she met the Golmorung's eyes, which seemed to be pleading with her. "I think he means they need our help to protect the village. Okune, take LoTur and Suarez and loop around to the left. I'll go right with Cantu, Lash, and the commander. Engage any Kitanes you encounter. Wound them if you can, but you're clear to employ lethal force when necessary."

Commander Predashi's mouth tightened at the orders, but she didn't speak up to countermand them. Alina gave the woman credit for knowing there wasn't time to quibble over niceties. Too many lives were at stake, their own included.

"Stay here," she told the Golmorung, patting her hand in the air to indicate he should hunker down in the shadows beneath the hut.

The frog emerged from between the stilts, however, and brandished one of the scooped clubs she'd seen in the carvings. A pouch hung from the belt looped around his waist, which bulged with whatever was inside. She sighed, but it was clear he intended to fight beside them. "Fine, but stay behind me," she said, hoping the Golmorung understood her hand motions.

Alina led her group to the right, looping around the village until they saw the first flashes of copper fur between house stilts. Cantu and Lash darted underneath the hut, while she and Predashi moved around the far side with the Golmorung close on their heels.

There were three Kitanes, with two of them carrying plasma rifles that seemed like they should be too heavy for the foxes' thin frames. The one without a weapon stood behind them, pointing out targets. Alina bared her teeth when she saw them launch globs of burning plasma toward one of the huts where she'd seen children only a few hours earlier.

She glanced into the shadows beneath the hut, found Cantu, and started to make a series of hand gestures for a coordinated attack. If they could neutralize the trio of Kitanes quickly, then it was possible Elder Hamman wouldn't know resistance had arrived in the village already.

Her carefully formulated plans fell to pieces when the Kitane directing shots screamed in agony. Alina snapped her eyes in that direction just in time to see the fox trying to reach back and stop the bright flames that ate through clothing, fur, and skin to sink into his back. The tormented shriek cut off suddenly, and the Kitane crumpled to the ground.

"What in the hell was that?" Commander Predashi asked hoarsely. She was looking at the Golmorung who had followed them, and the scooped club held in his hands.

"That was glormp," Alina sighed. She pulled her NK70 tight against her shoulder and fired off a three-round burst at the pair of Kitanes who were still standing. They were staring at their fallen comrade with shocked expressions, but she knew it wouldn't be long before they snapped out of it and looked for the source of the attack.

Cantu and Lash joined her, and within seconds both Kitanes were down before they could return fire. Unfortunately, they'd made so much noise that it was impossible their presence would go unnoticed now.

"What's glormp?" Predashi asked, still staring at the Gol-morung.

The frog reached into the bulging pouch at his side. Water splashed out around his wrist, and he was holding one of the small pearl-like objects when he pulled his hand back out. "Glo-rmp," he croaked proudly.

Alina quickly reached over and pushed his hand down. "Put it away, big fella." She watched carefully to make sure the danger-ous bead of fiery death was safely back in the water-filled pouch before she continued. "It's composed of some sort of chemical that ignites when exposed to the air, commander. As you saw, it's quite powerful."

Predashi snorted and finally took her eyes off the Gol-morung. "That's an understatement, lieutenant. I guess that means the natives aren't entirely helpless, then."

"Not at all," Alina replied with a tight smile.

"Incoming," Cantu hissed out from the shadows under the hut. He pointed toward the far edge of the village just as half a dozen Kitanes sprinted between two huts. "They're coming our way."

"Sent to find out what was causing so much noise, no doubt." Alina searched for a place to hide until the enemy arrived. The shadows under the huts would only keep them hidden from any-one who didn't look too hard, and she suspected the group head-ing toward them would be more vigilant. That left either retreat or...

"Can we get up there?" Predashi asked, voicing Alina's thought. She pointed up to the balcony around the hut, the floor of which was just above eye level for them. Strands of woven swamp grass hung from the railing, swaying in the breeze and providing some measure of cover.

"Cantu, I need a boost."

"You got it, lieutenant." He pushed his rifle behind his back and then crouched down next to one of the stilts. The sharp barnacles and slimy mold would make those impossible to climb without sustaining injuries.

Alina placed her boot in his cupped hands, and then pushed off with her other leg at the same moment that Cantu lifted. The extra momentum allowed her to leap high enough to vault over the low railing, and then she reached down to help him climb up.

It took less than a minute for Lash and Predashi to follow, and the Golmorung merely leaped up on his powerful legs. He croaked out a few words shortly after landing beside Alina, and she followed the direction of his gaze to see a pair of eyes peering at them through a woven curtain. She waved for the person inside to stay down and hoped they understood her meaning.

"They just went behind that hut," Cantu hissed out in a whisper as he pointed at the nearest structure. He and Predashi were hunkering as low as they could, hoping to remain hidden behind the strands of grass rope. Alina and the Golmorung moved around the edge of the hut, where they would be out of sight for a few extra seconds.

A pair of Kitanes sprinted out from behind the hut, but the others remained behind cover. With a series of barks, the scouts spotted the fallen warriors and began searching for whoever had killed them. As Alina had suspected, they first peered into the deep shadows beneath the hut.

She ground her teeth together in frustration. She'd hoped

the entire group would come out into the open. With most of them still behind cover, it was going to make this much more difficult. The danger was compounded by now having to worry about the innocent person inside the hut possibly being hurt if the Kitanes fired in their direction.

"Glormp?"

Alina started to wave the Golmorung away, but then she stopped as an idea came to her. She let a smile spread across her lips as she hissed to get Cantu's attention. He and Lash came over to listen to her plan. "And they call me crazy," Cantu laughed. He reached out.

"It will work," Lash said. He held out his tiny hand, waiting expectantly.

Alina motioned to the Golmorung, pointed to his pouch, and then tapped the open palms. "Glormp."

The frog stared at her for a moment until understanding dawned. He dipped his hand into the water-filled pouch, extracted two of the small orbs, and placed them carefully on the open hands.

"Go!" she hissed urgently.

Cantu and Lash sprinted across the balcony. The sound of their rapid footsteps made the Kitanes look up just as the orbs were dropped onto their heads. Exclamations of surprise turned into pained yelps when the glormp ignited and burned with the fury of a thousand suns.

"That was close," Cantu said, rubbing his palm against his pants as if afraid some of the chemical might remain.

Alina's focus was elsewhere, though. The yelps of their companions drew out the four Kitanes who had remained hidden. She and Predashi had their rifles ready, and they fired as soon as coppery fur came into view. One of the Kitane stuttered back as he was hit by a three-round burst, while another was hit in the leg and fell with a scream.

The Golmorung flung another glormp orb, which landed in the grass between the two remaining Kitanes. They stared at it uncertainly, and then fled when the orb ignited and burned with blinding light for several seconds.

"They'll be bringing friends when they return," Predashi said.

"They'll be expecting that glormp stuff, too," Cantu added.

Alina glanced at the hut's window to find the pair of eyes staring past her at the Kitanes who had fallen to their NK70's. Small eyes, she thought, which likely belonged to one of the village's children. "Let them come," she said. "Okune, status report."

Her earpiece hissed with static for half a second before he spoke. "Clear so far, lieutenant. We engaged with two hostiles but managed to dispatch them silently. That was right after you guys made so much noise the first time. All okay over there?"

"We're fine," she said. "Seven hostiles down but two got away and we're expecting more company soon."

"Uh, it might be a while before your guests arrive," Okune said. "The Golmorungs have been using some weird kind of weapon that flings out molten metal or something. Whatever it is, it burns hot and bright for a few seconds, and it's killed a few of the Kitanes near us."

"That's glormp," she told him, smiling when he repeated the name questioningly. "Just don't get too close if you see a small pearlescent orb, because that's what ignites in air."

"Well, it's working. There are about twenty Golmorungs standing near that big stone monolith at the center of the village, and they've been holding off the Kitanes with that glormp stuff.

Elder Hamman is looking pretty pissed about it."

"You can see him?" she asked, leaning over to peer around the edge of the hut as if she might find the elder nearby. She could see part of the monolith and a few of the Golmorungs surrounding it, but none of the Kitanes. "We need to take him out, Okune. He's the brains behind this attack, and the rest of the Kitanes might scatter if he's no longer goading them on."

"He's got six guards around him, lieutenant, and all of them are toting those plasma rifles. We might be able to sneak around... Wait! He's pulling out something that looks like a comm device."

Alina sucked in a breath and squeezed her eyes shut, wishing she could see what Okune was seeing. Was Elder Hamman about to call in another large group to help him wipe out the Golmorung village? Commander Predashi said he'd only brought along about half the number they'd seen in the cavern, but who could say how many other nearby mountain caves might have been filled with Kitane invaders.

"He's speaking into it, so it's definitely a comm device. It's huge, though. Almost the size of two NK70 magazines taped together."

"Could we disrupt their communications?" Lash asked. Alina wasn't surprised the rest of the squad had been listening in.

Cantu grunted a negative. "We brought a short-range scrambler with the rest of our gear, but we had to leave it behind when we commandeered the shuttle. There wasn't room in our packs."

"The odds that it might disrupt whatever signal they're using are minimal, anyway," Predashi said. "We have no idea what spectrum they're broadcasting on, or if their devices use radio waves at all."

"He's pissed about something," Okune said, interrupting the discussion. "Uh, lieutenant? He's looking up at the sky and shouting."

Alina couldn't stop herself from craning her head to look up. There were a few wispy clouds overhead, but nothing that might explain why Elder Hamman would be looking in that direction while talking on his comms.

"The ships in orbit," Predashi said through clenched teeth. She raised her hand to point toward the western horizon. Alina followed her finger and saw the faint shape of a boxy ship that was barely visible through the atmospheric haze.

"That's weird," Okune said in confusion. "The Kitanes suddenly stopped firing at the Golmorungs. I think they're retreating."

A heartbeat later, there was a tiny flash from the barely visible ship. Alina began to wonder if it might be launching more shuttles to bring Kitane soldiers down to join the fight.

That thought was banished when something slammed into the marsh half a mile away. Even at that distance they could hear the sizzle as superheated plasma boiled away the water.

"They're firing from orbit!" Cantu shouted.

Commander Predashi's face had gone pale, and now her eyes met Alina's. That shot might have missed the target, but it wouldn't take long for the ships in orbit to dial in on the Golmorung village. When that happened, there would be nothing to prevent the Kitane from wiping out the natives, and the Infantry squad right beside them.

34 - Kerrigan

Lyle was struggling to keep up with the Infantry squad as they raced along *Intrepid*'s arching spine. There was a stitch in his side that was growing more painful by the second, and his lungs were burning as he tried to suck in enough oxygen to maintain the sprint. Life as a starship captain didn't offer a lot of opportunities for calisthenics, and he was regretting that mightily in the current moment.

"The reactor room is open," Commander Berger reported triumphantly over the comms. "We've secured three Kitanes who were inside, and I'm happy to report that Lieutenant Saunders is alive. He'll need to visit the medical bay for a head wound and probable concussion, though."

"Glad to hear it," Lyle puffed. He was very happy that the officer hadn't been killed in the first attempt to retake control of the ship's reactors. That joy was compounded by finally knowing how many Kitanes were still loose on *Intrepid*. With three in the reactor room, there must only be four of them involved in the assault on the bridge.

"I wish I had good news, as well," Lieutenant Commander Cottlen said. "The bridge feeds are still down, captain, and we're still not receiving any response to our attempts to communicate with the officers on duty there. I think it's time to initiate Protocol Delta Niner Seven."

Lyle grimaced and forced himself to slow down. When Lieutenant Galbraith looked over her shoulder and began to slow as well, he waved for her to continue without him. "I concur, XO. Initiate the system now."

Protocol Delta Niner Seven was one of the emergency programs that could be activated in dire circumstances. The bridge falling to enemy forces was one of the catastrophic situations it had been designed for, but it hadn't been used in more than twenty years. The last known activation of the protocol was during the tail end of the Unification Wars, when American Alliance forces had boarded and seized control of a Latin Confederation destroyer. That action had caused some diplomatic issues when the two factions merged with others to become the North American Alliance a little more than a year later.

"The program has been initiated," Cottlen reported after a short pause. "Awaiting your authorization now, captain."

Lyle lifted his chin and spoke in a loud, clear voice. "Computer, this is Captain Lyle Kerrigan granting approval for Protocol Delta Niner Seven. Authorization code Madrid Seven Dash Charlie Two Six."

Silence fell, with only the sound of his laboring breaths filling the corridor as he grasped his side and began to jog forward again. After a delay that seemed to take minutes but was only five seconds, a series of confirming chirps sounded.

"Your code is acknowledged and accepted," Commander Cottlen reported. "Primary system controls have been transferred to CIC until the bridge can be secured."

"See what you can do to restore the camera feeds," Lyle said through deep breaths. "It would help if we could see what we're about to stumble into."

"We're working on that now, captain. I also have the third squad on the way to rendezvous with you."

Lyle nodded, unable to use any more breath to speak. He knew his temporary XO was likely monitoring his pathetic progress on *Intrepid*'s security feeds. Knowing that his officers could be watching made him dig deep for a little more speed.

A short time later, he was grateful to find Lieutenant Galbraith's squad waiting for him at the very top of the arch. The rest of the run to the forward section would be downhill and slightly easier.

"You... didn't have... to wait... for me," he puffed out as he bent over and rested his hands on his knees.

"We're waiting on squad three, captain."

Lyle tried to push down his annoyance that none of the soldiers were breathing any harder than if they'd been on a pleasant walk along Kraken's promenade. He resolved to do more cardio training when this was all over, so that he wouldn't put on such a shameful performance in the event of another emergency.

He was able to rest for only half a minute before they heard the sound of approaching footsteps. Far more than he'd expected. Lyle straightened up when squad three exited the cargo drum, followed by more than a dozen of the WayLin miners. Sumarongs, Panosh, Dubuks, and a single Telbrith formed the group, each of them carrying a large canister that tapered down to a rounded point.

"They volunteered to help," squad three's sergeant said with a shrug.

"You'll need us," one of the Dubuks said. He hefted the canister that rested on his shoulder. "These sonic drills can cut through the hardest rock in the galaxy. We'll breach any doors between you and the hijackers quicker than those could." He nodded toward the plasma cutter assembly two of Galbraith's squad were carrying.

"We're good in a fight, too," a Sumarong added, flexing her long hands to show off the claws that extended from her fingertips.

Lieutenant Galbraith pressed her lips together in a frown and looked over at Lyle. "Your call, captain."

"Let them come," he said. "We don't have time to debate the issue."

"Fine, you can tag along." Galbraith stepped forward to jab a finger into the Sumarong's chest. "But you keep those claws sheathed unless I tell you to use them. The same goes for all of you. If you can't follow my commands, then turn around and go back to where you came from."

"We will follow orders," one of the Dubuks promised. "Our lives are at risk, as well."

Lyle waved a hand, motioning everyone to start moving. The stitch in his side had begun to ebb, but he knew it wouldn't take long for it to come back with a vengeance. At least he'd managed to catch his breath during the short break.

It took another twenty minutes to reach a maintenance access area, where they found metal stairs that were rarely used during day-to-day operations. The bridge was only two levels up from where *Intrepid*'s spine opened onto the forward section, however, so Lyle was able to keep up with the Infantry and miners as they pumped their legs to quickly climb the steep stairs two at a time.

Galbraith held up a hand to bring them all to a halt once they'd reached the top. "This door opens onto the bridge deck corridor," she said quietly, pointing to it. "XO, do we have the security feeds back online?"

"Negative, lieutenant. It appears as if the equipment itself has been damaged."

She clicked her tongue in disappointment. "Cho, pop out there and see what we're dealing with."

Sergeant Cho quickly moved to the door and pressed a series of buttons on the access pad. Because of the high security on this deck, even a simple maintenance access door was locked. The Infantry squads had an emergency code that could be used to open almost any door on *Intrepid* in the event of an emergency, though.

The door had barely begun to open when the air was filled with the staccato sound of weapons fire. Galbraith yanked Cho back just as several bullets pinged off the bulkhead where his head would have been if he'd leaned forward to look outside.

"Those are NK70's," Sergeant Simmons growled. "How did they get our guns?"

"It's only one NK70," Cho said.

"How do you know that?" Galbraith asked.

"Because I recognize the sound of it. Simmons and I were doing some target practice last week, and Sergeant Major Bauer was testing one of the rifles that continually misfires. He told me the Armory has replaced half a dozen parts in that NK70, but they couldn't seem to solve the problem." Cho pointed toward the door and the gun still firing on the other side of it. "The gun he was using made that same kind of stutter, with third shot in each burst sounding muted."

Every person in the tight confines of the maintenance area closed their eyes and tilted their heads to listen. The Kitane pulling the trigger seemed intent on keeping them bottled up, so it didn't take long for heads to start to nod in recognition of what Cho had pointed out. Lyle heard it himself on the fourth or fifth three-round burst; the last shot was slightly muffled as if the rifle was as tired as he was after the long run from the rear section.

"That still doesn't explain how the Kitanes got their hands on it," Galbraith muttered.

"The sergeant major must have left it on the range to come back and work on it some more," Cho shrugged. "The Kitanes probably got lucky and found it when they were scavenging while we were all occupied with the situation in Engineering."

"However they got it," Lyle said, "we need to neutralize that shooter if we're going to reach the bridge."

Cho held up a finger. "Hold that thought, captain." A few bursts later, they all heard the gun make a grinding noise when it jammed while pulling a bullet from the clip. Cho grinned around at everyone. "I guess the sergeant major didn't figure out the problem yet."

"Good thing for us," Galbraith said, lifting her own NK70. "Simmons, take the lead."

Lyle hung back with the miners while the Infantry soldiers stormed out into the corridor. There was a flurry of shouts, followed by several guns shooting simultaneously.

"All clear," Galbraith called out.

When he entered the corridor, Lyle frowned at the sight of a Kitane slumped against the bulkhead. The fox's feet were splayed out, the jammed weapon still clutched in one hand, and his face was frozen in a wide-mouthed expression of shock.

Galbraith stepped in front of the body and motioned to the miners. "You're up! The bridge doors are locked down and not responding to our security codes, so let's see what those sonic drills can do."

The miners chattered excitedly as they hurried forward and took up positions in front of the wide doors that led onto the bridge. They hefted the canisters onto their shoulders, and with a flip of a switch the rounded points retracted to expose a wide mouth. The sonic waves that blasted out of them were nearly invisible, but the metal on the doors began to vibrate and ripple like water around a stone thrown into a pond.

Lyle turned his back on the process so that he didn't have to look at the dead Kitane. "XO, what's the status on our engines?"

"The reactors are in the process of spinning up now, captain. Commander Berger said we should have enough power to ignite the engines in just under four minutes."

"That's excellent news," he said as he pulled out his tablet. The countdown to a collision with the asteroid was still ticking down, and there wasn't as much time as he would have liked. "Will we be able to avoid the asteroid?"

"Navigation is telling me it's going to be tight, but as long as everything continues running smoothly we should escape with a dented hull at worst. At least we'll have the power necessary to shut compartments in the event of a breach now."

Lyle closed his eyes and sent a silent prayer of thanks out into the universe. His people were safe, and the disaster could be avoided. Once they were able to retake the bridge, *Intrepid* would be fully under his command once more, and they could begin sorting out the mess left behind.

"Those sonic drills are awesome!" Sergeant Simmons laughed. "We need a couple, lieutenant."

"I'll put in a requisition," she said wryly.

Lyle turned around to check the miners' progress, careful to keep his eyes from straying to the corpse in the corridor. With a dozen sonic drills in operation, an opening was already appearing in the doors. He thought it might be large enough for someone to comfortably pass through within another minute.

There was a sudden flash of reddish-brown, and one of the miners cried out in pain as he stumbled back. His sonic drill jerked on his shoulder as he struggled to keep his feet. Unfortunately, it was still active. Another miner screamed as the powerful sonic wave touched her arm, which erupted in a bloody mess.

"Shut down!" Galbraith shouted. "Shut down those bloody drills and pull back!"

Before any of them could follow her command, a Kitane arm stabbed out from the ragged opening in the bridge doors. Lyle was shocked to see a makeshift spear with a jagged head that had been crudely sharpened. It was dangerous enough to gouge out a wound when the Telbrith couldn't retreat fast enough.

Galbraith had her weapon at her shoulder in an instant, and she let loose with a burst of bullets that ripped into the Kitane arm before it could pull back to safety. There was a high-pitched yelp, followed by growling barks from the other Kitanes holding the bridge. Lyle was about to order the Infantry soldiers to storm through the small opening cut by the sonic drills, but he was suddenly shoved back by a pair from squad three.

The corridor was abruptly filled with blinding, flashing lights and a loud shrieking noise that threatened to rupture his eardrums. Lyle was thrown to the deck, and the world around him became a blur.

35 - Predashi

Indira gazed toward where the orbital round had hit. Steam was still rising up from the water that rushed in to fill the void where much of the liquid had been cooked off by the superheated burst. A warm breeze had wafted toward them in the seconds after the hit, and she knew that if the impact had been any closer to the Golmorung village the heat would have been intense enough to leave first-degree burns on any exposed skin.

"We need to evacuate these people," Cantu said suddenly. "Before the next round hits even closer."

Lieutenant Ballard turned to the Golmorung who had stayed close to them. She began speaking slowly, using gregarious hand gestures to try and reinforce the meaning of what she was trying to get across. When the Golmorung only stared at her in what seemed to be an uncomprehending silence, Indira motioned to Lash. "You said their language is similar to an old Telbrith dialect?"

"Yes, one that has not been used outside of the Telbrith home world in well over five hundred sequences. The similarities aren't perfect, but the parts of the Golmorung language I've heard so far would lead me to conclude that there is a seventy-two percent similarity. Enough to make me wonder if there was some contact between the races in the distant past." Lash's flow of words finally stopped, and he tapped just below his mandibles. "The real question is how such contact could be made while the Auricle protections were still in place around this system. Could the Telbrith have ventured to this world in the murky depths of time before the Auricle obelisks first appeared?"

Indira pinched the bridge of her nose and blew out an exasperated breath. "We can debate the implications later, Lash. Can you try to talk to him and explain that his people need to flee the village? Quicker would be better." She glanced out at the horizon, where the hazy outline of the orbiting ship could be seen more clearly. The Kitanes on board must have dropped into a very low orbit to be visible from the surface.

Lash began speaking in a language that seemed to well up from deep within his chest. Indira noticed that every member of the squad reached up to rub the place behind their ear where the implants were vibrating in an attempt to translate his speech. Much like the Golmorung tongue, the ancient Telbrith dialect was not one of the programmed languages. But it was close enough to one that the implant did its best.

Lieutenant Ballard didn't allow herself to be distracted, though. She was speaking over the comms with the other group of soldiers in a quiet voice while her eyes scanned around for any sign of Kitane warriors who might still be nearby.

The Golmorung was silent for a while once Lash finished speaking. He spoke a few words before disappearing with a powerful leap that splashed all of them with water. "I believe he understood enough to decipher the meaning of my warning," Lash said.

"Okune said all the Kitanes fled with Elder Hamman just before the orbital bombardment began," Ballard said. "Let's pair off and do a sweep of the village to be sure, though. If you spot any Golmorungs trying to hide in their huts, do your best to get them to leave with the others."

Indira was paired off with Cantu, who led her toward a hut to their left while Ballard and Lash went right. She kept her NK70 in a guard position across her chest as she followed the sergeant, ready to raise it and fire at the first sign of danger. The Kitanes had proven to be adept liars, and she couldn't help thinking that mindset would lend itself to leaving behind troops hidden in huts and ready to spring out in an ambush.

"Why haven't they fired again?" Cantu asked once they'd cleared the first hut. He paused on the balcony to look out toward the horizon.

"Are you disappointed?"

"No," he said distractedly. "I just can't shake the feeling that there has to be a reason behind it, though."

"They're probably giving Elder Hamman time to retreat far enough from the village that his forces aren't in danger from the next blast."

"Maybe." Cantu shrugged and pulled his attention from the orbiting ship. "I just hope that first shot wasn't designed to make the Golmorungs flee, goading them right into a larger group of Kitanes waiting to slaughter them outside the marsh."

Indira grunted in shock, wondering why that thought hadn't occurred to her. It was the sort of tactical trickery she might expect from the foxes now, but it was hard to leave behind the last two weeks of thinking the Kitanes were relatively primitive and lacking in warfare skills.

She found herself looking out to the horizon more and more as they cleared several more huts. The second ship was just coming into view, and she projected that it would be able to join an orbital bombardment within the half hour. Indira wondered if that was the reason for the long delay after the first shot, though it would seem pointless to warn the Golmorungs of what was coming and then give them so much time to clear out before the attack commenced full force.

They discovered a pair of Golmorungs in the fifth hut. Indira suspected they were mother and child, but she still had no way to tell which of the frogs was male or female. For all she knew, they were all asexual and there were no separate genders. She forced those thoughts aside as she tried to gesture for the pair to follow them out of the hut.

It took far too long, but the mother finally led her child out onto the balcony. There was a deep croaking voice nearby, and the mother snatched her child and sprang away in a leap that carried them a dozen yards away. Indira smothered her yelp of surprise, while Cantu laughed nervously. "I guess dad found his family," he said, pointing to where the pair they'd just goaded out of the hut were effusively greeting another Golmorung.

Indira happened to glance out toward the horizon only a second before there was another flash from the ship hovering there. "Get down!" she shouted, just before the air seemed to pulse around them. The shockwave hit half a second before the noise of the orbital round slamming into the marsh nearby, and it tossed them off the balcony like ragdolls.

Cantu's body cushioned her fall, and the air whooshed out of his mouth when her elbow slammed against his chest. Indira groaned as she rolled off him, then lifted a hand to touch her upper lip. Her fingers were spotted with blood when she pulled them away, but the lack of pain reassured her that her nose wasn't broken.

"No offense, commander, but I really wish you were a little lighter."

She snorted a surprised laugh, then lightly slapped the back of her hand against his chest. "Well, I wish you had more padding, Cantu. Because you make a crappy cushion."

"I'll be sure to grab extra dessert before missions from now on," he said through a pained grin.

Indira struggled to rise, having to pause on her hands and knees for a few moments before getting to her feet. A quick survey showed that she wasn't injured anywhere else, and the only blood came from her battered nose. "Are you okay, sergeant?"

"I'm good," Cantu said, waving a hand lazily through the air. "I just need to get my breath back."

"You'll have time for that later," she said as she held out a hand. He grabbed on, and she pulled him upright with a grunt of effort. "We need to check on the others."

Cantu tapped his ear as he stood. "The lieutenant is fine. She just ordered everyone to leave the village and rendezvous at the shuttle. It sounds like that strike was much closer than the first one."

Indira nodded as she looked over at a pillar of steam rising behind the nearest huts. The orbital round had still hit outside the village, but it was only a matter of a hundred feet or so this time around. The Kitanes on the ship would be dialed in on the next shot or the one after that at the latest, and then this village would become a smoldering pile of debris.

Before they retreated, she dragged Cantu around the hut they'd been thrown from. Indira was relieved to find that the trio of Golmorungs had fled, and that none of them had apparently been injured by the shockwave. With that concern settled, she allowed Cantu to set a quick pace back toward the foothills.

They met Lash and Ballard not far outside the village. The

Tiké was as unruffled as always, but the lieutenant had a huge red welt on her forehead with several bleeding scratches around it. "Barnacles," she said in response to a questioning look. "I was standing too close to one of the support poles when that shock-wave hit."

Indira winced at the imagined pain from her head slamming into the barnacle-encrusted stilt. It could have been much worse, however. "How long was that?" she asked. "Between the two orbital strikes?"

"A little more than thirteen minutes," Lash responded.

"Too long," Ballard said through a frown. "I can't claim to have any experience with orbital bombardments, but it seems like they'd normally happen at a much faster pace."

"The average rate of fire during the Unification Wars was seventy-nine seconds," Indira said. "Those figures come from three separate attacks by two different factions."

Ballard nodded, but her gaze was distant. "We have to assume there's a reason for the delay, but I can't think of one."

"I can," Lash said. Indira glanced at him and then had to clamp her jaw shut to keep from laughing. The small insectile alien bounced as he ran, like some cartoon creation in a children's entertainment program. "The crew of that ship could be too small to allow for efficient use of the systems."

Ballard grunted in reply. Whatever thoughts she might have on his suggestion were diverted when they arrived at the edges of the marsh. The need for a speedy retreat from the village had trumped the desire to stay dry, so all of them were glad to pause for a moment and pull off their boots to dump out the water that had seeped in over the tops.

Indira was tempted to pull off her socks, as well, but without knowing how much more running might be in her future she decided that would be a bad idea. She settled for squeezing her feet to wring out as much of the moisture as she could before sliding them back into the still damp boots.

Okune, LoTur, and Suarez caught up to them during the short break. There was a brief round of hand clasps and fist bumps as the squad members welcomed them with relief, before the lieutenant barked an order to keep moving.

"Have you heard from MakTur?" LoTur asked, obviously concerned about his brother.

"They're already at the shuttle," Ballard told him. "Lash, I know you're holding back in order to stay with us. Race ahead and start warming up the engines."

"Yes, lieutenant." The Tiké suddenly sprinted ahead, leaving them all behind with apparent ease.

"Are we taking the fight to Elder Hamman?" Cantu asked. "I've got a few things I'd like to say to him about firing on civilians, not to mention about how he tried to use us to do his dirty work."

Ballard shook her head. "We're going to fight, but not here." She met Indira's eyes with a mischievous glint. "What do you think about Lash's idea that the crews on those ships are too small, commander?"

Indira had been considering it during their halt, so she didn't have to think it over. "It makes sense, lieutenant. Based off our observations and the state of those ships when we approached Waldruun, I'd put money on his hunch being correct."

"So would I," Ballard said with a nod. "With that in mind, how do you feel about getting a closer look at one of those ships, commander?"

A smile spread across Indira's lips, and she glanced at the horizon with buzzing anticipation. "I say it's about damn time."

36 - Ballard

Alina held one arm up over her head, with her palm pressed tightly against the low ceiling to provide stability as the shuttle passed through an area of extreme turbulence. She ran her eyes across the members of her squad, stopping on the two who were injured. "How's that wound feeling, MakTur?"

"It stings a little, lieutenant, but I'm ready to fight."

She visually checked his bandages and was glad to see there were only small dots of blood seeping through. "You'll be rear guard duty with Suarez, then."

"Aw, lieutenant, rear guard?" Suarez looked up from where she was checking over her rifle with a pained expression. "I wanted to shoot some of those foxes and get some revenge for what they've done."

"You'll have your chance. The Kitanes have proven themselves to be sneaky little bastards, so I'll be surprised if they don't try to take us from the rear at least once during the boarding."

Cantu snickered at her words. Okune punched his shoulder and shot him a glare, but Alina ignored the short exchange. She knew all too well which of her words had set him off. It took a supreme effort of willpower not to roll her eyes at his juvenile humor, but she appreciated how his brief moment of levity relaxed some of the tension among the squad.

"What about me, lieutenant?"

Alina slowly shuffled over to where Gundar was sitting with his back propped up against the bulkhead. The flight had smoothed out once the shuttle was through the last vestiges of planetary atmosphere, so she was able to crouch in front of the injured man and peer into his uncovered eye. "We need someone to stay with the shuttle, Gundar. If those foxes retake it while we're out storming their ship, any hope of retreat is cut off in the event we've misjudged the situation."

A wave of irritation and anger passed across the half of his face not obscured by bandages, but she noted more than a little relief there, as well. "I'd rather be fighting them with the rest of you, lieutenant."

"I know you would," she told him, squeezing his knee in a show of support. "Who knows? You might end up having to make a stand around the airlock and wind up with more kills than the rest of us combined."

Gundar gave her a wan smile in response. Both of them knew the chances of his being able to stand up to an assault like that were miniscule at best, but they also knew the odds of it happening were just as low. Alina personally suspected there wouldn't be more than forty or fifty Kitanes on each of the orbiting ships.

She left the squad to finish their preparations and moved toward the front of the shuttle. Commander Predashi was hunched over one console while Lash contentedly stood in front of the other. They were speaking in low voices, and as Alina got closer she overheard enough to know that the Tiké was giving Predashi a quick tutorial on the systems.

Her eyes drifted to the huddled lump of their prisoner. Tamma seemed to still be unconscious, but Alina suspected it must be a ruse by now. Either way, the Kitane's hands and feet were secured so that she couldn't give them any trouble.

"Have they spotted us yet?" she asked once she was standing

between the consoles.

"If they have, they're not reacting in any way," Predashi said.

"They will likely think this shuttle carries their brethren," Lash added. "I suspect the supply runs performed while we were training groups of Kitanes in the caverns were merely trips to these orbiting ships."

"Let's hope you're right," Alina muttered under her breath. The operation would go a lot smoother if they could make a quick entry and hit the crew of their chosen ship with the kind of shock and awe that would lead to a quick victory.

She dropped to one knee to get a better look at the small display that was showing the ship they had decided to target. Commander Predashi had selected it because it was the lead ship of the pair, and the one that had already fired from orbit twice. Lash was confident he knew which systems would allow the shuttle to attach to what they guessed was an airlock, providing them an entry into the ship they hoped to control before the other could learn of the attack and send help.

Several tense minutes passed as they got closer and closer to the boxy ship. They were already much closer than Tamma had brought them during the arrival on Waldruun, and Alina was able to see more clearly the poor condition of the hull plating across much of the ship. There were visible gaps between a few of the panels, where atmosphere must be leaking out into space unless the interior sections had been sealed off.

"This thing is going to be a maze to get through," she said in exasperation. "Especially without any schematics to provide guidance."

"I had the opportunity to board several cargo vessels during our WayLin contracts in Gliese 649," Predashi told her. "Each of them was of a different design, and yet they followed a similar blueprint. Power and engines are always near the rear, while the bridge or primary control center is near the bow. I think we can assume it'll be similar here."

"The Qualtide followed the same pattern, commander." Lash buzzed in what Alina had come to recognize as his lecturing voice. "We'll want to move toward the port side of the bow, lieutenant. The Qualtide primarily used their left-most arm, which led to most of their designs favoring that side. They recognized the weakness of their less dominant right sides and would have fortified that portion of their bridge as a result."

Alina could picture it in her mind's eye. The majority of humanity was right-handed, which had influenced design for millennia. Throughout centuries of battle, armor had often been designed to better defend the left side of the body. Shields had been carried there, as well, to add further protection. If Lash was correct about the vanished race which had built these ships, then she would expect to find the entry to their bridge on the far left side of the ship. The bulkheads on the right side would be more fortified because of an instinctual feeling of weakness.

"One minute to contact," Lash said, breaking into her thoughts.

Alina shook herself back into focus as she moved toward the rear section of the shuttle. "Fifty seconds! Line up by the airlock in your assigned groupings."

She stood aside as the squad stormed through the opening. Okune would lead Lash, LoTur, and MakTur in one group, while she had Cantu, Commander Predashi, and Suarez in the other. The hope was that they could stick together throughout much of the assault, but it was better to have defined teams for the inevitable need to separate.

Alina moved among her squad as they shuffled into place, checking their gear and performing a final inspection of their armor plating. She dropped her fist onto the shoulder of each member of the squad as they passed her checks, then took up her position to the left of the hatch door.

The countdown in her head expired several seconds before she felt the braking thrusters fire to slow their approach. Everyone swayed with the sudden momentum shift, then they were thrown forward when the shuttle slammed against the side of the ship with a deafening screech of metal on metal.

"We have a good seal!" Commander Predashi called out.

Okune almost instantly reached out to spin the hatch locking mechanism. In less than five seconds, the door was swinging open.

Alina was surprised that the hatch door on the ship they'd just forcefully docked with was also swinging open. She pointed her NK70 into the opening until she saw the room beyond it was empty, then motioned the squad to enter.

Lash and Predashi joined them less than a minute after the airlock chamber had been swept and cleared. "The shuttle is locked in place," Lash told her as he held his rifle across his chest. The NK70 looked far too large for his half-sized body, but he had no difficulty using it.

"Good luck, guys," Gundar called out from just inside the shuttle. "I'll make sure you still have a ride off this rust bucket in case worse comes to worst."

Alina tapped her ear as she looked around at her squad. "Comms up?" There was a chorus of confirmation, which she heard in stereo since it also came through the earpiece. "Stay tight, keep your finger on the trigger, and remember the mission."

"Save the frogs," Cantu said with a nod.

"Which we do by seizing control of this ship to stop them from firing another round from orbit."

The ship seemed to shake beneath their feet, and Alina flexed her knees in response. She looked at the deck in confusion and wondered if the Kitanes had already detected their incursion and initiated countermeasures.

"Seventeen minutes once again," Lash said. It took only a second for his meaning to hit. There were mutters of anger that the Kitanes had fired on the Golmorung village for a third time, interspersed with disgust that they hadn't arrived swiftly enough to prevent it.

"That gives us a mission clock," Alina said loudly, forcing the squad to quiet down. "We need to have control of this ship within the next seventeen minutes, or at least find a way to prevent them from firing on the planet again."

There's still the other ship to deal with, she reminded herself. They couldn't do anything about that until this one was under control, however, so she just had to hope the crew of the second ship would be as bad at aiming as this one had been so far. This latest round might have hit the village, but she doubted it would have been fully dialed-in for maximum damage yet after the first two blasts were so off target.

Alina waved to the oval door that led out of the airlock chamber. "Lash, you're the one who knows these controls. Get that door open."

"Yes, lieutenant." The Tiké scuttled forward quickly, and his small hands flew across a series of switches and knobs set into the wall. It didn't take long before the thick, metallic door retracted with a muffled squeal of protest.

Okune charged out with his half of the squad, then barked a hushed "Clear!" over the comms.

Alina stepped out to find herself in a long corridor that stretched out for a hundred yards in either direction. She bit on her lip at the apparent emptiness of the ship, surprised there weren't at least a few Kitanes racing toward the airlock to greet the shuttle they would think was bringing friends.

She was tempted to immediately change up the plan and send Okune's group toward the rear of the ship. Engineering might be an easier target to take control of than the bridge, but the systems on this alien ship would be gibberish to most of them. She needed Lash with her, since he was the only one who could reliably decipher the controls. There was no way she'd rely on Tamma to help them unless it was the last option.

She motioned for Cantu and LoTur to take the lead. "The bridge is our target. Take down anyone who gets in the way." The clock in her head was ticking down, and she swore she wouldn't fail the Golmorungs. She owed them a debt after almost helping invaders push them off their world, and she swore to herself that she wasn't leaving this ship until that debt was paid.

Alina pulled her rifle tight against her shoulder as the squad moved quickly along the corridor. She kept her eyes constantly roving around, checking every door and shadowed alcove in the bulkheads for any sign of a crew member. The ship was too quiet, and that was ratcheting up the tension in her body with every step.

Her senses tingled a warning only a second before the door at the end of the corridor slid open. Alina threw herself against the bulkhead as a pair of Kitanes rushed through the opening and fired off sizzling plasma rounds. There were shouts of dismay peppered by yelps of pain as members of her squad were hit or grazed by the attack.

The long corridor had suddenly become a killbox.

37 - Kerrigan

The blurriness in his vision cleared after several seconds, and Lyle shook his head to clear it further as he crawled to his hands and knees. His ears were ringing from the aural assault, and the continued strobing flashes of light from the flashbang grenades gave the scene an eerie quality.

Most of the WayLin miners were shaken just as badly as he had been, but the two Infantry squads had fared better. They'd been trained to endure situations like this. Lieutenant Galbraith and a few others were firing through the ragged holes ripped in the bridge doors by the sonic drills. They squeezed off three-round bursts in quick succession, then fell back to allow Sergeants Cho and Simmons to squeeze through the openings and enter the bridge.

Lyle staggered forward to join them, but an arm pressed against his chest to hold him back. "Stay out here until we're sure it's clear, captain," the soldier restraining him said authoritatively.

Galbraith shot him a glance that told him to obey her underling, then ducked to follow her squad into the bridge. The staccato sound of gunfire was muted by the effects of the flashbang grenades someone had tossed through the openings in the door, and Lyle strained to hear any sounds of return fire.

Not knowing what was happening through that door was the hardest part as he was forced to wait outside the bridge with the miners and third Infantry squad. He was desperate to find out what state his officers were in. The worry that some of them might have been injured or even killed when the Kitanes took the bridge had been weighing on him during the long run from the rear section of *Intrepid*.

After what seemed to be a lifetime, the sound of gunfire slowly ebbed shortly after the lights and noise from the flash-bangs finally cut off. There was silence for a few heartbeats before Lieutenant Galbraith passed word that the bridge was secure. The arm holding him back finally dropped, and the soldier waved him forward.

Lyle stumbled over the outflung legs of the Kitane they'd encountered in the corridor when he rushed forward. One of the miners reached out to keep him on his feet, and he shot the Dubuk a grateful nod of thanks.

Simmons helped him crawl through one of the narrow openings torn into the bridge door, and then Lyle was able to stand upright and jerk on the hem of his uniform as he took in the chaos that awaited him.

The first thing he saw were sprays of blood across several of the consoles arrayed near the front of the bridge. It wasn't enough to suggest someone had been killed, but more than enough that his heart dropped at the thought of an officer receiving grievous injury. There were smashed screens and dented panels, too, as if the Kitanes had vented their frustration or anger on the equipment.

His command chair was tilted to the side in a way that shouldn't have been possible, and it looked as though the Kitanes had attacked the comfortable cushioning with their crudely made spears. Several of the displays set into the wide arms were cracked, as well, with exposed wires dangling from where one had been ripped out by force.

Two Kitanes were sprawled in poses of death between his chair and the main consoles. Both had been peppered with bullets, which suggested they had fought to the end even though their spears would have been of little use against soldiers carrying firearms. He could almost respect their tenacity, if not for the fact that they had tried to forcefully take his ship and would have left hundreds behind to likely die with no hope of rescue in this desolate portion of space.

Then he finally spotted the first of the bridge officers. Ensign Larkin was hunched down beside his station at the rear of the bridge. One of the Infantry soldiers was applying bandages to a wound on the young officer's upper arm, but he began to struggle to stand when he spotted the captain.

"At ease, ensign," Lyle said, waving for Larkin to remain where he was. The young man would have a nasty scar, but the wound would be easily treated. "Where are the others?" he asked, finding the bridge empty of any other officers.

"Through here, captain," Lieutenant Galbraith called out. She stood beside the doors that opened onto the conference room he used for meetings with his senior staff.

Lyle couldn't hold back a shaky laugh of relief when he saw the rest of his bridge officers in the room. Ensign Nuñes and Lieutenant de Windt were being treated for slightly serious injuries, but the others seemed to merely be ruffled and shaken by their ordeal.

Except for Lieutenant Stebbins, who stood over the final Kitane with a stun gun pressed against the fox's head. The Helm officer greeted his captain with a short nod. "He refuses to talk, captain."

The Kitane's eyes gleamed as his gaze darted to Lyle. "You are the captain here? You think you have won, but we will still take this ship from you. My people are strong!"

Galbraith snorted as she ambled around the table to get closer to the prisoner. "You don't look so strong from where I'm standing. Three of your friends are dead, while we've captured the group who tried to take control of our reactors. It's over."

"It's not over," the Kitane hissed at her. "Elder Hamman will come with our ships. With many more Kitane warriors."

"Let him try," Galbraith said through a fierce grin. "My squads need some more target practice."

Lyle placed a hand on her shoulder, then tilted his head to the side. Galbraith understood and moved back from the prisoner so he could take her place. "Tell me about Elder Hamman," he said gently, sitting in the chair nearest the Kitane. "Why did he or she send you here to try and take our ship?"

The fox's face rippled with what he suspected was repugnance. "You are weak! The Kitanes take what they want from the weak so that we can survive and grow strong. When Elder Hamman comes, you will wish you had followed our commands and let us have your puny ship."

"They're scavengers," Lieutenant Stebbins said, his lips pulling up distastefully.

"That seems likely," Lyle agreed. He wanted to pepper the Kitane with more questions, but it was clear the fox would continue hurling threats and insults at them instead of providing any real information. "Lieutenant Galbraith, have this one put with the three we captured in Engineering."

"Aye, captain." She motioned to a pair of soldiers, who stepped forward to grab hold of the Kitane's arms and force him up out of the chair. The fox spat vitriol and insults at them as he was dragged through the bridge.

Lyle saw the WayLin miners lurking just outside the doors that had been wrenched open. As far as they could be with the damage from the sonic drills, anyway. "I want to thank each of you for assisting in our efforts to secure *Intrepid* against the Kitanes."

"It was the least we could do," one of the Panosh said. "As we told you earlier, it wasn't just your lives at stake."

"Besides," a Dubuk added through a pointy grin, "this was a lot more exciting than listening to Marl tell us another story about his imaginary exploits in station brothels." His words kicked off a round of laughter while another Dubuk protested with a smile on his face.

Their expressions sobered when Lyle stepped forward to crouch down to check on the two who had been injured. The man stabbed by one of the Kitane spears held a hand over the wound, but he waved away any concern. It was the woman whose arm had been mangled by the sonic drill who needed immediate medical attention. She was pale and sweating, but still conscious.

"Medical teams are less than a minute out, captain. These two are at the top of their list. I'll have squad three escort the rest of them back to the cargo drum," Galbraith said.

"Excellent." Lyle tucked his hands behind his back and looked over the chaos on the bridge one more time. "Commander Cottlen, I suspect we may have to run everything from CIC for a few shifts, until repairs can be effected here."

"We can handle that, captain," his XO said through the earpiece. "I'll dispatch a repair crew to assess the damage and begin the necessary repairs."

"Let them finish with the reactor room first," Lyle said. "I'd much rather have Engineering back at one hundred percent before we pull people off to focus on the bridge."

"Understood. I'll see what I can do about speeding up that process at least." Cottlen paused for a second, and when he spoke again his voice was lowered so that others in CIC wouldn't overhear. "Are you alright, captain? We still don't have visuals on the bridge deck, but it sounded pretty hot and heavy for a while there."

Lyle chuckled and touched the bump on his forehead that he'd sustained when one of the Infantry grunts threw him down before the flashbangs were tossed into the bridge. "I'm fine, Commander. We do need medical crews up here to see to some of the bridge officers."

"Already on the way," Cottlen assured him.

Reassured that everything was under control for the moment, Lyle waved Lieutenant Galbraith over. "Did any of your people sustain injury during the assault?"

"Just a few cuts and bruises," Galbraith said. "It would have been much worse if those damn foxes had managed to get into the Armory."

"Did they attempt to access it?"

Her head jerked down in a nod as she unconsciously reached up to touch her earpiece. "Sergeant Major Bauer checked the logs, and someone tried to brute force their way through the security panel right around the time we were responding to the first alert from Engineering. The sergeant major's team set up a rotating security program, however, that changes the codes on a frequent but random basis. That prevented the Kitanes from breaking in."

Lyle blew out a deep sigh. "Remind me to commend the

sergeant major for being so paranoid."

"Will do, captain," Galbraith laughed. "But like he once told me, 'it's not paranoia if someone's really trying to get you, Lizzie'. He's never going to let us forget he was right."

Lyle chuckled along with her, but he thought Sergeant Major Bauer could teach everyone on *Intrepid* a few things about being prepared, even if the need was exceedingly rare. One fully functional NK70 in the hands of the Kitane would have proven disastrous. As it was, they'd already damaged the ship in various ways, and it would take days to complete repairs.

The one bright spot was the image on the main viewscreen. The asteroid that had drifted into their path was large enough to take up much of the screen. It was a behemoth that would have caused devastating damage if *Intrepid* had collided with it, and he could only think the Kitanes had no idea it was there when they launched their attempts to wrest control of his ship.

His shoulders relaxed a tiny fraction as the asteroid began to drift away from their corrected course. The deck plates were vibrating with an unusual intensity as the newly ignited engines burned hard to take the ship out of danger. One of the few functional displays on the bridge told him the margin would be slim, but there should be nearly a hundred yards of breathing space between *Intrepid* and the nearest point of the tumbling space rock.

As the medical crews treated the miners and his officers, Lyle's thoughts turned to Commander Predashi and Lieutenant Ballard. The attack might have been thwarted on *Intrepid*, but he could only wonder how they were faring against a larger number of Kitanes. Their prisoner's warning of Elder Hamman had left him with a disquieting sense that the Kitanes might be a bigger threat than he'd expected.

38 - Predashi

When the Kitanes charged through the doorway, Indira was slow to recognize the threat. The Infantry soldiers around her threw themselves against bulkheads to get any amount of cover they could find and make themselves more difficult targets, but she froze in the middle of the corridor for a second longer than she should have.

She was hit just as she turned in search of cover. The glob of plasma splashed against her upper back with a force that felt like she had been lightly punched. She scrambled to crouch down behind a bundle of conduits running up a narrow vertical divider in the bulkhead. Parts of her body were still exposed, but she presented a small enough target that she should be ignored.

Pain began seeping through her adrenaline-fueled panic while she was struggling to catch her breath. It was minor at first, and she thought she'd maybe pulled a muscle during her mad scramble. That thought was quickly banished when a burning sensation radiated out from where she'd felt the impact earlier.

The corridor was filled with the sounds of weapons fire as the Infantry squad began to return fire. Several of the soldiers were shouting, either hurling insults or trying to coordinate their defense. Another pair of Kitanes had appeared through the door, so that four of them were now firing plasma bursts down the long corridor which presented few places to hide.

All of it faded into the background for Indira as she struggled against the pain raging through her body. Sweat began to pour down her face as she bit down on her tongue to hold in a shriek of agony. Her fists were clenched so tightly against her chest that sharp points of stinging pain flared up where her fingernails broke through skin. Indira barely even realized that her body was beginning to shake violently as the plasma burned through her skin.

Eons seemed to pass, each second drawing out into a century as the supreme torment in her back continued to worsen. Indira was barely aware of the hands that grabbed her arms and pushed her down onto the deck. The coolness of the bare metal against her cheek was a microscopic spot of pleasure lost in the sea of suffering.

"Pour some water on it," a voice said, the words barely getting through the fog of pain that clouded her mind.

"Water won't help," another voice insisted. "We need to get the plasma out of the wound before it eats all the way down to her shoulder blade."

Indira finally screamed when another spike of pain joined the burning agony in her upper back.

"Hold her!"

"I've almost got it. Keep her still, or I'll cut her worse than I need to."

"She's trying to shake us off."

"MakTur, use your full weight. I'm pretty sure the commander will accept a few bruises in exchange for saving her life."

Indira writhed beneath the suffocating weight that held her down, trying to escape the rising pain that flared out from her back. Through it all, she never stopped screaming.

"Got it!"

Something sizzled against the deck a few feet away, distracting Indira from her pain for a brief moment. There was a series of sharp jabs across her back, and then the pain began to slowly fade. It was still agonizing torture, but it retreated enough that she could think again.

"Can you hear me, commander?"

She realized that question had been shouted at her several times already. Indira opened her mouth to respond, but her throat was so raw from screaming that she could only croak out a barely audible answer.

Lieutenant Ballard's face appeared in her vision, and the woman's eyes filled with relief when Indira met her gaze. "Hold tight, commander. We're almost done."

Some of the weight lifted from her back, but then she had to suffer being manhandled while someone pinched and squeezed the skin of her upper back. After a minute or so, bandages were wrapped around her wounds. There were several moments when an errant movement made the pain spike, but for the most part her back was beginning to feel numb and disconnected from the rest of her body.

"Secure the arm," Okune said. "If she moves it around too much, those stitches are going to come out. They're not exactly very good."

"Hey, you took the same first aid course I did," Cantu protested. "I'd like to see you do better in these conditions."

"They'll do for now," Ballard said sharply. "We need to hurry up, before more of the Kitanes come to check on their friends."

Finally, two pairs of hands helped Indira into a sitting position. She tried to protest when her right arm was pulled tight against her chest and then bandages were wrapped around her torso to hold it there. Her words were ignored, though.

Ballard crouched down in front of her, and their eyes met for a second. "LoTur and Suarez, help the commander back to the shuttle."

"No," Indira croaked. She worked saliva into her mouth and then tried again. "No!"

"You've been very badly injured, commander." Ballard gingerly touched her right shoulder. "I know you can't feel much of it through the painkiller, but you took a plasma round on your shoulder blade. It did a lot of damage before we were able to get it out," she said, casting a glance at the viscous glob on the deck plates not far away.

"I'm staying with you," Indira said through clenched teeth. The pain was still radiating out from the upper right portion of her back, but it had been dulled enough that she could somewhat ignore it and focus on their mission. "Unless one of you grunts knows how to drive a starship, you'll need me when we reach the bridge."

Lieutenant Ballard shook her head. "Lash can figure out the controls, commander."

"You'll need his skills elsewhere," Indira said. She reached out to grab the lieutenant's armor, pulling her closer. "I'm the only one who can fly this thing, and you know it. I'm going with you. That's an order, lieutenant."

Ballard clearly wanted to keep insisting that she retreat back to the shuttle, but she also knew Indira was right. Lash's ability to decipher the systems on the ship would be needed in dozens of places if they had any hope of putting an end to the Kitane aggression on the planet below. He couldn't be confined to the bridge, and she was the only other one who had any clue how to control the ship, as rudimentary as her knowledge might be.

"You'll stay at my back, commander, and let me know if the pain starts to get worse. That's non-negotiable."

Indira nodded gratefully, then held out her good arm until someone helped her up. A quick survey showed that a few others had taken hits, but their body armor had prevented all but minor injuries. "The Kitanes?"

"They've been neutralized," Suarez said with a tight smile. Her eyes flicked toward the end of the corridor, and when Indira followed the woman's gaze she spotted the crumpled bodies.

"We need to move," Ballard barked. She gingerly pulled Indira into position only a few feet behind her, then led the squad forward.

The door the Kitanes had come through led into another corridor, but this one was much shorter. There was only one other door, and it also stood open. "That's shoddy operational security," Okune snorted.

"Or too much wishful thinking that they'd succeed in taking us down," Cantu chuckled.

Ballard waved them into silence, then motioned for her sergeants to go through the open door. Okune charged through first, and Cantu had barely stepped over the threshold when he came to an abrupt stop. "Uh, lieutenant? You'll want to see this."

Indira stayed tight with Ballard as they moved forward. The lieutenant froze in the doorway just as Cantu had, and Indira tried to go up on her toes to see over the other woman's shoulder. She hissed as the movement sent a sharp jolt of pain out from her wound, but that was forgotten when she got a glimpse of what was beyond the doorway.

There was a counter in the middle of the room, which held a corpse. It had once been a Golmorung, before some lunatic had sliced it open from neck to groin. The skin had been pulled back so the organs could be removed, and they now rested in shallow containers beside the body. The smell was enough to make Indira retch, and she had to press her arm against her nose to block it out.

"Who does something like this?" LoTur asked in stunned disbelief.

"It had to be one or all of those Kitanes we just killed," Suarez guessed. She pointed to four bedrolls spread out against the far wall, and the disgust on her face made it clear how she felt about anyone who could live in the same room where they had butchered another being.

Everyone took in the gruesome sight for several silent seconds, and it was Lash who finally broke them out of it. "The bridge is this way," he said, pointing to the portside door. He had found the controls to open it while the others were in a shocked stupor.

"Let's go," Ballard said, her jaw clenching as she took point.

Indira finally dragged her eyes away from the dissected Golmorung and stayed close to the lieutenant. Knowing what atrocities the Kitanes were capable of helped her push the pain down a little more, and it heightened her determination to put an end to their invasion of Waldruun.

The squad moved through twisting corridors for the next twenty minutes. Every step took them closer to the bridge, and yet they saw no other sign of the Kitanes who must be on board the ship. Lash felt certain they would need a skeleton crew of at least twenty to operate the ship, and they'd only seen four so far.

Ballard held up a fist to bring them to a halt when they reached a wide doorway. It was larger than any other they'd seen on their journey through the alien ship, which suggested it opened into an important area. "This has to be it," the lieutenant said in a low voice. "Lash, can you get it open?"

The Tiké scuttled forward to look over the control panel beside the door. After half a minute of close examination, he finally nodded.

"When those doors open," Ballard hissed, "we go in hot. Anything that moves, you put it down. I don't want to give them any chance to scuttle this ship or launch another round at the planet. Understood?"

"Yes, lieutenant," everyone responded in hoarse whispers.

"You should hang back here, commander."

Indira chuckled and nodded in agreement. She still carried one of the NK70s, but her ability to use it was severely hampered with one arm out of commission. "I won't fight you on that, lieutenant. Good luck in there."

The Infantry squad flanked the doorway with their weapons held in a ready position. Lieutenant Ballard held out a hand with all her fingers splayed open, then began to lower them in a silent countdown. As soon as she'd made a fist, Lash's hand moved swiftly across the control panel.

With a loud *thunk*, followed by an almost deafening squeal, the bridge doors began to slide open.

39 - Ballard

Alina knew the smart play was to hold back and see if any of the Kitanes were waiting to ambush them, but the sight of the butchered Golmorung had left her incensed. That anger was still roiling deep inside her chest when they reached the bridge, so as soon as the doors opened, she burst through them.

Plasma rounds sizzled as they flew past, but Alina dodged and threw herself into a forward roll. She came up on one knee and pulled her NK70 against her shoulder. Her finger tightened on the trigger before she consciously picked out a target. She was relying on instincts honed through hundreds of hours of training and combat simulations on *Intrepid*.

Her first three-round burst missed, but the second swiftly followed and peppered a Kitane trying to crouch behind one of the consoles that filled the small bridge. Blood sprayed as the fox fell backward and released his plasma rifle to slide across the deck.

"Five hostiles!" Cantu shouted out at almost the same moment.

"Make that four," she amended with deep satisfaction. She had already shifted her aim to target another of the Kitanes still firing globs of plasma in their direction. Before she could pull the trigger, though, two of her squad scored simultaneous hits.

MakTur roared angrily as he spread his legs and stood in the open doorway, with LoTur standing solidly beside him. He fired bursts from his NK70 as quickly as he could pull the trigger, but his ear-splitting roars did more to distract their foes. Alina thought she saw one of the Kitanes shivering with terror as they focused on the most obvious threat in the room.

That's a mistake, she thought. As she continued to fire, she noticed Suarez and Lash sneaking around the edges of the room. The Kitanes were so focused on MakTur that they didn't even seem aware their flanks were exposed. Alina waited for Suarez and Lash to reach optimal positions, then stood and began furiously squeezing her trigger to add a deadly fusillade to those already being spewed by the Panosh brothers.

A third Kitane fell to their bullets seconds before the pincer attack was launched. Suarez and Lash easily killed the last pair of foxes, taking them from the side before any kind of defense could be mounted.

With their rifles at rest, a heavy silence fell on the bridge. Alina's ears were full of the sound of her heavy breathing, and she waited for the adrenaline high to fade. "Did anyone get hit?"

"Sort of," Cantu said, shrugging as he held up a hand to show a nasty red burn across the back of it. "Just a graze, lieutenant."

Okune had a few more blackened spots on his armor, but MakTur and LoTur had somehow come through the brief fight without being hit. There were sizzling globs of plasma dotting the walls and deck around them, but the Kitanes must have been so frightened by the rageful display that their aim was thrown off.

Alina swept the room with her eyes, looking for any cubbies or nooks where an attacker might be waiting to spring out at them. The bridge was small, though, and already felt cramped with just the seven of them inside. It got even more claustrophobic when Commander Predashi shuffled in.

"Drag those bodies out," the commander ordered, pointing to a few of the fallen Kitanes who were blocking access to the consoles.

While her squad set about that gruesome task, Alina waved Lash over to join Predashi at the first console. "What do you think, commander? Can we control this rust bucket?"

The two put their heads together and spoke in low mutters that she couldn't hear. Alina shuffled her feet nervously, hoping they hadn't just gone through all this for nothing. Almost nothing, she amended. Even without the ability to fly the ship, they could still stop it from firing on the planet below. Scuttling the ship would have to wait until they repeated the boarding process on the other vessel in orbit over Waldruun, except the Kitanes there would be expecting them by the time their shuttle crossed the space between the ships.

"I believe we will be able to master these controls," Lash said after a very tense couple of minutes. "The commander and I will need some time to examine these consoles to be sure, lieutenant."

"What about the weapons system?" she pushed. "Can we shut that down from here?"

There was silence broken only by low mutters as the two conferred and examined the console again, until Lash turned back to her. "The orbital cannon appears to be controlled from a different part of the ship, lieutenant. However, we do have access to a bank of smaller turrets. There are half a dozen along the port side of the ship and another half dozen to starboard."

"Excellent. Do they have enough range to hit the other vessel in orbit over Waldruun?"

Commander Predashi nodded slowly, not looking up from whatever screen she was examining. "They look to be fairly low-powered, but the other ship is practically riding our ass. The real problem is that I don't know how many of these cannons are operational. The maintenance aboard this ship has been abysmal from everything I've seen, and I'm not finding any kind of logs to show routine work being performed to keep the individual parts in working order."

Alina groaned in dismay and wondered if they'd made a mistake in boarding this ship first. If the other ship had functional weapons, they could be blown to atoms before they did more than annoy them with a paltry attack.

"These two are reporting as operational," Lash said, his finger moving across the small display. "They are ideally placed for a surprise attack, as well."

"Do it," Alina said.

Commander Predashi looked up at her with a wry smirk. Her face was still pale and covered in a sheen of pain-induced sweat, but her eyes were bright with excitement at the opportunity to study an alien vessel. "Your purview ends with the boarding assault, lieutenant. Command of a captured vessel falls to me as the senior officer on board."

"Yes, ma'am," Alina said, squaring her shoulders and lifting her chin. "I apologize for overstepping."

"Accepted," Predashi said with a wave of her hand. "I agree with you, by the way. Let's give those bastards a taste of their own medicine, Lash."

The Tiké hummed to himself, a steady buzzing noise that was oddly soothing to her ears. His hands moved across the consoles as he sought out the buttons and switches he needed, and then the ship shuddered as the first turret fired.

"That's a hit!" Predashi said, raising her good arm in celebration. "Dead center on their bow, Lash. Keep it coming."

Alina pushed down the elation that threatened to suffuse her face with joy. "MakTur, stay with Lash and the commander, just in case there are more Kitanes lurking nearby who try to retake the bridge."

"Where will you be, lieutenant?" the Panosh soldier asked in his rumbling voice.

"We're going to find whatever passes for Engineering on this relic," she said, looking around at all the old-fashioned switches and dials that covered the bridge consoles. The displays here were just as small as those in the shuttle, which quashed her hopes that the technology might be more advanced on the larger ships.

"I can assist you with that," Lash said. The Tiké moved to another console and brought up an image on a display.

Alina joined him and bent over to examine the screen, which seemed to show a wire-frame schematic of a boxy vessel. "This is the ship we're on?"

"It is, lieutenant." Lash flipped, pressed, and turned controls for several seconds until bright orange dots began to flicker on the schematic. "And these are the life signs aboard the vessel."

She gasped in surprise and bent closer to study the image. "Kitane life signs?"

"All life signs," Lash clarified. He tapped the bow portion with a tiny finger. "This cluster will be all of us, while these others toward the rear of the ship I suspect are the Kitane crew who are still active."

Alina counted no more than half a dozen slowly pulsing dots. It seemed far too few for the size of crew they had expected to find on the ship. "Is there any way to zoom in so I can see which corridors will get us there faster?"

Lash lifted his carapace in a shrug. "None that I know of, lieutenant. Sorry."

She dropped a hand onto his shoulder. "Don't apologize, Lash. We have more information than we did before. Okay, squad, you heard the man. We've got six Kitanes still standing, and they all seem to be near where I'd expect to find Engineering."

"Let's finish this extermination job," Cantu said, shaking his NK70 in a show of anticipation.

Alina opened her mouth to berate him for such a bloodthirsty remark, but then she flashed back on the image of the dissected Golmorung. The smell of that room was still in her nose, and she knew that none of the Kitanes on this ship could possibly be unaware of what had gone on there.

"Pick your shots carefully," Commander Predashi barked while Alina was frozen in thought. "I don't need one of you grunts putting a hole in the reactor or destroying the engines."

"The commander's right," Alina said. "We'll shoot back if we're attacked, but we focus on quick incapacitation. Those Kitane bastards can't be allowed to launch another plasma round at the village below."

Without another word, she led half of her squad out of the bridge at a slow jog. She wanted to reach the aft portion of the ship as quickly as possible, but she didn't want to be sprinting so fast that they fell into a trap before she had time to spot it.

As she ran, she felt the vibrations through her boots each time the working cannon turrets fired. Each shot made the smile on her face grow larger. Her squad had been lured to this planet under false pretenses, but they'd discovered the truth in time to set things rights.

40 - Kerrigan

The docking bay was a hive of activity, and Lyle stood at the center of it. A dozen crew members were bustling around one of *Intrepid*'s two shuttles, which had just returned from its first trip to ferry miners to the asteroid they would call home for the length of their contracts with WayLin Mining Consortium. Off to the side, another group of miners was waiting for the boarding call, with all of their possessions gathered around them in bags and crates.

Lyle watched with a critical eye and expressionless face while his crew went about their tasks. The trip had been delayed after the Kitane attempts to seize control of *Intrepid*, so that they were running nearly two days behind schedule. He was pleased with the prompt efficiency on display, especially when the shuttle was prepped and ready for departure only minutes after it arrived.

"The second shuttle has just lifted from the asteroid," Lieutenant Commander Cottlen reported in his ear. "ETA for return to *Intrepid* is seven minutes."

Throughout those minutes, Lyle stood with his hands tucked at the small of his back. He presented a calm and unruffled exterior, which he hoped hid the roiling concerns deep inside. *Intrepid* might have escaped Kitane aggression relatively unscathed, but he still had no idea how Commander Predashi and Lieutenant Ballard's Infantry squad were faring. The uncertainty had given him plenty of sleepless hours through the last stages of this voyage.

Docking bay officers attended to the miners when it was time, hustling them on board the shuttle and helping to carry any baggage that was too bulky for someone to lift alone. It was a smooth process that was completed within minutes. Lyle allowed a small smile to touch his lips as the shuttle lifted from the deck and passed through the blue shimmer of the shield that protected the docking bay and kept everything from being sucked out into space.

Only thirty seconds later, the other shuttle arrived with a burst of thrust to slow its forward momentum as it passed through the shield. The pilot touched down with a display of skill that would have left anyone thinking this was merely one of thousands of trips they'd flown instead of the first real use the shuttles had seen since the ship launched from Earth. The passengers within would have barely felt their arrival.

Lyle strode forward as a group of crew members swarmed the shuttle, performing quick checks of the hull and verifying fuel levels. The shuttle door rose silently as they worked, allowing the three passengers within to descend a short set of stairs that extended out from beneath the opening.

At the forefront of the new arrivals was a willowy Edryne. Lyle couldn't help but compare the woman to Bosanlek, the aide who worked at the embassy on Kraken. She was slightly taller, with the same delicate air of fragility, but her skin was pale pink instead of Bos's milky blue.

"Administrator Jainn, welcome to *Intrepid.*"

She dipped her head in a shallow bow. "Captain Kerrigan, it is a pleasure to finally meet you. I have heard good things about your ship over the last several phases."

"I hope our lateness doesn't sour your opinion," Lyle said

through an apologetic smile. "There were delays that were beyond our control."

The WayLin administrator lifted a hand with long, thin fingers to dismiss his worries. "The fact that you were able to so swiftly dispense with those who tried to take over your ship speaks well of you, captain. I will be sure to include my praise for your handling of that situation in my report."

"Then you should also make note that a group of your miners assisted our efforts. Without them, *Intrepid* may have faced greater damage and higher casualties." He motioned to the cluster of miners that was arriving through the doors at that moment. Lieutenant Galbraith had coordinated it so the group who used their sonic drills were scheduled to take this shuttle over to the asteroid. "One of your miners suffered a serious injury in the process, I'm afraid, but our medical bay treated her to the best of our ability."

"Yes, I've already received reports about these heroics," Administrator Jainn said. Her voice was somber, but the smile on her tiny mouth took away any harshness. "Rest assured that they will receive commendations for their actions, captain. More importantly, as I'm sure they'd agree, WayLin's executive committee has approved a small pay raise for each of them."

Lyle felt relief that the miners wouldn't be punished for helping to retake *Intrepid*'s bridge. He hadn't really thought it likely, but his experience with corporations on Earth was that they were unpredictable on how they viewed any action that wasn't directly in the company's interests. "Speaking of pay," he said, sliding into the next topic that had given him hours of worry during the last days of the trip. "I will understand if WayLin feels that our delayed arrival merits a penalty of some sort, but I hope we can negotiate better terms than those outlined in the contract."

The Edryne woman laughed, a surprisingly deep, booming sound coming from her slim body. "There will be no penalties accrued, Captain Kerrigan. Quite the opposite, I assure you. The WayLin executive committee also wished for me to express that your actions have shown humans can be trusted to place just as much importance on the lives of others as they do on themselves. In light of that, I have been directed to deposit a five percent bonus into your account."

His eyebrows climbed his forehead in surprise at her announcement. Five percent of their contract rate would be a significant number of credits, enough to partially cover the expense of the powered armor suits Lieutenant Galbraith was still urging him to procure for the Infantry squads. "I don't know what to say, administrator. Thank you."

"No, captain," she said, dropping a hand onto his shoulder and bowing deeply. "We at WayLin Mining Consortium owe you and your crew our deepest gratitude. Without your swift action and capable response to unexpected aggression within your own vessel, many lives would have been lost. WayLin may value profit and efficiency, but our workforce is the prime asset in achieving those goals."

The miners who had clustered nearby added their approval with hearty cheers, and even the wounded Dubuk was hammering the fist of her good arm against her chest in applause. The crew members going about their tasks were assaulted with hearty slaps on the back and even a hug here and there, leaving shocked faces and flushed cheeks.

"Now, while these men and women board the shuttle," Administrator Jainn said officiously, "perhaps you'd be willing to entertain another contract offer. Our mining operations in the Orales system are outpacing the abilities of the transport company currently contracted there. If *Intrepid* would agree to provide support for one phase, with the option of extending the contract on a phase-by-phase basis, the efficiency of the operation could be improved by nearly twenty-seven percent."

Lyle chuckled as she launched into a familiar spiel about the benefits and perks of working with Waylin Mining Consortium, and he listened with half an ear while he watched the miners being herded into the shuttle. More than a few of them paused in the doorway to wave a farewell, and he lifted a hand in return.

After ten minutes, he was finally able to part from Administrator Jainn. He promised to consider the contract she had offered, which came with a fairly decent payout. The real profits would come with the four percent bump for each extra phase they continued the work, however, and that was a time commitment he wasn't willing to accept just yet.

He stood back as the shuttle lifted from the deck and passed through the shimmering barrier. The first shuttle was already visible as it returned from the mining outpost to retrieve another load of miners and gear. Lyle could also see a handful of small mining vessels in the distance, making their way toward *Intrepid*. They would be working as tugboats for the next several hours, detaching and moving the full cargo drums so they could be unloaded on the asteroid.

Pleased with the progress so far, Lyle departed the docking bay and headed for the elevator. Getting them back online had been low on the task of repairs, but it had finally been accomplished shortly before their arrival at the asteroid. He greatly enjoyed not having to climb stairs anymore when he needed to transit the decks.

When Lyle entered the bridge, he strode to his command chair and lowered himself into it. The new cushioning was firmer than he was used to, and it hadn't had a chance to mold itself to his shape yet. He shifted uncomfortably for a moment while his eyes scanned the displays in the arms of the chair. "XO, what's the status on the unloading?"

His earpiece crackled for half a second when the channel opened in CIC. "The first cargo drum has been detached and the move is in process. Transport of the miners and their gear is proceeding slightly ahead of schedule, as well. Barring any unexpected obstacles, everything should be completed within the next fifteen hours."

Once again satisfied by the efficiency and skill of his crew, he acknowledged the estimated time and settled back to keep an eye on the progress throughout the day and night. Their ability to work through several shifts was enhanced due to his decision to double the size of the crew, and the speed in this particular instance was making that decision even more beneficial.

Lyle's thoughts turned once more to Indira Predashi and the predicament she might have found herself in. It had taken every ounce of self-control not to order the use of the wrinkle drive to take them to Waldruun to launch an immediate rescue as soon as *Intrepid* was back under their control. That and the disappointment he suspected he might find in her eyes if he gave in to such an impulsive act.

He wouldn't have to wait much longer, though. Lyle had plenty of work to keep his mind occupied through much of the wait, as well. Now that they were in orbit around the asteroid, *Intrepid* was able to access the WayLin communications array. The moment that process was complete, a flood of messages began to arrive.

Most of the messages, and nearly all of those marked "urgent", came from Paine Wingate. Lyle chuckled as he began reading through them, finding warnings of the duplicitous nature of the Kitanes inside. It appeared as though Wingate had been able to discover something about the scavenging race a few days before the attack on his ship was launched.

He sent off a quick reassurance that *Intrepid* had weathered the danger. After a moment's thought, he also asked Wingate to speak with Eslop about how to handle the four prisoners they'd taken. *Intrepid* hadn't been designed to hold prisoners, so Lieutenant Galbraith had been forced to lock the foxes into the quarters they'd been given when they boarded the ship. An Infantry soldier was on guard at their door at all times, and there were frequent inspections to make sure the Kitanes hadn't found a way to escape.

Only a handful of hours had passed by the time Lyle completed the tasks that had awaited his attention, and he sighed deeply as he stared at the viewscreen. The first cargo drum had been emptied and was on the way back to *Intrepid*. That left two more to be unloaded, and then they could set a course for Waldruun. He hoped to find Indira safe. Their relationship had only begun to move beyond the professional, and he was eager to be reunited with her again.

41 - Predashi

Indira tried to reach out to flip one of the switches on the far right edge of the console, then grunted when she remembered her right arm was swaddled against her chest beneath the bandages. She had to twist her torso so that she could reach over with her left hand to complete the action.

She was thankful that her left hand was dominant, so that she wasn't further slowed by trying to force her brain to work with the only option available. It also helped that Lash had been correct about the Qualtide favoring a design that was oriented around the left side of the consoles. The majority of her work could be done without having to twist and turn to reach the less important switches, buttons, and dials on the opposite end.

"Hull integrity has been restored in starboard section seven," Lash reported from the console beside her. "Lieutenant Ballard is sending the repair team over to the next rupture."

Indira nodded in acknowledgment but kept her focus on her own assignments. Repairing this old relic of a ship to the point where they might feel comfortable using it to leave the system was proving to be a monumental task.

One that wasn't helped by the damage they'd taken during the brief but harrowing fight against the other ship. The Kitanes had only returned fire with three plasma cannons, but that was one more than their ship had available. Their surprise attack to begin the hostilities gave them the edge, however, especially once Lash was able to access Engineering and increase the power being routed to the weapons. It had taken fifty-nine shots, but they finally disabled the other ship's working cannons and also put a round through their aft section. That hull breach had forced the sparse Kitane crew to abandon Engineering. When Lieutenant Ballard led a boarding action, all fourteen crew members had been found huddling in a section of living quarters near midship. The bridge of the second vessel had been open to space, as well, though it appeared to have happened long ago. That coupled with fewer crew members than necessary explained the poor performance of the orbital bombardment.

Now, they were hard at work on making this ship space worthy, since it had been determined to be the one closest to whole. That didn't say a lot since there were weeks of work waiting to be completed just to reach a minimal safety threshold. Indira was tempted to send Lash and Ballard in the shuttle to find help, but she needed the Tiké's help deciphering the systems she wasn't familiar with. And no one else could fly the shuttle, except for their prisoner.

Reminded of Tamma, Indira turned her head to cast a side-eye glance at the Kitane woman. Her feet were still bound, but her hands had been freed so that she could point out switches and buttons whenever Lash asked her to explain parts of the console that he hadn't figured out yet. So far, their prisoner had been honest and helpful, though she was also sulky and refused to cooperate occasionally.

Matters on the ground were far less settled. Once they'd wrested control of the gun capable of firing plasma rounds at the planet, Lieutenant Ballard had sent one final shot toward the cavern where the Kitanes had been holed up. She'd hit close enough to make the threat obvious, but not so close that lives should have been endangered inside the caves. They weren't sure if the message had been received, but their scans of the planet so far showed no signs of continuing hostilities. The Golmorung villages they could see from orbit, which dotted the marshes and lakes of the continent spread out below them, were peaceful.

The village they'd fought to save had survived the third orbital strike mostly intact. A handful of huts had been burned by the plasma round, but the watery marsh had prevented the fires from spreading. The frogs were already in the process of removing the debris and rebuilding.

"Commander, it's time for a break."

Indira looked up to find Gundar standing at her side. The man's face was still covered in bandages just as her chest and back were, but he didn't look as close to death as he had when they first arrived on this ship. "Just a few more minutes, Gundar. I think I'm finally getting the hang of reading these diagnostic reports."

He placed a restraining hand on her wrist when she tried to get back to work. "Sorry, ma'am, but the lieutenant ordered me to make sure you take the agreed-upon breaks."

Indira pulled her lips up in a snarl, but she quickly banished the rage. She knew the Infantry squad leader was merely trying to protect her from herself. Her body was still healing from the wounds she'd sustained and pushing it beyond normal limits would do more damage than good.

"Lash, will you be okay in here while I'm resting?"

"We'll be fine, commander," he said, motioning to their prisoner. "Tamma and I are beginning to develop an understanding of each other, and I believe our pace of cooperation will increase."

Gundar snorted in disgust at working with one of the Kitanes, and Indira nudged him with her elbow. The Kitane woman had accelerated their repair process quite a bit, so she'd earned some small measure of goodwill. If they could shave even a day off the process and return to the space station to establish contact with *Intrepid*, it would all be worthwhile.

When they left the bridge, Indira's shoulders slumped with exhaustion. She didn't like to show weakness around any member of the crew, but Gundar was the one man she felt could understand what she was feeling. They'd received the worst injuries during the mission, and both of them would likely face extended stays in a medical bay once they were back on *Intrepid*.

"How are you holding up, commander?" he asked in a gentle voice.

"Well enough," she said. Then she sighed and ran her hand through her tangled hair. "It hurts like hell, to be honest. Especially with the pain meds being dialed back."

Gundar nodded, and he winced as the movement irritated his own injuries. "The lieutenant didn't want me to tell you this, but we're running low on everything, ma'am, not just the pain killers. If we don't get this ship operational within the next three or four days, we'll have to cut the rations again."

Her stomach rumbled as if triggered by his words. They were already eating half of the calories they should be taking in every day. Working for only a few hours left them exhausted more than it should have, and that was further slowing the repair process. Water was the only resource they had plenty of, since the tanks aboard the ship had been nearly full when they took it.

"We'll complete everything in time," she said firmly. "Lash and I are figuring out more systems every hour, and the hull repairs are almost complete. Once we can turn our full focus on the engines, we can figure out why the power management systems aren't feeding the wrinkle drive as much juice as they should be."

"I hope so, commander. We're not exactly in a position to call for help."

They were interrupted by the sound of rapid footsteps, and Indira tensed as they turned to face whoever was running toward them. She still had nightmares about a Kitane bursting out from hidden compartments and attacking while their guards were down.

Lash appeared around a corner and slid to a stop. His mandibles were spread in a joyful grin. "Commander! You need to return to the bridge."

Gundar held out a hand and shook his head. "The lieutenant ordered –"

"The lieutenant will not mind this time," Lash said playfully. "Come on. Both of you!"

Indira traded looks with Gundar when the Tiké sprinted back in the direction of the bridge. She shrugged and began to follow him, increasing her pace to a light jog despite the jolts that sent waves of discomfort out from her shoulder blade.

As she ran, scenarios began to race through her head. The urgency in Lash's voice made her suspect something bad had happened, but the joy on his face countered that. Was it possible he had finally convinced Tamma to give up some major discovery which would allow them to understand the systems that still remained shrouded in mystery?

Gundar grunted with each step as they neared the bridge, and Indira had to bite down on her cheek to keep from doing the same thing. Their injuries had restricted both of them to most-ly sedentary activities since the boarding action, and for her that had meant hours and hours spent sitting in front of a bridge console. Physical fitness had fallen to the wayside, and this jog was showing just how out of shape she was.

Those thoughts fled the moment she entered the bridge and bent over her console to look at the small screen Lash was pointing at. Her jaw dropped in shock, and she rubbed her eyes in case she might be imagining what she saw on the screen. When the familiar shape of the ship that was their home was still there when she looked again, she let out a whoop of joy.

42 - Ballard

The sleekly modern shuttle touched down in the clearing with a hissing burst of thrust to slow the descent at just the right moment. Alina felt the muffled thud as it settled on the grass ten yards from the boxy old Qualtide shuttle her squad had used to reach the planet. The contrast between *Intrepid*'s shuttle and the one stolen by the Kitanes made it look even more outdated.

Air hissed out as the door began to lift on the side of the shuttle, and she walked forward to greet the new arrivals. She kept one hand draped over the butt of her NK70, which hung across her chest where it could easily be snapped up into a shooting position. Suarez and the Panosh brothers were keeping an eye on the small crowd of Kitanes at her back, but she didn't trust the foxes enough to let her guard down fully.

Captain Kerrigan exited the shuttle, and she had to bite down on her tongue to keep a joyous grin from spreading across her face. Alina hadn't realized how much she missed her shipmates until that moment.

Commander Predashi must have felt the same, because she brushed by to throw the captain a quick salute before pulling him in for a brief one-armed hug. Alina smirked at the shocked but pleased expression on her captain's face, but then scoffed when she saw the woman exiting the shuttle behind him.

"You just couldn't wait to come down here and say 'I told you so', could you?"

Lisbet Galbraith ambled across the grass with an arrogant

swagger. "Hey, you're the one who fought so hard to take the reins on what you called a 'diplomatic rescue mission'. It's not my fault you swallowed their lies so easily."

Alina rolled her eyes. "Because you divined the truth so much faster than I did, right? No... wait... you didn't realize the Kitanes were up to no good until they already controlled the reactor room on *Intrepid*!"

Galbraith snorted and gave her an innocent look. "Well, at least the senior officer in my care didn't end up wounded."

They both glanced over to where the captain and his XO were speaking in low voices. Commander Predashi's arm was now in a makeshift sling instead of being bound against her chest, but flashes of pain crossed her face whenever she tried to move it. "Okay, you win that one."

They finally burst out laughing, and Galbraith reached out to clasp her forearm in a quick greeting. "All jokes aside, you did fantastic work down here, Alina. I don't know if I could have done it better."

"You couldn't," she said with a wink. "It sounds like you faced some tough times, as well, Lizzie. We both got to experience taking the bridge of a ship out of hostile hands, only you had twice as many troops to do it with."

Galbraith chuckled, and her eyes strayed to a pair of Infantry soldiers flanking the shuttle door. Both of them were from the newly created squad. "I talked the captain into it because I thought those miners were going to be the death of me, but it turns out I should have been focusing my paranoia in a different direction."

"We both should have been more aware of the possibilities for betrayal," Alina conceded. "Sergeant Major Bauer is never going to let us live that down."

"I know!" Galbraith laughed and wiped her eye. "I told Captain Kerrigan the same thing after we took the bridge back from the Kitanes."

They fell into companionable silence for a short time, until Captain Kerrigan finished his discussion with Commander Predashi. Alina couldn't help but witness their hands brush together in a fond gesture before the captain walked over to join her and Galbraith.

"Lieutenant Ballard, I hear that I owe you a debt of gratitude. Without the valiant efforts of yourself and the Infantry squad under your command, my XO tells me that she likely wouldn't be with us any longer."

"Commander Predashi was only injured because I allowed her to join us on the boarding mission, captain."

He smiled fondly and leaned in to lower his voice. "We both know that was a fight you never would have won, lieutenant. The commander always gets her way."

Alina fought to hold back a grin. "Yes, captain. She does."

"Now, let's turn to the business at hand. I see a contingent of the Kitanes are here. Are the Golmorungs sending any representatives?"

His eyes darted past her shoulder, where Alina could almost feel the hateful glare of Elder Hamman boring into her. He was surrounded by half a dozen Kitane warriors, but they were only carrying spears today. There was a stack of plasma rifles near the group, however, which her squad had carefully examined and verified weren't loaded.

"The Golmorung chief should be here shortly," she said. "I sent Sergeant Cantu to their village as soon as we had word that your shuttle departed *Intrepid*. I didn't think it prudent to have both groups waiting here together."

"Probably wise," Kerrigan muttered. He was focused on the group of Kitanes, and his eyes roved over them taking in every detail. "The scarred one will be Elder Hamman, I presume?"

Alina stiffened in surprise. "He is, captain. Did the commander tell you about him?"

Kerrigan chuckled and shook his head. "One of those who briefly held our bridge threatened that an Elder Hamman would be coming to take *Intrepid* with many more Kitanes at his side. That one looks like an old warrior, so it seemed to fit."

She still couldn't believe how thoroughly the Kitanes had hoodwinked them. Luring her squad to Waldruun and almost convincing them to do the dirty work of killing the locals was bad enough. Finding out about the attempts to wrest control of *Intrepid* made her feel twice as gullible. She didn't like to think what would have happened if the Qualtide shuttle had allowed Tamma to transport more of her brethren to the space station to be left behind with *Intrepid*.

The lack of numbers seemed to have been the Kitanes' weakness from the beginning. From the little that Lash had been able to prod out of Tamma, the foxes had suffered grievous losses during the battle in which they eradicated the Qualtide and stole their two remaining ships. Their own vessel, pilfered from some other race so long ago that Tamma's own grandmother hadn't yet been born, had been all but vaporized by return fire during the battle. The survivors transferred to the stolen ships, but their numbers were barely sufficient to keep them running. If the Kitanes had been less greedy and consolidated their survivors on a single ship, they might have managed to thrive.

As it was, they drifted from star to star for nearly twenty sequences until they encountered a lonely craft adrift in space. The Golmorung crew had been either dead or close to it when the Kitanes forced their way inside. Tamma hadn't been part of that operation, but Alina suspected any Golmorungs still alive had been swiftly dispatched by the boarders. Once that was done, it was a simple matter to retrace the path of the ship, which had originated from Waldruun in the nearest system. The technology and construction of the ship had apparently been so poor that it was a wonder the Auricle obelisks had even given them the option of leaving the system and losing their protection.

Alina was shaken from her thoughts by the wet slap of wide feet that announced the arrival of the Golmorung chieftain. Cantu was puffing heavily at his side, and she grinned at the thought that he'd likely had to run to keep up with the powerful leaps the frogs were capable of.

She walked over to greet the chief, then motioned toward the newly arrived humans. "Captain Kerrigan, this is the chief of the Golmorung village the Kitanes attacked. From the few words our implants are able to translate, it seems as though he speaks for a coalition of nearby settlements in these negotiations."

The Golmorung launched into a croaking speech, and Alina chuckled when she saw the captain and squad members guarding his shuttle touch their implants with shock. The steady vibration as it worked to translate the words had become normal to her, so that she barely noticed the feeling anymore. They were able to understand maybe one word in ten, but it seemed clear the chief was welcoming the captain to his world and expressing optimistic hopes of a satisfactory settlement with the invaders.

"Enough talk!" Elder Hamman snarled out after several minutes. "Is this all you humans do? Talk, talk, talk! I regret that I ever sent Tamma in search of the great warriors we'd heard tales of."

"Our people are quite capable of fighting, as you've learned to your peril," Captain Kerrigan said, his shoulders stiff with restrained distaste. "But only when it's necessary and all diplomatic routes have been exhausted first. Perhaps if the Kitanes had less need for battle and a little more openness to talk, then you wouldn't find yourself in the current predicament."

Elder Hamman snarled in response, but wisely held his tongue. Alina thought it was mostly because of the captain's reminder of how dire their situation was. From what they'd been able to determine, there were fewer than two hundred Kitanes alive on the planet. More losses to fighting would all but spell certain doom for the race. *Unless there are others scavenging deeper in the galaxy*, she thought.

"The tent has been prepared, captain," Galbraith said. She motioned to where white canvas peeked out above *Intrepid*'s shuttle.

"Thank you, lieutenant." Captain Kerrigan looked at the leaders of the two races, then held out a hand in a welcoming gesture. "If you'll follow me, we can offer refreshment while the three of us work to find a peaceful resolution that will satisfy all parties."

The Golmorung chieftain happily walked beside the captain, while Elder Hamman reluctantly followed. The repugnance on his face when he looked at the Golmorung told Alina that her captain was in for a difficult process. She and Commander Predashi had decided to keep knowledge of the dissected Golmorung aboard the ship they'd taken secret for now, in fear that it might sabotage the negotiations before they began.

"Now the fun begins," Galbraith whispered.

Alina groaned through a wan smile. "Paper, rock, scissors to determine who takes the first watch?"

Galbraith's eyes narrowed as she stared toward the tent for a few moments. "Deal. Loser's squad takes the first three hours."

Alina dropped her fist into an open palm and lifted one eyebrow. "Ready when you are."

43 - Wingate

"Then everything has been resolved peacefully in the end?" X'Zak asked gently, walking over to set a tray down on the table in front of the couch where Paine was seated.

"Captain Kerrigan has begun the process, at the very least. The remaining Kitanes have all been consolidated in one place on Waldruun, and the Golmorungs agreed to allow them to live in the forested valleys they preferred to avoid. Their need for humidity keeps them close to water except during times of great need."

"What if the Kitanes grow violent again now that your people are leaving the planet?" The Kr'Sal ambassador poured out steaming red liquid into two cups as she spoke.

Paine gratefully took the cup she passed to him and blew on the liquid to cool it. "Now that their plasma rifles have been confiscated, Captain Kerrigan thinks they'll adhere to the treaty. Long enough for a delegation to be sent out from Kraken, anyway. Wyeth, the Telbrith ambassador, will be leading it. These Golmorungs apparently speak a language similar to an old Telbrith dialect, and he's quite eager to discover if there might be some distant connection between their races."

X'Zak sipped her drink while she gazed at him fondly. "What of these plasma rifles? Does your captain know where they might have come from? I've heard of plasma-based weaponry being used in deeper parts of the galaxy, but to my knowledge this is the first time such a thing has been seen in this sector."

Paine shrugged and took a small sip. The liquid was still piping hot, but he enjoyed the spicy flavor that washed over his tongue. There was an enticing sweetness beneath that heat which lingered in his mouth long after he swallowed. "It would seem these Kitanes have lived as scavengers of sorts for many generations. They've drifted through space, stealing whatever they could take from anyone weaker than themselves. Unfortunately, that same lifestyle is what led to their numbers dwindling to so few in the present moment."

"Hmm, it is a cautionary tale for many of us," X'Zak said. She placed her cup on the tray and then leaned back against the couch cushion. Her hand drifted toward his, until her fingers were lightly tracing along his bare wrist. "I suppose I can take solace in the fact that my people played some small part in this drama."

"Hmm?" Paine asked, his thoughts fragmenting as he enjoyed her touch.

"The Kitanes sought out *Intrepid* because they'd heard of human exploits to free the slaves my people took, yes? Had that not happened, they might have requested aid from some other race. One less filled with morals and integrity, perhaps."

"I suppose that's true," Paine said. He smiled at her over the rim of his cup as he drained it. "You and I never would have met, either. I probably owe F'Mosh a thank you for that alone."

She laughed lightly, with a purr deep in her throat that sent a chill up his spine. Paine had found himself spending more and more time in the Kr'Sal embassy over the last dozen cycles. While his initial visits had only been an hour or so, filled with pleasant chit-chat about their respective cultures, he had taken to staying much longer in recent cycles. X'Zak had even hinted at retiring to his quarters at some point, to continue getting to know each other in a more relaxed setting.

"Your *Intrepid* will return to Kraken soon, then?" she asked, taking the empty cup from him to set it next to hers on the table.

Paine's tongue was still tingling from the aftereffects of the drink. He kept meaning to ask the name of it, but his thoughts were always otherwise occupied while he was in X'Zak's presence. "Captain Kerrigan is making a brief detour to the nearest space station to replenish supplies, but then they'll come straight to Kraken. Eslop has already assigned a shipyard berth for the Qualtide ship, and he's verified that it rightfully belongs to us due to galactic salvage laws. Since the race who built the ships is sadly no more, there is no one to dispute the claim."

"The human fleet grows," she hissed in a near whisper. Her clawed finger ran up the arm of his jacket, slowing as she reached the collar of his shirt. "That seems a just reward for the great pains your people have suffered in their quest to right the wrongs that were almost perpetrated."

"Mmm, I agree," Paine hummed. His eyelids felt heavy, and he allowed them to drift shut as he enjoyed the warmth of her body against his side. The pleasant tingle in his mouth seemed to be enhanced by her touch, and he greatly appreciated the combination of pleasures.

"You will be able to open your home world to other races soon," she said, her warm breath tickling his ear as she moved closer.

"Maybe," he mumbled. Paine wanted to discuss all the preparations he still hoped to complete before Earth was brought into the galactic community, but he was finding it hard to think about anything other than her touch. When her dry lips pressed against his skin, the surge of sensations raced through his body like an electric shock.

"Wouldn't you like to share that triumphant moment with those you care about the most, Paine?" X'Zak gently scraped her claws down one cheek while her tongue darted out to lightly touch the other, sending a shiver down his spine. "I'd very much like to see the world you came from. Would you show it to me?"

"Love to," he slurred. The heaviness of his eyelids had spread to his limbs, and his hands were beginning to feel disconnected from his body. A warning voice deep in his mind yelled at him to get out of there, but the thought of moving away from the Kr'Sal woman was ridiculous. He enjoyed being with X'Zak, and the growing closeness of their relationship brought him far too much joy.

"You could show me all your favorite places," she said. "I could meet the old colleagues you have told me so much about. Won't they be shocked to find out you're responsible for humanity's first meeting with other races?"

"...be awshum..." he said, his words slurred by a tongue that refused to move in the way he wanted.

"We can so much, Paine." X'Zak's breath was on his lips now, but he barely felt it when she kissed him. "You and I can be together in every way that matters. All you need to do is tell me how to find your world. How to find Earth."

The warning voice deep in his head screamed out again, but it was a faint sensation easily ignored. While Paine luxuriated in the touch of her fingers and lips, he began to speak.

JOIN THE MAILING LIST

You'll get my monthly newsletter, which includes information on my latest projects as well as sneak peeks at new releases and short stories I share months before they appear anywhere else.

https://www.timrangnow.com/newsletter/

By The Author

SCIENCE FICTION

<u>Guild Series</u>

Vagabond

Indomitable

Waterloo

Resolute

<u>Rim Jumper Series</u>

Prime Example

Viridian Skies

Pirate's Nest

Nebulous Loyalties

Fraying Edges

Chain Reaction

Galaxy's Edge

Dark Matters

Regent's Rise

<u>Intrepid Saga</u>

Wayward Stars

Stolen Stars

Shattered Stars

URBAN FANTASY

Jack Dahlish Series

Lost Souls

Memory and Sorrow

Dark Deception

Fateful Knights

Awakenings

Reckoning

Bad Blood

Rising Storm

Last Call

Watchers Series

Rite of Passage

Old Wounds

Reign of Fire

About The Author

Tim Rangnow is the best-selling author of the Jack Dahlish series, which features a man able to see through the masks that hide the supernatural creatures who live in San Antonio. Jack is tasked with keeping the city, and the world, safe from those who break the long-standing Covenants.

The story continues in the Watcher series, which follows a group of dedicated Watchers as they strive to keep powerful and dangerous Relics out of the hands of humans and Nox alike who would use them for evil.

Tim also enjoys writing science fiction novels. The Guild series is a space opera that takes place in the near future, while the Rim Jumper series includes action, adventure, and a rebellion against a powerful Hegemony that rules human-settled space.